Remember, Vengeance is mine;
I will repay, says the Lord.
Rom 12 v 19

23259

BUCHANAN

The case of

The Bodies in the Marina

Alex Willis

First published in Great Britain by Mount Pleasant Press 2015

The story contained between the covers of this book is a work of fiction, sweat, and perseverance over several years. Characters, place names, locations, and incidents are either the product of the author's imagination or are used fictitiously. Any resemblance to actual persons, living or dead, or locals is entirely coincidental.

ISBN 13-978-151700-525-2
ISBN 10-151700-5252-6

Text set in Garamond 12 point.

Foreword

I was delighted and honoured when asked to write this foreword for the book *Buchanan* by Alex Willis.

Many times, when police work is featured in films, television programmes, or in the printed word, the policeman or policewoman is shown as either a drunkard, racist, sexist, and in some cases a gun-toting super hero.

In reality, the above is so far removed from everyday life. The policemen and women with whom I came into contact during my twenty-six years in the service proved to me, over and over, that they were hard working, caring professionals.

I have personally experienced their dedication to defending the nation against those who seek to subvert our free society for their own depraved ends.

I believe this book, although a work of fiction, shows this to be the case.

ACC Gillian Atkins, QPM (Retired)

This book is dedicated to my parents, Alex and Hilda, without whose encouragement and direction I would have never arrived at where I am today.

1

It was half time and an excited peace prevailed; Ibrox was rocking, the pub was heaving, and Rangers were ahead two goals to one. Buchanan nodded to the bartender for another pint of McEwan's Export, his sixth. 'Just going for a pee, Tam; off to make room for the next one,' he laughed, while swaying between the crowded tables.

It took a few moments for his eyes to become accustomed to the dimly-lit corridor. A single fly-spattered bulb hung from the ceiling at the far end. He could have found the Gents in the dark, though. The smell of stale urine mixed with tobacco smoke got stronger the closer he got.

He leaned on the door, stuffed a cigarette in his mouth, lit it, and almost fell through. Two men were standing outside one of the cubicles, engrossed in the display on their mobile phones. Buchanan, bleary-eyed, stared at them. They looked familiar, but nature called and he made his way to the urinal unzipping as he crossed the wet floor.

To relieve the boredom as the patrons went about their ablutions, the management of the establishment had installed plastic-covered humorous cartoons above the urinals.

Buchanan started to read a caption but was distracted by the reflection of one of the men; he suddenly remembered where he had seen him before. Momentarily sobered by the revelation he zipped up, turned, and stared.

'Ah, know you,' he said, taking a step towards the man who hurriedly stuck the phone in his jacket pocket. 'You're Davie Shelton; you're a nonce. I read it in *The Herald*.'

'Then you'll remember I was found not guilty.'

'That was bullshit, man. The children were too afraid of you. If it was up to me, I'd have ripped your balls off and stuffed them up your arse.'

The other man made to leave, then stopped. Buchanan looked at him and saw the scar running from his left ear across to the corner of his mouth turn from bright red to white.

'You and who else – your mother?'

'You threatening me? Do you have any idea who you're talking to?'

'Couldn't give a shite.'

Buchanan stared into his eyes. He knew that look; he'd seen it in the eyes of every Glasgow thug who thought they could get the better of Jack Buchanan. They'd all lost. He took a step closer, throwing his half-smoked cigarette into the overfull paper towel basket. 'And what you looking at on those phones? better not be what I think it is.'

Before he had time to react, Scarface threw a punch. His ring cut Buchanan's cheek below the right eye. Buchanan grabbed the errant wrist and, twisting the arm up Scarface's back, rammed him face-first, hard, against the tiled wall. Scarface slumped to the floor cursing Buchanan, while holding his face, blood dribbling through his fingers.

He turned in time to see Shelton flick open a cut-throat razor. Buchanan kicked him in the groin and drove a right uppercut into his face. Shelton collapsed to the floor. He lay there writhing in pain while holding his crotch and screaming obscenities.

'Take a razor to my face, would you? I'll show you!' As he spoke Buchanan kicked Shelton in the face. Blood and teeth flew across the floor. 'That'll teach you, you bastard.'

He was about to kick Shelton again when the toilet door opened and a fresh-faced youth stumbled in. Seeing smoke billowing from the wastepaper basket and the carnage of Shelton and his friend lying on the floor holding their blood-soaked faces, he backed off, pulled a phone from his pocket, and ran out.

Full of self-indignant fury, Buchanan took aim with his size twelves to kick Shelton again. In doing so he slipped on the blood-spattered floor and fell back, hitting his head on the edge of a cubicle door. He landed hard; his head bounced twice on the tile-covered floor, where he lay, deathly still, blood pouring from his head wound.

Scarface got to his feet and helped Shelton up. 'Come on, Davie, we've got to get out of here, that lad's probably called the police.'

Shelton got to his feet, looked down at Buchanan, and kicked him hard in the ribs. He was about to have another go when the sound of a police siren echoed through a broken ceiling vent.

'Come on, Davie, hurry! We can't be found here.'

Staggering like a couple of Friday night drunks they pushed their way out through the back door of the pub, through the crowd of smokers, and into the side alley.

The sound of more police cars approaching spurred them on down the alley, out into the road, and under the wheels of a speeding police car.

2

'Oh, you're awake, Inspector Buchanan,' said the nurse.

'Where am I?'

'You're in the Royal; you fell and hit your head.'

'How long have I been here?'

'Two days.'

'Shite, two days – my wife?'

'Not to worry, I believe your office contacted her and told her it wasn't serious, you'd just bumped your head. I'll get Doctor Aswan.'

She was back in four minutes with the diminutive Dr Aswan.

As the doctor approached, Buchanan did his best to prop himself up on one elbow.

'How are we today, Inspector Buchanan?'

'My head feels like there's a bunch of Clydeside riveters on piecework banging around in there. What happened to me?'

'That's what we hoped you'd tell us. You were found lying in a pool of blood on the floor of the men's toilets in Porter's bar. Apparently, you slipped and hit your head on the floor.'

'So, it wasn't a dream then,' said Buchanan, gingerly touching his bandaged scalp.

'We did a scan while you were unconscious. Don't worry; you've a thick skull, nothing wrong that a period of rest won't cure. We did have to staple your scalp back together though, and that will be tender for several weeks. The staples can come out next week, providing you behave yourself.'

'What about the pain in my head?'

'We'll give you something for that,' said the nurse, as the doctor moved on to his next patient.

'A wee dram would go down nicely.'

'This is the Royal Infirmary, Inspector, not your local.'

4

'Pity,' replied Buchanan, closing his eyes and drifting off to sleep.

♦

'Inspector Buchanan,' said the nurse, waking him from his slumbers, 'there's someone here to see you.'

'Good afternoon, Buchanan.'

Buchanan opened his eyes and focussed on the uniform that was Assistant Chief Constable Anderson.

'Good afternoon, sir. Sorry I can't stand to attention, lying down is the best I can achieve.'

'What on earth happened, man? My best DCI found lying on a toilet floor in a pool of blood, and drunk to boot – plus two dead men in the street under a police car. Every five minutes the Chief Constable's on the phone wanting to know just what the hell's going on. The newspapers are having a field day, and I've got to give a news conference in front of the cameras this afternoon.'

Anderson walked over to the window, looked down to Warnock Street, and smiled. A harried TV crew were arguing with a traffic warden. 'Do you realise,' he said, while continuing to watch the street spectacle, 'I've got just eighteen months to go to retirement and me with an unblemished record.'

'It wasn't my fault.'

Anderson turned away from the window and looked at Buchanan. 'No – so whose blood and teeth were spattered on the toilet floor of Porter's bar?'

'They were looking at pictures on a mobile phone.'

'That's not a crime; my grandchildren are on theirs, texting, all hours. I'm sorry, Buchanan, but I've got no choice, the press are baying for blood and you have become a problem I don't need –'

'Wait a minute, don't say something you may regret. Do you know who those two shites were?'

5

'Who, the men under the police car? No – forensics are still working on it.'

'One was Davie Shelton, can't remember the name of the other one.

'Shelton – that name rings a bell. Wasn't he the nonce, got off the charge if I remember rightly, had a good solicitor?'

'Randal, that's who the other bastard was; he was Shelton's lawyer,' said Buchanan, sitting up in bed, momentarily forgetting the pain in his head.

'Well,' said Anderson, rubbing his hands together, 'this puts a different light on the matter. All the same we can't have you wandering around being ambushed by the press.' He looked at his watch. 'Right – I've got to go back to headquarters. First thing, must get forensics to confirm the identities, and then, oh, I think a discreet leak to the press before the press conference, and finally, to find you somewhere to hide till this all blows over. Oh, by the way, how is Mrs Buchanan?'

'She's fine.'

'Does she know about your injury?'

'Apparently, Personnel called her and said there was no need to rush home.'

'Where is she?'

'In France, visiting her mother – as soon as my head clears I'll give her a call.'

'Great, I'll be off, and Buchanan – good work.'

Anderson walked off, muttering to himself, 'Two nonces off the street; that's one for the good guys.'

◆

Suitably anaesthetised, Buchanan sat up in his hospital bed and watched the televised news conference. Anderson had stage-managed the situation brilliantly, just in time for the TV network one o'clock news. The identities and histories of the two men had been previously leaked to the press. So instead of the police actions – Buchanan's in particular – being the focus of the press's attention, it was instead the activities of Shelton and his lawyer that took the brunt of their questions.

Buchanan watched while Anderson, with a grave look on his face, announced that the deceased's' mobile phones had been located and he was able to confirm that there were indecent photographs of children contained in both phones' memories.

Pressed for confirmation of the injured policeman's name, Anderson said it was being withheld pending full recovery from his injuries and all police enquiries were complete.

◆

Three hours later Anderson was seated at Buchanan's bedside.

'You watched the news conference?'

'Yes, thought it went off quite well.'

'I thought so, too. The press are after you, though; you won't have any peace when you get out of here.'

'How did they find out my name?'

'Guesswork, and a pub full of Rangers' supporters?'

'Ah, I forgot about that – who won, by the way?'

'Haven't a clue. Golf's my game – ever play it?'

'Me, chase a wee ball round the green? Never.'

'That's a pity, it's a great way to network and meet the right kind of people.'

'I'm not rolling up my trouser leg for anyone.'

Anderson shook his head. 'You don't understand, Buchanan. How are you ever going to get promoted if you don't mix with the right people?'

'Listen, I'm a policeman first; the only people I mix with are honest criminals. It's those people who think they are above the law that I concentrate my efforts on.'

'I'm sorry you take it that way, Buchanan, but if you ever change your mind all you have to do is ask.'

That'll be a snowy day in hell, thought Buchanan.

'Right, down to business. We've had a talk at headquarters; you said your wife's mother lives in France?'

'Yes, just outside Dieppe.'

'And your sister-in-law lives in Eastbourne?'

'Yes – why do I feel like I'm being shunted into a siding? You're not sending me on gardening leave – are you?'

'No, of course not, we've got something better in mind,' chuckled Anderson. 'We've arranged for you to be seconded to East Sussex.'

'East Sussex, but –'

'No buts, Buchanan.'

'What about the inquest? There's bound to be one.'

'Don't worry; I've had a word with McKenzie at the Procurator Fiscal's office. He says since you weren't actually involved with the two men being run over, they may not have to call you to give evidence – though you'll probably have to give a written statement.'

'Well, if that's the way he looks at it – but East Sussex?'

'Come on, man, it's not a foreign country, and besides I hear the local beer's fine.'

'So, what's this case that requires the services of an old Glasgow cop? Some old dear had her knitting needles swiped?'

'On the morning of the 30th March, a woman's body was fished out of Sovereign Harbour in Eastbourne. Then a week later, a DS was found in his car.'

'Asleep, or was he drunk?'

'Neither. He was in his car when it was pulled from the same harbour.'

'Was he on duty – on leave?'

'Not sure, you'll have to ask.'

'Are they related – the deaths, that is?'

'That's what their Internal Affairs wants you – if you accept the secondment – to find out.'

'What choice do I have?'

'Disciplinary hearing, your record being leaked to the press, career finished.'

'I'll go home and pack my bags.'

'I thought you'd see sense.'

'But – don't they have someone in-house who could take care of it?'

'Half the department is down with the trots, apparently. They were going to get someone from the Met, but he came down with measles.'

'Not a very healthy bunch, are they?'

'Their ACC and I go back many years. Last week she told me she was looking for an outsider to take over the investigation – felt an outsider would get better results.'

'And that's how I come to get volunteered?'

'There's that, and the fact that Shelton had friends in high places. I thought it would be good for your health to get some sea air – do you understand where I'm coming from?'

'Let me stay here, I'll sort this out.'

'No, we have a team already working on the case, almost ready to make arrests. In fact, your presence could jeopardise the whole investigation – that's why we need you out of the limelight.'

'Two birds with one stone, eh?'

'Knowing how you work, Buchanan, I really think you're the man for the job – except for one thing.'

'And what's that?'

'It's your use of English, or should I say Glaswegian. If you want to get ahead down south, you'll have to moderate how you speak; they don't provide interpreters for staff.'

Buchanan smiled, nodded his head and thought: *the same old bullshit.*

3

It was a wet and windy Monday – Buchanan's first day back at work after three days in hospital and a few days to consider his situation. He drove into the staff car park and saw that his personal slot had been commandeered by Fergusson's BMW. He shook his head and smiled, *so much for the gentle farewell.* He parked in the visitor bay, then headed for the first floor and the staff canteen; he needed coffee.

On the way to the lift, his path was blocked by a police cadet holding an empty beer glass. Collecting for something? mused Buchanan.

He lifted his coffee cup to his lips in an attempt to avoid reaching in to his pocket, but failed. 'What's it for?' he asked, dropping his loose change into the almost empty glass.

'Someone's leaving, works on the second floor. He's being put out to pasture; rumour has it the ACC is glad to be rid of the old duffer.'

Buchanan raised his eyebrows in surprise and asked, 'What's he done, this old duffer?'

The cadet shrugged and said, 'Not sure, only been told he's being put out to pasture.'

'What's his name?'

'Thanks, sir,' he said, looking disappointedly at the assortment of pennies and five pence pieces, 'I think his name is Buchanan; don't know his first name. Would you like to sign the card?'

Buchanan grinned, took out his Conway 388, and selecting a nice open area on the card he wrote, *Will ye no come back again? Best wishes Jack Buchanan.*

The young cadet looked at the card, squinted at the handwriting, then blushed and said, 'Oh, it's you!'

'Aye, laddie, it's me, and see I get that money back.'

Coffee in hand Buchanan headed to the lift to the second floor and his office.

Fergusson's feet were on his desk, his backside in Buchanan's chair. 'You're back!' he said, startled.

'Didn't realise I'd gone,' replied Buchanan, leaning against the door frame.

'The Chief said I could have your office, said you were off down south.'

'The rumours of my departure are much exaggerated.'

Fergusson stood. 'Just remembered, I have a meeting to go to.'

Buchanan put up his hand, shook his head, and said, 'Don't bother yourself, sit back down. I'll be away in the morning, just stopped in to get my briefcase. I'll find a hot desk down on the first floor if I need one.'

Fergusson sat back in the chair, relaxed, and asked, 'How's Karen?'

'She's fine, talked to her last night.'

'What's she say about you going down to Sussex?'

'She thinks it's great news. Her mother lives just outside Dieppe and Dieppe is only a short ferry ride from Newhaven.'

'And Newhaven is only a short drive from Eastbourne?'

'Got it in one.'

'That's you scuppered then. She'll never want to come back up here to Glasgow.'

'I'm scuppered anyway. Why do you think you've got my office and car parking space so quickly? It's like the lad downstairs said, I'm being put out to pasture. I'm an embarrassment to the division. Do you know what Karen called me?'

'I could come up with a few guesses.'

'An anachronism in the 21st century – me!' he said, pointing to his chest. 'The best DCI on the division, at least that's what the old duffer upstairs said.'

Fergusson laughed. 'Old duffer, that's a new one on me. Oh, have you sorted out your accommodation down south yet?'

'Yes, Karen's sister owns a house in the Marina – perfect for the investigation. She and her husband are off working in Paris and won't be back for four months, so we've rented the house till the summer.'

'Convenient – you living at the scene of the crime.'

'I suppose it is, never really gave it a thought.'

'Best of both worlds,' said Fergusson, standing, 'but Jack, I really do have a meeting to go to.'

'OK then, away you go. I'll see you around some time.'

Buchanan listened to the sound of Fergusson's footsteps retreating down the hall and took a slow, farewell look round his office – now Fergusson's, he reminded himself. He let out a long, slow breath. It had been thoroughly sanitised. Gone were his books from the oak bookshelf, probably now in cardboard boxes in the post room waiting for a forwarding address; as were no doubt the pictures of his passing out parade and the photo of him meeting the Prince of Wales in the Long Room at the Oval. The photo of the *Carrick* tied up at Clydeside still hung from the wall between the windows.

He walked round the desk and lifted the picture from its hook. All that remained was a shadow. *My legacy* he said to himself, *a bloody shadow on the wall.*

He shook his head, swallowed the last of his coffee, and threw the crumpled paper cup into the bin. He opened his briefcase and carefully placed the picture of the *Carrick* inside.

4

'Lew-es, this is Lew-es,' intoned the conductor in a pleasant Edinburgh accent, 'please mind the gap between the train and the platform when alighting and make sure you take all your personal items with you when you leave the train.'

While the conductor continued with his *ad hoc* dissertation on which platform for which train, Buchanan pulled his bags from the luggage rack, pushed through the throng of students getting on, and stepped off the train.

He had been told he would be met at Lewes station, but as the train left for Eastbourne he was the only one on the platform. Buchanan stood for a moment, wondering whether to go up the stairs to the booking office or down into the car park. He chose the car park; after all it was easier to go down the short flight of steps and they would just have to come and find him.

Five minutes later he saw a silver Mitsubishi Evo turn into the car park, head his way, and stop in front of him.

'Inspector Buchanan?' said the tall, slim, female driver as she got out of the car. Her long brown hair was pulled back in a ponytail, revealing a face that would look quite natural smiling out from *Elle*.

'Aye, and for your information, lass, it's Detective *Chief* Inspector Buchanan.'

'Sorry, sir, I'll remember that in future. I'm to drive you to headquarters; the Chief wants to have a word with you. I'll put your cases in the boot for you.'

'Thank you. I'll do this case – it's heavy, and fragile,' Buchanan said, as he picked up the smaller of the two. 'Nice car you've got there,' he remarked, stepping back to have a look.

Opening the boot and picking up the larger of his cases, she said, 'And for *your* information, Detective Chief Inspector Buchanan, it's Detective Sergeant Street.'

'Oops, sorry lass, I thought you were just a chauffeur.'

'No, I'm not, and this is your car. You've got it on loan from Traffic till you are finished with your investigation. I hope it's good enough for you.'

'Point taken, sorry.'

The sound of bottles clinking could be heard as he carefully placed the other case in the boot.

It was a strange experience for Buchanan to be chauffeured to work. He could get used to this, he thought, if it wasn't for the fact that he *did* enjoy driving – and especially powerful cars like this one.

♦

At headquarters, Street parked the car in a reserved slot, escorted Buchanan into the building and up in the lift to the Assistant Chief Constable's outer office.

The secretary looked at her phone. 'Assistant Chief Constable Atkins is busy. Would you take a seat?'

Looking around the room Buchanan realised there were certain benefits to higher ranks. One's own secretary, a private office with carpets on the floor, even fresh flowers and – if the view from the chief's window was anywhere as good as the secretary's – he might just be tempted to go for a promotion.

Looking away from the view of the Cuckmere valley his eyes settled on the roll of honour of photos of past Chief Constables. He recognised the picture of Henry Solomon, the only Chief Constable to be murdered on duty while interviewing a suspect. His own face could be there on the wall one-day Buchanan mused, then the thought of a rolled-up trouser leg floated into his consciousness and he shook his head. *You daft auld bugger, you don't belong behind a desk.*

14

Moments later the lamp went out on the desk phone and the secretary called through to say Detective Chief Inspector Buchanan had arrived.

The ACC stood when they entered the room. She walked round her ample desk and shook hands with him.

'Welcome to East Sussex, Buchanan. Hope the flight down was comfortable, no turbulence?'

'Actually, it was the seven thirty-seven from Glasgow Central. I don't fly if I can avoid it; you get a much better breakfast on the train.'

'A man with a sense of humour, good. Keep your nose clean and we'll get along fine.'

'I'll be waiting downstairs, Ma'am,' said Street, turning to leave.

Atkins nodded as she closed the door behind her.

'Fine girl that,' she said. 'I'm sure you two will get along very well.'

'I work alone,' said a startled Buchanan, halfway into his chair.

'It might be the way things are done in Glasgow, but while you're working for me you'll work as a team, do you understand? And Buchanan, just because I'm one DS down doesn't mean you're an expense I can afford. I expect you to earn your keep; I want results and fast.'

Buchanan nodded in agreement. No point in upsetting her at their first meeting – plenty of time to do that later.

'And another thing, it's common knowledge that I'm being considered for promotion to the position of Chief Constable and having this matter of a dead DS in the news is not good – especially since I now have this new superannuated level of bureaucracy of Crime Commissioner to contend with.'

Through years of service in the police force Buchanan had learned that ranks above inspector spent most of their working day behind a desk, while as an inspector himself he had a virtual free hand in the field and he wasn't intending to change his *modus operandi* now.

'What are your plans for the investigation, Buchanan?'

He felt like saying rounding up the usual suspects but instead said, 'I'll read the case notes first, then set up an incident room and go from there.'

'I don't want you spending too much time on the dead woman; coroner's report says it was either an accident or suicide. Stupid girl, should have watched where she was going.'

Buchanan's first reaction was to say something in defence of the dead girl but he kept quiet while the Assistant Chief continued with her edict.

'The death of one of our own is another matter: saps the energy from the force, cripples morale, everyone spends the day looking over their shoulder wondering if they'll they be next. What's needed is someone who can get to the core of the problem, not be deflected by innuendo or rumour: someone with a thick skin. Anderson says you're the man for the job, and I trust his judgement. It won't be easy for you, Buchanan; my people close ranks when trouble camps at the gate. In view of that fact I've sent a memo round telling everyone to extend whatever help you require. I've retrieved the case notes from the archives for you. It'll give you something to read if you can't sleep.'

'Thanks, that's just what I need.'

'And, about the incident room; John Street in Brighton is well equipped. There are plenty of office spaces and you'll find several rooms to choose for your incident room, all fully equipped with the latest technology. And of course, there are plenty of excellent restaurants to eat at.'

Buchanan was about to decline the offer, but said instead, 'I would like to get settled into my accommodation first and have a look around the scenes of crime before deciding what resources I'll require.'

'Good man, I'll hear from you tomorrow afternoon then. Just give tech services a call and they'll set things up for you. Where are you staying?'

'I've taken a house on the Marina, thought it might help to be close to the action.'

'Hmm, not sure that's wise. The drive along the A27 can be hell when there's an accident and the A259 can be worse – usually full of tourists. Have you signed the rental agreement yet? If not we'll find you somewhere in Lewes or Brighton, much closer to HQ.'

Buchanan put on a suitably worried face, shook his head, and said, 'Oh, if only I'd known before all the arrangements had been made. I can't cancel now.'

'Well, it'll just have to be. I pity you, though; I've driven those roads before. You'll have to make an early start in the mornings. I'm giving you two PC's for the legwork, can't afford any more than that – I've got the new Amex stadium to look after now. You'll have to organise your own secretarial staff to look after HOLMES. Will there be anything else you require, Buchanan?'

'No Ma'am, four's a nice round number and should do nicely.'

'Right then,' she said, standing and reaching out to shake his hand. 'Good to meet you, Buchanan. Keep me posted on your investigations.'

Not bloody likely thought Buchanan as he made his way to the stairs; no way was he ever going to commute to an office. He was an outside man. *'Work the coal face. Never polish your arse in a chair,'* his old sergeant in the Gorbals had said.

Buchanan smiled at the memory as he walked down the stairs with the case notes. It was going to be an interesting evening: a new case, a new car, a new town, and a new partner, now *that* was going to be very interesting indeed.

♦

The HQ office door closed silently behind Buchanan as he walked over to his car. Street was standing by the passenger door waiting for him.

'All sorted?'

'A work in progress. Can I give you a lift somewhere, lass?'

She shook her head slowly, looked at him, and then down at her watch. 'We've still got at least an hour before knocking off and in case it's slipped your mind we're supposed to be working together on this investigation.'

Ignoring her comment, he said, 'Do you know the Sovereign Harbour?'

'I've been there for dinner a couple of times.'

'Any restaurants do takeaway?'

'There's a really good Thai restaurant, I'm sure they do – why?'

'It's going to be a long night,' he said, holding up the bundle of case-note papers.

'Should you be taking those out of the building?'

'How else are they going to get read? Besides, the Chief gave them to me?'

'It's on your head,' she said, wondering what she had got herself into. After all he was supposed to be one of the best. Highly recommended by their chief constable and all Buchanan could think of was putting his feet up and having dinner.

'Listen, lass, I'm heading for the Marina and a takeaway. Then I'm going to go through these case notes,' he said, climbing into his car. 'And for your information I'm hypoglycaemic: I have to eat at regular intervals, or I turn into a bear with a sore head.'

'Oh, that makes sense now you explain it,' she said, getting into the passenger seat. 'But I can't quit this early.'

'It's all right, lass, we can go through the notes together till it's your knocking-off time, then I'll drive you home. Where do you live?

'Polegate. I share a flat with a friend.'

'That's just outside Eastbourne?'

'You know the area well?'

'My wife's sister lives in the Marina, it's her house we're renting. I've only been down here a few times, but my memory for places is quite good.'

'Look, if we are going to work together you'd better think of something better to call me than *lass,* she said, as they put on their seat belts. 'We're partners, remember?'

'Point taken; how's Detective Sergeant Street sound?' he said, adjusting his seat and mirrors.

'A bit of a mouthful; everyone goes by their first name in this division. Just call me Jill.'

'Er – ok.' He was silent for a minute, then burst out laughing.

'What's so funny?'

'Your name, or actually both our names. Don't you see?'

'See what?'

'Buchanan and Street, Buchanan Street. It's the main shopping street in Glasgow.'

'You missed the obvious one.'

'What's that?'

'Our first names – Jack and Jill. You know, the children's rhyme, Jack and Jill went up the hill?'

'To fetch a pail of water,' he said, laughing again. Then he nodded sagely as a cold chill ran down his spine. He remembered the next two lines of the children's rhyme and thought; *murder isn't childish business.*

'Turn right here and when we get to the bottom of the hill take the first left at the roundabout and go through the tunnel. So, what do I call you? And don't say *sir* – I had enough of that bullshit in the MDP.'

'You were in the Ministry of Defense Police? You surprise me. Why did you leave?'

'Pending government cutbacks would've severely limited promotion opportunities.'

'I'm sorry to disappoint you, Street, but *sir* is still the appropriate title.'

'OK. So much for equality, *sir*.'

He ignored the jibe and asked, 'Were you firearms trained?'

'Why? Do you want me to shoot someone?'

'No, of course not, just curious.'

'As a matter of fact, I was. Before I joined CID, I was a member of an armed response unit.'

'Why's that? East Sussex doesn't make me think of gangsters and shootouts.'

'Next to the MET, Sussex has the highest gun crime in the country, mostly with legally held shotguns. Then we have Gatwick and Shoreham airports on our patch and, although we don't get directly involved, along the coast to the east we have the Dungeness nuclear power station. Going west we have the ports of Newhaven and Shoreham.'

'Why'd you leave? With today's rising crime rate I'd have thought that it would have kept you plenty busy.'

'You try wearing a twenty-kilo flak jacket while sitting in a police car for up to twelve hours at a time, with the only respite an occasional sandwich and cup of coffee at Starbucks.'

'Ever shoot someone?'

'I'd rather not talk about it, if you don't mind.'

'Fair enough. What do you know about the case we're on?'

'First left at the roundabout, that's the A27, Eastbourne is about 14 miles.'

'Thanks.'

'As far as the case goes, I just know what's been in the papers and the talk around the office.'

'Did you know the dead officer?'

'Met him in the canteen once or twice.'

'What was your impression?'

'Egotistical chauvinist.'

'That's interesting; did he hit on the other women officers?'

'It didn't matter what rank they were, if it had a skirt on he would chase it.'

'Like a moth tae th' flame, his ardour he wid risk.'

'Sorry, you'll have to translate that for me.'

> *'Like a moth to the flame*
> *his ardour he would risk*
> *on the turn of the ankle or the flash of a skirt*
> *he'd bet it all to play his game.'*

'Robert Burns?'

'No,' he laughed, 'that, my lass, is a Jack Buchanan original.'

'You're incorrigible.'

They drove along the A27 in silence, Buchanan imagining Street in body armour holding a Heckler & Koch MP7, but the image of Laura Croft kept getting in the way. He glanced sideways at her, smiled, and realised working with a partner might not be a bad thing after all.

'Fancy the chief's job?' he asked.

'Sorry, I was miles away, and, yes, I was thinking about the ACC's rank, and the privileges that come with it. I could quite happily have a slice of that cake. In the meantime, there are many hours of studying ahead. I don't plan to stay a sergeant all of my career and, a Buchanan or not, nothing is going to stand in the way of my promotion.'

Little did she realise what chaos being hooked up with Buchanan would cause.

He slowed at the lights as they turned green.

'This is Polegate. Take the left lane, follow the road to the roundabout, then follow the A27 dual carriageway to the end.

When you get there take the A22 and follow the signs for Eastbourne; I'll tell you when to turn off.'

'You're a good navigator.'

'And you're a bad driver: you didn't keep to the speed limit once. You're lucky we didn't see any of the Traffic boys – their HQ's in Polegate.'

'Nah, they'd see the number plate and know it was one of their own.'

'Detective Chief Inspector Buchanan, this is East Sussex, not Glasgow. We play by the rules down here.'

'Point taken; I'll watch the speed limit signs in future.'

'Good.'

And ignore them, he thought.

'Turn left at the fourth roundabout, then follow the signs to the harbour.'

'Your wish is my command.'

They drove past the shopping centre and turned off Pevensey Road into the Marina complex.

'This is where you sister-in-law lives? Nice,' said Street, as they pulled into a private car park.

'It has three floors,' said Buchanan, opening the front door. 'Leave the cases at the foot of the stairs; I'll take them up later.'

'What about the incident room?'

'I'm going to set it up on Hammonds Drive. No need to commute to Brighton.'

'What will the Chief say? She's probably expecting you to set one up in Brighton.'

'Ah, spider-woman, who can forget *her*? What *can* she say? I'm the SIO, and this Marina is the centre of the action. Makes sense to have the incident room close to the action.'

'How late are we working this evening?' asked Street, looking at the digital clock on the cooker.

'What's the matter? Worried you'll have to work some overtime?'

'I've changed my mind; this is exciting. I'm intrigued to see how the mind of a Buchanan works.'

'Right,' said Buchanan, smiling, 'enough of the wind-up, let's get to work. We'll use the table in the conservatory for now.'

They walked through the kitchen and into the conservatory. Buchanan laid the case notes on the table: the dead woman's on the left and the dead DS's on the right.

'I could do with a coffee,' said Street.

'Good idea, mine's black.'

'Things never change,' she said, walking back into the kitchen.

'Pardon? I didn't hear that.'

'You weren't meant to.'

'Let's start with the dead woman,' said Buchanan, sipping his coffee and opening the slender folder.

'Wonder what her name is – was?' said Street, correcting herself. 'Not much there to look at, the folder that is.'

'Enough if it was just an accident.'

'And you don't think it was?'

'Two deaths in the Marina within a few days of each other. It's a case of busses.'

'Busses? What do you mean?'

'You get none for ages and then two come along at once. The Marina has been there since 1993 and up to now with only one death – some drunk on a bicycle falling in. Then two within a week – not very likely,' he said, thumbing through the assorted notes.

He picked up the coroner's report. 'Ever read one of these?'

She nodded. 'Once, when I'd just been made up to DS, I had to help with the investigation of a suspicious death. Not exactly bedtime reading.'

'Oh, they're not so bad,' he said, casually flicking through the pages, 'just think of it as a report from the mechanic on what went wrong with your car engine just after it blew up. It's just a list of facts with an opinion at the end.'

'You read it, and then give me *your* opinion.'

'Chicken!' he said, laughing. 'Right, let's see.' He read for a few moments, muttering as he worked his way through the document.

'Well, what's it say?'

Buchanan stopped mumbling and read out loud, 'The coroner's report states that the assistant divisional surgeon, Dr Alois Metzger, arrived on the scene at 06:55 on the 30th of March. The temperature was -0.5 C, overcast sky, no rain had fallen and the ground was damp with melting frost.'

'Quite a detailed report,' said Street. 'Can you summarise – or we'll be here all evening.'

'OK, I'll do my best. Let's see now,' he said, flicking through the pages again, 'ah, here we are. Dr Metzger says that he had been called in at the request of PC Ambrose, who was on the scene when he arrived. Also in attendance were PC Johnston and PCSO Fisher: they had pulled the body from the water and secured the area. DS Nichols arrived before the body was removed to the mortuary and assumed overall control of the investigation.'

'Be interesting to see what he thought of the incident,' said Street.

'We'll have to get hold of his investigation notes for that. The body had been observed floating in the harbour by a member of the public: a Mrs Ferranti, who was out walking her dog.' He stopped talking for a moment while studying the report. 'That's odd.'

'What's odd?'

'It usually takes several days before a body floats to the surface. She must have been wearing bulky clothing to make her body float,' he said, leafing through the report.

'What *was* she wearing? Does it say?'

'Ah, here it is: she was wearing an orange sailing coat. No life jacket, though.' Buchanan studied the report then continued with the narration. 'After removal from the water the body was covered by a plastic sheet, borrowed from a decorator, Mr Frank Field, who had just arrived to do some painting in one of the local apartments.

'The body and scene had been preserved from contamination and photographs had been taken. The body was then removed to the mortuary where the assistant divisional surgeon performed the autopsy. The autopsy information makes up the remainder of this report.'

Buchanan turned to the last page and read the surgeon's conclusion: 'In summary, my opinion is the cause of death was from drowning, which was compounded by the deceased being under the influence of cocaine and a substantial amount of alcohol at the time of immersion.'

'Poor kid, what a way to go. Well, what do you think? Accident or suicide? Certainly not murder.'

He looked at his watch. 'I'm getting hungry, that's what I think. What about you?' He got up and walked into the kitchen.

She shook her head and picked up the report. 'The report says she died from drowning; she hadn't eaten a proper meal during at least the past eight hours. It suggests she was snacking on food, rather than eating a prepared meal. The stomach contained traces of pork sausage meat, puff pastry, green and black olives, pineapple, and cheese. She must have been hungry to eat that stuff.'

'I know what that feels like,' said Buchanan, thumbing through a pile of takeaway brochures. 'She had traces of alcohol and cocaine in her blood. She was either drunk, stoned, or both, when she went in – it's no wonder she drowned. What about her identity or identifying marks on the body?'

Street grimaced at the surgeon's remarks about the state of the dead woman's liver.

'Have a look at page three; surgeon says there was nothing out of the ordinary.'

Street turned over the page and read the surgeon's notes. 'Age estimated late 20s to early 30s, dark-skinned, suggesting mid-Eastern origins, shoulder-length black hair, brown eyes and she had all her teeth. There was a small butterfly tattooed on the inner right thigh, and she was three months' pregnant.' She went silent and stared at the floor.

'What's the matter,' said Buchanan, picking up the kitchen phone, 'is it because she was pregnant?'

'That poor baby, it never had a chance.'

'Two hundred thousand a year never have a chance, but that's not our concern right now. We have to keep focussed.'

Street blew her nose. 'No name or anything to identify the body. Don't you think that a bit odd?'

He shook his head. 'Probably dropped her handbag when she fell in. It'll be lying on the bottom of the harbour somewhere.'

'So you don't think it's murder then? And I suppose the detective drowned while looking for the purse?'

'Interesting idea. Now, what do you want to eat?'

'What do I want to eat? What about work? We're supposed to be investigating two deaths.'

'There's plenty of time for that. Let's get the food ordered first, *then* we can discuss the case, all right?'

'If you insist. Not sure what I want though, what do you suggest?'

'How about we forget Thai, and just order one of my favourite Glasgow dishes? Keep things nice and simple.'

'What, deep-fried Mars bars? Not likely, I prefer mine from the refrigerator.'

He grinned at her and dialled the number for a local Indian takeaway.

'Oh well,' she said, as she scanned the remaining case notes. 'There sure isn't much to go on, is there?'

'What do they say?' he said, from the kitchen.

'Johnston and Fisher said they searched the area for the missing handbag and found nothing.'

'That's not surprising,' said Buchanan. 'The body was pulled from where it was found, not necessarily from where it went in.'

'That makes sense.'

'Yeah, two chicken tikka masalas, pilau rice and garlic naan breads. Thirty minutes? Great, let me get my wallet.'

'That's not a Scottish dish – that's Indian.'

'Actually, it was invented by a Pakistani chef in a Glasgow restaurant in 1971.'

'You could have fooled me'.

'Still not sure if it was an accident, suicide, or murder?' said Buchanan, opening his wallet.

'I'm confused. She hasn't been sexually assaulted, there was no bruising or lacerations found on the body, she was fully dressed, including that orange sailing coat. Maybe the fact that she was pregnant had a part to play. Can't get my head round why she was wearing an orange sailing coat at a party.'

'Perhaps she nipped out for a cigarette and the coat was all that was available to keep her warm.'

'Makes sense.'

'Remember the coroner's report?'

'It concludes the death to be a misadventure complicated by the presence of alcohol and illicit drugs.'

'Ah, but was it?' interrupted Buchanan. 'Where are her shoes and let's not forget the handbag.'

'Like you said, the handbag is probably lying on the bottom along with her shoes, just where she went in.'

Buchanan read out his card number, hung up the phone and returned to the conservatory.

'Let's look at the facts as we have them,' said Street. 'She was fully dressed, except for shoes and handbag. She hadn't been assaulted, but had been drinking and had a significant quantity of cocaine in her blood. Lastly, she had not eaten a proper meal for at least eight hours – only snacks – before she drowned.'

'Conclusion, lass?'

'Sounds like she'd been partying,' said Street.

'Just what I was thinking. But where, when, and with whom? And, was it the case she just simply fell in, or did someone push her?'

'She probably just fell in and drowned.'

'Did you look at the photos of her nails?'

'Quite striking. Lovely design, I thought.'

'Perfect condition, like she had just come from the nail parlour. Tell me, do you swim?'

'Yes, once a week at the Sovereign Centre, and when the weather is nice in the summer I go in the sea. Why?'

'Ever get pushed into a pool?'

'When we were young, a group of us used to go swimming in the river. One of the lads thought it was fun to push me in when I was too scared to jump.'

'What'd you do?'

'I'd be angry and chase him when I got out.'

'Your first reaction was?'

'Oh, now I see where you're coming from. I'd grab something, – a branch, or a rock – to pull myself out.'

'Right – and our victim, did she grab for something? Look at the photos of her nails again: think about her floundering in the cold harbour water, gasping for breath. Grabbing for a handhold when all she can feel is the wet, slimy, concrete sides of the harbour walls.'

'No, she couldn't have, there's no damage to her nails at all. If she had, they would have been torn and also there would be vestiges of whatever had been growing on the harbour walls left under what remained of the nails. She must have been unconscious when she went in – that poor girl.'

'Then that means someone put her in the harbour while she was still alive, a case of cold, pre-meditated murder. So now we have to ask ourselves a couple of questions.'

'Like, when and how did she get to the harbour?' said Street.

'Just so; not likely she walked, though, especially in her condition. If she took public transport it's possible someone saw her or was with her, same goes with a taxi, more items for us to check up on. Also, I think it would be a good idea to check the local restaurants and see if there were any parties going on. You never know, she could have been a guest at one of them. Or maybe she was working in one of the restaurants.'

'That coat just doesn't fit in, does it?'

'Maybe one of the restaurant staff owned it, and she grabbed it to go outside for some fresh air.'

'Report says she didn't smoke.'

'That's not what I meant.'

'Suppose she lived in the Marina? Lots of renters here.'

'Anybody check on that?'

Street had another look through the case notes. 'Looks like nothing was followed up on.'

'Or was it?'

'What do you mean?'

'Who was the SIO?'

'Nichols, but he only had a week to investigate, and maybe he was a slow starter.'

'Or maybe he was hiding something.'

'Like his relationship with the dead girl?'

'It's a possibility.' Buchanan was silent for a moment. 'Well, at least it gives us a clean slate to start from.'

'Then you're sure it was murder?'

'Yes, lass, it's definitely murder, by person or persons unknown.'

'This will be my first murder case. Not sure if I should be excited or scared.'

'One thing we haven't thought of.'

'What's that?' said Street.

'She could have been driven to the harbour by a boyfriend, they had an argument; he got angry and pushed her in. Of course, she could have just passed out, fell in and drowned, but I don't think either case is very likely.'

'And she was left-handed; at least I think she was.'

'Why do you say that, lass?'

'If you go to a nail bar to have your nails done, you'd expect the patterns of the nails on both hands to look identical; hers aren't. The nails on the right hand are symmetrical while the patterns on the left-hand shows signs of an unsteady hand: ergo she was left-handed and did her own nails.'

'Well spotted, lass. That's one up to you.'

'Didn't realise this was a competition.' Street smiled and relaxed as the doorbell rang announcing the arrival of their curries.

'I'll get the door,' said Buchanan. 'What do you want to drink with your dinner?'

'Is there any diet lemonade? If not, water will do.'

'It's after hours – we're technically off duty. I fancy a nice cold beer,' he said, looking in the fridge. 'There are a couple of packs of French beer in here. Would you like one?'

'As long as you don't expect me to keep up with you, a beer will be fine.'

Street dished out their dinners, carried the plates through to the conservatory, and laid them on the table.

'Not bad for an English version of a Scottish delicacy.'

'Not bad, wherever it's from. Good choice, sir. Hadn't realised just how hungry I was.'

They ate in a contented silence, she carefully tasting each mouthful while he ate like a bear devouring its last meal before hibernating.

He certainly was an enigma, she thought. He was not a tall man as some policemen were these days, but then he wasn't short either, about five-eleven. Nor was he fat or thin, he just had a presence – he occupied space. The sum of his being was greater than the man with whom she had just spent most of the day. She now saw he was a confident, contented being, who loved his work and made it clear he relished the upcoming challenge. She suddenly realised she liked him, faults and all.

'How long have you been in the force?' he asked.

'I joined the MDP after college, thinking I had a career path up to a senior rank. When they put a promotion freeze in place, I transferred to civilian duty.'

'What rank were you?'

'Sergeant. I'd just started studying for my Inspector's exam.'

'I'm suitably impressed.'

'I chose armed response as it was similar duties to military policing. Couldn't hack walking the beat.'

'There's nothing wrong with walking the beat. Everyone joining the force has to wear out some shoe leather first. I did it and it didn't do me any harm. But tell me, how'd you come to the Chief's attention?'

'It was a few years ago at Gatwick Airport; we were waiting for some American dignitaries. As the visitors were being escorted through the arrival hall, some crank in the crowd lunged out with a knife. I tackled him to the ground and disarmed him, then managed to dislocate his shoulder,' she smiled. 'But he deserved that, and in the kerfuffle, I accidently knocked the Chief over.'

'Bet she was furious.'

'No, in fact she said afterwards it was reassuring for her to see her force in action first hand. *Defending the nation against, those who seek to subvert our free society for their own depraved ends.* A few months later I was summoned to her office. She had read my transfer request and history and decided to approve my transfer to CID. What about you – how did you get to be a Chief Inspector?'

'My family on my father's side were shipbuilders; that is to say they worked on Clydeside in the yards. My mother's family were miners. My father saw there was no future in either profession and got me into the police. I've spent all my working life in the Glasgow force, worked my way up through the ranks till I got to where I am today, and happy in it.'

'Why are you in Eastbourne, then, if you have spent your entire career in Glasgow? Wouldn't it have made more sense for you to have stayed there?'

Buchanan opened another beer and told Street about the fight in Porter's toilets.

'And you kicked his teeth out! It's a wonder you're not in jail. You'd never get away with that down here,' she said, shaking her head. 'Although there are times when I'd like to just belt one of those drunken arseholes we meet outside the clubs on Saturday nights.'

'Language: there's a man present.'

She laughed. 'Do you have any children?'

The laughter left his face; he looked down at the floor, shook his head slowly and said, 'No, we tried, went to all the doctors that would listen, but nothing. We've just learned to live with the disappointment and get on with life.'

'I'm sorry to hear that. What about adoption?'

'We never thought of it at first, too wrapped up in our disappointment. Then, when we did, I was too old.'

'You're never too old to adopt, that's what I read in a magazine.'

'Maybe, but what about you? Any boyfriends? Girlfriends, even?'

'Certainly not. How could you think such a thing? Besides, my personal life is my own business.'

'Sorry lass, just making conversation.'

She was silent for a moment. Buchanan watched a tear form in her eye. She picked up a napkin and blew her nose, 'Right, let's get back to work.'

'And now for something completely different,' said Buchanan, trying to lighten the mood. 'I see the good Dr Metzger attended once again – that's what I like, continuity in an investigation.' He put down the coroner's report and picked up a newspaper clipping from the *Eastbourne Herald* and read:

> *'Police were called to Sovereign Harbour on Monday, April 6th, regarding a report from the harbour master's office about a submerged car. The area was cordoned off while the Sussex Police Specialist Search Unit was called out to search the vehicle prior to it being recovered. Upon searching the vehicle, the body of Detective Sergeant Arthur Nichols was discovered, still strapped in by his seatbelt. Speculation is that he accidentally reversed into the harbour. It is suspected he hit his head and was knocked unconscious and was unable to get out of the car in time.*

'Another accident, sir?' queried Street.

'Let's have a look at the good doctor's report. Impact wound to the right temple. Probable cause: impact on driver window. Particles of window glass embedded in scalp, commensurate with an impact of the head onto the glass. Blood test confirmed the presence of alcohol in the blood, BAC measured .097. Deceased unconscious when submerged; cause of death drowning while incapacitated.'

'And that's it?' asked Street. 'Just who is this doctor?'

'That's something we are going to look into. But in the meantime, let's decide on a course of action. I think we'll start with the death of the maiden. Tomorrow after breakfast we'll go look at where she was pulled from the water, then on to the harbour master and find out if the harbour has a current and, if so, what direction it flows in.'

'Why, what will that tell us?'

'We know where she was pulled out and how long she was in the water, so hopefully we should be able to extrapolate where and when she went in.'

'I see, and if we know where and when we can see who might have been around. Maybe we'll get lucky and see something on a CCTV camera recording.'

'Exactly. And another thing, can we get the mortuary photo of the girl touched up to make her look like she might have done on the day before she died? Then we'll get our PC's to take the photo of her and the tattoo round the local tattoo parlours and see if anyone recognises her. Can't be too many tattoo parlours in a town this small.'

'I could do that if I had access to a computer. Photography is one of my hobbies. I do weddings and I know how to, shall we say, enhance what people look like on their special day.'

'Wouldn't you require special software?'

'Shouldn't be an issue, there's a programme on the server for that. I used it when I was stuck at work one evening and had to get some wedding photos to the bride for the next morning before they went on honeymoon.'

Buchanan smiled at her. 'Good. As soon as we get operational in the morning, can you make that a priority?'

'I was just wondering, sir. Could it be possible that it's more than a coincidence they both died at the Marina? Suppose they were having an affair and Nichols was the father of her child. She confronted him at the harbour, there was an argument, and he told her he wasn't interested in being a father. He left in anger and she killed herself. Then, a week later, full of remorse. he does the same thing?'

'That's an interesting hypothesis. We would need a DNA check to see if he was the father.'

'Should be straightforward. Do you want me to pursue it?'

'OK, but after you have retouched her photograph. I want to find out her identity as soon as possible. I still think there's a great deal more to this case than we have information on and I'm still sure she is the key to the whole matter.'

'Oh dear, what *can* the matter be?' said Street.

'Two dead stiffs in the mortuary, they've been there from Monday till Saturday.'

'Sir, this is no joking matter – and we've got *three* dead bodies.'

Buchanan nodded. 'Yes, you're right. Even that poor wee three-month unborn baby has a part to play in this mystery.' He stretched out his arms, yawned and said, "I think I'm all in for the day. Where did you say your car's parked?'

'I left it in Traffic's car park when I picked up your car this morning; it's a short walk from my flat.'

'In that case I'll call you a taxi – I shouldn't be driving.'

'Where and when shall we meet in the morning?'

'Let's meet at the Harbour House in the Marina – breakfast starts at eight. Gives us a chance to see what stirs in the morning. Then I think, a visit to the harbour master's office, after that a walk round the harbour to reconnoitre where our fair maiden and DS Nichols went for their unintentional swim. And I suppose at some point we should have a look at Nichols' car.'

5

Street had walked into a very quiet restaurant. Would Buchanan still be here, or would his impatience to get on with the case have him out in the Marina already?

'Good morning. Are you here for breakfast?' asked the waitress.

'Yes, but I'm meeting someone and I'm running late,' Street grimaced, looking at her watch. 'Supposed to be here at eight – hope he's still here.'

'That'll be the gentleman at table seven, if you'll follow me,' said the waitress. 'Not many people come out for breakfast this early, we're usually quiet at this time of the day.'

Partially relieved that Buchanan hadn't gone on without her, yet nervous as to what he would say, she followed the waitress through the restaurant to Buchanan's table.

'Good morning, sir, sorry I'm late; train overshot the platform at the Hampden Park crossing. I had to turn around and go the long way round.'

'I'll come back in a minute when you've decided,' said the waitress dropping her order pad back into the pocket on her apron.

'Let's see,' said Buchanan, grinning, 'Hampden Park and back in one night and you're only half an hour late – remarkable timing. Not even I, in my nice new Evo, could do that. What do you want for breakfast?'

'Thanks, I won't be late again,' she said, with a sigh of relief, not fully understanding his reference to Hampden Park. 'Scrambled eggs on toast would be fine, oh – and could I have a black coffee?'

The waitress came out of hiding, looked at Street, relaxed, smiled, and said, 'Have you decided what you would like?'

'Yes,' interrupted Buchanan, 'the lass would like scrambled eggs on toast with coffee. I'll have the Harbour House breakfast, and I'll have coffee as well.'

'Any juices? We have orange and grapefruit.'

'Orange juice, please,' said Street.

'Sir?'

'I'll have a large one and bring the coffees when you bring the juices, please.'

'I'll be right back with your drinks,' said the waitress, scribbling on her order pad.

'Rough night, lass?'

'I couldn't get to sleep and when I finally did manage to drop off I dreamt I was looking out of my bedroom window. It was pouring with rain and there was a baby in a pram crying. Its mother was standing beside the pram shouting something at me but I couldn't hear what she was saying – and I couldn't find my shoes.'

Buchanan smiled and shook his head slowly. 'It might be your first, but it won't be your last dream about a corpse. I think you are going to do just fine.'

'Why do you say that? I haven't even done twenty-four hours on this case yet.'

'You care, that's what makes the difference.'

'Thanks, that makes me feel a lot better. But what do *you* do? Do you dream about your corpses?'

'My clients? Yes, I do.'

'Why do you call them clients? They're dead.'

He smiled at her. 'If I don't look after them, who will?'

They were interrupted by the waitress bringing their drinks.

'Two orange juices and two coffees. Your breakfasts will be out in a few minutes. Milk and sugar is on the table. Can I get you anything else?'

Buchanan shook his head. 'No thanks, we're fine.'

Street poured a drop of milk in her coffee and started stirring, 'you were saying.'

'Why do I call them clients? I just do. I suppose it makes the work a little bit more personal, like you're helping a friend in need.'

He looked up at the ceiling as though inspecting the work of the night spiders, then said,

Those who served in life
known and unknown, seen and unseen
now no longer struggle in servitude
but rest under warm elysian fields

Some crawled on their knees
Their master's whims to please
But no joy was there to find
But toil, trouble and a merciless grind

Others marched ahead
Through trials and travails
Fearless and determined
To stay on the rails

Unlocking the door, some stepped right in
to become entwined in our very DNA
we loved them for all time, but then time ran out
and departing they ripped out our hearts.'

'Another one of your poems?'

'I'm still working on it.'

'It's lovely – you really surprise me. But it's not just a poem, is it?'

He shook his head. 'Later. This isn't the place to talk about it.'

The waitress returned carrying their breakfasts and set them on the table. 'Will there be anything else?'

Buchanan, with his knife and fork in hand, shook his head.

'I'd like another coffee, please,' said Street.

As they ate in a contented silence a group of four dock workers entered and walked over to a far window table.

'Will that be all for you, sir, madam?' asked the waitress on her way to the group that had just entered.

'Yes – thanks.'

'I'll be right over with your bill.'

'If you'll excuse me, I need to powder my nose,' said Street. She returned five minutes later to an empty table.

'The gentleman you were with has gone outside, said he'd be right back,' said the waitress placing the bill on the table.

Street looked out of the window and saw Buchanan leaning on the railing, smoking.

♦

'Didn't know you smoked,' said Street, when Buchanan returned.

'I don't – and don't say anything to my wife. I quit last month.'

'I never started.'

'It's tough after smoking on and off for the best part of thirty years.'

'So I've heard. Where shall we start?'

'My treat,' said Buchanan picking up the bill from the table.

'Thanks.'

'Can you tell me, miss,' Buchanan said to the waitress, while taking his wallet out of his jacket pocket, 'where the harbour master's office is?'

'Oh yes, if you look out the window, it's that large bluish building over to the right – the one across the harbour. Going sailing?' she said, as she plugged Buchanan's card into the reader.

'No, we want to have a word with the harbour master.'

'You don't have to go all the way over there,' she said, 'some of the team are at that table by the window having breakfast. I'm sure they wouldn't mind being disturbed'.

Buchanan turned round to look at them; they were all dressed in blue work clothes. A woman, with long copper red hair cascading down on to her shoulders, sat with her back to Buchanan. Two wiry-looking young lads with their sleeves rolled up exposing well-toned biceps were seated at either side of the table. A large, swarthy male, apparently holding court, faced Buchanan.

Putting his receipt in his wallet, Buchanan placed a two-pound coin on the table and stood up. 'Time to go to work, lass.'

Street looked at the tip and added another two pounds.

♦

'Excuse me for interrupting your breakfast. I was wondering if you could answer a couple of questions?'

'If I can,' replied the swarthy male.

'I'm looking into the business of the drowned woman and policeman in the harbour last month.'

'You the press?' the man asked, pressing his fists down onto the table and leaning his bulk forward. 'We've had enough of you people poking your noses in around here.'

'Relax, Dan, I'll handle this.' The woman turned to face Buchanan, her green eyes assessing him. She smiled. 'That's police business; you'll have to take it up with them.'

'Excuse me, Ma'am, but we *are* the police.' Buchanan took out his warrant card and showed it to the assembled group. 'Detective Chief Inspector Buchanan and this,' he said, turning to Street, 'is Detective Sergeant Street. Who might you be?'

'Mary Riley. I'm sitting in for the harbour master – he's away on a training exercise. How can I help?'

Buchanan put his warrant card away. 'As I said, we're investigating the recent deaths in the Marina.'

'Then you'll know we've already answered the police questions. We didn't know anything then and we don't know anything now,' interrupted Dan.

'All right, Dan, try this one for size. Is there a current in the harbour? Does the water move around?'

'Not per se. When we get strong westerlies, the boats get buffeted at their docks and move around a bit, but that's all.'

'So, if I fell in and drowned, my body would just stay where it fell in?'

'That depends where you fell in,' Dan replied. 'For instance, if you fell in just outside the restaurant, you probably would just stay there. On the other hand, if you fell off the bridge between the north and south harbours and we were topping up the inner harbour, you could float quite a few metres with the current.'

'Do you pump sea water back into the harbour to keep it topped up?'

'No, when the tide starts to fall from its high point, we partially open both the outer and inner lock gates and top up the harbour direct from the sea. At high tide, the water in the inner harbour is anywhere up to two metres below the level of the sea, so we just let it flow back in a controlled manner.'

'Why fill when the tide is falling? Why not let it fill as the tide rises?' asked Street.

'For a very good reason,' interrupted Mary Riley. 'If there was to be a problem with the lock gates – say for some reason they stuck open – not only would the inner harbour water level rise too high, but most of the surrounding countryside would be flooded. With us doing the filling on a falling tide the worst that could happen is the inner harbour would drain. Doing it this way would give us time to ship the temporary drop gates and prevent flooding when the tide turned and started to rise again.'

'Very interesting, thank you. Oh, one more question,' said Buchanan. 'If someone fell in the water from the bridge and the water levels were adjusting between the north and south harbours, do you have any idea how far the body might travel?'

'The flow is the fastest directly under the bridge,' said Dan. 'As you pass the edges of the bridge the water spreads out sideways and the speed slows dramatically.'

'So not very far then? What – about twenty metres?'

'Slightly more if there's a large variation in the flow.'

'The dead woman was pulled from the harbour at seven in the morning and she had been in the water for about eight hours, any ideas where she might have gone in?'

The two Biceps stared at each other and shook their heads. Dan thought, and Mary Riley said, 'At a guess, the bridge is where she went in. We would have been topping up that evening and the flow would have been into the north harbour.'

'Thank you for your time. If we have any more questions, where would I find you?'

She smiled at him, and rolled the tip of her tongue round her lips. 'You'll find me in the office: it's the blue building above the locks.'

Buchanan smiled back at her; he'd had that sort of invitation before, and then as now replied, 'Thank you for your help; we'll be in touch if there are any further questions.'

He and Street left Harbour House and walked along the promenade, past the other restaurants.

'Where did you park your car, lass?'

'Across from the yacht club. I don't like the shopping centre car park, it's laid out backwards. It's the worst car park I've ever tried to park in. And you? Did you drive?'

'No, I had a lovely walk along the seafront. I understand from talking to my neighbour that there's a promenade on the other side of the locks that goes all the way to Eastbourne and on to

Beachy Head. Must do that someday, the exercise will do me good.' He patted his stomach and laughed.

They walked across the road and down the gravelled bank to the water's edge from where the dead woman had been pulled.

'Not much to see, is there, sir?'

'Not now there isn't.' Buchanan shook his head and grimaced as though there should still be tell-tale evidence lying on the ground to be discovered. After a few fruitless minutes of rummaging around, he said, 'Let's have a look at the bridge.'

Occasionally stopping to look for fish in the semi-clear water, they walked along the quayside.

'Interesting,' said Buchanan. 'Whoever put Nichols in the water wasn't trying to hide the car; it would show up very easily on a sunny day.'

'Could that have been a message to someone?'

'Or just a coincidence. Or, as the coroner implied, maybe it really *was* an accident.'

They walked past a cluster of crab pots and stopped where the harbour wall turned and ran parallel to the channel that led to the bridge.

'Well, what do you think, lass? Could this be the spot?'

Street looked back to where they'd just come from, then to her left and the bridge. 'If she had walked down here, maybe trying to hide from someone, these tall reeds would have partially hidden her. At least, that's what she might have thought.'

Buchanan turned around, looking for something.

'What are you looking for, sir?'

'Up there, on the corner of the building,' he said, pointing at a CCTV camera pod. 'I wonder what that saw on the fateful evening? I think a visit to the harbour master's office is called for, but in the meantime,' he continued, looking at his watch,' we've got visitors due at Hammonds Drive in a few minutes.'

♦

The visitors' parking bays in front of the office were occupied with a large unmarked white van and a police patrol car. Two uniformed officers were standing beside the patrol car talking with two civilians.

'These are our men,' said Buchanan, as he got out of the car. 'They're early, 'that's what I like.' Walking over to the impromptu gathering, he said, 'Buchanan,' more as a statement than an introduction.

The uniforms stood erect, while the civilians introduced themselves as Harrison and Palmer. 'We've got your office in the back of the van, sir. If you'll show us how you want it laid out we'll get on with the setup and get out of your way as quick as we can.'

'Follow me.'

Buchanan headed for the front door. He took three steps, stopped and turned to the uniforms, 'Be right with you – don't go away.'

Harrison and Palmer followed him into the office and up the stairs to the incident room.

'I'd like two desks under the window, facing each other, with room enough for a couple of chairs between, the other two desks, put them where they're shown on the sketch. He passed them a sketch of the room layout. 'Put the filing cabinets, printer and fax wherever they fit best, the white boards on the right of the door as you enter, OK, Palmer?'

'Yes, sir, looks straightforward enough. We'll get right on it, should be done within the hour.'

Buchanan walked back down to the car park and gestured to Street and the two constables to follow him into the building. 'No point in getting in their way, we'll use the time to get acquainted.'

He led them through to the long since closed canteen, stopped with his back to the window and looked at the two PC's. They visibly stiffened to attention, looking nervous.

'Detective Sergeant Street has already introduced herself. I'm Detective Chief Inspector Buchanan. I'm the SIO on this case, Detective Sergeant Street is assisting me and you two are assisting us. Is that clear?'

Two heads nodded. 'Yes, sir.'

'I grew up in Glasgow, in what used to be called the Mean City. My beat was the Gorbals. I walked many a mile on my own through wind, rain and snow, both day and night. I've done it all, there were no fancy air-conditioned panda cars for me. I've been sworn at, spat at, and even urinated on. I've had my nose broken more than once, been stabbed twice, slashed at by drunks with broken bottles and narrowly missed having my face opened by a cut-throat razor. So I don't want to hear any stories about the job being tough. Is that understood?'

Not waiting for an answer he addressed the PC on the right. 'What's your name?"

'Hunter, sir,'

'First name?'

'It's Stephen, sir.'

'And yours?' he asked the PC on the left.

The young PC grimaced and replied, 'Dexter, sir.'

'And your first name?'

'Morris, sir.' He shrugged, then grinned.

'You poor sod, who did that to you?'

'It was my mother, sir; she loved the Morse TV programmes and John Thaw in particular.'

'Morris Dexter.' Buchanan laughed and shook his head.

'Sorry, sir.'

'No, no. Don't be sorry, son, I think it's bloody brilliant; it'll do your career no end of good. But I'll warn you: never, ever, put a foot wrong. No one will forget you, and it'll be for all the wrong reasons.'

Dexter visibly relaxed.

'Right, let's get to work.' Buchanan pulled out a chair and sat down, still chuckling to himself.

'Who's for coffee?' asked Street, 'Stephen, can you give me a hand, please.

Coffees in hand, they sat round the table and waited for Buchanan to speak.

'Right, what do either of you know about the deaths in the Marina?'

'Not much,' replied Hunter, 'being PC's we don't get to hear much of what goes on in CID. We did hear about the dead policeman, though.'

Just then Palmer came into the canteen. 'We're finished in the office, sir, if you'd like to come and have a look then we can be on our way.'

'Street, bring Hunter and Dexter up to speed on the investigation. I'll be right back.'

Palmer and Harrison had done an excellent job. Gone was the empty box-like room, now replaced by a very compact and efficient-looking incident room. Buchanan walked over to the desk on the left and picked up the phone.

'Just dial nine for an outside line, sir,' said Palmer, 'your phone is on the company exchange. I've left you an internal directory on the desk.'

Buchanan nodded and said, 'Thanks Palmer, this should do very nicely.'

Returning to the canteen, he said, 'Right team, we're in business! Follow me to our new incident room.

♦

Buchanan sat, swivelled and looked out the window. 'Street, I want you to get on with the girl's picture. How long will it take?'

'I'll have to scan in the photo, find the software, and then touch-up the picture: say about an hour.'

'That'll have to do. In the meantime, Dexter and Hunter, as soon as DS Street is done with the photo of the dead girl, I want you to get into town and find out if any taxis brought a woman fitting our girl's description out to the Marina on the 29th of March, the day before she was pulled from the water. Then do the same with the busses; there can't be many of them that come this way. Next go round to all the tattoo parlours in town and see if anyone recognises the photo of the girl or the tattoo. Finally, check with the letting agencies and see if anyone has rented property to our girl. You'll probably draw a blank on that but I want all avenues explored. Got that?'

'Yes, sir,' they replied.

As the door closed behind them, Street asked, 'What's next, sir?'

'When you're done with the photo we'll go talk with Nichols' compatriots; maybe they can shed some light on his affairs.'

Buchanan followed Street down the corridor and into the main office. The room was laid out in a modern open plan arrangement: a row of cubicles down each window wall and rows of filing cabinets back to back ran the whole length of the middle of the room. Street walked over to one of the occupied cubicles.

'Hello, John.'

'Hiya, Jill. Who's your new partner?'

'This is DCI Buchanan, he's – we're investigating the death of DS Nichols.'

John stood. 'DI Hanbury. Welcome to Sussex, sir.'

'Thanks. Did you know DS Nichols?'

'As much as anyone could. He kept mostly to himself.'

'Did he have any friends?'

'Not that I'm aware of, sir. Although there was talk once of an aunt he looked after – not sure if she's even still alive.'

'What about bad habits? I know about his womanising. Did he drink?'

'Don't want to speak ill of the dead, sir. But he did occasionally let his hair down. His drinking didn't seem to affect his work – although one time he disappeared for a couple of days.'

'What did he say when he came back?'

'Something about a sick relative, needed to find someone to look after them.'

'When was that?' said Buchanan.

'Mid-March, I think. About two weeks before he died.'

'Anyone here know anything about him?'

'I doubt it; he really was a loner.'

'What about the cases he was working on before he died? Who picked them up?'

'You're in luck there: that's me, I got the lot.'

'What was he working on?' asked Buchanan.

'A series of robberies: at various industrial sites, one at a local stable, and another at a jeweller's in town. There also was a knifing assault outside a night club in Terminus Road and a couple of car thefts in Meads – one of which was a brand-new Audi.'

'Anything about the dead girl in the Marina?'

'I thought that was an accident?'

'Not as far as I'm concerned.'

'I reviewed all of his case notes; there was nothing about the dead girl.'

'What about the stuff in his office – you know, the contents of his desk drawers, etcetera?'

'They'll all be in the exhibit store room, sir. Only the case notes were passed to me. Jill can show you the way to the store room.'

'Right. Thanks, Hanbury.'

'Any time,' said Hanbury to Buchanan's back as he headed for the door.

♦

'Can I help?' asked the clerk behind the counter of the exhibit room.

'Yes. We'd like to see the contents of DS Nichols' office, please. We're investigating his death.'

'If you'll just sign the register, I'll take you to where you can view the items.'

They followed the clerk through to the back where there was a small room with a table and two chairs in front of a mesh-covered window.

'If you'd like to sit at the desk, sir, I'll bring the boxes in to you.'

'Thanks.'

The clerk returned a few minutes later with a blue trolley laden with four large cardboard boxes.

Street looked at the boxes, then at Buchanan's face, and said, 'I'll get the coffees. This is going to take a while.'

'Sorry, Ma'am, no drinks or food in here, it's the rules,' said the clerk.

She shrugged her shoulders and opened the top boxes.

'Nothing on our dead girl?' said Buchanan, as he went through the first box.'

'Nothing here either about our dead woman, do you think Nichols was working on her case in secret?'

'Just a hunch,' said Buchanan, initialling the evidence bag and dropping Nichols' keys in his pocket. He looked longingly at the half-empty bottle of Jack Daniels in the bottom of the second box.

'At least he had good taste in whiskey,' said Street.

'Ah – this looks interesting,' said Buchanan, finding Nichols' office diary at the bottom. He pushed the empty box out of the way and opened the diary at the last week in December.

Street came over and stood behind him while he read the limited number of entries. 'It's all symbols, sir. What do you think

49

they mean – and why would he not just write down the information?'

'I suppose he didn't want anyone to know what he was up to. Look at this: DTout@1930 and here's another sbret@2345.'

'They're not Masonic, are they?'

'I wouldn't know.'

'Could the letters be an abbreviation for an email address?' suggested Street.

He flicked further through the diary and found many more similar entries.

'Or, how about it's nothing more than shorthand for someone's initials and what time he's meeting them?'

Buchanan shrugged. 'They could be, not sure though.' He stood, looked at the contents of the boxes now spread out over the table and shook his head. 'There's something missing, Street. What is it?'

She looked over the contents and shrugged. 'Not sure, sir. You've got his keys, his diary, and his whiskey. The rest are just papers: an out-of-date copy of the *Eastbourne Herald,* a copy of the tide tables, February's *Sea Angler* magazine and a copy of *Friday Ad.* Just stuff.'

Buchanan reached for his cigarettes in his inside jacket pocket, his hand hesitated, then retreated to his side. He smiled. 'I have it – or at least I know what one of the missing items is.'

Street looked up. 'What is it, sir? What's missing?'

'It's obvious, lass. Where's his phone? Everyone has a phone – where's his?'

Street rummaged through the papers, looked inside the boxes, and found nothing. 'And what else?'

'His pocket notebook, lass. Although that would only have information he was prepared to share. I'll be right back.'

He returned a few minutes later with a smile on his face, holding Nichols' mobile phone above his head like an Olympic torch.

'Seek and ye shall find. It was in a drawer at the reception desk. The clerk said it was private property and didn't belong in the evidence room; he was going to send it on, but hadn't quite got round to it yet.' Buchanan stared at the screen for a moment.

'Shall I, sir?' said Street, putting out her hand. 'A friend has a similar model.'

He handed her the phone.

Street pressed the power on key, but nothing happened. "I'll send it off for analysis; maybe we'll get lucky and be able to retrace Nichols' movements.'

'You can do that?' said Buchanan.

'I can't, but the lab can,' said Street. 'It's surprising just what details can be found on old phones.'

'While you're at it, get on to his phone service provider's accounts and get them to give you a copy of the last six months' bills. Also, see if you can get them to provide you with a list of who has called him recently, I want to know who he's been keeping in touch with.'

'Yes, sir,' she said, putting the phone in an evidence bag.

'Right,' said Buchanan, 'grab the papers and the diary. We'll take them with us. We'd better head down to Personnel and retrieve Nichols' home address before leaving, and I suppose at some point we should have a look at his car.'

◆

'Yes, sir? What can I do for you?' asked the clerk behind the counter in Personnel.

'I'd like the home address of DS Nichols, please.'

'And you are?'

'DCI Buchanan and DS Street.'

'Thank you, sir. Need to be careful these days, you never know who's up to what, if you follow my meaning.'

Buchanan shook his head. 'Access to this station is by appointment only, man. No one can get in here who's not authorised.'

The clerk pursed his lips, and looked down at his computer screen. 'Ah, here it is. I'll write it down for you, so you can ask directions if you get lost.'

Buchanan was about to say something rude then saw the funny side of the remark and chuckled.

'Sir, I think I should get on with the girl's photo and get the DNA tests moving,' said Street.

'Good idea. In the meantime, I'm headed for the harbour office – I want to have a look at the CCTV tapes. It's just possible that we might get lucky and see something.'

He turned to go then stopped. 'Street, also find out where the morgue is. I want to talk to Doctor Metzger, there's something bothering me about his report.'

♦

Buchanan parked his car beside the yacht club and headed for the harbour office. He stopped at the bridge and wondered if this was going to be the moment the case started to reveal its secrets.

He stared at the water and imagined a lake with mist flowing over its surface, an arm rising up through the mist, with a hand clutching a scroll. He took the scroll and there, in beautiful Edwardian script, was the answer to the question of who killed the girl. He, smiled at his daydream, and told himself to keep picking at the coal face.

The path turned under a block of flats and into an underground car park. It took him a few moments to figure out how to work his way through the vehicles and up the ramp to the harbour office.

Before climbing the steps, he walked over to the nearest lock. The outer gates were open and he saw a small sailboat making its way, slowly, towards them. Directly below him was a large sport fishing boat. At the stern a crowd of fishermen were standing round a small gutting table, watching one of the crew clean and bag their catches.

An alarm sounded and the lock gates closed as the sailboat tied up to the pontoon. With a deafening roar the lock started to fill. Buchanan watched till the fishing boat untied and departed for its berth. Then he turned and walked slowly over to the harbour office and up the stairs.

'Can I help?' asked the lock-keeper.

'Yes, I'm looking for the harbour office.'

'You've found it.'

'Oh, looks more like a control room.'

'It's both, what you see in front is the control room, the offices are at the back, behind you.'

'That makes sense now you explain it.'

'Who would you like to see?'

'I would like to have a word with the assistant harbour master if she's in, please'

'And who shall I say is calling?'

'Detective Chief Inspector Buchanan.'

'Oh – just a minute, sir.'

The lock-keeper picked up the phone and dialled. The sound of a ringing phone came from a partially open door on Buchanan's left.

'She'll be right out, she's on another call.'

'Thanks.'

A few minutes later Mary Riley came out of her office. She'd done her make-up, observed Buchanan, realising just how pretty she was.

'Inspector, I hadn't expected to see you again so soon – what a pleasant surprise. What can I do for you?'

'I was wondering if your CCTV cameras around the harbour are working? If they are I would like to see the tape from the camera by the bridge between the north and south harbours for the night of the 29th and the early hours of the 30th of March.'

'Certainly – but they're not tapes. Everything is digitally recorded and stored on our server. If you'll follow me into my office I can have a look for you.'

> *My, my, my,*
> *said the spider to the fly,*
> *would you come with me*
> *I've something for you to see*

Buchanan mused as he followed her into her office.

She closed the door behind them, walked over to her desk, and sat down in front of her computer. 'The 29th,' she said, looking at the screen, 'yes that would be camera 28. What time did you say?'

'I didn't say what time: in fact, we're not sure. Could we try sometime after ten pm?'

She pressed the keys on her computer; Buchanan stood beside her and looked at the scene on the screen, hoping something of interest would emerge.

'Is this what you're looking for?' she said. looking up at him.

He hadn't noticed till now how green her eyes were; also, she'd got a smudge of lipstick on one of her well-kept upper teeth. He tried to ignore the fact she'd undone the top button on her blouse. Attempting to get back on the subject, he said, 'What time is that on the screen?'

'Ten past three in the afternoon.'

'How do you make time pass – on the screen?'

'Here,' she said, standing up, 'let me help you. You sit here and I'll show you how to find what you are looking for.'

She stepped behind the chair while Buchanan sat down and concentrated on the view of the bridge. It was an excellent view; he could clearly see both sides of the bridge from about thirty feet back and it was clear all the way across to the lower edges of the apartments opposite. The residents on the first floor had either fitted blinds or nets to the insides of the windows to keep the prying eye of the camera out of their living rooms.

To the right, the area of tall reeds and the water's edge was clearly visible. If anyone had been standing there, Buchanan felt they would be easy to identify.

'Just use the mouse to advance the time.'

Buchanan wasn't a Luddite but no matter where he moved the mouse nothing changed on the screen.

'Here, let me help,' she said, reaching over and placing her hand on top of his. He felt her breasts pushing into his shoulder as she operated the roller on the mouse. Her long red hair caressed his face and tumbled down onto the desk in front of him, almost covering the keyboard. She smelt of sunshine and roses.

'See how easy it is to make time pass? Just use your finger to push the roller ball, a little to go slow, a lot to go fast, just be gentle and you'll find what you are looking for.'

He could feel his pulse racing and his breathing was getting deeper. *Get out Jack, you're getting into deep water,* he said to himself.

He cleared his throat. 'Would it be possible for you to make a copy of the recording from between eight pm till four am the following morning for me? That way I could have one of my men go through it.'

'I'd have to burn that to DVD,' she said, grinning.

'Fine, that would do nicely. How long will it take?' he said standing up, trying to hide his discomfort.

'I'll do it now, shouldn't be more than a few minutes.'

♦

Two DVD's later Buchanan returned to the incident room. He held them up. 'Homework for this evening, lass.'

'Need company?'

'Not really, especially after my meeting with the assistant harbour master.'

'Was dragon lady being awkward about the DVD's?' said Street, picking off a long strand of red hair from the front of his jacket.

'It's not what you're thinking.'

'I'm not thinking anything. So what about the DVD's? Are you going to sit up all night and watch them yourself?'

'There's eight hours to watch – do you want to stay that late?'

'I feel another takeaway looming, and this time *I'll* choose what we eat. Besides, if your prognosis is correct, we shouldn't have to watch all the way till four am.'

'Good point. How did you do with your enquiries?'

'I called the hospital – that's where the morgue is. I was told the bodies are still in the fridges. And you'll like this, sir. Doctor Metzger is not the regular pathologist. He was standing in for the regular doctor who was away at a conference.'

'Well done, Street, the mists are clearing. I see a raised arm.'

'Pardon, sir?'

'Never mind. How did you get on with the DNA tests?'

'The best I could get out of them was five working days; they don't do it in house anymore.'

'Well, that's a start,' he said. 'Anything from Hunter and Dexter?'

'Nothing yet; there's a lot of taxi firms in town and who knows how many tattoo parlours there are.'

Buchanan sat down at his desk, turned on the computer, and inserted the first of the DVD's.

'Coffee?'

'Black, hot and tall,' he replied. 'This is going to be a long night.'

'Weren't you going to call the Chief, sir?'

Before Buchanan could answer, the phone rang. He punched the speaker button. 'Buchanan.'

'Buchanan, this is Assistant Chief Constable Atkins. I've been all over the building – where the hell are you?'

Street grimaced; Buchanan put his finger to his lips and made a face at her.

'I'm in the incident room, Ma'am.'

'And just where might that be?'

Buchanan wasn't a fool; he knew that she knew where the incident room was. How else could she know the extension number?

'Been busy, Ma'am. Making progress on the dead girl: we think we know where she was killed. I was going to call you later this afternoon when we get the results of our enquiries.'

'I told you not to waste your time on her; she either committed suicide or simply fell in. I want to see you in my office – this is not good enough. What time is it?'

Buchanan looked up at the clock on the wall. 'It's ten after four – be with you in twenty minutes.'

'No, you won't, you'll never make it here before five. I'm off to Glyndebourne this evening and I'm not going to be late because of you. Be here at nine tomorrow morning.'

'Yes, Ma'am, that suits me fine,' said Buchanan, smiling at Street. 'I was planning to be in at HQ tomorrow morning anyway.'

'About time you got down to proper police work. Don't be late.' She hung up.

Buchanan shrugged, picked up his coffee, and went back to staring at the screen.

Street smiled but said nothing. 'Shall I do something about dinner, sir?'

'In a minute. Where's Hunter and Dexter? They should have been back by now.'

Ten minutes later the peace was disturbed by their return.

'Well, anything?'

They shook their heads.

'We went to all the taxi firms,' said Hunter. 'No record of any fares to the Marina matching the girl.'

'We walked the taxi rank at the station,' added Dexter, 'just in case someone recognised the girl. Then on to the bus terminus, but nothing.'

'What about the letting agencies, Hunter?'

'Nothing on the books, sir.'

'But that doesn't mean she wasn't a student,' said Dexter. 'Some of them stay privately with families.'

'What about the tattoo? Anyone recognise it?'

'None of the ones we checked. A couple were closed, we'll get those tomorrow.'

'Right,' said Buchanan, 'first job tomorrow morning for you two is to go to all the student letting agents and see what you can find. Then go round all the harbour restaurants and see if anyone recognises the girl.'

'Yes. sir, see you tomorrow.'

'Street, I'll be back in a few minutes, left my mobile at home charging.'

♦

'Excuse me, Mr Buchanan,' said Johnston, the next-door neighbour. 'The wife and I were wondering if everything was all right – you know, with all these police around?'

Buchanan smiled and said, 'Everything's fine, those policemen work for me. I'm investigating the two deaths in the Marina.'

'So you *are* a policeman! I knew it. I said to Mary: I bet he's a policeman.'

'Detective Chief Inspector Buchanan. I'm renting the house from my wife's sister while they're away.'

'About time someone looked into what's been happening in the Marina. We were wondering when the police would get round to catching the culprits.'

'We, sir?'

'Oh, some of us down at the yacht club thought it was strange that two people could die there within a few days of each other and nothing was done about it, especially when you consider what goes on in the Marina.'

'And just what might these goings on be, sir?'

'Well, you know, all sorts of things: drugs, cigarette smuggling, there was even talk of people trafficking.'

'Do you have any evidence of these activities, sir?'

Johnston shrugged. 'Not first hand, but it's common knowledge that strange things happen around the Marina at night.'

'Did anyone report these strange happenings to the police, sir?'

Johnston shook his head. 'I don't know.'

'Can I suggest that the next time you hear stories like that you call the police'

Johnston nodded. 'Yes, certainly.'

♦

'What do you think, sir?' said Street, when Buchanan recounted Johnston's speculations. 'Could these sorts of things be going on in the Marina?'

Buchanan said, 'Small communities thrive on gossip. I'm sure that's all it is.'

But was it all just gossip, he wondered. What community didn't have drug problems? There definitely had been firearms offences committed in the past, and people had drowned, so why not people trafficking? He decided to keep his speculations to himself. In the meantime there were two deaths to investigate and hours of DVD to watch.

Street ordered pizza for them and sat down beside Buchanan to watch with him. It wasn't till about one-thirty in the morning that they thought they saw what they had been waiting for. The bridge rose and a large power boat, with only its navigation lights showing, slid silently past. As it passed the camera it was apparent there was a party going on inside as people could be seen seated in the well-lit cabin with glasses in their hands.

As it was about to pass out of sight, Buchanan exclaimed, 'What the –'

He'd just seen what looked like a dark figure standing on the swimming platform with a bundle at its feet. But as he stared at the figure the camera was blinded by what appeared to be a car headlight reflecting off of the apartment windows. By the time the camera refocused on the boat, the swimming platform was clear.

They ran the DVD back and forwards several times and each time came to the same conclusion. They were both sure someone had pushed something – or someone – off of the yacht's swimming platform.

'Tomorrow, Street, the very first thing we do is to find out who owns that yacht

6

Street looked at her clock. Seven-fifteen. It could only be one person: Buchanan.

'Are you awake, lass?'

'Of course, I am. I was just about to leave the house.'

'Good. As soon as you get here, we're off to the harbour office, we need to find out who owns that yacht.

'Need someone to save you from the clutches of dragon lady? Shall I bring my pistol and body armour?'

'That won't be necessary; I can look after myself, thank you very much.'

♦

'Good morning, sir. Can I help?'

'Are you the duty lock-keeper?'

'Yes, sir.'

'We're looking for the owner of a large motor yacht that entered the north harbour early in the morning of the 30th of March.'

'I wasn't on duty that evening,' the lock-keeper said, looking up at the roster chart on the wall behind him. 'That would've been Dan. You're lucky – he's on duty this morning, should be here soon.'

They waited patiently for Dan to arrive by watching boats come and go through the locks.

He arrived at seven fifty-five on his bicycle. At eight o'clock they followed Dan up the stairs to the office.

'The 30th you say, about one in the morning? That would have been the *Moonstone*, owned by Sir Nathan Greyspear. He owns Greyspear Yachts.'

'That name rings a bell. Is that the same Greyspear Yachts that are built on the Clyde?'

'Not sure, sir, all I know is he owns the *Moonstone*.'

'Do you log all entries to the Marina?'

'Not all, mostly those after hours, and always if they are visitors. HMRC likes to know what's coming and going at night, worried the Exchequer might lose out on its pound of flesh.'

'Can you tell me where to find Sir Nathan?'

'He owns a house in the north harbour, on Auckland Drive. You can't miss the house, it's the largest one on the drive.'

'Right then, lass,' said Buchanan, as they got into the car, 'let's pay a visit to Sir Nathan.'

'Shouldn't you be going somewhere else first, sir?'

'Oh, damn. Spider Woman,' said Buchanan said looking at the clock on the dashboard. 'That's ok, there's plenty of time, not due there till nine – we've twenty–five minutes. Fasten your seatbelt, lass, were going for a drive.'

The drive out of the Marina was a frustrating one for Buchanan. White vans delivering and mothers with prams made him conscious of the fact that he wasn't the only person up and about. When they finally got on to the A27 he turned on his siren and blue lights.

'Is that legitimate?'

'Urgent police business, lass.'

'I looked up Sir Nathan Greyspear on the net last night.'

'And?'

'He does own Greyspear Yachts, started it from scratch. It's now the largest private yacht building company in the UK. He also owns a string of very successful racehorses.'

'The more I learn about Sir Nathan Greyspear, the more he interests me.'

For once the A27 was quiet and they arrived in the HQ car park with ten minutes to spare.

'Good morning,' Buchanan said to Atkins' secretary. 'Is she in?'

The secretary shook her head. 'Not yet. She called to say that she was running a bit late this morning.'

Buchanan grinned. 'We'll just nip down to the canteen for a quick coffee, then; we'll be back in a couple of minutes.'

They returned twenty minutes later to find Atkins had arrived and was in her office.

The secretary picked up her phone. 'Inspector Buchanan and DS Street are here, Ma'am, shall I send them in?' She nodded to Buchanan. 'She says to go right in and don't speak too loudly,' she added, smiling.

Buchanan noticed the open bottle of aspirins and the large black coffee on Atkins' desk.

'What time is this, Buchanan?' she said, wincing at the sound of her own raised voice. 'I said nine sharp, not nine-fifteen.'

'Sorry Ma'am, overslept, had a late one last night.' he replied. 'We spent most of the evening looking at CCTV footage, won't let it happen again.'

'I should think not. I demand punctuality from my staff, and Buchanan, I want you to understand I command a right good crew in this division. Can't run a sloppy ship, have a reputation to maintain – after all, it's the taxpayers who fund our operation. Must give them value for their money. Have I said something that amuses you, Street?'

'No, Ma'am, just remembered something from my school days, that's all.'

'Right then, if we're all paying attention we can get down to business. Where are you in the investigation? Was DS Nichols' death an accident?'

Buchanan drew in a deep breath and shook his head. 'It's early days on that, Ma'am. We're concentrating on the death of the girl.'

'Buchanan,' she winced, 'how many times do I have to say that her death was probably accidental? It's Nichols' death that I want you to concentrate on.'

'We have DVD evidence that points to the girl's death being a deliberate act of murder.'

'What's this evidence? Where did it come from?'

'One of the CCTV cameras in the Marina shows what looks like a body being pushed off a private yacht as it passed the area where the girl's body was recovered.'

'I'd like to see that.'

Buchanan pulled a copy of the DVD from an evidence bag and handed it to Atkins, who slid it into the slot on her laptop.

'About one am, Ma'am,' said Street.

Buchanan and Street waited in silence as Atkins ran the DVD to the spot where the *Moonstone* came into view.

'Not very conclusive, Buchanan. No name on the yacht to be seen, blurry figures in the dark, no clear shot of faces and at the supposed crucial moment the video goes blank and when it comes back there's nothing. You'll have to do better that this to convince me.'

'We do have a name for the yacht, Ma'am,' said Street. 'It's called the *Moonstone* and it's owned by a Sir Nathan Greyspear.'

Atkins leaned back in her chair, shaking her head slowly from side to side. 'Now I know you're way out of your depth. Sir Nathan is a well-respected member of society, had lunch with him not two weeks ago. It's not at all likely that he killed this girl. He's a patron of the arts, a board member and financial supporter of several local charities.'

'None the less, Ma'am, his yacht passed the scene of the crime close to the time of death.'

Atkins thought for a moment. 'What do you plan to do, Buchanan?'

'Go and have a word with Sir Nathan, see what he has to say.'

'Tread very lightly, Buchanan, he has friends in high places. Wouldn't want to see an ignominious end to your career. What else are you working on?'

'The two PC's are doing the rounds to see if anyone recognises the girl or her tattoo. So far we've drawn a complete blank.'

'A bit of a waste of time and resources, don't you think?'

'Just eliminating the improbable, Ma'am. I'm sure with your experience and knowledge you know that, after sifting through evidence, what's left – however strange and improbable – must be the facts. It's just like panning for gold.'

♦

'We're very, very, good, and be it understood, she commands a right good crew,' Buchanan sang loudly, with laughter in his voice, as they walked across the car park to his car.

'Now that's Gilbert and Sullivan,' said Street, 'I remember it from school. Where are we off to now?'

'I think it's time to have a look at DS Nichols' house.'

♦

Nichols' house turned out to be a large detached house on a side street off Westham village High Street. Buchanan parked his car in Nichols' driveway and walked up to the front door.

'He's not there,' said a voice from the other side of the garden hedge. 'He had an accident a few weeks ago: died, the paper said, drowned in his car.'

Buchanan and Street walked over to the gap in the hedge and introduced themselves.

'DCI Buchanan and DS Street, Sussex CID,' said Buchanan, showing his warrant card.

'Agnes Saunders,' said the neighbour, continuing with her narrative. 'He was such a nice young man, pity he had the accident. We'll miss him, he was always so helpful to the neighbours – fixed my washing machine, and wouldn't take a penny for his troubles.'

'Did he have any friends?'

'Not that I remember, though he did sometimes have a barbeque on a Saturday if the weather was good.'

'Alone?'

'Mostly, dear, though a few weeks before he died he had a group of people over for a dinner party. Very posh they were.'

'Did he do the cooking?'

'No, dear, he had it catered. He had servants, young girls, all dressed in pretty dresses, with starched white aprons. They were really cheeky though, when they thought no one was watching they would sneak out the back and have a cigarette and a gossip.'

'Can you remember when this was?'

She shook her head. 'Sorry, Inspector. Oh, wait a minute, aren't I the silly one? It was March 8th – finals day at Crufts. I got up to make a cup of tea before they announced Best in Show and there they were, smoking and gossiping.'

'Did you by any chance hear what they were talking about?'

'I didn't want to hear, Inspector, but they were right outside my kitchen window. They were saying something about a play, or it might have been a film, they saw. I'm sorry, dear, my memory isn't what it used to be.'

'We all have our off days, Ma'am' said Buchanan. 'Did you by any chance see who the caterer was?'

'Sorry, no.'

'Do you know if they were work friends?' asked Street.

'Not sure, dear. I was never introduced to any of them.'

'Do you think you would recognise any of them again?'

'I doubt it, dear, I only saw them as they got out of the taxis.'

'That's all right Mrs Saunders,' said Buchanan.

'Oh, there was a good-looking one that looked familiar, looked like the chap who played – oh what's his name – oh that's it, now I remember: Bret Chance.'

'Was that the name of the actor or the character, Mrs Johnson?' asked Street.

'The character. He was the owner of the horse stables in the television show called – oh, my memory, what was it called?'

'Everslea?' suggested Street.

66

'Yes, that was it.'

'Thank you, Mrs Saunders. We'll get in touch if we have any further questions.'

'What do you think of that, sir?' asked Street.

'Fancies of an old woman. Someone once mistook me for Brian Cox, pestered me till I showed them my warrant card.'

'What, Brian Cox the TV presenter and scientist?'

'No, lass, the actor.'

Street looked at Buchanan's face. 'There is a resemblance, and with your accent I can see how the mistake could be made.'

'Thanks.'

They retraced their steps to the front door; Buchanan took Nichols keys, opened it and went in.

Street sniffed the air and said, 'Bit stuffy, but I suppose that's what happens when a house is shut up for a long time.'

Buchanan bent down and picked up the post that was lying on the floor under the letter flap. He looked at the dates and postmarks. 'No one has been here for a few weeks. In fact, looking at these postmarks, I would say no one has been here since he died.'

'Anything interesting?'

'Mostly bills that'll never get paid – hmm.'

'What did you find?'

'An invitation to a Federation Dinner in Bournemouth next month. C'mon we can't spend all day at this. I think we'll try upstairs first.'

Buchanan tried the front bedroom and Street the rear; they met on the landing.

'Find anything, sir?'

'No, and you?'

'Rear bedroom must be the guest room; bed's been slept in and roughly made-up. The bedding hasn't been washed. Pillow stills sells of perfume.'

'Street, put the pillow in an evidence bag. Let's see if forensics can identify the scent, and get a DNA sample – you may be right about the girl and Nichols. Also I think it would be a good idea to have the SCI's go over the house and see if we get any other surprises.'

'Yes, sir.'

'We'll have a cursory look around downstairs then I think it must be lunchtime. Somewhere nice before we disturb Sir Nathan. Know anywhere close?'

'Smugglers – it's just down the road, past the castle, almost on the way to the Marina. Has some of the best pub food around.'

♦

Buchanan turned to Street as they drove along Auckland Drive to the only house that fitted the description of Sir Nathan Greyspear's home and said, 'I smell money, lass'

'And money is the root of all evil.'

Buchanan shook his head. 'You've made the same mistake almost everyone makes. It's not *money is the root of all evil*; rather the correct quotation is: *for the love of money is a root of all evils.*'

'Whatever.'

He pulled up in front of a set of very imposing stainless-steel gates. 'Quite a pile, as they say.' Winding down his window he pressed the call button on the gate intercom.

A garbled ringing came from the speaker to be replaced by a disembodied voice. 'Sir Nathan Greyspear's residence. Who's calling, please?'

'Detective Chief Inspector Buchanan, Sussex CID. I'd like a word with Sir Nathan.'

'I'm sorry, sir. Sir Nathan is away at the moment.'

'And where might *away* be?'

'Head office, it's in Greenock, that's in–'

'Scotland,' interrupted Buchanan. 'Is the *Moonstone* here?'

'Yes, sir.'

'Good, we'd like to have a look at her.'

'Sales enquiries are dealt with from our London office. Shall I get you the number?'

'Listen, son, this is a murder investigation and the only number you'll get is my size twelve boot up your arse if you don't let us in.'

'One moment, sir.'

'What's funny, sir?' asked Street.

'The music on hold: it's the BBC shipping forecast theme, *Sailing By*. And I bet he's calling Sir Nathan.'

They didn't get as far as the forecast before the voice returned. 'Sir Nathan's apologies that he's not here to greet you. If you drive through to the front of the house, I'll take you down to the *Moonstone*.'

There was an audible hum as the gates slowly hinged inwards to reveal a gravelled driveway curving round to the front of the house. Buchanan resisted the urge to spin the wheels in the gravel and parked at the front door.

The butler was standing at the foot of the front steps of the house waiting for them. 'If you'll follow me, sir, Captain Bracewell is waiting for you.'

They followed the butler round to the back of the house and down to the dock. Bracewell was talking on his phone while pacing up and down the side deck of the *Moonstone*. He hung up and stepped down onto the dock as Buchanan approached.

'Detective Chief Inspector Buchanan, and Detective Sergeant Street, Sussex CID.'

'Can I see some identification, please?' said Bracewell, putting down the book he was reading. 'Can't be too careful, these yachts are very valuable.'

'You mean to say people would steal one of these? Every town in the country has their fair share of horse thieves –, but a boat this size? How on earth do you get it into the harbour?'

69

'Inspector, if a few Somali pirates in a rusty fishing boat can pirate a super tanker, what chance has a boat the size of *Moonstone*? And the narrowest part of the harbour is the drawbridge between the north and south harbours, but even there we have a metre on both sides. Now, how may I help, Inspector?'

'Can you tell me where you were on the morning of the 30th of March?'

'Straight to the jugular, eh? I was here on the *Moonstone*. Why?'

'Were you and the *Moonstone* out sailing the previous evening, the 29th?'

'Yes. We were out on a demonstration sail. Sir Nathan was showing some prospective buyers how the *Moonstone* performs at sea.'

'How many people on board?'

'I'll have to check the log book.'

'Could we do that, please? And I'd like a list of all on board that night, with their addresses.'

'Not sure I can do that.'

'And why not?'

'I only get the names of the guests. That's so I can make sure we have the necessary life-saving equipment and food and drink on board.'

'Let's start with the list of names, then. I suppose your sales office will have the contact details?'

'I should think so, unless Sir Nathan invited any guests himself. If you'll follow me on board I'll get the log book.'

Buchanan read down the list then handed it to Street.

'How about crew? How many were there?'

'Including me, there were five, plus the caterers.'

'How many caterers? And do you have a list of their names?'

'No, but I remember there were four of them. I spent most of the evening in the wheelhouse. Sir Nathan likes it that way.'

'Most of the evening?'

'Yes, all except for when I greeted the guests in the main saloon. That was prior to us leaving harbour.'

'So you don't know where your guests were during the trip?'

'Inspector, they were all grown-ups. They had the run of the whole boat.'

'Including cabins?'

'As I said, they were all grown-ups.'

'How about CCTV?'

'Bridge only.'

'Who was with you in the wheelhouse when you returned to the harbour?'

'Apart from crew, two guests.'

'Who were the guests?'

'Mr and Mrs Carstairs.'

'What were they doing?'

'I was showing the Carstairs how the *Moonstone* handles in tight quarters.'

'And you were on the bridge the whole time?'

'Other than for the call of nature, I did have to leave for a moment.'

'Why was that?'

'Two of the guests, Bashir and Silverstein, were getting vocal.'

'What about?'

'Something personal.'

'Did they come to blows?'

'No, just raised voices lubricated with a little too much brandy. Apparently they've known each other for years and the argument is an ongoing discussion they have whenever they get together. Sir Nathan stepped in and calmed the waters; they're his friends, I believe.'

'What about their partners, did they get involved?'

'The wives? No, they sat with the other women in the main saloon.'

'When was the argument?'

'As we returned to the harbour.'

'And Sir Nathan, other than the time he was with Bashir and Silverstein, where was he?'

'Not sure, but it's his yacht so probably with his guests.'

'Where were the crew?'

'I was at the helm. Russell, Colin, and Andy were out on the side decks keeping a lookout, and I think John was in the engine room.'

Buchanan took out the picture of the dead girl and showed it to Bracewell. 'Ever seen this girl?'

Bracewell looked at the photo for a moment. 'She does look familiar. Is she an actor?'

'Not that we're aware of. She was pulled from the Marina on the morning after you were out with the *Moonstone*.'

Bracewell shrugged. 'What's that have to do with the *Moonstone*?'

'That's what we are trying to ascertain. Did all the guests leave when you returned?'

'We logged them all onboard at the start of the evening and off when we returned. Your dead girl wasn't any of my guests, Inspector.'

'How about the caterers?' asked Street.

'Haven't a clue – once we'd tied up they were no longer my responsibility. As soon as we'd done that they left. I checked all the cabins before I shut down the *Moonstone* for the night. I was the only one on board.'

'Captain, I'm going to keep this guest list. You can have it back when our enquiries are complete.'

'You can keep it, Inspector, it's an extract from the log; I've got the original.'

'Could we have a look around while we're here, Captain? I've never seen such luxury.'

'Certainly, Inspector.'

'How do you know your way around, Captain? There's more twists and turns on the yacht than Hampton Court maze.

'It helps to be there while the yacht is being built, and I'm good with directions.'

'How often are the decks washed down, Captain?'

'After every trip out, or once a week, whichever comes first.'

'Thanks, Captain, we've seen what we need for now.'

◆

'What do you think, Street? We have our suspects. Now all we need to do is eliminate the improbable,' said Buchanan, as he read through the Smugglers' lunch menu while sipping on his whiskey

'Pity there's not more of them, sir. By my count we have seventeen suspects.'

'Not quite that many, Street. The crew were busy on deck, with one of them in the engine room. Sir Nathan and Bracewell were on the bridge with the Carstairs. Bashir and Silverstein were arguing and let's not forget the poor unfortunate dead girl. According to Bracewell nine of them have alibis. Of course, Bracewell could be lying and that would make them all suspects.'

'Either way that's still a lot of names to check up on.'

'Can I take your order?' asked the waitress.

'What do you fancy, Street?'

'Could I have a small salad, please?'

'And, sir?'

'I'll have a BLT.'

'White or brown seeded bread?'

'Brown, please.'

'Anything to drink?'

'Er, I'll have – another whiskey. Street?'

'Lemonade will be fine.'

'I'll be right back with your drinks.'

'Did you notice any names in particular on the list, Street?'

73

'You mean Dr Metzger?'

'What's wrong, lass? You've gone white as a ghost.'

'Nothing, just a memory from my past. It'll pass, it always does.'

'You sure you're OK?'

'Yes.'

They ate their lunch in silence; Buchanan watched Street push the last tomato round her plate.

'Penny for your thoughts.'

'Sorry, I was miles away. Let's get going, I've lost my appetite.'

'OK, if you're really sure,' replied Buchanan, throwing back the remains of his whiskey. 'Wonder if it's the same doctor who performed the autopsy?'

'One way to find out.'

'You're right, I think we'll head for the hospital and pay our respects to the deceased, also see if the elusive Doctor Metzger is available.'

'You're going to park *here*?' said Street, as Buchanan backed in beside an ambulance at the emergency entrance.

'I'm not paying to park. This is official business, lass.'

Buchanan followed Street down to the mortuary.

'Is Doctor Metzger around?' he asked one of the white-coated attendants.

'And you are?'

'Detective Chief Inspector Buchanan, Sussex CID. We're investigating the recent deaths in the Marina.'

'Doctor Mansell. How can I help?'

'Sorry Doctor, you all look the same to me. I had hoped to talk with Doctor Metzger; he did the autopsies.'

'Ah, he was here earlier. Not sure if he's gone back to his practice: he has his clinic in Meads. We use him when we are short of a pathologist. Would you like his address?'

'Before you do that – did you review his findings?'

'Inspector, we have been very busy. Five off of Beachy Head in the last two weeks and, with the recent flu outbreak, we are full to overflowing. I simply don't have time to review someone else's work.'

'This is a double murder inquiry, Doctor.'

'Inspector, it's getting late and I have had a long day, but – I suppose I could give you half an hour.'

'That's more like it. Your office?'

'Follow me; I'll get the records on the way.'

'It's the inspector's death I'm more interested in, Doctor. The report says he had window glass embedded in his head. Was it caused by him bumping his head or someone breaking the glass on to his head?'

Mansell read through Metzger's report for a moment before replying. 'You raise a very interesting point, Inspector. Car side window glass is very tough so it's not likely he hit his head and broke it; more likely something hit the glass. Would need to have a look at the impact area, want to join me?'

'No time like the present.'

♦

'Well, what do you think, Doctor?' said Buchanan, grimacing as Mansell peeled back the flesh from the late Nichols' head.

'How the hell did he miss this?' said Mansell. 'Definite impact area to the right temple, no doubt about it, Inspector. See the damage? Someone hit the window, breaking the glass and causing immediate unconsciousness to your detective. You're looking for a blunt instrument, surface area about fifty by fifty millimetres.'

'Club hammer?' suggested Buchanan. 'None found at the scene, pity.'

'Want me to look at the girl?' asked Mansell.

'Might as well.'

Mansell pulled out the drawer and unzipped the body bag. Street fainted.

'Here – drink this,' said Buchanan, after picking Street off the floor and seating her in Mansell's office chair.'

'Sorry, sir. It was – it was – that poor child: it never had a chance. How could they do such a terrible thing?' she said, bursting into tears.

'No, it's my fault,' said Mansell, 'I should have warned you that we don't always return the deceased's organs and tissue samples to the body cavity after the post mortem.'

'That's all right, Doctor; my issue, not yours.'

'You sure you're all right?' asked Buchanan.

'Yes, thanks. Shouldn't let things like that get to me, I thought I was over all that.'

'Over what?'

'Nothing – really, it's nothing. It was something that happened a long time ago. Look, can we get out of here? This place gives me the creeps.'

'Sure, let's get back to the office. We need to contact Greyspear's office and get the addresses of his guests. Then I suppose I should call Spider Woman and let her know we are now investigating a double murder.'

7

Buchanan squinted at the digits on the alarm clock. They glared back at him in luminescent green: two fifty-nine. For a moment he wondered why the alarm had gone off so early. Then he realised it wasn't the alarm clock: it was his mobile phone.

He groped for the flashing display and pressed the answer key. 'Buchanan.'

'Detective Chief Inspector Buchanan, so sorry to wake you at this early hour. This is Amy at the Force Control Centre. We've just had a call from PC Hunter.'

'And that's why you're waking me at this time of the night?'

'Yes, I mean no, sir. It's about your partner, DS Street.'

'What about the lass?'

'She's in trouble, sir. PC Hunter says DS Street is sitting on the edge of the cliff at Beachy Head.'

A cold chill ran down Buchanan's spine. 'What's wrong with the lass?'

'I don't know, sir. All we know is PC Hunter asks would you call him, immediately, please.'

Buchanan hung up from the call, scrolled through his contact list and dialed Hunter's number.

'PC Hunter.'

'It's Buchanan. What's going on? And what are you doing out on Beachy Head at three in the morning?'

'It's DS Street, sir. We found her sitting on the edge of the cliff.'

'We?'

'Sorry, sir, I'm out as an observer with Martin Sorel of the Beachy Head Chaplaincy. That's how we found her.'

'Who's with her? You haven't left her alone, have you?'

'No, sir, one of the chaplains is with her right now and there's a second close by.'

'Good.'

'She's quite distressed, sir. She won't listen to us but mumbled something about you, though. That's why we called.'

'Why would she want me? I'm her boss, not her father confessor.'

'Not sure, sir. Every time one of the chaplains approaches her she moves closer to the edge. They've called for a mental health nurse.'

'Why, for heaven's sake?'

'Apparently, it's the procedure they follow, sir.'

'I'm on my way. How do I find you?' said Buchanan, throwing back the blankets.

'Where are you coming from, sir?'

'The Marina.'

'Drive along the sea front till you get to the end of King Edward's Parade; there'll be a school on the left – it's called Meads. At the school the road turns sharp right on to Jukes Drive, follow it up the hill. Watch for the double bend at the top; that will bring you out on to Beachy Head Road. Take the first on the left off Beachy Head Road and I'll flag you down. How will we know your car, sir?'

'I'll have my blue lights on.'

'No siren please, sir, it can make a disturbed person very nervous.'

'Be there in ten minutes.'

He made it in six and a half and almost ran into Hunter standing in the middle of the road, waving a torch.

'Where is she, Hunter?' asked Buchanan, getting out of his car.

'If you'll follow me, I'll take you over to her, but please, sir, no sudden movements.'

'Does she know I'm coming?'

'She does.'

Buchanan walked briskly behind Hunter, their long moonlit shadows scudding along beside them over the undulating ground. Hunter stopped beside a figure dressed in a bright yellow coat. The words Beachy Head Chaplaincy were clearly visible, printed in large silver letters on a bright red patch on the back of the coat.

'Inspector Buchanan.'

'Martin Sorel. Thanks for coming at such short notice, sir. If she'll talk to you, let her talk – it will help divert her mind from what's troubling her.'

'Do you know how long she's been sitting there?'

'No. We only spotted her twenty minutes ago. She's sitting on a ledge just below the cliff edge. Your PC recognised her and called your control centre.'

'Has she given any indication of why she's here?'

'No, sir. We did try to get her to talk but she says she just wants to be left alone to think.'

'Have you tried to restrain her?'

'We never do that, sir: too dangerous for the distressed person, and us. Some of these people are determined to jump, whether anyone is holding them or not.'

'All right, I'll give it a try. Just hope I'm not too late to convince her to change her mind.'

'Go careful, sir – We'll be praying for you.'

'Thanks, but I'm not sure what good that'll do.'

'You'd be surprised if I told you how often it makes a difference.'

◆

'Hello, lass.'

'I told them I wanted to be left alone.'

'I'll just sit here if that's all right with you?'

'Suit yourself.'

'Why didn't you tell me something was bothering you?'

'You're a man. You wouldn't understand.'

'Wouldn't understand – understand what? Like why you are sitting on the edge of Beachy Head at three in the morning?'

'Do you know what some people call it?'

'What, Beachy Head? No, I'm sorry, I don't.'

'The Gaping Mouth of Hell.'

'And you, do you have a name for this place?'

'Elysium, that's what I call it.'

'Really?'

'Can't you see it, sir?'

'I suppose I can, a little.'

> *In Elysium there falls not rain,*
> *nor hail, nor snow,*
> *but Oceanus breathes ever with a West wind*
> *that sings softly from the sea,*
> *and gives fresh life to all men.*

'That's beautiful. More of your poetry, sir?'

'No, lass, that's from Homer's *Odyssey* – Listen, it does sound like a wonderful place to go –when the time is right – but I don't think this is it for you. You have your whole life ahead of you.'

'It would be so easy – see?' she said, standing up and moving closer to the edge.

'Jill – please; come away from the edge.'

'On windy days I like to come up here and watch the seagulls; they're so free. They just step off the edge, open their wings and let the wind lift them up. They have no worries, nothing to do but fly.

'Jill, please come sit back down, you're scaring me.'

'You called me Jill – why?'

'How the hell do I know? I'm out of my depth, I'm not trained for this.'

'Sorry.'

'That's all right.'

'Haven't you ever wondered what it would be like?'

'Wondered what – what it would be like? You're not making sense.'

'Ever been on a tall building and got that urge to just step off? See, all I have to do is lean forward a bit; I can see the bottom, it's a long way to fly. You put your left leg out, you put your left leg in, you do the–'

'For God's sake, stop it – You'll go over the edge.'

'For God's sake? What's He ever done for me? Where was He when I needed Him?'

'To do what you're contemplating would be wrong, you must know that.'

'Huh, you're sounding just like the Mother Superior at my old school. She said that God would wipe away all my tears. I ran out of tissues years ago waiting for Him.'

'You never told me you'd been in a convent.'

'It wasn't a convent. It was a private school for children of diplomats.'

'Look, lass – please, at least move away from the cliff edge and sit down.'

'OK, but keep your distance.'

'Thanks. Now what's this about diplomats and tears?'

'My father was a colonel in the army; my mother held the rank of major. When they retired from the army they joined the diplomatic core and were posted to Hong Kong.'

'How old were you then?'

'I was born there; I don't remember anything about it. Except for the photographs, I might as well never have been there. When I was four, my parents were posted to New Zealand. When I was eight we were sent to Belfast, then on to Belgrade in Serbia.'

'Can you speak any Serbian?'

'A little; it comes in handy with the day job. You'd be surprised how many foreign students we get in Eastbourne. After Serbia my parents were posted to the embassy in Tehran. Because of the unrest in Iran, I was packed off to a boarding school in England.'

'Did you stay with relatives during the holidays while your parents were abroad?'

Street shook her head; tears started to run down her cheeks.

'Sorry, I'm intruding in your personal affairs.'

'That's all right,' she answered, while blowing her nose. 'And to answer your question: no, I stayed at the school during the holidays.'

'On your own?'

'Yes – unfortunately.'

'How long were your parents in Tehran?'

'They had been there two years when they were killed in a hit and run accident. They died the day before my fourteenth birthday.'

'I'm sorry. I didn't realise.'

'You weren't to know.'

'Did you have any other family to go to?'

'My dad had a distant cousin living in Scotland; they said I could go up and live with them if I wanted.'

'But that's no reason to be contemplating – well, you know what I mean.'

'You mean jumping off Beachy Head? No, I realise it's not.'

'Then what's the problem? I can't help you if you won't talk about it. Was it anything to do with the visit to the mortuary yesterday?'

Street nodded and Buchanan saw the tears return.

'I'm not sure – I've never spoken to anyone about it before.'

'Try me, I'm a good listener.' He removed a small silver flask from his jacket pocket and offered it to her.

She shook her head.

'It's only water with a dash of whiskey.'

Street reached out and took the offered flask. 'Thanks,' she said, taking a swig. 'One night at boarding school – about six months after my parents died – I'd cried myself to sleep again. I woke thinking there was someone in the room.'

'I remember thinking when I was a wee lad that there were monsters living under my bed, and if I were to stick my leg out they'd bite it off.'

Buchanan looked at Street's crestfallen face. 'Sorry, lass, I'm being insensitive.'

She sniffed. 'I opened my eyes and stared into the gloom, but I couldn't see anything or anyone. But – I couldn't shake off the feeling that someone was watching me. I turned over and there he was: Mr Salter, the PE teacher, in his pyjamas and dressing gown. He said he'd heard me crying and wondered if he could help. I was petrified; I didn't know what to say.'

'You poor, wee lass.'

'He forced his way into my bed. I tried to stop him but he was too strong – he said it would make me feel better.'

'Did you say anything to anyone in the morning?'

'No. I was too frightened and embarrassed. I went to lock my door the next night, but he had taken the key. He kept creeping back into my room at night after everyone had gone to sleep; I dreaded going to bed. I'd started to get sick, kept vomiting, couldn't eat without throwing up. I thought he was killing me.'

'The bastard! I'd like to get my hands on him. You know, it's not too late to make a complaint: he can still be charged.'

'It *is* too late.'

'Why do you say that?'

'He's dead.'

'How did he die?'

She hesitated. 'I – shot him. I couldn't put up with him attacking me anymore. I – I was desperate.'

'You shot him? With what?'

'My mother's service pistol. I found it when looking through her effects that were returned by the Embassy. It was the one she let me use when we went to do target practice. I was their only child and next of kin.'

'What happened? Were you arrested?'

'No. The doctor and Mother Superior fixed everything; they were more worried about the school's reputation than me. Mr Salter was single with no family to inquire as to his whereabouts. The doctor signed off the death as a heart attack and had the body cremated. They told me never to speak of the killing or they would have me arrested for murder and that was the end of it – or so they thought.'

'What do you mean?'

'I kept getting sicker – I lost weight, had no appetite. One day I fainted and fell down a flight of stairs.'

'Were you hurt badly?'

'No. I was taken to the infirmary, where the doctor examined me. Mother Superior was there as well; they said I was a stupid girl. I had no idea what they meant; I was just terrified about what was happening to me.'

'Did they say anything about what was wrong with you?'

'No. I was given a pill, a glass of milk and sent back to my room. It was supposed to make me feel better, the doctor said. But I just got worse. During the following week I was often doubled over in pain that made me cry. I collapsed and fainted four times and finally was taken back to the infirmary.

'I'll never forget the stupid grin on the doctor's face. The bastard gave me another pill and sent me back to my room again. He said I was to wait, that it wouldn't take long. I'd no idea what "wouldn't take long" meant till the next morning. I woke with a tremendous cramp and passed what I thought was a lot of blood.'

'You sure you want to go on?'

She nodded. 'I was rushed back to the infirmary. That's when they told me I had been three months pregnant. I went to pieces when they told me it was a foetus I'd passed. It was – just like the one we saw in the mortuary yesterday.'

84

'Oh, lass, if I'd only known.'

'It would have been his fifteenth birthday today.'

'But you were raped.'

'Doesn't matter. He would still have been my child, my only family.'

'How do you know it was a boy?"

'I don't.'

'And you'd had no idea you were pregnant?'

'How would I? I'd led a sheltered life – never had a boyfriend. I just spent my childhood travelling with my parents till I ended up in the boarding school.'

'What happened after that?'

'I rebelled against the authority of Mother Superior and became unruly. So I was expelled.'

'You mean you were put out in the street?'

'Not quite. The school contacted the solicitor who had handled my parents' affairs and she arranged for me to go to another school.'

'How was it?'

'Great. It was co-ed. No private rooms, just dorms.'

'Make friends?'

'A few, but when I went to university I sort of lost track of them.'

'What happened to the gun?'

'Not sure. Probably still in the bottom of one of the boxes of my parents' things. Although it's been nearly fifteen years since they died, I still can't bring myself to go through the boxes. Too many unanswered questions.'

'You do realise, don't you, that to do what you have been contemplating would be an admission of defeat? The doctor would have won, and the death of your child would be for nothing.'

'I know that. I've been here before. This is as far as I ever get – I just can't screw up the courage to go through with it.'

'And you've never spoken to anyone about what happened to you?'

'Never. You're the first one outside the school who knows. Are you going to arrest me?'

'No, lass, especially after what you've just told me.'

'Thanks. It's just sometimes it gets too much for me; I can't cope with the memories. I'm too frightened to get help. I tried phoning the Samaritans once but got scared they might turn me in for what I did – so I hung up.'

'Surely you know the Samaritans would never do that?'

'I realise that now.'

'My wife, Karen, and I are always available if you need to talk.'

'What's she like, Karen?'

'Why don't you find out for yourself? Come and have dinner with us this Saturday, she'll be back from France then.'

'But what will she think of me? She's married to you, a chief inspector and me – I 'm just a policewoman who's admitted murdering someone.'

'It was self-preservation, lass. She'll probably put her arms round you and give you a big hug. Honestly, she'll understand.'

'Are you sure?'

'Of course, I am. But I can't fix your problem. I'm not trained for that.'

'But what will I do then? I can't go on like this.'

'The chaplain called a mental health nurse; she's over there if you wanted to talk. Maybe she could help you?'

'You think I need help, that much?'

'No, of course not, you're as sane as me. Tell you what; if we have a talk with the division Family Liaison Officer I'm sure she will be able to put you in touch with someone who can help.'

'But won't I have to admit to what I've done?'

'You'd only have to tell them you were abused as a child.'

'What if they ask what I did?'

'There would be no need. The perpetrator is long dead and there is no evidence to contradict the death certificate. Besides, what you say will be covered by client-counsellor confidentiality.'

'Are you sure? Can I really believe it?'

'Of course you can, lass.'

She gave a sigh of relief and smiled. 'For the first time in my life I feel as though a great weight has come off my shoulders. Thanks.'

'You're welcome. Now we've got a busy day tomorrow: oops, should have said today! Our flight to Glasgow leaves at ten-twenty. Or actually on second thoughts, you shouldn't be going anywhere, not after tonight. I think you need some time off to think.'

'No,' she said shaking her head, 'thinking's the last thing on my mind. I need to keep busy; it's the only thing that keeps me sane.'

'If you're sure?'

'Of course I am.'

'OK, but I warn you, the first sign of distress, you're off duty. Do I make myself clear?'

She smiled, nodded, and asked, 'Where shall we meet?'

'I'll pick you up on the way, about seven o'clock; should give us time for breakfast before the flight.'

'All well, sir?' asked Sorel, as Buchanan and Street walked back to the car.'

'Yes, thanks to you and your team.'

'Good'.

'Where's PC Hunter?'

'He left, sir; said something about an early start in the morning.'

'Stephen was here?'

'He's the one that found you, lass.'

'How embarrassing. He didn't hear what I said, did he?'

'No, lass, that's strictly between you and me.'

8

'Remind me again, why we're going to Glasgow?' asked Street, as they drove up the M23 to Gatwick airport. 'I thought Greyspear's office is in Eastbourne?'

'The registered office is, but the receptionist said he was at the factory in Greenock and won't be back for a couple of weeks. And while we are up there, I want to check in with my old boss. Also, it will do you good to get away for the day, especially after last night.'

'Don't remind me, please.'

'My lips are sealed.'

♦

'Quite a pleasant view of the river,' said Street, as the taxi wound its way from Greenock station through the late morning traffic. 'Looks like a lovely place for a holiday.'

'You would think differently if you knew what the town used to look like,' said Buchanan. 'When I was a lad, you couldn't see the river for ships being built. The noise of riveting hammers filled the air from morning till night. Once the river Clyde was synonymous with shipbuilding; now, sadly, not much is left except the memory.'

The taxi pulled up in front of a newly-constructed factory on the edge of the Clyde. Opening the reception door Buchanan and Street were greeted by a pervasive aroma of polyester resin. A sign on the wall at the foot of an impressive stainless steel and teak staircase informed them that Greyspear's reception was situated on the first floor.

At least the atmosphere here was free from the smell of resin. Another view of a river thought Buchanan as they waited for Greyspear.

The secretary put down the phone and said, 'Sir Nathan is saying goodbye to a client, he will be with you shortly.'

Saying, good buy, or goodbye, wondered Buchanan.

♦

Greyspear was not what Buchanan expected. Though they were about the same height, he could imagine Greyspear stepping out on to Murrayfield with a ball under his arm, ready to lead his team to victory.

'Inspector,' said Greyspear, shaking Buchanan's hand, 'what can I do for you and your assistant?'

'DS Street, sir,' said Street, fighting the urge to curtsey.

'We're investigating the deaths of two people in the Sovereign Harbour last month.'

'I read about that in the paper but what has it to do with me?' he said, making a shrugging gesture with his hands.

'I'm referring to the 29th and 30th of March, sir. I believe you were out on the *Moonstone*?'

'Hmm – yes, so I was. But we didn't see anything and none of my guests were missing.'

'It's not one of your guests we are trying to identify. We think the dead woman may have been one of the catering crew,' said Street, handing Greyspear the photo of the dead girl.

Greyspear looked at the photo for a moment, shook his head and said, 'sorry, inspector, don't recognise her.'

'Did you engage the caterers, sir?'

'No, I don't get involved in those arrangements. You need to talk with my PA.'

'And where may we find her, sir?'

'I'm afraid you've just missed her – she's gone into Glasgow to do some shopping.'

'We'd like to have a word with her. When will she be back?'

'She won't be back here today. When she's finished she's going back to the office.'

'Would that be here in Greenock, or the London office, sir?'

'Neither. The London office mainly deals with sales and marketing and, as you can see, design and building is done here on the Clyde. These days with fibre broadband there's no reason to commute to London so I have my office in my home. We do have regional sales offices in Eastbourne, Poole, and Falmouth.'

'Are you married, sir?' asked Buchanan.

Greyspear shook his head. 'My wife died some years ago – she did in a car accident. Why would you want to know that?'

'You were listed as unaccompanied on the guest list.'

'That's life, Inspector.'

'I'm sorry to hear about your loss. Captain Bracewell was only able to provide us with a list of names of your guests on board that evening. We would like to interview each of them. Could you provide us with their addresses?'

'Once again, you'll need to talk with my PA.'

'What was the purpose for you going out on the *Moonstone* on the 29th, sir?' asked Buchanan, opening his briefcase and taking out the list of names Bracewell had given him.

'Partially business, and partially pleasure, Inspector; one of my guests was interested in ordering an FBC40.'

'FBC40, sir?'

'That's the model number, FB stands for fly bridge, C stands for cruiser, and the 40 is its length in metres.'

'And which of your guests was interested in the FBC40?'

'That was Harry Carstairs.'

'Do you know where he was when you returned to the Marina?'

'Yes, he and Yasmine were in the wheelhouse watching us dock.'

'Yasmine – she would be his wife?' said Buchanan, looking at the list of names.

'Yes.'

'What does he do for a living?'

'He used to fly for Virgin Atlantic.'

'Used to?'

'He's retired, runs his own executive jet company. He said he was looking to branch out into yacht chartering.'

'What can you tell me about the other guests?' said Buchanan, showing Greyspear the list.

'Not much I'm afraid,' he said, studying it. 'Richardson's an accountant, partner in a firm in Eastbourne. Silverstein is a CPA, and Bashir is a venture capitalist. Dr Metzger owns a private clinic in Meads.'

'Your captain said Silverstein and Bashir were arguing.'

'As per usual. They are actually good friends.'

'What about Dean Maxton and Rachael Angelous? They're actors, aren't they?'

'Yes, must have come along with one of the other guests.'

'What about partners – wives?'

'Not sure; from what I remember the women spent their time in the main saloon.'

'And you, sir, where did you spend your time?'

'On the bridge with the Carstairs. Couldn't ignore a potential customer.'

'Notice anything out of the ordinary during the trip?' asked Street.

'No,' said Greyspear, shaking his head. 'As I said. I was preoccupied with the Carstairs on the bridge for most of the trip.'

'And that was it? The purpose of going out was to show Carstairs how the yacht performed at sea?'

'Yes. Since we were taking the Carstairs out anyway I had my PA invite some business acquaintances for the day. Nothing sinister in that, is there, Inspector?'

'Someone died on that trip, sir.'

'Ah, that's your assumption, and it had nothing to do with me, I can assure you.'

'I think I'll be the judge of that, sir. Tell me, why go out at night? I would have thought that a day trip would have been more useful.'

'It was daytime when we went out.'

'Where did you go?'

'We motored along the coast to the Isle of Wight and back.'

'Did you go into any ports along the way?'

'No.'

'Stop to pick up anything?'

'Of course not. Inspector, I don't like your insinuations. You've seen my house, the *Moonstone*, and this factory. Do I look like I need to supplement my income with a spot of smuggling?'

'Sorry, sir, it's what I'm paid to do. Nothing personal about it.'

'And for your information the house is mine, the *Moonstone* belongs to the company and the factory is funded by a business support grant from the Scottish Government.'

'So you could —'

'Inspector — our order books are full for the next five years. Every yacht ordered comes with a twenty percent non-refundable deposit. The *Moonstone* is our latest and largest motor yacht, and as of this morning we have firm orders for five of them. Cash flow is not an issue. Getting trained, experienced laminators and ship fitters is my biggest headache.'

'How much does a forty-metre yacht cost?' asked Street. 'And please, I know the old saying about if you have to ask.'

'We could build you a very fine forty metre cruiser for about fifteen million.'

'I think I'll wait for Santa Claus.'

'Would you like to see the factory before you go, Inspector?'

'We have time. Oh — would you happen to have a brochure of the *Moonstone*? It would help us to familiarise ourselves with the interior.'

Greyspear, shrugged and reached for a brochure lying on his desk. In doing so he knocked a well-thumbed novel on the floor.

Buchanan bent down and picked it up, and looking at the front cover read, *The Penitent Heart*. Food for the soul, sir?'

'You could say that, Inspector. Just something to read while travelling – flying bores me.'

Buchanan slipped the brochure into his briefcase. 'Me too, sir. I much prefer to travel by train.'

'If you'll follow me I'll show you round the factory.'

Greyspear led them through the laminating shop and on to the fitting-out bays.

'What's that over there?' asked Street.

'That's a new venture for us. We are well known for our motor launches; that's the mould for our new sailing yacht.'

'It's huge! How big is it and where do you get the mould from? Or am I missing the obvious?' asked Street.

'Let's see. To answer your questions in order, firstly, the yacht when complete will be 105 feet long with its bowsprit; the hull is only ninety-five. We made the mould from a plug.'

'I'm sure that makes sense to your workers, but I'm lost.'

'To make a plug for a hull, we make a mock-up of the shape of the hull upside down, and then cover it in fibreglass and resin. Next, we pull the fibreglass off of the plug and there's the mould.'

'Must be quite wasteful to make something that big and then throwing it away?'

'Ah, but we didn't throw the plug away. Instead of making timber patterns for the yacht's hull, we used steel frames. We set these steel frames on timber bearers, just like you would do in traditional wooden boat construction. Then, instead of covering the frames with planks, we fastened horizontal strips of cedar to the frames. Next, we covered the cedar strips with a combination of cedar veneers, laid down diagonally, and glued on with epoxy. To finish we applied a protective coat of Kevlar, carbon fibre and epoxy. So instead of throwing away an expensive chunk of timber and labour, we have a very useful hull for a yacht. When all the resins and glues have cured, the hull is sanded and sprayed with epoxy paint.'

'Quite a lot of work for one boat. I can see why you'd make a proper hull for the plug.'

'The original hull has already been rolled over and attached to its keel. The yacht's in the fitting-out area now; you'll get a glimpse of it as we go through the factory. Hope to launch it in two weeks' time.'

'Must cost a fortune to start a new project like that,' said Street.

'It's not so expensive, especially since the boat is already sold.'

'They're taking a big risk, sir, your customers?'

'Not really, Inspector, the design's been around for many years. The original was by Herreshoff, a highly-respected name in the world of yacht design. We took that original design and stretched it to its present size.'

'Quite an impressive set-up,' said Buchanan. 'Thank you for the tour, Sir Nathan. Big difference from when my father worked in the shipyards.'

'You're welcome. And Inspector, I can assure you that none of my guests or staff were missing when we returned. Your dead girl is nothing to do with me. Probably just some visitor to the Marina who'd had too much to drink and simply fell in and drowned.'

♦

'What was the method of applying the resin called?' queried Street, as the taxi headed for the station.

'Vacuum resin infusion.'

'Thought so. How about we try a spot of tea infusion?'

'I'd prefer beer ingestion.'

Buchanan had to wait till he got to the airport.

♦

'This was where you worked?' asked Street as they entered Buchanan's former Police HQ. 'And not a pub in sight.'

'There is – it's just down the road.'

'I might have known.'

'Let's get a coffee, lass. Then we'll go see Ferguson. Maybe he can shine a light on our illustrious Sir Nathan Greyspear.'

'Is that all?'

'No, lass, I've a funny feeling all's not well.'

'Jack!' said Ferguson, as Buchanan and Street walked into his office. 'You're not coming back, are you?'

'No,' said Buchanan, smiling and shaking his head. 'Relax, we're just up to see a witness about a case we're working on.'

'Thought you were investigating the death of a DS in Sussex?'

'We are. Oh, this is DS Street; we're working on the case together.'

'Stewart Ferguson,' he said, extending his hand.

'Jill Street.'

'Who's the witness, Jack?'

'Sir Nathan Greyspear. Heard of him?'

'Not the Greyspear who builds those super yachts in Greenock?'

'The very same. Why – do you know him?'

'Not personally, only know his firm employs a lot of local people. He's a bit of a local hero.'

'Why do you say that?'

'He emptied the dole office of no-hopers, many with families, and trained them to be yacht fitters.'

'Quite a man.'

'I suppose your impending suspension will make your investigations a bit redundant, then?'

'What suspension?'

'Oh shit, don't tell me you don't know? It's all round the office.'

'No one has said anything to me. Are you sure it's me they're talking about?'

'Last week, I had to go up and see the boss. When I got to his office I had to wait – secretary said he was on the phone and couldn't be disturbed. It was a hot day and he had his door propped open a bit. I wasn't trying to listen, but he got quite agitated with whoever he was speaking to. I couldn't hear what the other person was saying, but the boss clearly said there was no option – you were to be suspended.'

'Are you sure? Were those his exact words?'

'Hmm, what he said was: *I have no option, I'll have to suspend him from duty*. I just assumed it was you. Remember Porter's bar?'

'How could I forget? I'm going to have words with him about this. He can't suspend me, especially when I'm in the middle of a double murder investigation.'

'Relax, Jack. You can't.'

'Can't? Just watch me.'

'Jack, what I mean is you can't – he's not here. He's gone to the States for a few days. His secretary said he's gone to a convention.'

'C'mon, lass, let's get out of here. Suspension or not, we've got a job to do and I need a beer.'

♦

'Isn't that Greyspear?' said Street, as they waited to board the plane for the flight back to Gatwick.

'Where?' said Buchanan.

'Over there, by the toilets; he looks like he's waiting for someone.'

They watched as a tall elegant blonde exited the Ladies and stopped to talk with Greyspear. He reached out to hold her but she pushed his hands away. He tried again, but with the same result. She said something while shaking her head and then walked off. He went to follow but stopped, turned and went into the executive lounge instead.

'What do you think of that, sir? Could she be his secretary?'

'It's possible. He owns the company and figures he owns the secretary as well. I pity her, though she does look like she can take care of herself. Did you see how she pushed him away?'

'It's not right; she shouldn't have to defend herself against a predator like Greyspear. And her a married woman. Did you see her right hand? She was wearing a wedding band.

9

This time the gates opened as soon as Buchanan announced their presence. They drove in, parked in front of the front door. The butler was waiting in front of the open front door.

'Good morning, Inspector,' said the butler, 'if you'll follow me I'll show you through to Sir Nathan's office.'

Most of the view through the window consisted of the *Moonstone*, leaving a partial view of sunshine on the water with smaller boats tied at docks on the far side of the lagoon. Once again Buchanan thought of office life, till his daydream was interrupted by the arrival of the tall, elegant blonde they'd seen the previous day arguing with Greyspear.

'Good morning, Inspector. Sir Nathan has informed me you would like the list of those guests who were on board the *Moonstone* on the 29th of March, and their addresses.'

'That's correct – names and addresses.'

'I'm not sure I can do that.'

'And why not?'

'Client information is commercially sensitive and covered by the Data Protection Act. Captain Bracewell shouldn't have given you those names.'

'I'm aware of the Data Protection Act, but this is a double murder investigation. I could get a court order, Mrs –?'

'Richardson, Susan Richardson.'

'Thank you, Mrs Richardson.'

'I thought that might be the case. I'll be right back.'

The sound of muffled voices came through the open office door. Buchanan shrugged his shoulders at Street. She shook her head.

Susan Richardson returned a few minutes later. 'Please keep the list confidential, Inspector,' she said, handing him a manila folder.

'Thank you, Mrs Richardson. We'll take good care of this.'

Buchanan opened the folder and looked at the list of names. He nodded his head in agreement as he checked the list against the mental note he had made of the one Bracewell had given him. 'What about the caterers? There's no mention of them in here?'

'You'll have to ask my husband. He made those arrangements.'

'Who invited Dean Maxton and Rachael Angelous?' asked Buchanan as he handed the list to Street.

'I'm not sure, possibly the Carstairs. They spend most of their working life mixing with celebrities. Mr Carstairs operates an executive jet service.'

'Hmm – so we have been informed,' said Street, looking up from the typed list. 'You're married to Rodney Richardson?'

'Oh, a smart detective: knows two and two equals four. Yes, I'm married to Rodney Richardson.'

'Sometimes two plus two equals five, Mrs Richardson. You were with Sir Nathan in Glasgow yesterday?' Buchanan asked.

'Inspector, I'm Sir Nathan's PA. Where he goes, I follow.'

'Do you recognise this person?' Street handed Susan Richardson the photo of the dead girl.

'Should I? No, I'm sorry – although she does look familiar. Is she an actress?'

'I believe the word is actor, Mrs Richardson; they get quite touchy about that.'

'Is your husband at work this morning?' asked Street.

'Yes, of course he is. Surely you don't suspect him of anything, do you?'

'No, Ma'am. We're primarily interested in the names of the caterers.'

'Where does he work, Mrs Richardson?'

'His firm's in Meads, Inspector – it's across from Lloyds. Well, it used to be till they closed the branch. But you won't find him in his office today – he's gone to London, won't be back till late tomorrow evening.'

'And Sir Nathan, is he available?'

'No, and he won't be for a few days.'

'A few days?'

'He is off to Hong Kong tomorrow.'

'And will you be going with him?'

'No. My mother's not well, and besides, why do you think I would?

'It's just, you said: "where he goes, I follow".'

'In an ideal world – Now, if you're done with the inquisition, I have an office to manage.'

'Not quite. Can you tell me where you were when the *Moonstone* arrived back in the harbour on the morning of the 30th of March?'

'I would have been in the steward's pantry. Any time we go out for a demonstration, on the return I have to account for all the items consumed – mostly alcohol.'

'Was your husband with you?'

'I suppose so; he had the catering staff to look after.'

'Why were you in the pantry and not with Sir Nathan?'

'Like any business, sales and marketing expenses are tax deductible.'

'Anybody with you, or see you?'

'I don't remember.'

'How about the caterers, or the galley staff? Surely they'd be busy clearing up?'

'I was too busy to notice.'

'So no one can corroborate your story?'

'No, I have no alibi.'

♦

'Did we tread on toes there, sir?'

'Remember, lass, if you're going to walk on broken glass, always put your shoes on first.'

'What's on the bill for tomorrow, sir?'

'Be a good idea to spend the day going over the case notes.'

10

In spite of the April sunshine, Buchanan arrived at Hammonds Drive with his own personal cloud of doom. How *could* they suspend him? Whose toes had he trodden on? What'd he done to deserve being suspended?

'Morning, lass,' he responded to Street's welcome.

'I'll get the coffees. You look like you could do with one.'

'I need more than coffee.'

'You're on duty.'

'Thanks, lass,' he said, unscrewing his flask and pouring a good measure into his cup. 'Heard from the dynamic duo?'

'They're in the canteen, I told them to wait till you've had your coffee.'

Buchanan looked at his drink, thought for a moment, smiled and said, 'Thanks.'

As if on cue, Dexter and Hunter walked in.

'Well, what did you find out? Any trace of the maiden?'

Dexter shook his head and Hunter said, 'We think we have a lead on the tattoo.'

'*Think*. You're not paid to think, that's my job.'

Ignoring the jibe, Dexter said, 'One of the tattoo parlour owners said he recognised the design as one by a French artist working in Dieppe.'

'Well done – now we're getting somewhere! Anything else?'

'No.'

'Right. You're both local, aren't you?'

'Yes, sir,' said Hunter.

'Have you checked the harbour restaurants yet?'

'No, sir, not yet,' replied Hunter.

'Then might I suggest you do. Find out if anyone was having a private party – maybe she was a guest.'

As Dexter and Hunter left the office, Buchanan asked, 'Any word on the DNA tests?'

'Results came in before you arrived. Negative on Nichols being the father, but the girl did stay at his house. DNA on the pillow from the back bedroom matched.'

'How about the other bedroom? Did forensics find any trace on Nichols' pillows?'

'Nada, they slept alone.'

'Interesting: they knew each other but slept in separate bedrooms. Was he protecting her against the father of the child? Did she tell Nichols who the father was? Is that the reason for his demise?'

'Maybe they had a falling out and he did her in.'

Buchanan shook his head. 'No, we've been down that road before. I don't think so. Now, before we get interrupted we've got work to do. Where's that brochure Greyspear gave us?'

'Should be in your briefcase.'

Buchanan opened the case and carefully took it out.

'Thinking of heading out to sea?'

'I wish,' said Buchanan. 'I think it will be a good idea if we feed the information we have into Mycroft.'

'Mycroft? Don't you mean HOLMES?'

'No, lass. HOLMES is nothing but a mishmash of zeros and ones running around in a computer. Mycroft is – and I quote the greatest detectives of all times – *the application of the problem to one's own little grey cells.*'

'That's Poirot, and I'm sure he never said that.'

'Doesn't matter – it takes time and people to load HOLMES. And in case it's slipped your wonderful powers of deduction, we still don't have any data entry clerks.'

'I'm sure we'll have them soon.'

'Maybe, maybe not; in the meantime let's get started. Read out the list of names Bracewell gave us.'

Street read while Buchanan wrote down a vertical list of names on the whiteboard. Then using the brochure Greyspear gave them, he wrote the names of each area of the *Moonstone* across the top of the whiteboard. He finished off by drawing horizontal and vertical lines, creating a grid.

'There. Now all we have to do is put a mark where each person was at the moment the *Moonstone* passed through the drawbridge,' said Buchanan. 'The odd one out will be our killer.'

'What about the crew? Shouldn't we add their names as well?'

'Good idea,' said Buchanan, picking up the marker pen.

'That's brilliant, so simple.'

'If only. Remember they'd all be partying the best part of the day. It will be a miracle if half of them remember where they were as they entered the Marina.'

Further prognostications were prevented by the ringing of Street's phone.

'DS Street. Yes Ma'am, he's here – yes, I'll tell him.'

'Spider Woman?' mouthed Buchanan.

'You've been summoned to the web. I'll drive – where are your keys?'

♦

As Street drove, Buchanan chewed on his personal bumblebee, while muttering to himself. Once in the ACC's secretary's office Buchanan paced up and down. He could no longer imagine his photo on the wall.

'She does know I'm here?'

'Yes, sir. She's on the phone – shouldn't be long.'

Buchanan continued with his pacing. This summons could mean only one thing. But try as he may he couldn't think of why he should be suspended. The fight in Porter's toilets had been while off duty and in self-defence. He hadn't even been wearing a uniform – not that he had one. Randal had started the fight and when it came to the issue of the two men's demise, he reasoned it was their own guilt and stupidity that drove them to run out into the road and under the police car.

The secretary's phone buzzed and she picked up. 'Yes, Ma'am – he has DS Street with him – I'll send him right in.'

'I heard,' said Buchanan, hand on the door handle.

'Come in, Buchanan.'

Buchanan approached the ACC's desk and stood like a naughty boy in front of the headmistress.

'For goodness sake, sit down.'

'Yes, Ma'am.'

'What's the matter with you?'

'Nothing. Bit tired that's all, didn't sleep well.'

'Well, to the business at hand.'

'My suspension.'

'Your what?'

'Isn't that why I've been summoned?'

'No, of course it isn't! Why would you think that?'

'It's just – it's just, when we were in Glasgow I was told I was going to be suspended.'

'By whom?'

'Fergusson – he's one of the DS's.'

'They're winding you up, Buchanan. As far as I'm concerned you're still on duty. Now what about your visit to – Greenock, was it?'

'Yes, Ma'am. We went to interview Sir Nathan.'

'Still chasing the death of the girl?'

'Not just. We now have definite information that the girl and Nichols knew each other. In fact she was staying with Nichols in his house.'

'You're certain of that?'

Buchanan went through the details of the investigation. He included the results of the forensic examination of Nichols' house and the fact that the dead girl's baby wasn't his.

'What's next, Buchanan?'

'Standard police work: we will be interviewing everyone on the list to determine where they were at the moment the *Moonstone* went past the bridge.'

'Do you still require the two PC's?'

'I've sent them round the harbour restaurants on the off chance they may turn up something, although I think they'll draw a blank.'

'What about the tattoo?'

'Ah, yes. One of the Eastbourne tattoo parlours identified it as being done by a French parlour in Dieppe. I was thinking of sending Street to investigate; she speaks better French than I do.'

'What about protocol? You know the gendarmes won't appreciate you, or Street, poking around on their turf?'

'She'll just be there as a day visitor. If anyone asks, she can say she's going to visit with my wife and just happened to be looking for a tattoo for herself. If she finds out anything that may lead us to our killer, I'll go through the proper channels.'

'Good. Anything else?'

Buchanan shook his head. 'No, Ma'am.'

'Good work so far, Buchanan. Keep me posted.'

♦

'Fancy a coffee, sir? The Cavendish van's just pulled into the car park.'

'Yeah, and see if they've got any sandwiches left – tuna will do.'

Street returned with their coffees and Buchanan's sandwich.

'Thanks, lass, I'll get the next.'

'Who's first on the list, sir?'

'I want to talk to Greyspear again but since he's not available we'll start with Richardson –, mister that is.'

♦

Richardson's office was on the corner of Mead Street and Grafton and was blessed with ample parking at the side. Buchanan ignored the gravelled private parking space and stopped on a double yellow line.

The entrance door was midway in the shop front and set back from the glass-fronted office. Enough space for the homeless to set up home, thought Buchanan. Stencilled on the inside of the window in gold letters was: *Richardson and Hendricks Chartered Accountants*. Buchanan looked through the spotless window. There were six desks, all polished mahogany; each was equipped with a computer replete with double-flat screen.

Walking into the office they were greeted with the relaxed atmosphere of a well-managed office.

The severe-looking woman seated at the desk by the door looked up and asked, 'Can I help?'

'Yes, we're here to see Rodney Richardson.'

'Do you have an appointment?' she asked, looking at her screen. A concerned frown wrinkled her brow.

'Sussex CID. We'd like to have a word with Mr Richardson in private. We won't keep him long.'

She pressed a button on her keyboard and spoke into an almost invisible headset.'

'Mr Richardson – thank you – and the same to you. There's a couple of police officers here to see you. No, they haven't.' She turned to Buchanan and Street. 'Mr Richardson wants to know the purpose of your visit; he's extremely busy.'

'Tell him we're investigating a death in the Marina.'

'It's about a death in the Marina – OK.' She nodded to them. 'He says to go right up. Take the lift, it's quicker.'

'Very impressive office – the carpet is deep enough to hide a pony,' said Street, as they exited the lift to be greeted by another polished mahogany desk. This time, there was just a discrete laptop and a face that could be the twin of the one on the ground floor. Richardson's secretary, thought Buchanan.

'Mr Richardson says he'll see you in a minute.'

'Always thought of accountants as being dull and sitting at desks with piles of ledgers in front of them,' said Street, while they waited.

'Must be a perk of being a secretary,' said Buchanan, while looking out the window over the rooftops to Pevensey Bay. 'What's that in the bay, Street? Looks like a sort of tower.'

'That's the Sovereign light, replaced a light ship.'

'Excuse me, Inspector, Mr Richardson will see you now.'

The secretary shut the door behind them.

Richardson looked up from his screen. 'How can I help?'

'Can you tell us where you were on the evening of the 29th of March?'

Richardson moved the mouse on his desk and clicked a couple of times.

'Yes, as a matter of fact I can,' he said, looking up and smiling. 'I was on the *Moonstone*, as a guest of Sir Nathan Greyspear. But you knew that already.'

'Did he invite you, sir?'

Richardson frowned. 'No, not directly.'

'What do you mean, sir?'

'My wife, she's his secretary. I went along for the ride, that's all.'

'Did you spend the day with your wife, or mix with the guests?

'Inspector, I was too busy to mix with anyone. Ask my wife, I was with her the whole time.'

'And the caterers, did you organise that?'

'Not exactly, I know someone who provides that service.'

'Could we have their name and contact details, sir?' requested Street.

'I'm afraid that's not possible. I mean, I don't have them. I usually run into him when a bunch of us meet up for coffee. He travels a lot – in Europe.'

Richardson reached into his pocket and took out a handkerchief to wipe the drops of sweat that had formed on his forehead.

'Mr Richardson, I simply want a name and contact details of your associate.'

'I told you, I can't,' he said, the sweat reforming. 'He travels in Europe and I only see him when he's in town.'

'Does he have a name?'

'He calls himself Abosa.'

'Surname?'

'Just Abosa.'

'How do you get in contact?'

'He'll call me when he's in town and we'll meet for a drink.'

'When did you last meet him?'

'A few weeks ago. I was in a restaurant having dinner and he walked in.'

'Did you say hello?'

'We were just finishing, he sat and had a drink with us.'

'Was he alone?'

'Yes, although I had the impression he was meeting someone and they were late.'

'Can we have his description, please? And the name of the restaurant and date of your meeting.'

♦

'The plot thickens, lass,' said Buchanan, as he stared out the office window. 'I want you to go to the restaurant Richardson had dinner at and see if anyone remembers him. Wish we had Richardson's photo, it would make identification much easier.'

'No problem, I have it already.'

'How'd you manage that?'

'The arrogant sod has his photo all over his company website. I simply copied and uploaded to my phone.'

'Well done, and when you're there ask if anybody remembers this mysterious Abosa. If so, get a description. Maybe he's known to us or maybe someone at immigration will remember him.'

'And you, sir?'

'I'm off to Newhaven to pick up Mrs Buchanan. You're still OK for dinner tomorrow?'

'Oh, I'd forgotten! Er – yes, why not? What time?'

'Seven-thirty?'

11

'How'd you get on at the restaurant?'

'I talked to the manager and asked him to check his records. I showed him Richardson's picture and he recognised him immediately.'

'So he *was* there.'

'Not only was he there on the evening in question, he was also there last night, sitting with his back to me as I talked with the manager.'

'Did he see you?'

'I doubt it; he was busy looking at the menu. But wait – it gets better: last night he wasn't with his wife.'

'Oh?'

'I asked the manager if Richardson usually dined alone.'

'And?' said Buchanan, rubbing his hands together.

'He said he was usually with a lady. I asked for a description of his guest, and guess what?'

'What?'

'It definitely wasn't his wife – more a description of his secretary. And it gets better still. The person Richardson met, this Abosa fellow, is known to the manager.'

'What did he tell you about Abosa?'

'He runs an employment agency, somewhere in Budapest. Abosa calls in regularly to local restaurants to see if they need any workers. Apparently it's all legal.'

'How does it work?'

'The workers are employed by the agency in Budapest. When it comes to charging the restaurant, they are usually charged rates 20 percent lower than what the equivalent local agencies would charge the restaurant.'

'What about wages?'

'This is where the unfairness comes in. The workers are sometimes paid more than they would get at home, but substantially less than the going rate in Eastbourne.'

'So everyone wins?' said Buchanan.

'Not everyone. How about all those school-leavers looking for their first jobs? Where's the work for them? I wandered round the back of the restaurant and had a chat with one of the waitresses.'

'Get her name?'

'Ilka. She said the agency organises staff transportation and the first three months' accommodation. They only get paid when they have worked off their advance. The real stinker in the pudding is, unless they are willing to do extra duties, they get let go with no money for their three months of work. On top of all that the agency holds their passports – preventing them from doing a runner.'

'What do they live on during these three months?'

'Tips. Remember that the next time you're out to dinner.'

'I don't need to guess what the extra duties will entail,' said Buchanan.

'It gets even worse.'

'Do I want to know?'

'There are unscrupulous agencies that get some of these girls, and it's mostly girls, hooked on drugs and then forces them into prostitution to fund their habit.'

'Did Ilka say if she had been asked to do extra duties?'

'She said she's only heard stories from friends who returned to Hungary.'

'Did you show her the picture of our girl?'

'She said she didn't recognise her, but I wasn't sure if she was telling the truth.'

'I think we'll pay her a visit, see if we can help her memory.'

'She's off for a couple of days, be back at work next Wednesday.'

'Right, put that in the diary for Wednesday and I think,' he said yawning, 'we're done for today. What time's dinner?'

'You said seven-thirty.'

'Right, see you this evening.'

♦

'It's really nice of you to invite me to dinner, Mrs Buchanan.'

'It's Karen, please call me Karen. You may call him *sir* if that makes you feel more comfortable.'

'Thanks, Karen. Can I help with anything?'

'Yes, the trifle needs putting together. The cream needs whipping. I can't stand it when the cream dries out and turns into a solid lump.'

'If you two are going to the kitchen, I'm going to catch up on the news,' said Buchanan

Twenty minutes later Karen came out of the kitchen and said, 'Jack, we're low on milk, pop out and get some, would you?'

'We've got plenty – there's two pints in the fridge.'

'Jack, I said we're low on milk.'

'Oh, silly me, of course we are.'

When he returned Street and Karen were sitting on the settee, a box of tissues open on the coffee table.

He looked at Karen, she shook her head as if to say, don't ask. Street was hugging a pillow and sobbing quietly.

12

'How was the weekend?'

'You were there Saturday. You saw what happened.'

'Yes, Karen has that effect on people.'

'I felt a complete fool breaking down in front of you.'

'That's all right, I don't mind. After all, it was my suggestion for you two to meet.'

'She's invited me back, wants to introduce me to some of her friends at church.'

'Will you go?'

'Don't know, feels weird talking about the past, especially after all these years.'

'Just like lancing a boil.'

'That's what Karen said.'

'Smart lady.'

'Of course she is; she married you.'

'Enough of that, young lady!'

'Do you go?'

'Where?'

'To church?'

'Me? Nah, I'm usually too busy.'

'It's just down the road.'

'Maybe someday. In the meantime we've got work to do.'

'Where first?'

'Let's go down the list. Who's next?'

'Mr and Mrs Silverstein; they live in Meads.'

♦

Buchanan rang the doorbell and the chimes of Big Ben escaped through the letterbox. The sound of Schubert being played on a cello drifted down from an upstairs bedroom.

The door was opened by a petite, well-dressed middle-aged woman whose hair looked like it had just been coiffured for an advert in *Vogue*.

'Mrs Silverstein?'

'Yes.'

'Chief Inspector Buchanan, Sussex CID, and this is Detective Sergeant Street. I wonder if we could come in and ask you a few questions?'

'What about?'

'Could we step inside, please?'

'Yes, of course, this way.'

She led them to the back of the house, through the living room and into the conservatory. 'It's much warmer in here; we don't have the heating on during the day.'

'This is a lovely house, Mrs Silverstein, so peaceful,' said Street.

'Thank you, dear.'

'Who's the artist in the family?' said Buchanan.

'My husband. He took up painting while recovering from a heart attack. He said the one in the hall was of a dream he had while in hospital. Do you paint?'

'No, never tried. My talents lie in a different direction.'

'Can I get you something to drink? Kettle's just boiled.'

Street interrupted Buchanan before he could say no. 'Yes please, Mrs Silverstein, tea would be lovely.'

Mrs Silverstein returned a few minutes later with the tea, accompanied by a young woman carrying a tray with a plate of scones, butter, and a pot of strawberry jam. 'This is my daughter, Deborah.'

'Was that you playing the cello?'

Deborah smiled. 'Yes.'

'You're very good.'

'Thanks. I'm performing it at St Martin's next weekend.'

'Lucky audience.'

'Now, how can I help, Inspector?' said Mrs Silverstein, sitting down with the sun to her back.

'Will you need anything else, mum?' asked Deborah.

'No dear, you can go back to your practicing.

'You went out for a sail on Sir Nathan Greyspear's yacht on the 29th of March?'

The sound of the cello from upstairs resumed. 'I do remember going out on Sir Nathan's yacht. Don't remember which day but I could check the calendar,' she said, getting up from her chair. She returned a few minutes later and said, 'Yes, it was the 29th, lovely weather for the time of year.'

'Do you remember much about the day?' asked Street.

'The weather was nice. I spent most of the trip inside talking with the other ladies.'

'Do you remember who was with you just before you docked?' asked Buchanan.

'Hmm. Aakifah was sitting on my right and that lovely actress, Rachael Angelous, was sitting opposite, beside Rosalind Metzger.'

'Anyone else?' asked Buchanan. 'For instance, Mrs Richardson, was she with you?'

'Don't think so. She did pop in and out as the day went on. I think she was making sure everyone had what they wanted, being the perfect hostess.'

'Where was your husband?'

'He and Achmed were in the lounge.'

'What were they doing?'

'What were they doing?' she said, laughing. 'What they always do when they're together. They were arguing about the West Bank and who owned it.'

'They're friends?'

116

'Of course, they are.' She laughed again. 'They've known each other for years.'

'What about Dean Maxton, Rodney Richardson or the Carstairs? Did you see anything of them during the day?'

She shook her head. 'They could have danced naked through the saloon and we wouldn't have noticed them, we were too busy talking. That Rachael was so full of stories about what they get up to when on location.'

'Do you recall seeing this person?' asked Street, passing Mrs Silverstein the picture of the dead girl.

She looked at it. 'No, sorry.'

'How about this one?' said Street, showing her a photo of Nichols.

'Sorry, no.'

'Thank you, Mrs Silverstein,' said Buchanan. 'Can you tell me where we would find your husband?'

'He's gone to London. I think he said he'd a meeting at Lloyds in the morning then he was going on to another meeting in the afternoon. I don't remember where, though. He should be in his office in town, tomorrow.'

'Where is his office?' asked Buchanan.

'Lushington Road. I'm not sure of the number. I do remember it's on the left, just before you come to Cornfield Road.'

'Thank you, Mrs Silverstein,' said Buchanan again. 'We'll get in touch with your husband tomorrow. Goodbye.'

'On to the Bashir's?' asked Street.

'Why not. We'll probably draw a blank with the husband; he'll most likely be at work. Where do they live?'

Street opened her notebook and said, 'In Willingdon, just below the Downs.'

Achmed Bashir was at work, though not in London like Silverstein. He was in his office in the rear of their expansive house.

117

Whereas Sarah Silverstein was petite and compact, Aakifah Bashir was tall and slender. She wore a long, flowing, jade-green satin gown, embroidered with peacocks. She had long, dark hair down to her waist and eyes that any Persian princess would envy.

'My husband is on a conference call and I can't interrupt him,' she explained. 'He should be finished soon.'

'We can wait.'

'Can I get you something to drink, while you wait?'

Buchanan looked at Street and grimaced.

'Could I have tea?' asked Street.

'Certainly, and sir?'

Buchanan looked flustered; he'd prefer a whiskey. 'Tea will be fine, thanks.'

She returned a few minutes later and said, 'My daughter, Ayesha, will bring in the tea when it's ready, should be with us shortly.'

Relaxing into an enormous armchair, she kicked off her slippers, pulled her long legs up beside her and immediately covered them with her robe. A perfect picture of a Persian princess, thought Buchanan.

Moments later a perfect copy of Aakifah Bashir, except for being twenty years younger, entered carrying an engraved gilt tray with glass cups held in little gold-plated holders.

'Thank you, Ayesha. Put it on the table, I'll serve.'

Buchanan was perplexed. He was used to a mug with a teabag and a slosh of milk.

'Inspector, I see you're not used to traditional Iranian tea?'

'No, Ma'am.'

'We drink it all the time. Sometimes we add a stick of cinnamon.'

Buchanan watched as Aakifah Bashir poured the tea through a strainer into the glass cups, with not a drop of milk in sight.

'If you'll excuse me,' said Ayesha, picking up a copy of *The Penitent Heart* from the table, and curling up in an armchair.

118

That's the second time I've seen that book recently, thought Buchanan. 'What's the odds on that?'

'Mrs Bashir,' began Buchanan, 'do you remember where you were on the 29th of March?'

'Ah, yes. We were out on Sir Nathan's lovely yacht.'

'Do you know Sir Nathan?'

'Not directly, I believe he and my husband have a business arrangement.'

'What kind of business arrangement?'

'I'm sorry Inspector; you'll have to ask my husband.'

'Can you remember where you were just before the end of the evening – just before the *Moonstone* tied up at her berth?'

'Where I was most of the day.'

'And where would that be?'

'I think it is called the main saloon.'

'Anyone else with you?'

Street wrote in her notebook while Aakifah Bashir recounted a similar story to that of Sarah Silverstein.

'And you don't remember anything out of the ordinary?'

'Inspector, the whole day was out of the ordinary. What luxury!'

'Do you remember seeing either of these people?' He passed her the photos of the dead girl and Nichols.

She shook her head and then said, 'Ayesha, go see if your father is available. I'm sure the Inspector has better things to do with his time than sit and drink tea.'

Achmed Bashir, with his daughter, walked into the room followed by the fragrance of an expensive Cuban cigar.

Buchanan and Street stood.

'Achmed, these police officers want to know about the day we went out on Sir Nathan's yacht.'

'Detective Chief Inspector Buchanan,' said Buchanan, 'and this is Detective Sergeant Street. We are investigating the death of a young woman in Sovereign Harbour on the morning of the 30th of March.'

'Inspector, as my wife has probably told you, we were out at sea all day.'

'Where were you when the yacht returned, especially just prior to tying up at the dock?'

'I was in the lounge, talking with Aaron Silverstein.'

'Anyone else with you?'

'No, just the two of us.'

'What about Sir Nathan?'

'Ah, he may have come in to see how we were. I think the raised voices may have disturbed him.'

'Pleasant conversation, was it, sir?'

Bashir looked at Buchanan and smiled. 'Inspector, please don't be confused between an argument of anger with one of passion. We both feel very passionate about the West Bank.'

Street passed the photo of the dead girl to Bashir. 'Do you recognise this person, sir?'

Bashir looked at the photo and thought for a moment. 'She does look familiar. It's the hair and the eyes. Yes, I think she may have served us drinks at some point.'

'Did you talk to her?'

'No, why should I?'

'To order drinks, perhaps?'

'Maybe, but that's not having a conversation. She was just a waitress.'

'And this one, sir? Did you see him on the yacht?'

'Er – no. I'm certain he wasn't.'

'But you do recognise him?'

'I saw his picture in the *Herald*; wasn't he the policeman who had the accident in the harbour?'

♦

'Just a waitress,' muttered Buchanan, as they headed to the office.

'Well, we now have our first positive sighting of the dead girl on board,' said Street, 'and more than likely one of the guests must be the murderer.'

'It's looking that way.'

'You're not convinced, sir?'

> *Many a corner*
> *Turned left or right*
> *Can lead you*
> *Into the darkest of night*
>
> *This way and that*
> *You shuttle and dart*
> *Cherchez la femme*
> *You cry from your heart*
>
> *Deceived by your senses*
> *You fret and squirm*
> *Only to return*
> *To whence you begun.'*

'You think we've missed something? Why?' said Street.

'Not sure, something – something significant and I can't quite grasp it. I need a drink – let's go for lunch. We'll have a council of war.'

◆

They parked in the Smugglers' car park, went into the bar and sat at a table close to the fire.

'Whiskey, please' said Buchanan to the waitress.

'Diet lemonade,' said Street.

'And would you like a menu, sir?'

'Bring it with the drinks, will you?'

Buchanan threw his drink back in one gulp.

'Thought you're supposed to sip whiskey?'

'I'll sip the next. Now let's order our food and we can get on with the business at hand.'

'Where will we start?'

They ate lunch and discussed the case, without a resolution or suspect.

'Before we drive all the way to Shoreham airport, I'll call Carstairs and make sure he's not off flying,' said Buchanan.

♦

Street turned off Cecil Pashley Way and into a private car park. She parked between a bright yellow Ferrari and a highly-polished grey Maserati. A painted sign on the grey steel door informed them that the office of *Carstair* was third door on the left at the top of the stairs.

Buchanan knocked, and entered. This was a working office. There were three desks: one covered with piles of packages and papers, the two others empty. One desk had a typical office chair, the other an empty aircraft ejector seat. A bent propeller blade hung from the ceiling and a smashed cockpit window was fastened to the wall like a trophy. The far wall consisted of a full-width window, which looked down into a vast hanger. Buchanan walked over and saw the hanger contained two executive jets, both in the *Carstair* livery.

'He's in his trailer,' said a voice from behind the papers.

Street went round the pile. Her search revealed a curvaceous brunette reclining in a seat from a first-class BA cabin. She had a coffee in one hand and a book in the other.

That's the third time I've seen that book, thought Buchanan.

'They have lunch at this time. Trailer's at the side of the hanger: out the door and turn right.'

122

'Short on words, wasn't she?' remarked Street.

'"Trailer" didn't really portray the magnificence of the Carstairs' residence.

Street opened the white picket gate for Buchanan. They climbed the steps to what they assumed was the front door. Buchanan pushed the door bell and waited. The door was opened by a tall Asian woman.

'Inspector Buchanan, Sussex CID, and this is Detective Sergeant Street. We'd like to have a word with Mr Carstairs.'

'Come in, he's on the veranda.'

'Never realised caravans could be quite this luxurious,' said Buchanan, as they followed her through the trailer.

'It's what the Americans call a "double wide", Inspector. Harry bought it from a US airman who was stationed at Mildenhall. The guy was desperate to dispose of it so Harry got it for a song.'

They stepped out of the cool of the trailer and out onto the veranda.

'Harry, this is –'

'DCI Buchanan and DS Street.'

Carstairs sat up from his recliner, took off his Ray-Ban sunglasses and squinted as his eyes adjusted to the sunshine. 'Didn't think police budgets extended to hiring executive jets, Inspector.'

'We're not here to hire a jet, sir. We're investigating a death in the Sovereign Harbour, Eastbourne, on the morning of the 30th of March.'

'Wasn't that the day we were out with Sir Nathan, Yasmin?'

'You're Mrs–?'

'Carstairs, yes, and we went out with Sir Nathan on the 29th of March.'

'How was the weather?'

'The weather was fine, plenty of sunshine as I remember, just a bit of wind.'

'Did you take the helm?'

'Not much while we were out – the *Moonstone* is equipped with autopilot.'

'Can you tell me where you were just before you returned to the dock?' asked Buchanan.

'On the bridge; the captain was showing us how easy the *Moonstone* is to dock.'

'Did you leave the bridge at any time?'

'During the day we were shown round the yacht, we're thinking about leasing one.'

'Be a bit expensive to run, wouldn't it?'

'Won't be much different than flying a modern Gulfstream, of which we have three.'

'I only saw two in the hanger.'

'The third is in maintenance. We always have at least two in service.'

'Do you still fly?' asked Buchanan.

'Yes.'

'I understand you retired from Virgin?'

'Did twenty-five years with them; got tired of the routine. Could say I took a leaf out of Sir Richard's book and followed in his footsteps.'

'Why live at the airport?'

'Technically we don't live here. This is the company headquarters and this,' he said, sweeping his arm across the expanse of the open fields and runways, 'is my executive view, from my executive office. Due to the irregularity of our schedules our pilots need somewhere to sleep between flights, hence the bedrooms.'

'How many pilots fly for you?'

'Just two of us full-time, then when we're pushed, we contract others in as needed.'

'Who's the other pilot? Is he here?'

'I am,' said Yasmin Carstairs.

'You're a pilot? But you're a woman!' said Buchanan.

'Well observed, Inspector.'

'How long have you been flying?' asked Street.

'I joined the RAF from college and went on to fly jets. I was a pilot in a tornado bomber before I left. I met Harry in London and he offered me the job of flying with him. The rest is history.'

'Did you bring Dean Maxton and Rachael Angelous with you on the 29th of March?' asked Buchanan.

'Yes.'

'How do you know them?'

'They're clients.'

'Did you invite them?'

'No, we got a call from Greyspear's office asking us if we could bring them along.'

'Would that have been Mrs Richardson?' asked Buchanan.

'Yes.'

'Why do you think she asked you to bring them? I understand most actors have their own dedicated chauffeurs.'

'We were booked to fly them back from the Ann Arbor film festival. We flew in at six and had Nancy drive us over.'

'Nancy?' said Buchanan.

'She's my PA, Inspector. I expect you met her upstairs in the office.'

'Why do you think they were invited?'

'Friends of Greyspear, I suppose.'

'Are you a friend as well?'

'We have a contract with Greyspear Yachts. We fly Sir Nathan where and when he wants.'

'Bit expensive?'

'Not really, inspector. Especially when you balance the cost of first class airfares and the restrictions airline schedules impose.'

'Can we have Maxton's contact details?' asked Street.

'We don't have that sort of information. You'll have to contact their agent.'

'Well, do you have their agent's contact details?'

'Yes. I'll get them for you.'

She returned a few minutes later and handed Street a sheet of paper.

'Jack Kleinman Agency, Wardour Street London.'

Street handed them the pictures of the dead girl and Nichols. 'Recognise either of them?'

The Carstairs shook their heads.

'Thank you, Mr and Mrs Carstairs. We'll be in touch if we have further questions.'

'No problem, Inspector. Let us know the next time you plan to visit and we'll take you up for a spin in the Gulfstream.'

♦

'Street, when we get back to the office, get on the phone and find out if Kleinman is available. Tell him we want to have a chat with Maxton and Angelous. I want to get all the preliminary questioning done before the end of the week.'

'Figure out what's missing yet?'

'What'd you mean, lass?'

'You said this morning that you'd missed something.'

'Ah, that. They're all lying.'

'You mean they weren't out on the *Moonstone*?'

'No, they probably *were* all out on the *Moonstone*. What I missed was they're all keeping a secret.'

13

'Kleinman called, sir,' said Street, as Buchanan walked into the office. 'He gave me Maxton's home number. I set up a meeting with them tomorrow morning at ten.'

'Them? Are they married?'

'Don't know.'

'Excellent. In the meantime, I think we'll use today to take stock of where we are. How are you doing with HOLMES, all up to date?'

'Yes. How about Mycroft? How's he doing – are his little grey cells behaving themselves?'

'I need some fresh air, back in a moment.'

'Karen knows.'

'Knows what?'

'That you're still smoking.'

Buchanan stopped at the door, turned and stared absently at the floor.

'I – I didn't say a word, honestly. It's your hands: you need to wash them more often,' said Street.

Buchanan sighed then returned to his desk. 'Get me a coffee, will you? No, don't bother, let's go for some real fresh air. My treat.'

'Where?'

'Starbucks, the one down by the garage.'

♦

'Anything from our dynamic duo?' asked Buchanan, as he delivered their coffees. 'You did tell them to check the restaurants, didn't you?'

'Yes. Stephen called and said they are almost done.'

'They're coming here?'

'No, I said to wait for us at the office.'

'Good.'

'Disappointed Karen knows you're still smoking?'

'A bit. Feel like I've let her down.'

'Don't worry; she says she still loves you, warts 'n all.'

Buchanan smiled and shook his head. 'You know, if you were – ah, never mind.'

'Never mind what?'

'Nothing – just a mad thought from a tired old man.'

'If you didn't–'

'Didn't smoke? Was that what you were about to say?'

'My lips are sealed; won't say another word about the subject.'

'Good. Let's get back to the office and see what Dexter and Hunter have got for us.'

◆

'For goodness' sake, don't stand there like you're on parade. Sit down.'

'Yes, sir.'

'Well? What did you find out?'

'Nothing on the tattoo,' said Hunter.

'Or the photo of the girl,' added Dexter.

'Just as I thought.'

'We did the rounds of the restaurants last night,' continued Dexter. 'None of the managers recognised the girl.'

'What about this chap Abosa?'

'Drew a blank at most restaurants.'

'Except for a couple,' said Hunter. 'When we described Abosa the managers looked wary, and clammed right up.'

◆

'We're in the wrong business, lass,' said Buchanan, as they waited for the gates at Maxton's house to swing back.

'Then who'd bang up the bad guys?'

'You're watching too many cop shows on TV.'

'Seen any of Maxton's movies?' asked Street.

'No, don't have time for the movies.'

'He plays a cop in one.'

'Really, any good?'

'Not bad, script let him down. He had to work hard to be convincing.'

'When did you see that?'

'Last night, watched it online.'

'Well, let's see how good he is in real life,' said Buchanan, as they walked up to the front of the Maxton residence.

The front door was opened by a young woman. She led them into what Street assumed was the lounge.

'Dad said he'll be right with you and to offer you something to drink.'

Buchanan and Street sat on the settee drinking their coffees and staring out of the plate glass windows at the expanse of garden. Maxton's daughter sat in an armchair reading from a book that to Buchanan's eyes was becoming a point of interest.

As if on a director's cue at the Oscars, Maxton and Angelous walked, arm-in-arm, into the lounge. Buchanan and Street stood.

'Inspector,' said Maxton, offering his hand. 'Dean Maxton – and this is my wife, Rachael Angelous. How may we assist you?'

'As you are probably aware, sir, we are investigating the death in the Marina of a young woman on the morning of 30th of March.'

'Ah, yes, we'd heard.'

'And who told you that, sir?'

'Andy – Andrew Kleinman, our agent. Your secretary told him that's why you wanted to talk to us.'

'That was Detective Sergeant Street, sir. My rank doesn't warrant a secretary. You came with the Carstairs?'

'That's right. They'd just flown us back from the Ann Arbor film festival.'

'Were you getting an award?'

'No,' said Rachael Angelous. 'Inspector, in our business if you're not seen breathing regularly you're assumed to be dead. End of career.'

'Can either of you remember where you were just before you docked?' asked Buchanan.

'I was in the lounge with the ladies,' said Rachael.

'Who was with you?'

'Let's see. Ruth Silverstein was sitting opposite me and Aakifah Bashir was sitting beside her – and Rosalind Metzger was beside me. We were having a good natter – what girls do best when they are together, Inspector.'

'And you, sir, do you recall where you were?' Buchanan caught a slight sideways movement of Maxton's eyes towards his wife.

'Inspector, in spite of what you may see me do on screen, I'm afraid I'm not a good sailor. I was lying down in one of the cabins. Dr Metzger gave me some tablets to help with my nausea and, like an idiot, I took a double dose and downed them with a shot of whiskey. Didn't wake till we tied up.'

'Can anyone corroborate that, sir?'

'No. I'm afraid not.'

'Do either of you recognise this girl?' asked Street, showing them the photograph.

They both shook their heads.

♦

They were approaching the Drusilla's roundabout when Buchanan's mobile began to ring. He let it ring till it went to answerphone. A minute later Street's phone rang.

'Yes Ma'am – he's driving. Yes, I'll tell him – right away, Ma'am.'

'What's up?'

'We're wanted. A body of a young girl has just been reported found in Abbots Wood.'

'Where's that?'

'We can get to it from the A27. I'll tell you where to turn off. Hunter and Dexter are waiting for us.'

♦

They turned off the A27 at Wilmington and followed the twisting narrow lane to Abbots Wood. For once Buchanan resisted the temptation to put his foot down and even earned a couple of polite nods from the horse riders they'd passed

'Turn here – this is Abbots Wood,' directed Street.

Buchanan stood on the brakes and came to an immediate halt at the police cordon. He ran the window down and announced to the constable, 'Chief Inspector Buchanan.'

'Yes, sir, one moment, sir,' said the constable, lifting the cordon tape to allow Buchanan to drive through.

'The car park is up the road,' said Street, 'just behind the trees.

Slowing for the speed bumps, Buchanan negotiated his way up the road and turned right onto a gravelled parking space, just managing to avoid the mud puddle. He parked beside a fleet of police vans and cars.

They were getting out of the car as Dexter and Hunter approached.

'Good afternoon, sir, 'said Dexter. 'The body is over there, in the undergrowth.' He pointed to the group of police and suited individuals in blue coveralls.

'Who found it?'

Dexter looked at his notebook. 'A Mrs Soames; she's in the incident van waiting to be interviewed.'

'Walking her dog, I suppose?'

'What else, sir?'

'When was the body discovered?'

Dexter looked back down at his notebook. 'About ten-thirty this morning, sir. Mrs Soames says she comes here regularly to walk her dog. She parked across from the toilets. That's her car beside the police van, the blue Mercedes. She got out, changed her shoes, visited the toilet, and started her walk. She let her dog off the lead and it immediately ran off into the undergrowth. When it wouldn't return to her calling, she went into the undergrowth to find out what had got the dog so agitated.'

'That's when she found the body?' asked Street.

'Yes. She grabbed the dog's collar, *and rushed* – her words – back to the car and called 999.'

'Didn't she check to see whether the girl was all right first? She might have just fallen, or had an epileptic seizure, why did she assume the girl was dead?' asked Buchanan.

Dexter flipped through a couple of pages in his notebook and read: '*I knew she was dead. I'm a nurse, I've seen plenty in my time.*'

'Hmm, suppose that makes sense. Who's with the body?'

'Doctor Mansell.'

'Right, lass; let's go see what the good Doctor Mansell has to say.'

'We'll need to put these on first,' Street said, holding up a blue coverall for Buchanan. Buchanan pulled on his coveralls, locked the car, and pocketed the keys before walking over to the doctor.

'Good afternoon, Doctor.'

'Ah, Inspector, Sergeant. So sad, and her so young.'

Street walked carefully over to the corpse, crouching down to get a closer look. Kneeling beside the body, she exclaimed, 'That's Ilka – the waitress I talked to last Friday. '

'Are you sure?' asked Buchanan.

Street nodded.

'What can you tell us, Doctor? Time of death?' asked Buchanan

'She was strangled. I'd say she was eastern European and in her late twenties. Death occurred sometime between seven and midnight. I can tell you more when I get her back to the morgue.'

'Was she killed here?'

'Most likely, I will be surer of that when I've finished looking at the body in the morgue, the livor mortis will confirm.'

'How do you know she was strangled? She looks like she could be sleeping.'

'See the red spots, Sergeant? Like little pinpricks on her eyelids?'

'Yes.'

'They're called petechiae. Simply put, it's caused when the lungs can't get oxygen. Under this condition, the body tries to move oxygenated blood to vital organs. The increased blood pressure can be too stressful for the blood vessels and they just simply burst.'

'Oh – and you can tell the cause of death just from that?'

'That and the finger marks on the back of her neck. Someone put their hand over her mouth and smothered her. Should be able to get a DNA sample of the killer.'

'How's that?'

'She bit the hand that killed her – killer's blood on her teeth.'

Street and Buchanan returned to Dexter and Hunter. 'Anything been found, Hunter?'

'Nothing obvious sir, forensics have just got started. There's a lot to look at. Abbots Wood is a very popular venue for families, dog walkers and photographers.'

'What time does the park open and close?'

'It's open from eight to eight daily at this time of the year. Next month it closes at nine.'

'So our killer arrived while the park was still open?'

'Looks that way.'

'Most likely to have been just before closing,' said Buchanan, looking round for a CCTV camera. 'Street, as soon as the doctor confirms time of death we'll get on to the local paper.'

'The *Herald*?' interrupted Street.

'Whatever. We'll put in an appeal, asking for anyone who was in the park at the time to get in touch with us. Quite possibly we'll get lucky, maybe someone will remember them, or have taken a photo of our killer or perhaps their car.'

'What about tyre tracks, sir?'

'Not much point, Dexter, there must be fifty to choose from.'

'Took a bit of a chance, sir,' said Hunter.

'What do you mean?'

'This is a very busy park. How did the killer know it would be empty?

'Maybe no-one noticed. Just imagine the situation. It's near to closing time, just a few dog walkers, maybe a travelling salesman emailing in his reports at the end of a busy day. A family who've finished their nature walk, climbing into the family car. Everyone is busy. Then a car is driven in and parked. A couple get out, maybe busy in conversation. He puts his arm round her waist, pulls her close and they walk off into the undergrowth for a private conversation.'

'Wouldn't she be arguing, trying to get away?' asked Hunter.

'Not necessarily. He could have been telling her how good she was at her job, going to get a promotion and a raise in pay.'

'Suppose he was married and they were lovers, off to the woods for – well, you know what I mean,' said Dexter, blushing as he realised Street was standing beside him.

'All a possibility,' said Buchanan. 'Street, I think a visit to the restaurant where she worked is in order. You two,' he said to Dexter and Hunter, 'take Abosa's description round the other restaurants in town and shake a few trees, see what falls out.'

'Meet at the office in the morning, sir?' said Dexter.

'No, lad, we've got three deaths now – I want to see you back at Hammonds Drive at five. Got that?'

'Yes, sir.'

♦

Buchanan parked on the double yellow lines in front of the restaurant. It was still early, with only three couples seated strategically inside.

'Table for two?' asked the waitress.

'I'd like to see your manager,' said Buchanan, showing her his warrant card.

'Just a minute and I'll see if he's here. He sometimes goes over to our sister restaurant at this time of day.'

She returned a few minutes later, followed by a short, bald-headed man who looked like he sampled the whole restaurant menu daily.'

'Inspector Buchanan and this is Detective Sergeant Street. We're investigating a murder that took place in the Marina in March.'

'Tony Andreotti, Inspector,' the man said, shaking hands with Buchanan. 'So, what's that got to do with me?'

'It's about someone who works here – or at least did up till a few days ago.'

'What do you mean – *used* to work here? I haven't let anyone go in – in months.'

'I spoke with Ilka last week.' said Street.

'So?'

'So? She's now on her way to the morgue,' said Buchanan. 'She was found dead in Abbots Wood this morning. When did you last see her?'

'I saw her on Saturday. She asked for a couple of days off.'

'Can you account for your movements yesterday evening? Between – say, six and nine pm?'

'I was here, where I always am.'

'Not shuttling between restaurants?'

'Not last night, the other restaurant was closed. Dead, you say? What happened to her?'

'That's what we are investigating, sir,' said Street.

'What can you tell me about Ilka, sir?'

'Not much. She's – was – a good worker, never late, never missed a day of work. Cheerful, that best describes her.'

'Married?'

'Not that I'm aware of.'

'Was she seeing anyone?'

'Don't think so. She kept mainly to herself.'

'We'll need her home address, sir.'

'I'll get it for you.'

He returned a few minutes later, looking perplexed. 'I'm sorry, Inspector, I don't seem to have an address for her – all I can find is a mobile number.'

'For goodness' sake man! Someone must know where she lived?'

'I'll ask Alice – maybe she knows.' He turned and walked between the tables to the waitress they'd met earlier. She followed Andreotti back.

'Alice, this is Inspector – er?'

'Buchanan. Alice, do you know where Ilka lived?'

'She lived with me – we shared a flat on Pevensey Road. Why?'

'I've some sad news for you,' said Street. 'Ilka was found dead in Abbots Wood this morning.'

'Dead – but how?'

'She was strangled. When did you last see her?'

'Saturday evening at Jukes.'

'Jukes?'

'Sorry, Inspector. Jukes is a night club.'

'Was she with anyone?'

'Don't know, it was busy, payday weekend.'

'Did she have a boyfriend?' asked Buchanan.

'No, don't remember anyone who you would call a boyfriend. She did have some friends though; at least I suppose you'd call them friends.'

'What do you mean?'

'When we went clubbing, she always hung around with the same crowd.'

'All male?'

'Mostly, but I'm sure they were just friends.'

'Anyone in particular?'

She shook her head.

'How often did she go clubbing?'

'Most Friday and Saturday nights.'

'What about work?'

'Service ends at nine; most clubs don't get going till close on eleven.'

'We'd like to have a look at her room.'

'No problem, any time.'

'DS Street will call tomorrow morning.'

'Make it after ten, I need my sleep.'

'Do you know someone called Abosa, sir?' asked Buchanan.

'You don't think,' said Andreotti, his eyes opening wide, 'that he had anything to do with her death?'

'So you do know him?

'Known him for years. I doubt he's your murderer, Inspector.'

'I didn't say he was. We'd just like to have a word with him.'

'To eliminate him from your enquiries?' asked Andreotti.

'Can you tell me how to get in touch with him, sir?' said Buchanan, avoiding Andreotti's cliché.

'Never needed to – he'd just show up.'

'How often?'

'Maybe twice a month, nothing regular.'

'When did you last see him?'

'Two, maybe three, weeks ago.'

'So, you might expect him soon?'

Andreotti shrugged, 'I suppose it's possible.'

'How do you pay him?'

'I get a PayPal invoice once a month.'

'You wouldn't happen to have a photo of him, would you, sir?'

Andreotti shook his head then, remembering something, said, 'Yes, I do. Well, he's in a photo that one of our guests took last year. I'll get it for you.'

He returned a few minutes later with a photo of a group of diners seated round a large table.

'Which one is Abosa, sir?'

'The one on the left, seated at the table beside the girl with the party hat.'

Buchanan showed the photo to Alice. 'Do you recognise this person – the one on the left?'

'Yes, he sometimes has dinner here and I think I've seen him in Jukes.'

'Can we borrow this photo, sir?' asked Buchanan.

'Certainly. I would like it back, though.'

'No problem, DS Street will return it first thing in the morning.'

'Thank you, Inspector. Can I interest you in something from the menu – on the house?'

'No thank you, sir. We'll get something on the way back to the station.'

They parked outside Domino's in the Langney shopping centre.

While they waited for their takeaway pizzas, Buchanan said, 'Street, I want you to work your magic on that photo and have Abosa's picture circulated. I want him picked up: he's got a lot of questions to answer. And get on to Immigration at Newhaven – maybe we'll get lucky and he'll get stopped.'

♦

'Where's Dexter and Hunter, Street?' asked Buchanan, as she opened the pizza boxes.

'Just saw them park their car, should be here in a moment.'

'Good. I don't want to be here all night; we've got a lot of ground to cover.'

'Where shall we start?' said Street, as Buchanan folded two slices of hot pizza and winced as it touched his lips. He shook his head as he tried to chew an oversized mouthful. Street waited for his reply as Dexter and Hunter entered the room.

'Dinner's ready: Hawaiian on the left, spicy meat in the middle and veggie on the right. Drinks are in the machine in the canteen.'

'Thanks, Jill,' said Hunter.

'Right,' said Buchanan, as he wiped the leftover tomato stains from his mouth. 'Let's get started. We now have three deaths to investigate. I'm still sure the death of the girl in the Marina is the key to solving the case. Nichols' death is part of the mystery but the death of this third victim bothers me. We've missed something. We've trod on toes somewhere, and I want to find out whose toes.'

'Abosa's, sir?' suggested Street. 'I talked with the girl on Friday night and by Tuesday she's dead.'

'It's possible, Street.'

'Could he have been on the yacht the night the first girl died?' asked Hunter.

'If he was, no one saw him, or admitted to seeing him,' said Street.

'Let's start at the beginning,' said Buchanan. 'On the night of the 29th, or early the 30th of March, victim number one is pushed off of the transom of the *Moonstone*. The body is recovered the next morning. She has drowned and was three months' pregnant. A week later DS Nichols is found dead in his car submerged in the same Marina.'

'And just a few yards from where the first victim was recovered,' said Hunter.

'Correct, though we have no evidence to say those two locations are connected. Though from looking at the scene, if Nichols was following up a lead he would have probably chosen that location to park as it was close to where the girl died.'

'Suppose he was meeting someone – someone who knew something about the girl?' said Dexter.

'Go on.'

'Maybe the killer was getting worried that Nichols was closing in on him and he got Nichols down there to kill him.'

'Nichols was definitely waiting for someone,' said Hunter. 'Forensics said his car was parked prior to being pushed into the Marina.'

'So what we are saying is,' surmised Street, 'the killer contacted Nichols, arranged to meet him at the Marina. Hit him through the window with a hammer then pushed the car into the water?'

'Doesn't quite add up,' said Buchanan. 'Can't see a trained detective just sitting in his car and not noticing what is going on around him.'

'I know,' said Street, 'suppose Nichols knew and trusted the killer? They met, the killer climbed in the car with Nichols to talk. He knew Nichols' pre-delectation for alcohol and gave him a drink spiked with Rohipnal.'

'Well done, Street, that works.'

'And maybe the dose wasn't strong enough and, while the killer is about to push Nichols' car into the Marina, Nichols starts to come round and the killer hits him with the hammer,' added Dexter.

'Well done, Dexter, well done,' said Buchanan. 'Now all we have to do is to figure out why a hammer is just lying about for our killer to use. Can't see someone just casually walking around with a two-pound club hammer in their pocket.'

'Oh,' said Dexter, his shoulders slumping.

'Don't take it to heart, lad, you've done brilliantly. Why don't you and Hunter go back to the Marina and see what you can

140

ferret out?' said Buchanan, rubbing his hands together. 'We now have established a working thesis for how all three victims died.'

'And we know from forensics that the girl and Nichols knew each other,' said Street, excitedly. 'Also he was not the father of her unborn child, nor did he kill her.'

'OK, now we're getting somewhere,' said Buchanan. 'We know someone on the *Moonstone* killed the first girl. So?'

'Did they kill Nichols and the second girl as well?' said Hunter.

'Exactly,' said Buchanan.

'We've never established why all those people were on the *Moonstone*,' said Street. 'Why were they invited in the first place? What do they have in common?'

'The Carstairs were there as potential customers,' said Dexter, picking up the last piece of pizza.

'And the rest, as far as I can see, are just a random group of wealthy local businessmen and their wives.'

'The obvious thing is money,' said Hunter.

'But why them? Eastbourne is full of wealthy retired families. What else brought them together?' said Street. 'We know the Bashirs and Silversteins have known each other for a long time, and the Carstairs ferry Maxton and Angelous to film sets.'

'And let's not forget the Carstairs fly Greyspear and his PA to shows,' said Buchanan.

'Richardson is married to Greyspear's PA,' said Street.

'But what, other than money, is the common factor in all of this? Don't forget Nichols and the two girls are part of this equation,' said Buchanan. 'Hunter, Dexter, as part of tomorrow's investigations, I want you to go interview all of them. Find out why they know each other and take photos of Nichols and the two dead girls with you, see who recognises any of them.'

'And the photo of Abosa, sir?' said Hunter.

'Why not? It's time we shook the tree. Talking of which, find out anything during your travels this evening?'

'We've started a list of the restaurants and managers in town that displayed a recognition of Abosa's photo, though some deny actually knowing him.'

'And?'

'Of those we checked, six definitely said they knew Abosa, and three denied any knowledge of him – though they were quite agitated when they saw his photo.'

'We've still to interview Mr Silverstein,' said Street, 'and Dr Metzger and his wife.'

'You two know anything about Dr Metzger?' asked Buchanan.

'He runs a private clinic in Meads,' said Hunter. 'He's well known and respected in town.'

'Drives a vintage silver Rolls Royce,' added Dexter. 'Has a bit of a reputation with the ladies. His older patients dote on him.'

'What kind of clinic is it?' asked Buchanan.

'It's one of those places where women go for female issues,' said Dexter.

'Abortions?' asked Buchanan.

'I suppose so,' replied Dexter, a grin growing on his face. 'Metzger is the German word for butcher.'

'Quite an appropriate name for a doctor who performs abortions,' added Street.

'It's just a name, Jill, no need to get worked up about it.'

'Dexter,' interrupted Buchanan, 'leave it alone.'

'Sorry, Jill.'

'That's OK.'

'To work,' said Buchanan, standing. He walked over to one of the large whiteboards, picked up a pen and printed the name Greyspear in the middle. Directly below he drew three rectangles. In the first he printed 1 GS Yachts; in the other two he printed 2 GS stables, and 3 GS? On the right of the board he drew a column of six rectangles. In the first he wrote Aaron Silverstein, in the rectangle below he wrote Ruth Silverstein. In the box directly below that he entered the name Deborah Silverstein.

Buchanan filled the next three boxes with the names of the Bashirs.

Next, he drew three double sets of boxes across the bottom of the board and entered the names, as he had done for the Silversteins and the Bashirs, of Metzger, Carstairs and Maxton, leaving the bottom rows of boxes empty in case of additional names of children.

On the left he drew a list of boxes and entered the names of Rodney Richardson, Susan Richardson, his own name, Buchanan, and in the last box he wrote Street.

'Don't be downhearted that I've left you off of the board,' Buchanan said to Dexter and Hunter. 'You're better off out of this mess.

Lastly, Buchanan drew a series of four boxes across the top of the board. In the first he wrote Girl 1, in the second he wrote Nichols, and in the third, Ilka; the fourth he left blank.

'So you think there'll be a fourth, sir?' said Hunter.

'Just in case, laddie, you never know.'

Buchanan completed his homage to crime by adding another row of boxes under the top row. In the box below Girl 1, he wrote baby, in the next box he wrote Abosa. Like the row above he left the remaining boxes blank.

'What about the crew of the *Moonstone*?' asked Dexter.

'And the caterers, sir? Shouldn't we include them?' added Dexter.

Buchanan shook his head and said, 'I don't think they are part of the picture, other than Girl 1, of course.'

'Oh,' said Dexter, looking puzzled.

'You're correct in connecting them to the case, they all do have a part to play, but the names on the board are the main cast.'

Dexter smiled.

'What next, sir?' asked Street.

'This,' said Buchanan, picking up a blue pen. He drew lines between the names of family groups. Then with a green pen he

143

joined the boxes for business groupings and finally an orange one for crime connections.

Buchanan put down the orange pen and picked up a red pen. 'This one,' he said wielding the pen like a sword, 'will be the one that joins all these parties together. Then we'll know who killed who and why. Tomorrow, while you two,' he looked at Dexter and Hunter, 'are out interviewing the families, I am going to see Mr Silverstein at his office, and Dr Metzger, probably at his clinic and hopefully his wife, wherever she may be. Street, I want you to see what you can dig up on Sir Nathan's past. I want us all to meet up back here at, say, six o'clock.'

Reading the looks of disappointment on Dexter and Hunter's faces, Buchanan said, 'Instead of pizza, do either of you fancy a Chinese takeaway? I'm buying.'

They didn't have to answer; their smiles said it all.

14

Buchanan for once bought the coffees and wandered into the office to find Street at her desk, engrossed in the computer display.

'What's got your attention?' he asked, as he set her coffee down.

'Sir Nathan. He really is a busy boy.'

'Explain, please?'

'Not only does he own Greyspear Yachts, he also owns Castlewood. It's run as an equestrian centre and golf and country club. There's private stabling, training facilities up to Olympic standards, and he has several of his own horses, plus a couple of racehorses.'

'Winners?'

'Apparently so; his horses enjoy many firsts, and a few places.'

'Where's the stables located?'

'You'll like this. It's on a side road, a few hundred yards from the Abbots Wood entrance.'

'Well done, Street. Well done.'

'So, now I expect you'll want to know where Sir Nathan was when Ilka was dumped?'

'China: that's what his secretary said.'

'I wonder, sir, I wonder. You remember when we went to his office to get the list of guests? We heard whispered voices in the other room, if you recall? Suppose Sir Nathan didn't really go to China?'

'What'd you suggest?'

'I'll call *Carstair* and ask; they supposedly fly him everywhere.'

'Great, good work; be very interested in what you find out. In the meantime I'm going to call and see if Aaron Silverstein is in this morning.'

Buchanan grinned as he put the phone down and looked up at Street. Once again she was engrossed in the display on her screen.

'Silverstein will be in his office after lunch. What'd you find?'

'Carstairs's Nancy said all three planes are out on charter, no flights to China though.'

'Could have gone commercial, I suppose. No, that won't work: too many airlines to check. Street, I think I'll pay another visit to Sir Nathan, after I've talked with Silverstein and Metzger.'

'I've found something else on Sir Nathan.'

'What's that?'

'He has a record.'

'What for?'

'GBH. It was while he was in the army.'

'Explain?'

'It was twenty years ago, according to the records. He came home on unexpected leave and caught his girlfriend with another man. Greyspear pleaded self-defence, said there had been an argument and the other chap came at him with a knife. He, Greyspear, put the other chap in hospital for a couple of months. Apparently, it was touch and go whether a manslaughter charge would be brought against him.'

'Did he go to jail?'

'No, the jammy bugger, his CO got him out. The report said Greyspear was required for a Special Ops mission, and he was whisked away.'

'Pays to know the right people, I suppose.'

'Yep.'

'Sir Nathan is fast becoming a person of extreme interest, Street. What else have you turned up?'

'He is a co-owner of a film company.'

'What, you mean like making movies?'

'Not quite, they produce advertising videos about the yachts they make. Here, let me show you.'

Street clicked to the YouTube site, typed in Greyspear Yachts and sat back to watch a FBC40 going through its paces in Poole Bay.

'They have videos of the whole range of yachts they build, sir.'

'That's impressive.'

'It is, especially when you look at the credits and see who gets mentioned.'

'What do you mean?'

'The helicopter shots – they're done by Carstair.'

'Thought they only flew executive jets?'

'No, they have a couple of Bell 407's.'

'What's a Bell 407?'

'No idea, one helicopter looks the same as all the others to me. I've also had a look at the stables, very impressive. The video shots of the horses out on the gallop are very professional. Here, have a look.'

'That building looks familiar,' said Buchanan, as the camera panned along a row of horseboxes, each with an inquisitive horse staring at the camera.'

'It should – it was used in several episodes of *Everslea*. Didn't think period drama was your cup of tea?'

'It isn't, but Karen was addicted to the show so I'd no choice but to watch it.'

'There's a better view of the stables if you watch some of the episodes,' Street said, as she clicked to a YouTube video.

Buchanan looked at his watch and was about to head for his desk when one of the actors caught his attention. 'Just a minute – isn't that Maxton?'

'Hold on, I'll check,' said Street, googling the IMDB website.

'Now this is what I like to see,' said Buchanan. 'Not only was Maxton in the series, so was Angelous.'

'They do make a nice couple, don't they?' said Street.

'Street, I've got a hunch, I see an arm rising through the mist. Can you find out who bankrolled the TV programme? In fact I want you to make it your number one priority to find out everything you can about the show.'

'And you, sir?'

'I'm off to see Aaron Silverstein and Doctor Metzger. I have a feeling we will each have something of interest to share when I return.'

♦

Buchanan parked on double yellow lines in front of Silverstein's office and noticed there were no customer parking spaces. The highly-polished brass name plaque on the door read: *A Silverstein CPA*. He climbed the steps, pushed open the inner spotless glass door and walked over to the young lady behind an enormous mahogany desk.

'Yes, sir, can I help?'

'Detective Chief Inspector Buchanan, to see Mr Silverstein, please.'

She consulted a large, leather covered, appointments diary. 'Ah, yes – he knows you're expected, but he's still in conference and said would you mind waiting? I'll buzz him to let him know you're here. Would you like a drink while you wait?'

Buchanan almost said a glass of brandy and a cigar, but settled for a black coffee. As he sipped it, he looked at his surroundings, and then said. 'Must be quite an honour to be working in such plush surroundings?'

She looked away from her computer screen. 'Yes it is.'

'Mr Silverstein must be quite successful to afford such a fancy office?'

'I suppose he is.'

'Worked for Mr Silverstein long?'

'About five years.'

'As a receptionist?'

'No.'

'Secretary?'

'May I see your warrant card, Inspector?'

'Oops, stepped over the line there, sorry. Just me being a policeman too long' said Buchanan as he took out his warrant card.

'Thank you, Inspector. And for your information, my name is Angela, and I'm Mr Silverstein's PA.'

'That makes sense.'

He returned to his chair and took stock of the room. Polished mahogany wood-panelled walls, drapes that would look at home in any country house and the carpets looked like real wool. As he lingered over his coffee he imagined the whiteboard in his office and the names. Mentally, he picked up the red pen and drew a line from Greyspear's name to Susan Richardson, to Greyspear Yachts, to the Greyspear stables, to the Greyspear film company, to Carstair and Harry and Yasmine Carstair, on to Dean Maxton and Rachael Angelous, where the pen hovered.

'Inspector,' said Silverstein's PA, interrupting Buchanan's musing, 'Mr Silverstein will see you now.'

Buchanan stood and followed her into the office of *A Silverstein CPA*.

'Inspector, good morning,' said Silverstein, as he stood up. 'My wife said you'd called – sorry I wasn't in. Please, have a seat. Can I offer you some refreshments?'

'No thank you, sir, your PA has already given me a cup of coffee.'

'Angela,' said Silverstein, 'no calls, please. Now Inspector, what can I do for you?'

'As you are probably aware, we are investigating two deaths that occurred in the Marina last March.'

'And what's that got to do with me?'

'Nothing, I hope. You were out on Sir Nathan's yacht on the 29th of March?'

'Ah – yes, such a lovely day.'

'Did you notice anything out of the ordinary?'

'Inspector, the whole day was out of the ordinary.'

'So your wife said, sir.'

'Yes, she enjoyed the day immensely.'

'Quite an office for a CPA,' said Buchanan, staring at one of the pictures on the wall behind Silverstein.

Silverstein turned to see which picture Buchanan was looking at. 'Ah, the Osborne. Yes, he's a local artist, got a couple of his at the house. Inspector, don't get misled by the luxury of what you see, this is still a working office, and the trip on Sir Nathan's yacht was a one off.'

'Who owns this building?'

'Why would you want to know that? Surely the ownership of this office has nothing to do with your enquiries?'

'Mr Silverstein, I ask the questions, and for your information I'm just being a policeman, doggedly following a scent.'

'If you must know, the building is owned by one of Sir Nathan's holding companies.'

'And your connection with Sir Nathan is, other than renting this office?'

'Sir Nathan's company is on our list of clients.'

'Tax returns, that sort of thing?'

'Precisely.'

'And Achmed Bashir, sir; what's your relationship with him and his family?'

'I suppose you'll find out anyway. We've been friends with the family for years. Achmed is a venture capitalist. Together our firms look after the financial affairs of Sir Nathan's holdings.'

The imaginary red pen moved on.

'You say your respective families have been friends for years, yet you and Mr Bashir are known to argue when you're together?'

'Ah yes,' Silverstein said, smiling, 'both our families emigrated to the UK in 1948 to avoid the fighting in Palestine. Our parents wanted us – their children – to grow up in a cosmopolitan environment away from strife. Achmed and I met at a fundraising rally for those displaced by the fighting. Neither of us takes sides in the conflict; other than to take pity on those who suffer from the constant bombardment of shells and rockets.'

'Do your families socialise often?'

'We have meals together from time to time. Our daughters are closer.'

'Oh, how's that?'

'They're both into horses, spend a lot of time at the stables. They compete in various horse trials.'

'Would that be Castlewood, Sir Nathan's stables?'

'As a matter of fact, yes'

'Does your firm look after the financial affairs of the Maxton's and the Carstair's?'

'That's confidential information, Inspector.'

'I'll take that as a yes. One final question, if you don't mind. Do you know Rodney Richardson?'

'I'm aware of his company. I believe his wife works for Sir Nathan.'

'And how about a Doctor Metzger?'

'Sorry Inspector, we've been in business in Eastbourne for many years. I am aware of him, but we can't be expected to look after everyone's financial affairs.'

'How about socially? He was listed on the guest list.'

'Not really. To be honest with you, Inspector, I'm not sure why, but there's something about the man that – ah, I'd rather not say. He just made me feel uncomfortable when I was introduced to him.'

'Did you see him when you were out on the *Moonstone*?'

'As we boarded, and at lunchtime, after that I was too busy talking with Achmed to notice.'

'Do you recognise any of these people?' Buchanan asked as he handed Silverstein the photos of the two girls, Abosa and Nichols.

Silverstein looked at the photos and shook his head slowly. 'No, sorry, Inspector. Although this one – the male – he looks familiar. Can't quite place him. Who is it?'

'His name was Detective Sergeant Nichols; his body was recovered from the Marina a week after your trip on the *Moonstone*.'

'Surely you don't think I had anything to do with his death, do you?'

'It's early days yet, sir, the investigation is still ongoing.'

Buchanan was about to get up when something caught his attention. Sitting on Silverstein's desk was a copy of *The Penitent Heart*, the same book he'd first seen Bracewell reading when they interviewed him on the *Moonstone*. It was also the same book he'd seen Nancy at Carstair reading and that young Ayesha Bashir picked up from the coffee table the day he'd interviewed her mother.

'One more question, Mr Silverstein. Do you read a lot?'

'That's an odd question to ask, Inspector.'

'In my business we ask lots of seemingly odd questions, sir.'

'Not really, I'm usually too busy with reading financial reports and the like. Why?

'This,' said Buchanan, picking up the copy of *The Penitent Heart* from Silverstein's desk. 'I've seen several copies of this book in the last few days. Wondered if I should get myself a copy to read?'

'Er – yes, it's my wife's; she left it here. I was going to take it home. She says it's a good story. Not quite my cup of tea, though.'

'And what might your cup of tea be, sir?'

'Inspector, the last book I read was the Chancellor's Budget.'

♦

Buchanan's next call was to see Doctor Metzger. The clinic was shielded by a high brick wall overtopped by a neatly-trimmed boxwood hedge. He drove through the impressive iron gates, parked in a visitor space and went into the reception area.

'Yes, can I help?'

'I'd like to see Doctor Metzger, please.'

'Do you have an appointment?'

'No.'

The receptionist consulted her computer screen, 'I'm sorry, he's fully booked this morning. He has time next Wednesday – would you like to make an appointment?'

Buchanan took out his warrant card. 'It's Detective Chief Inspector Buchanan. I won't keep him long.'

'Oh – ah, I'll – if you'd take a seat, I'll see if he has time to see you.'

Buchanan sat and smiled; the red pen quivered.

As far as surgery receptions went, this was the bleakest Buchanan had ever been in. Not what he expected from a private clinic.

The receptionist unplugged her headset and came over to Buchanan. 'Inspector, Doctor Metzger is with a patient. He says if you don't mind waiting, he will have a few moments for you shortly. In the meantime, can I get you something to drink while you wait?'

'No thanks, I'm fine.'

Buchanan sat and waited and watched the comings and goings of the clinic's patrons. He quickly realised that the majority of the patients were young women and most of them visibly pregnant. There were a few older women who looked none too pleased to be there.

Eventually a young man wearing a white doctor's coat came over, introducing himself as Doctor Payne, Doctor Metzger's partner.

'Doctor Metzger's apologies, Inspector, he's had a difficult procedure this morning and has just finished. If you'll follow me I'll take you through to his office.'

Payne swiped his ID card on the card reader and pulled the door open. Buchanan followed him into a completely different environment. Instead of a few basic chairs resting on a vinyl covered floor, this room had wall to wall carpet, armchairs and settees, all with small coffee tables adorned with flowers. The smell of freshly brewed coffee mingled with the piped sounds of waves gently washing on a far flung sandy beach. There were several women seated, drinking and reading various magazines. 'Inspector, not everyone appreciates what we do here. We need to provide full security for patients and staff while visiting.'

'Hence the secure waiting room?'

'Exactly.'

Buchanan followed Payne through, Buchanan noticed, another secure door and down a short passage. Payne stopped and knocked gently on a treatment room door. There was an audible sound of a magnetic lock releasing. Buchanan followed Payne into the room.

'Doctor Metzger, this is – sorry, I didn't get your name?'

Security breach thought Buchanan, *should have got my name.* 'Detective Chief Inspector Buchanan, Doctor,' he said, presenting his warrant card.

'How can I help, Inspector?'

Doctor Metzger wasn't what Buchanan expected. He'd imagined him to be an old, shrivelled, stooping man in his 70's. Instead, Buchanan estimated the doctor's age to be somewhere in his mid to late fifties. Metzger looked like he could compete in a triathlon and not be out of breath.

'Doctor, I understand you performed two autopsies at the Eastbourne DGH recently?'

'Inspector, I perform lots. Do you have any in particular in mind?'

Buchanan took out the photos of the dead girl and Nichols and passed them to Metzger.

Metzger looked at them and shook his head. 'Not sure about the girl. The male does look familiar – who was he?'

'His name was Detective Sergeant Nichols; his body was recovered from the Marina a week after your trip on the *Moonstone*.'

'Ah, now I remember. Head injury. He drowned, I believe was my diagnosis – didn't realise he was a policeman.'

'Anything else come to mind, sir?'

Metzger shook his head. 'No, sorry, Inspector. My detailed findings will be in my report. I'm sure you must have a copy somewhere in your records system.'

'I'm sure we will, sir. Can you tell me where you were when the *Moonstone* returned to the harbour?'

'Hmm, not sure. I'm not a good sailor, Inspector, so I was probably outside getting fresh air. Yes, that's it. I remember now. I watched the crew tie us up in the lock.'

'Do you remember seeing anyone helping on the pontoon?'

'A couple of the crew were – at least I assume they were crew. It was quite dark, Inspector. As the lock gates opened one of the crew – I think his name was John – slipped and fell in the engine room. I went to see if I could help.'

'You treated him in the engine room? Wouldn't the galley or a similar location be more suitable?'

'I've always been fascinated by large powerful machinery, so took the opportunity to poke around. Then when I came back up on deck we were tied up.'

'Thank you, Doctor.'

'Is there anything else I can help you with, Inspector?'

'No thank you, Doctor, not at the moment – er – although there is one thing,' said Buchanan, getting up from his chair. 'This clinic – do you mostly perform abortions?'

'No, we are what our brochures call, *A Full Service Clinic*.'

155

'Not just abortions, then?'

'Inspector, abortion is only one of the services we offer here. We also offer a full, well-woman service and, just to demonstrate to you we have a balanced outlook on pregnancy, we also offer advice on IVF treatment.'

'So, you look out for a woman's well-being?'

'We at the clinic believe if a woman is considering a termination, it is imperative that she finds the best help and advice available during this trying time. During the pre-termination counselling sessions, we emphasise that it is the woman's choice whether to terminate the unwanted pregnancy or continue to full term. Ultimately it is the woman's choice to proceed; we never coerce her into a decision.'

'And you say it's always her decision?'

'Yes, a woman's decision to terminate the pregnancy is *her choice*. I'm sure you realise, being a policeman, that pregnancy is not just an outcome of two people in a stable relationship. There is a darker side: incest, rape, emotional instability, and drug and alcohol abuse. All these scenarios can lead to an unwanted pregnancy.'

'Do they always have to end in an abortion?'

'Not always, but sometimes. For instance, in the case of foetal abnormality detected after twelve weeks, termination is the only sensible answer. We must always think of the woman's health and welfare.'

Buchanan could taste the bile rising in his throat. 'Thank you, Doctor Metzger. If I have any further questions, we will be in touch.'

'My door is always open. Doctor Payne will show you out.'

Payne opened the door. As Buchanan was about to leave the office he turned and asked, 'Doctor Metzger, do you know a Rodney Richardson?'

There was an awkward silence as the two doctors exchanged glances.

'Er – yes. He's the clinic's accountant. Why?'

'No particular reason, just connecting the boxes, that's all. How about someone called Abosa?'

The muscles on Metzger's face dropped. 'Ah, no, sorry Inspector, I don't.'

Buchanan swallowed; the red pen moved on.

♦

'Glad you're back,' said Street. 'How did your visits with Silverstein and Metzger go?'

Buchanan looked at his watch and said, 'It'll be dinner time soon. I would like Dexter and Hunter to be here when I go over my thoughts on where this investigation is going.'

'Shall I call them?'

'Yes, I feel a headache coming on,' he said, doing his best to imitate a hungry bear.

'Chinese takeaway, I think you said?'

'So I did. Where's the brochure?'

'Should I wait till they get here before ordering?'

'Where are they?'

'Walked over to Tesco's for a birthday card; it's Morris's wife's birthday today.'

'OK, in that case just order a set meal for four.'

'Just for four?'

Buchanan smiled. 'All right, make it for eight and don't forget the drinks – I'm not paying the canteen price.'

Street put the phone down and said, 'Dinner will be here in twenty minutes.'

'Good. Street, do you have a Kindle?'

'No, read my books on my phone. Why?'

'Can you have a look on Amazon and see if you can find a book for me?'

'Sure, what's it called?'

'*The Penitent Heart*.'

'You're not—?'

'No, of course not. The book has shown up four or five times in as many places this last week and I'm getting an idea.'

'An arm in the mist?' she said, smiling.

'Maybe.'

'Here it is,' she said, handing Buchanan her phone. 'Is this the book you're looking for?'

'That's the one; I wonder why it's so popular?' he said, passing the phone back.

'I'll order a copy for you. What's your Kindle address?'

◆

Street set up one of the small office tables with paper plates, plastic cutlery, and plastic cups she'd found in the defunct canteen.

They waited patiently for Buchanan to clear his plate before Street asked, 'So, how did the meeting with Silverstein go?'

'In a minute. I would like to hear from Dexter and Hunter before I go into that.'

'We went to see Mrs Silverstein first,' said Dexter. 'There is another family connection. Bashir and Silverstein's daughters both ride at Greyspear's stables; they're part of an amateur, international dressage team, expenses underwritten by Greyspear.'

'Flights provided by Carstair?' asked Street.

'The very same, Jill,' replied Dexter.

'What about the photos?' asked Buchanan.

'Silverstein's daughter said the first girl looked familiar but couldn't remember where from, said she might have seen the photo in the *Herald*.'

'That's not much help,' said Buchanan. 'Anything else?'

'The mothers both work at fundraising for a non-sectarian medical charity based in Gaza.'

'Did you ask them if they knew Dr Metzger?'

'No – why? Didn't think he was under investigation?'

Buchanan shook his head. 'Never mind, just a thought I had. Street, bring us up to date on what you found out about Greyspear.'

Street recounted what she'd found out about Greyspear's past.'

'And his stables are just a short drive from Abbots Wood,' said Hunter.

'What did his first wife die from, Jill?' asked Hunter.

'He said she died from cancer.'

'Did you check on that, Street?'

'Nope, should be easy to do, though.' she said, going over to her desk and computer.

'Anything?' asked Dexter.

'Lots. Death certificate confirms cause of death as cancer.'

'Did she die at home or in a hospice?' asked Buchanan.

'Why would that be an issue, sir?' asked Dexter.

'We'll see,' replied Buchanan. 'Anything else, Street?'

'I'll check the *Herald*.'

Hunter got up and cleared away the table, Dexter excused himself for a toilet break and Street continued to stare at her computer screen.

'Not much in the *Herald*, but the *Financial Times* had very in-depth article on Greyspear, and includes a bit about his late wife:

*After a short illness, the wife of Sir Nathan
Greyspear passed away peacefully at home in her
husband's arms yesterday evening.*

'Why would that be of interest, sir?' asked Dexter.

'Who knows? He seems to be a trifle unlucky with female acquaintances, that's all.'

'How were the visits to Silverstein and Metzger, sir?' asked Street, returning to the table.

Buchanan recounted his visits, but kept his thoughts on Metzger to himself.

'Sir,' said Dexter, looking longingly at the wall clock,' it's the wife's birthday today and I promised to take her out to the cinema this evening.'

Buchanan looked up at the clock and said, 'OK, it's been a long day. Tomorrow I want you and Hunter to do some background investigating on Dr Metzger.'

'I could help,' said Street.

'Er – no, lass. Tomorrow we're going back to see Sir Nathan. It's time he explained a few things he's been hiding from us – that is, if he's back.'

'He's not. I called his office earlier; his butler said he was away till Friday.'

'OK, Friday it will be. At least it will let us catch up on the paperwork. Should please Spider Woman.'

15

At nine twenty-five Buchanan and Street pulled up at the closed gates in front of Greyspear's house. Buchanan could see through the gates that he must be having a meeting as there were several expensive-looking cars parked in front of the house.

'Sir, that looks like Carstair's Maserati.'

'Interesting. Any of the others look familiar?'

'No, only recognised Carstair's car from the registration, CA51AIR.'

'Hmm, well spotted, Street'

Buchanan pressed the intercom and waited. Instead of the plumy sound of the butler's voice answering, the hum of the gate-opening motors welcomed them in to Greyspear's residence.

Buchanan parked between the Maserati and a dark blue Mercedes.

The front door was open, so they went in and stood in the entrance hall. They could hear voices coming from one of the rooms at the end of the hallway.

Buchanan beckoned Street to follow him down the hall. He was about to walk into the room when Greyspear walked out.

'Inspector! What the hell are you doing here? Who let you in?'

'Good morning, Sir Nathan. We're here to go over the statement you made when we visited you in Greenock, and *you* did.'

'I did?' said Greyspear, grappling for understanding 'I did *what?*'

'You let us in. I pressed the gate intercom and before I could announce myself the gate opened, and your front door was wide open.'

'I – I can't possibly talk to you just now, I've a very important meeting going on at the moment. You'll have to make an appointment.'

Greyspear put his hand under Buchanan's elbow and started to shepherd him down the hallway just as Silverstein came out of the same room.

'Inspector – I didn't realise you were joining us?'

Before Buchanan could reply, the rest of those at the meeting filed into the hall.

'He's not – are you, Inspector?' said Greyspear.

'No,' said Buchanan, a smile growing on his face. 'I'm just continuing with my investigations.' Turning back to Greyspear, he said, 'Aren't you going to introduce me to the new member of your group?'

'Inspector, this is a private meeting for –'

'A name will suffice.'

'Alex Willis, Inspector. You could say I'm a friend of the family.'

'Thank you, Mr Willis.'

'Satisfied, Inspector?'

Buchanan smiled. 'For now, Sir Nathan. But before we go, I would like a word with your secretary.'

'You can't.'

'And why not, sir?'

'Er – she's away.'

'Away where, sir?'

'Just away. I expect her back soon.'

'Shopping?'

'No, her mother is not well. I think she's gone to see her mother.'

'You think?'

'Yes, that's it. She's gone to be with her mother.'

'All the same, sir, I do have a couple of questions I need answers to.'

Greyspear turned to look at the assembled group in the hall.

'It's all right, we can wait, Nathan,' said Silverstein, coming to Greyspear's rescue. 'I'm sure the Inspector won't take long with his questions.'

Greyspear turned back to Buchanan, a look of indecision on his face, and glanced at his watch. 'All right, this way, we can talk in here.' He opened a door to a small room on the right. 'I can only spare a few minutes. Not only do I have a very important meeting in the other room, I have to be in Greenock first thing in the morning.'

'Thank you, Sir Nathan.'

'So, what is so pressing that you can't wait?'

'Do you recognise this person, sir?' Buchanan asked, showing Greyspear the photo of Nichols.

Greyspear's face froze, then he relaxed and frowned. He thought for a moment, then said, 'I'm not sure where or when I have seen him, but he does look familiar. Who is he?'

'He was Detective Sergeant Nichols.'

'Was?'

'Yes, sir, he was pulled from the Marina a week after the girl.'

'And you think I had something to do with it?'

'No, sir, I just wondered if you recognised him. Could he have been on the *Moonstone* the day you went out?'

'Not likely, unless he was hiding in one of the cabins, – but Captain Bracewell would have found him if he had been.'

Buchanan's questioning was interrupted by a knock on the door. Silverstein opened it and said, 'Nathan, we do need to get on. They are getting impatient waiting for us.'

'Inspector, I simply have to go and join the meeting.'

'Would that be with the investors, sir?'

Greyspear looked at Buchanan, breathed out and said, 'I have lots of meetings during my working day.'

'But not like this one.'

'Just what do you mean?'

'Well, would this one have anything to do with a book entitled *The Penitent Heart*?'

They watched as Greyspear's face went from a healthy pink, to grey, then to a shade of angry red. 'Who told you that?'

'Sir Nathan, I'm paid to be observant. I have seen that title in the hands of at least four of the people who were on the *Moonstone* the evening the girl disappeared. I look at the occupations of those same guests, add that to your resources and put it all together and *voila*, Sir Nathan's making a movie, plus, you just introduced us to the author. Am I correct?'

'I am assuming that all your investigations to this point are confidential?'

'Yes, except for what is shared internally for investigative purposes.'

'Then I suggest you keep your thoughts to yourself and I will consult my solicitor. I don't appreciate your line of enquiry, or your incessant insinuations. My butler will show you out, and the next time wait until you are invited.'

As they made their way back to the office, Street waited for the inevitable outburst.

'That self-opinionated, over-valued, toffee-nosed – *arrgghh*! Why do I let him get to me, Street? I'm going to have the *Moonstone* searched. He's hiding something and I mean to find out just what it is.'

'That's going to be expensive, and require a specialist team,' said Street.

'Nah, what we're looking for is going to be in plain view.'

'A handbag, or a pair of shoes perhaps?'

'You got it. I'm sure if they're anywhere they're still on the *Moonstone.*"

'You'll need a search warrant and I doubt you'll get one today.'

'I know, Street, I know, we'll set it up for Saturday. You heard Sir Nathan – he's going to be in Greenock then.'

'Do you still want me to do the rounds of the nightclubs on Friday?'

'Yes, can't let that door close.'

'If I'm going to be up till all hours Friday night, I'd like to get off early.'

'Shouldn't be a problem, Friday will probably be an office day.'

'Thanks.'

'Seriously, how are you doing on the Greyspear film studio?'

'Haven't found much yet. I was going to use this afternoon to do my research.'

'Good, in that case, after I've organised the search warrant for the *Moonstone*, I'll take a run out to Castlewood and see if it's as impressive as the TV version.'

'OK see you later.'

♦

As he accelerated up the A22, the sun came out and Buchanan felt on top of the world; he could taste victory. Tomorrow the specialist search team would go over the *Moonstone*, and certainly they would find the dead girl's handbag and probably her shoes, most likely somewhere at the back of the boat. Yes, he thought, that would make sense. The caterers would have used the crew quarters to change into what there was of their uniforms. Maybe Greyspear had wandered back down there and saw the girl on her own and tried it on with her, like he must have done numerous times with his secretary. Possibly he'd spiked the girl's drink, but he'd been disturbed, and, when the opportunity arose, he simply pushed her over the side.

A DNA sample from Greyspear would be required; just possibly he was the father of the child. Buchanan mused on: she'd refused to have an abortion, had become an embarrassment, didn't fit into Greyspear's plans. Yes, that all made sense. Why else would someone with Greyspear's clout associate with Doctor Metzger? Then a horrible thought came to Buchanan: suppose

165

this girl wasn't the only one? Suppose there really was a people trafficking operation going on? Young women from Eastern Europe being illegally brought into the country, sold into prostitution and done away with when they became difficult to control. But how did they get the women into the country?

Buchanan almost missed the Arlington turn-off, but thanks to the Mitsubishi's excellent brakes and handling he made the corner and continued with his thoughts. These women obviously didn't just fly into the UK and head for Eastbourne. Nor did they take the train or bus. That only left the channel and boats, but there was no commercial ferry from France to Eastbourne. Of course, there was the Newhaven to Dieppe ferry, but that would require wheeled transport and passports. So what was left?

This time Buchanan slowed and took the Bushy Wood turn-off and started to look for the Castlewood turn-off. So what kind of vessel would be suitable. he wondered? Then the obvious came to him. Why not a boat like the *Moonstone*? Someone with Greyspear's standing could come and go as he pleased. No one would think it odd, him going out for the day and returning after sunset. Buchanan made a mental note to check the harbour master's log to see how often the *Moonstone* went out and for how long; also he'd have to check the French ports to see if the *Moonstone* had put in to any of the harbours. No wonder Greyspear been so touchy at. Buchanan's jibe about picking up something while they were out in the channel. But how to prove any of his ideas? That was going to be quite a headache. First step was the search of the *Moonstone* and proving the girl had been on board on the 29th.

Castlewood was easy to find. A huge, green-painted, wrought-iron fence and gates that wouldn't look out of place in a country estate, with the name Castlewood in an arch over the entrance made the stables' presence obvious. Buchanan slowed and turned onto the gravelled driveway. On each side of the there were immaculate mowed verges. Half a mile up the driveway

Buchanan slowed even more too avoid a brace of peacocks casually sifting for insects in the gravel.

'You can't park here', shouted one of the stable lads, 'all visitors park over there.' She indicated a car park hidden behind a well-manicured hedge.

Buchanan dutifully drove over to the parking area, got out of the car, climbed the steps and opened the door. Once inside, he saw there was an office on his left up a flight of stairs and, to his surprise, there was a coffee shop through a set of glazed double doors on the right.

He chose the coffee shop, went in and ordered a large black coffee with a slice of carrot cake. Looking at the layout he realised the café had been designed so that one side looked out onto the car park and the opposite window looked directly into an indoor exercise ring. Buchanan pushed through swing doors out on to a veranda and walked over to a free table. The seating area was raised with a protective sturdy wooden half-wall separating the visitors from the horses being put through their paces. A large sign with red lettering stated that there was no access to the stables from the café.

Buchanan grinned, up to now his only experience of horses had been at the local stables as a lad; being this close to real thoroughbred horses gave him a whole new appreciation of the equine world.

He was just finishing his cake when two riders entered the ring and started to go through their dressage routines. Buchanan watched, fascinated. It wasn't until the end of the routine that he realised that the two riders were Deborah Silverstein and Ayesha Bashir. He waved at them and beckoned them over.

'Good afternoon, Inspector,' said Deborah.

'Good afternoon, ladies. That was quite a show – you two are very good.'

'Thank you,' said Deborah. 'We're practicing for a competition at the SSE Arena in Wembley next month.'

'I'm sure you'll both do fine,' said Buchanan.

'You here to ride, Inspector?' asked Ayesha.

'No,' he said, shaking his head, 'I like my feet to stay flat on the ground.'

'Then why are you here?'

'My wife is a fan of *Everslea* and I thought, being this close, I would have a look at where it's filmed.'

'We're fans, too,' said Deborah.' We even managed to get some walk-on parts last year; unfortunately, there were no speaking parts available.'

Buchanan smiled. 'Those are really fine horses you are riding.'

'They're not ours – they belong to Sir Nathan,' said Ayesha.

'Then you two are very lucky ladies. Does he look after the costs when you compete as well?'

'Yes.'

'Does he come and watch you when you are competing?'

'No, not very often, unfortunately he's usually too busy,' said Deborah.

'How about here, at the stables?'

'Sometimes.'

'Last few days, perhaps?'

'Inspector, I really think you're checking up on Sir Nathan. He couldn't have killed that poor girl, it's just not him. Honestly, Inspector, he's the kindest man in the world,' said Deborah.

'I glad to hear that, Deborah.'

'Debs, we've got to go,' said Ayesha. 'Sorry, Inspector, our horses need their rubdown.'

Buchanan watched them trot back across the ring and through the opening to what he supposed was the exit to the horse stalls.

He got up and walked through the café and climbed the stairs to the office. It wasn't what he expected. As a lad he'd spent many weekends helping at a local stable to make extra pocket money. There, they had no office – unless you called a phone tied to a post by bailing string in the tack room an office –, and no matter where you walked, the ground was always strewn with stray ends of hay and straw and the air always smelt of horse. Here in this office the floor was covered with a very expensive carpet and there were several large bouquets of lilies in crystal glass flowerpots.

'Good morning. Can I help you?' asked the receptionist.

'Er – yes – do you have any information on the costs of stabling a horse here?'

She glanced at the clock on the wall. 'Mrs Masterson should be back in a minute. If you'd like to take a seat, I'll buzz her and let her know you're waiting.'

'That won't be necessary at the moment; I'm just looking into the costs of stabling a horse.'

'Oh, that's all right. I'm afraid I'm only the receptionist. Mrs Masterson will be able to answer all your questions. Could I have your name, please?'

Buchanan was about to say 'Inspector', but instead said, 'Buchanan, Jack Buchanan.'

She pressed a couple of keys on her keypad. 'Mrs Masterson, there's a Mr Buchanan in reception inquiring about stabling his horse – yes, I'll tell him.' She nodded to him. 'Mrs Masterson will be right out.'

'Thanks.'

The receptionist returned to typing while Buchanan walked over to the window and sat on an overstuffed settee to await Mrs Masterson. Buchanan had always prided himself on creating a mental picture of a person based on their name. This time he was very, very, wrong. Instead of being short and broad in the beam with mousy brown hair, Mrs Masterson looked like she'd just stepped out of a clothing advertisement in an up-market horse magazine.

She strode across the floor and extended her hand, 'Mr Buchanan, Jacqueline Masterson. I understand you wish to stable your horse here?'

'Er – not quite. I'm just looking into the cost at this time. I'm thinking about getting back in the saddle again when I retire.'

She smiled. 'You don't look old enough to retire. But I'm sure we can help, if you'll follow me,' she said, turning and walking back to her office. Buchanan followed.

'Would you like something to drink, Mr Buchanan?'

'No thanks, I've just had a coffee next door.'

'Fine. Please sit.'

She waited for Buchanan to relax into the chair. 'Now, is it for just one horse?'

'It would be at this stage.'

She turned to a filing cabinet behind her, opened a drawer and took out an A4-sized glossy brochure. 'This will explain all the costs and services provided.'

Buchanan opened the brochure, flicked through to the section on stabling and was shocked to see the charges. 'Does this include their feed?'

'Yes and no. We do provide a standard feeding schedule. But most owners specify what their horses are to be fed and there's an extra charge for that. We also have a full-time veterinary practice in the grounds.'

'I understand that the television series *Everslea* is filmed here? Does that cause difficulties with the running of the stables?'

'No, Sir Nathan wouldn't allow that to happen.'

'Sir Nathan? Sir Nathan Greyspear?' Buchanan looked up from the brochure, feigning surprise. 'Is that the same Sir Nathan Greyspear who builds luxury yachts?'

'Er – yes. Do you own one?'

'No,' said Buchanan, trying to look as though he was contemplating what size yacht to purchase, 'not at the moment. Sir Nathan showed us round the factory where the yachts are built in Greenock last week. All that luxury!

'Yes, I can imagine. I'm afraid the closest I ever get is the cross-channel ferry.'

'Does Sir Nathan visit the stables often?'

'Why would you want to know that?' A look of concern showed on Jacqueline Masterson's face.

'Just curiosity, since it's his stables and I've seen how much care and detail go into building his yacht, I wondered if I would be likely to run into him whilst here?'

She relaxed and replied, 'When he's in town he always pays us a visit.'

'Would that be, say, once a month?'

'Yes.' The look of concern returned to her face.'

'In the last few days, for instance?'

'Mr Buchanan, or whoever you are, I don't think Sir Nathan's whereabouts are any of your business. Now, if there are no further questions about stabling your horse here, I've got another appointment.'

She stood and walked over to the door and opened it for Buchanan to exit.

Buchanan stood and, as he was about to walk out of the room, said, 'Mrs Masterson, I'm afraid I haven't been totally forthright with you.' He removed his warrant card from his pocket. 'Detective Chief Inspector Buchanan. I'm investigating the death of a young woman in Abbotts Wood a few days ago.'

'And you think Sir Nathan had something to do with *that*? You're barking up the wrong tree, Inspector. I've known Sir Nathan for years; he's the kindest, most gentle person I've ever met.'

'I'm glad to hear that, Mrs Masterson. One more question: are you by any chance related to Susan Richardson?'

'Yes, she's my sister.'

16

Buchanan walked into the office at seven am expecting to go straight to work, and the search of the *Moonstone*. But it wasn't to be.

'And why not, Dexter?'

'The specialist search team is down in Shoreham, big drugs bust on a freighter. There just weren't the personnel available.'

'Well, when will they be available?'

'Control says they may stand down some of the team later in the morning.'

'That's just great; I'm supposed to be driving my wife to the ferry at eleven.'

'Sorry.'

'That's all right, lad; it's not your fault.'

'I could drive her, and then join you at the *Moonstone*?'

Buchanan thought for a moment. 'No thanks, lad, I'll need you at the *Moonstone*. Where's Street?'

'She's – in the cells, sir.'

'Interviewing someone?'

'Not what I meant, sir. She's in cell eleven. She was brought in for being drunk and disorderly, I think.'

'I've told you before: I do the thinking on this team. You sure it's our lass?'

'Afraid so.'

'Cell eleven?' said Buchanan, shaking his head as he hurried out of the door.

♦

Buchanan stopped at the booking-in desk. 'Do you have the notes on DS Street?'

'Just a minute, sir.'

'What's so funny, Sergeant?'

'Who'd have thought she could have done what she did?'

'And just what is she *alleged* to have done?'

'Put two of Jukes' customers in A&E, that's all.'

'Let me see the report.'

Buchanan read through the booking-in report, shook his head, smiled and muttered, 'What a lass.'

'Do you want to interview her, sir?' asked the desk sergeant.

'Is she under arrest?'

'No, sir, just sleeping it off.'

'Lead the way.'

♦

'What on earth have you been up to, lass? Are you all right?'

'I'm fine – I think I've sprained my right wrist though,' she said, gently massaging it.

'Do you remember much of the evening?'

She shook her head. 'Sorry, sir, not much.'

'What *do* you remember?'

'I remember meeting up with Alice as she came out of the restaurant. We went to the Drakes Drum for a couple of drinks then on to Jukes. Don't remember much after that. Can I have a drink? I'm parched.'

Buchanan took a bottle from his pocket. 'Here, this'll do you good.'

She took a swig, looked at him and said, 'That carries a kick. Where's the water from, the Scottish Highlands?'

'That's my lass. Now, what do you remember? And what are you wearing on your feet?'

Street looked down. 'Flip-flops. Oh, now I remember, it's coming back to me. I was trying to get away from someone and I pushed them away and one of the Street Pastor ladies gave me some water to drink and these flip-flops to wear – I'd lost my shoes somewhere.'

'That's better. Anything else?'

173

'I do remember walking along to Jukes with Alice and going in. Someone asked me to dance, and next thing I was outside sitting on the curb trying to put on these flip-flops and sipping water. Then I was sitting in a police car and waking up in the cells this morning.'

'You don't remember being escorted out of the club? Then throwing one of your escorts into the crowd waiting to get in and punching the other one?'

'I did that? That why I'm in the cell? Have I been arrested?'

'No, not officially, you're here to cool off.'

'Where's Stephen?'

' –Stephen? Constable Hunter, you mean?'

'Yes.'

'Should be here in the station somewhere, I'll check.'

'If I haven't been arrested, can I get out of here?'

'Don't see why not.'

◆

'Dexter, where's Hunter?' Buchanan asked, when they got back to the incident room.

'At the DGH, sir.'

'Why?'

'Gone to interview the two men who were with Jill, sir.'

'They're still in the DGH?'

'That's what he's gone to find out.'

'It'll be a waste of time.'

'Why, sir?'

'Because, unless they're in the morgue, they'll have long since scarpered.'

'Why do you think that, sir?'

'How much did you have to drink last night, lass?'

'A couple at Drakes Drum, then one or two at Jukes, I think.'

'And do you think those drinks were enough to make you act the way you did?'

The colour drained from Street's face. 'Shit, that's what probably happened to Nichols.'

'And he didn't have someone looking out for him,' said Dexter.

'What do you mean by that?' asked Buchanan.

'Jill said she was going out clubbing last night, so Stephen said he'd keep an eye on her. If you remember I was at the cinema with the wife.'

Buchanan glanced at Street's face; she was staring off into the distance.

'If it's all right with you, sir,' said Dexter, 'I'd like to go and assist Stephen at the DGH?'

'Good idea, still think it's a waste of time though, Any word on the search team?'

'Oh yes, control called – we'll have a team at the harbour at twelve.'

'Good.' Buchanan glanced at his watch. 'We'll meet at Sir Nathan's house at ten to twelve.' He looked at Street. 'What you thinking about, lass?'

'What would have happened to me if I hadn't done what I did.'

'Don't forget, Hunter was watching after you.'

Street smiled for the first time that morning.

'That's better, lass. Fancy some breakfast? I'm famished.'

'Where?'

'Mac D's?'

Street screwed up her face.

'All right then, where do you recommend?'

'Bill's. It's open at eight, and they make the best breakfast in town.'

'Where's Bill's?'

'Terminus Road.'

'Let's go.'

They parked the car on Lismore Road and walked back to Terminus Road and Bill's.

'How did you get on at the stables, sir?' asked Street.

'It was a bit of an eye-opener. The last time I was in a stable was when I was a lad. A lot has changed in the world of horses.'

He recounted his visit and his meeting with Silverstein and Bashir's daughters and the fact that the stable manager was the sister of Susan Richardson.

'One big happy family, sir.'

'I wonder, Street. They're all are protecting Greyspear – not sure why, but they're all protecting him.'

'He is a bit of a dominant father figure.'

'But he doesn't fit the classic profile of a violent man, Street.'

'That's usually the way with them. All smiles and pleasantries to those not in the family circle, but rules those in his inner circle with a rod of iron.'

'You find out any more about him?'

'Played rugby while at university, and in the services. Left the Army and married into money. First wife inherited a plastics company.'

'What did they make?'

Street looked at her tablet, flicked through a couple of screens, and said, 'Children's toys. When costs rose Greyspear shifted the whole operation to China. Then sold that company and invested in boatbuilding.'

'That's a bit ironic, him making children's toys and not having any children. You said first wife – how many has he had?'

'Just two, both dead.'

'You said earlier the first died from cancer – what happened to the second?'

Street looked back at her tablet and said, 'Second wife died in a car crash, a head-on coming back from London.'

'Who was driving?'

'He was.'

'Had he been drinking?'

'I checked the accident report, doesn't say anything about him being breathalysed, or a blood test. Apparently the wife was in ICU and no-one thought to ask for a blood sample from him when he was brought in.'

'He has more lives than a cat. So his first wife's money set him up in business and he's rolled that up into the empire it is today.'

'Quite a man.'

'I hope so, Street. It'd be a pity if it's all a front for something sinister.'

'You still think he's got something to do with the first girl's death, sir?'

'He had the opportunity.'

'What about motive, sir?'

'Father of an inconvenient, illegitimate child, perhaps?'

'Maybe fifty years ago; today he'd be a hero.'

'Suppose he'd raped the girl and she was threatening to go to the police?'

'That'd work, but what reason would he have for killing Nichols?'

'Blackmail. We haven't checked into Nichols' background or bank account yet.'

'Then what about the second girl, Ilka? Why did she die?'

Their musings were interrupted by Buchanan's phone ringing.

'Buchanan. What is it, Dexter?' He looked at his watch. 'We'll be back in fifteen minutes. Wait for us – good.'

'What was good, sir?'

'They're back from the DGH where our two birds have flown the coop – and they've completed their background check on Metzger.'

♦

'Morning Jill, how are you?'

177

'Morning, Stephen. I'm fine, now that I've had a night's sleep and a good breakfast.'

'Glad to hear that. You didn't look too good last night.'

'Thanks. Just what a woman wants to hear first thing in the morning. How was the movie, Morris?'

'The missus enjoyed it.'

'And you – did you enjoy it?'

'Not really, more of a woman's movie. Crying into a hankie sort of stuff.'

'Hmm, can we get to business?' said Buchanan. 'I'll start.'

'I've already heard this,' said Street, 'so if you'll excuse me for a moment?'

Buchanan brought Dexter and Hunter up to date on his visit to the stables. 'Right, while Street is out powdering her nose, what did you find on the doctor?'

'There's not a lot to tell,' said Hunter. 'He's been in Eastbourne for the last fourteen years. The clinic has a clean bill of health, no reports of anything untoward.'

'Mrs Metzger, she around?'

'There isn't a Mrs Metzger,' replied Dexter.

'Then who was he with on the *Moonstone*?'

'That was his sister, sir.'

'He lives with his business partner, Dr Payne, in Meads,' said Hunter.

'What about before he came to Eastbourne?'

'He was a doctor at a private school.'

'Was?'

'He left under a cloud, something about signing a death certificate and cremating the deceased with undue haste.'

'Details?'

'I got this through the local newspaper. According to the article, the sports master died suddenly from a heart attack and Dr Metzger immediately signed the death certificate and had the poor master cremated the next day. Caused a bit of a stir in the village.'

'Where was this school?' asked Buchanan.

'The village is called Charlesward, it's seven miles out from Exeter, on the A30.'

'Did I miss anything?' asked Street, when she returned.

'In a minute,' said Buchanan. 'Before we go through the *Moonstone* I would like you two to go to the harbour office and see if they have a record of vessels arriving and departing in the Marina.'

'What time period, sir?' asked Hunter.

'See if they have records for the last six months: if not, get what you can.'

Buchanan waited for Dexter and Hunter to leave before he asked, 'Street, where was that school you attended?'

'Why?'

'No reason, just wondered.'

'You think Greyspear went there?'

'Maybe.'

She thought for a moment then said, 'It was near a village called Charlesward, that's all I remember, or ever want to remember. Why would you want to know that?'

'Nah, never mind,' said Buchanan. 'Let's get going, can't sit here all day.'

He was about to open the door when Atkins barged in.

'Ah, Buchanan, glad I caught you before you go and make a complete arse of yourself. What do you mean by searching Sir Nathan's yacht, and besmirching his reputation? And what's this I hear about DS Street,? Drunk and disorderly, fighting with the public and putting two citizens in hospital?'

'I believe we will find evidence on Sir Nathan's yacht to prove conclusively that the unidentified dead girl was onboard the night in question, and DS Street was fighting off her abductors.'

'Is that so, Street?'

To Street, this information was startling, She'd thought the two miscreants were just trying to pick her up, not abduct her.

'I'm not sure, Ma'am; the evening is a bit of a blur to me.'

'We believe DS Street had been given rohypnol in her drink,' interjected Buchanan. 'It looks like she was in the process of being abducted when PC Hunter stepped in, Ma'am.'

'And you put both of the miscreants in hospital, Street?'

'Apparently so, Ma'am.'

'And you don't remember what happened?'

Street shook her head. 'Sorry Ma'am, I'm afraid last night is a bit of a jumble of memories for me.'

Buchanan looked at the clock and was about to say they had to go when Atkins' phone rang.

'Yes? Ah, Sir Nathan, yes – I'm looking into the matter as we speak. I'll call you as soon as I hear what the inspector has to say. Sir Nathan, there's a phone ringing in the office – let me go out in the corridor.'

It was Buchanan's phone.

'Buchanan. They have? Fantastic news – where were they? Just as I thought. Anything else? OK, get back here as soon as you can. Oh, Hunter, what did you find out at the harbour office? You did? Get a copy while you're at it, you can sort it out here.'

Atkins returned to the room. 'As you have no doubt worked out, that was Sir Nathan Greyspear, and he's not a happy man. He says he is tired of being persecuted for something he knows nothing about, having his businesses brought into ill repute and having his family and friends pestered. I'm sorry, Buchanan. you've been a big disappointment to me. I'm going to have to hand the investigation over to one of my other detectives. I'm afraid you just don't have what it takes to work here in Sussex.'

'Hmm, that was PC Dexter on the phone, Ma'am. He says he and PC Hunter will be here in a few minutes with the dead girl's bag and shoes. Who do you want me to turn them over to – Ma'am?'

'What are you talking about, Buchanan? You don't know whose shoes and bag they've found – could be anybody's.'

'A DNA test should prove it, one way or another, Ma'am,' said Street.

'For your sakes, it had better. I'll wait till your constables arrive. Street, would you get me a coffee, please? Milk, no sugar.'

When Street had left for the coffee, Atkins asked, 'How's she coping? Not every day one has to fight off an attempted abduction.'

'She's had a hard life. I'm sure she'll deal with it in her own way, Ma'am.'

'Does she drink, have any friends?' asked Atkins, a look of worry growing on her face.

'Not that I've noticed. When we've been out she only drinks lemonade and she's become friends with my wife.'

'Your wife's not in the force, is she?'

'No, not unless you consider her being married to a career policeman. Karen – my wife – has a habit of befriending lonely souls, be them two or four-legged.'

'Your coffee, Ma'am.'

'Thanks, Street.'

'I've just seen Hunter and Dexter pull into the car park, sir.'

'Good, now we're getting somewhere.'

The peace was broken by the arrival of two excited PC's.

'Here they are, sir,' said Dexter, handing over two large evidence bags. One contained a pair of high-heeled shoes, the other a ladies' small evening bag.

Buchanan pulled on a pair of gloves and unzipped the shoe bag. He looked at the shoes for the size, and smiled. 'Size five, perfect, now the handbag.'

He unclasped the flap and carefully emptied the contents onto the table.

'Let's see what we've found. A small bunch of keys, an unopened pack of tissues, a coin purse containing," he counted

181

the coins, 'three pounds twenty-four in change, plus a five pound note. Damn, no credit cards. But there is this,' he exclaimed, holding an identity card high above his head.'

'Is that the sword, sir?' asked Street.

'Yes, lass, a sword it is indeed.'

'Would one of you explain what you're going on about, please?' said Atkins.

'This, Ma'am – is the identity card of the maiden in the lake, or I should say the unidentified girl murdered while on Sir Nathan's yacht, the morning of the 30th of March.'

'Let me see that,' said Atkins.

'Ah, if you don't mind, Ma'am, I'll hold and you can look. Fingerprinting and DNA testing are required first.'

'Olga Tratas,' said Atkins. 'Such a beautiful-looking woman. Are you sure she's the same person you've been looking for?'

Street passed the retouched photo of the dead girl to Atkins.

'Then there's no denying the fact. Buchanan, I want the DNA tests done as a priority.'

'And while you're at it, lass,' said Buchanan, picking up the FCB40 brochure from his desk and sliding it into an unused evidence bag, 'have this checked for Sir Nathan's DNA and fingerprints as well.'

'Yours will be on there too, sir,' said Street.

'Only on the top right-hand corner.'

'Buchanan, I see I owe you an apology. I should have never doubted you, but are you really sure Sir Nathan could be responsible for all three of these deaths?'

'He was on the yacht the night Olga Tratas was killed. He lives a fifteen-minute walk from where DS Nichols was found, and his stables are a short drive from Abbotts Wood, where the third girl, Ilka, was found.'

'Other than the *Moonstone*, do you have any witnesses to say he was in the vicinity of the harbour or Abbotts Wood at the time of their deaths? And further, do you even know *when* either DS Nichols or the Ilka girl died?'

'We are assuming Nichols was killed sometime between midnight and five in the morning.'

'Why?'

'Most of the restaurants and cinemas in the Marina usually close about eleven in the evening. Giving a couple of hours for staff to clean up and lock up, puts the earliest time the harbour in that area gets quiet is about one in the morning. So we can assume Nichols was still alive at one.'

'Anything on CCTV?'

'That's on my list of things to check on, Ma'am.'

'And the girl in the woods – can you determine a time for her death?'

'The woods are locked at seven in the evening. The doctor says Ilka was killed on the spot where she was found, and that she'd been dead at least fourteen hours when the body was discovered.'

'You're going to have to find motive and opportunity, Buchanan; you can't just assume anything. At this point it is only circumstantial.'

'That's all right, Ma'am, still plenty of investigating to do yet. We're only just getting under Sir Nathan's skin.'

'Wish you'd spend more time looking for Nichols' killer, not good for one of us to die like that and no-one be brought to book for it.'

'Dexter and Hunter are going to do some ferreting around the harbour tomorrow morning. Who knows what they'll find? They're good at using their nous.'

'They're what?'

'Nous, Ma'am, their intelligence.'

'Do you need any more resources?'

'Not at this time. I've got Dexter and Hunter for legwork, Street for online researching and myself for the one on one toe-treading.'

'What are your plans now we have an ID on the dead girl?'

'Go through everyone's statements again, make sure they were where they said they were at the relevant times, eliminate as many of them as I can. Then I'll focus on who's left, see who had motives. Right now, I'm still betting on Greyspear.'

'Go carefully, Buchanan. Greyspear has lots of friends in high places, wouldn't want to see your career go down in a blaze of flames.'

'I'll watch our backs, don't you worry about that, Ma'am.'

'Right, I'm late for another appointment,' said Atkins, standing to leave. 'Keep me posted, Buchanan.'

'Will do, Ma'am. I'll walk you down.'

'No need, Buchanan.'

'I need to drive Mrs Buchanan to the ferry, Ma'am, and I'm running late.' he said, looking at his watch, 'should just about make it.' He nodded to Street. 'Back in forty minutes.'

◆

'What makes him tick, Jill?' asked Dexter, as he watched Buchanan walk across the car park to his car.

'Dogged stubbornness and a self-assurance built on years of experience of being right.'

'Does it bother you he calls you "lass"?' asked Hunter.

'No, not really, sort of feels comfortable.'

'You're getting soft on him; remember, he's still the boss.'

'I know, and I'm glad he is. Remember what it was like to work under Arness?'

'How could I forget? Every report filled out in triplicate, with no spelling mistakes allowed.'

'And perfect punctuation,' added Hunter, 'reminded me of a grammar tutor I once had. And talking of reports, better get this info on boat movements into a readable form for the boss, though why he wants it I can't figure out.'

'Anyone fancy lunch?' asked Dexter.

'Where are you taking us, Morris?' asked Hunter.

'I was going to Macky D's. Want to come along?'

'No thanks, I packed a sandwich.'

'Bring me back a chocolate shake, Morris,' said Street. 'I've got too much work to do.'

'OK, back in a minute.'

'What are you working on, Jill?'

'The boss wanted me to look up information on Greyspear Studios.'

'Find much?'

'Fancy website, lots of commercial endorsements from companies that have had their advertising handled by the studio.'

'Didn't think film studios did advertising?'

'Greyspear does, all part of the empire I suppose. They're going to have to up their game though if they are going to start making movies. It said in one article I read that modern movies can cost anywhere up to £100 million.'

'That must sound like chicken feed to Greyspear – how much did one of those yachts cost?'

'He said fifteen to seventeen million, but that's not all profit, there's the cost of building the boat in the first place.'

'Didn't you say he's already sold five?'

'Yes, but he's very shrewd. I think he likes other people to invest their money: they take the risk and he takes the profit.'

'Sounds like a good businessman to me.'

'On that level I suppose he does. What you two doing tomorrow?'

'The boss wants us to poke around the Marina and see what turns up. Morris isn't too happy about that, he likes his Sundays off.'

'You won't be getting any days off unless you get that report done.'

♦

Dexter returned to find Street and Hunter busy at work.

'Jill, your shake,' he said, lifting the drink out of its brown paper bag.

'Thanks, Morris.'

'Did you show her?' he asked Hunter.

'Show her what, exactly?' queried Street.

'You mean you haven't shown her?'

'All right; what are you two up to?'

'Want to see what you got up to last night, Jill?'

'What do you mean, Morris?'

'Go on, show her, Stephen.'

'I thought we were going to keep that from her?'

'What *are* you two going on about?'

'Well, now the cat's out of the bag. I was keeping an eye on you last night, it was the boss's idea, didn't want you to get into trouble.'

'Apparently you didn't succeed.'

'Ah, but I didn't need to, you handled the situation perfectly.'

'Show her, Stephen, she won't believe you otherwise.'

'Show me *what*?'

'I had my video camera running as you exited Jukes, saw it all.'

'Let me see that!'

'OK, since you insist.' Hunter unclipped his camera from his uniform and plugged it into the reviewing stand. 'Here, see, you are being escorted out of the club, and here's where you realise all's not what it seems. See – you push one of them backwards over the barrier.'

'Shit, bet he didn't expect that to happen,' said Street, 'didn't look like those chaps in the queue took well to a gatecrasher. Just as well the door staff jumped in to stop the beating.'

'Watch, it gets better,' said Stephen.

As the fight in the queue was being brought under control the camera panned and focused in time to see Jill land a well-aimed punch to the belly of the other miscreant, who spun round in pain accidently kicking the door of a waiting taxi. The taxi driver jumped out and belted the person who he thought had just kicked his taxi door on purpose.

The camera shot then zoomed in on Jill being helped into a police car and driven away.

'So that's what happened to me last night! Those arseholes.'

'Forget it, Jill, it's all over, they got what they deserved.'

'Where are they now?'

'Want to go another round with them?'

'No, I want to find out just what they were up to.'

'Isn't it obvious? Besides you can't, they've scarpered. I checked with the hospital this morning and they've gone, best just forget it.'

'Forget what?' asked Buchanan as he walked into the office.

'Forget following up on the two miscreants who accosted Jill last night.'

'Why's that?'

'They're gone, sir. They did a runner from the hospital before we could get statements from them. Made some sort of excuse about needing to go to the toilet, and when our boys were talking to the nurse, the two of them scarpered.'

'Tell me – we did get their details, didn't we?'

'I'm sorry, sir, but we do have images.'

'How?'

'You remember you told me to keep an eye on Jill last night?' said Hunter.

'Yes.'

'Well, I joined one of the patrols and kept my camera running. When Jill came out of Jukes, I videoed the whole affair.'

'Good stuff, Hunter. Street, can you make mug shots of the miscreants? I have a feeling if I were to show them to Bracewell, he would be able to put names to the faces.'

'I'll get right on it, sir.'

'Hunter, do you have that list of boat movements in and out of the harbour?'

'Yes, sir. Just printed off a copy for you.'

Buchanan took the sheets of A4 from Hunter, had a cursory glance at the neat columns of boat names, arrival and departure times, rolled them up and put them in his inside jacket pocket. 'Well, there goes Sunday. Was going to spend the day reading *The Telegraph*.'

Street yawned.

'Now, let's sort out tomorrow's duties,' said Buchanan.

'But, sir, tomorrow's Sunday, and it's my turn to work in the crèche,' intoned Dexter.

'You got a second job, Dexter?'

'No, sir, it's church. I take turns in the crèche once a month, and it's my turn tomorrow.'

Buchanan looked at his watch and said, 'Right, in that case, I suppose it would do us all good to have a break. I'll see you all back here at seven sharp, Monday morning, and be ready for work. The fox has been in the henhouse too long.'

17

Unable to sleep, Buchanan got out of bed, dressed and left the house. At six in the morning – the sun hadn't fully risen and, except for the occasional dog walker and jogger, the north harbour appeared deserted. Not having any specific destination in mind, Buchanan walked through the twitten to the beach, turned right and headed along the seafront towards the harbour office.

The tide was ebbing and when he reached the lock gates he saw that the lock-keeper was in the process of topping up the inner harbour through the furthest lock. Buchanan could now see, by the rush of water entering the harbour through both open lock gates, why this was done on a falling tide. He walked over to the nearer lock gates and stopped on the central island between the locks. Reaching into his coat for a cigarette, he realised he still had Hunter's report in his inner pocket. He took out the report, glanced at it, and saw that Hunter had listed the boat movements in columns by name of vessel, date, time out, time back, and lastly type of vessel. Buchanan lit his cigarette, leaning on the railing to think.

Waiting to transit the first lock was a large red fishing boat. Buchanan glanced at her name then scanned through the report. The fishing boat *Sally B* went out on Mondays, Wednesdays and sometimes on Fridays, regular as clockwork. He looked through the report and saw what appeared to be a regular pattern for fishing boats. Pleasure craft were another matter; no matter how Buchanan scanned the list he couldn't determine any sensible pattern to their movements. As the English Channel continued to empty into the inner harbour he looked for a particular boat's name. He had to go back to the fifth page to find it: *Moonstone*, out at ten am on the 29th, returned at one am on the 30th of March.

Buchanan scanned back through the report; not till the last page did the name reappear. He looked at the date: 31st December.

The sound of rushing water diminished and was replaced by the hum of the hydraulic ram closing the lock gates. The barrier lifted and Buchanan crossed the gangway and continued his walk along the promenade.

For the first time since he had started the investigation he felt he was getting somewhere, though giving everyone the day off frustrated him. Finding the girl's – no, Olga Tratas's – shoes and bag on the *Moonstone* was just what the investigation needed. On Monday, after they had done a second search of the boatyard, he would send Dexter and Hunter out to Castlewood to see if they could find anyone who saw Greyspear around the stables the day of Ilka's killing. Street would continue gathering information on Greyspear's business empire and he would go and tread on Greyspear's toes, if he was around.

There was still the nagging issue of how the girls had been brought into the country. Was it possible they were smuggled in through Newhaven, inside a container? Buchanan knew from reading police reports and watching television news that some migrants, desperate to start a new life, climbed under lorries waiting to board the ferries at Calais. There had been unfortunate results for one young man, who fell off and was run over on the M25. But those migrants were willing and able to make this attempt on their own, with no coercion involved. The girls were a completely different matter, no hanging on to a lorry axel for them. So how did they get transported into the country?

The only conclusion Buchanan could arrive at was Greyspear and the *Moonstone*. But why would he run the risk of being caught, going to jail, possibly losing his business empire, and having a seventeen-million-pound yacht being confiscated? Arrogance was the only answer that presented itself to Buchanan. Besides, who'd search such a yacht as the *Moonstone* or even think someone with Greyspear's standing would be involved with human trafficking? Then he remembered other prominent people who'd had their public persona shredded when the scope of their evil deeds had been revealed. The fact that the *Moonstone* had only been out twice since December bothered him; it didn't fit into the scenario he was building in his mind.

His sojourn along the promenade was brought to an abrupt halt at the pier. Two large cranes had been installed either side of it. Buchanan remembered reading in the *Herald* that the cranes were there to remove the burnt-out structure on the pier.

He walked up onto Marine Parade, crossed over and wandered down Cade Street. It wasn't till he reached Seaside Road that he realised where he was headed. He looked at his watch and realised that Bill's would be open in twenty minutes: just what he needed.

The restaurant staff were putting out tables and chairs for those who chose to sit outside and smoke while they ate.

'We'll be open in a few minutes. Can I get you something to drink while you wait?' asked one of the waitresses.

'Black coffee, please,' requested Buchanan.

As he sipped his coffee he took out his phone to call Karen, and then remembered she was in France with her mother. He scrolled through his contacts, chose a number, pressed the dial key and waited for the phone to be answered.

'Hello.'

'Street, it's Buchanan. Fancy breakfast? I'm buying.'

'What time is it?'

'Just gone eight.'

'But it's Sunday, sir; my day to sleep in.'

'I could do with the company.'

'What about Hunter or Dexter?'

'They're boring.'

'Where are you, or should I guess?'

'Bill's, I'll wait to order.'

'Your table's ready, sir. If you'll follow me,' said the waitress.

'Don't be long, Street; I'm hungry.'

'What's new about that?'

♦

Buchanan was deep in Hunter's report when Street arrived.

'Morning, sir.'

'Morning, lass. Sleep well?'

'I was, till someone phoned.'

'I wonder who that could have been? Sorry, I didn't think. I just needed someone to talk to. My mind is going round in circles with this thing about Greyspear. Thanks for coming, lass.'

She looked at him, shook her head and said, 'That's OK.'

They ordered scrambled eggs, orange juice and coffee. While they waited for their breakfast, Street asked, 'What's got your mind so tied up in knots?'

'Been looking at the report, Stephen —I mean Hunter — put together on boat movements for the Marina. It's only for the last three months, but paints a good picture of what the lock activities are.'

Street looked at Buchanan, smiled, then said, 'And the *Moonstone*? Is she mentioned anywhere?'

'Here, have a look,' he said, passing her the report. 'Only twice: once on the evening in question, and the other on New Year's Eve.'

'Not exactly the pattern of a people trafficker, is it?' she said, thumbing through the pages.

'No, it's unfortunately not.'

'Maybe he paid someone not to record his comings and goings?'

'That's possible —but who?'

'That Dan fellow — he didn't take well to you asking him questions.'

'No, he didn't, did he? Maybe we should have another word with him, find out what his duty schedule is. Be interesting to find out how often he works nights.' Buchanan put down his cup and asked, 'Where's your car parked? I could do with a ride back to the Marina.'

'I took a taxi, bit too hung over to drive this morning.'

'Well, I guess it's a walk back along the promenade for me.'

'Want company? You could drive me home when we get to your house.'

'Perfect, didn't fancy the walk back on my own.'

By the time they'd finished breakfast and wandered back to the Marina the early sunshine had vanished, to be replaced by dark scudding clouds.

Once again Buchanan had to wait for the lock gates to close.

They looked down into the far side lock. It was empty except for two sailboats flying French flags. Buchanan walked back along the side of the lock and checked the yachts' names against Hunter's report.

'Are they on the list?' asked Street.

'No, but that's not surprising.'

'Were you thinking this was how the girls were smuggled into the country?'

'Wouldn't be the first time. There was an article in the *Herald* last November about a UK national who tried to smuggle a bunch of Albanians in.'

'Did he get caught?'

'Yep, and all those on board were arrested by Immigration. Most were deported.'

'Sir, do you see what I see?' said Street.

'Are you referring to the person climbing down the steps?'

They watched as Dan climbed down onto the pontoon against which the two French yachts were tied up and walked along it. He chatted with each of the yacht skippers, checking their passports. As he talked he filled out forms and had the skippers sign them.

'Interesting, very interesting,' said Buchanan.

'What is?'

'He's wearing a new coat.'

'Who?'

'Dan. I think we should definitely have another chat with him.'

Buchanan and Street waited for the gates to open and let the two French yachts make their way into the inner harbour, and Dan to make his way back up into the harbour office.

'Right, lass, let's go stand on some toes.'

Street followed Buchanan up the stairs and into the harbour office.

'Hello, can I help?' said the lock-keeper.

'Yes, can we have a word with Dan?'

'Who's asking?'

'Detective Chief Inspector Buchanan, Sussex CID.'

'Ah, just a minute,' he said, picking up the phone and dialling. 'Dan, there's a policeman here; he wants to talk to you. OK.' He put the phone down and said, 'He'll be out in a minute.'

Buchanan and Street watched a couple of fishing boats exit the lock and head out into the outer harbour while they waited.

'You want to talk to me?' said a voice from behind.

Buchanan and Street turned to see a red-faced Dan.

'Is there somewhere quiet we can talk?' asked Buchanan.

'The boss's office; she's not in today.'

'Lead on.'

They followed Dan into the office; Street shut the door behind them as he walked over to the window and stood facing them.

'Dan,' said Buchanan, I was wondering if you have remembered anything about the evening – no, I should say the morning – of the 30th of March.'

'Like what?'

'That's a nice coat you're wearing. Is it new?'

'Yes, why?'

'Do you remember when you purchased it?'

'No.'

'Bit strange, that. It must have cost quite a bit – it's one of those float coats, isn't it?'

'Yes.'

'And you don't remember when you purchased it?'

'No.'

'Ah well, I suppose we could have a look at your charge card statement, that would tell us.'

Small beads of sweat broke out on Dan's forehead. 'I paid cash for it.'

'What happened to the old one?'

'Gave it to charity.'

'Early on the morning of the 30th of March, were you on duty on your own?'

'No, there are always at least two of us on duty at night.'

'Who was with you?'

'Harry, but he left early – his wife called and said their child was sick and needed to go to the DGH.'

'What time did you go off duty?'

'Supposed to go off at midnight, but hung around till about four'

'Why?'

'I just told you. Harry went home early, I waited for George to come in.'

'What time did you leave?'

'Don't remember.'

'After the *Moonstone* returned?'

'Er – yes, but why would you want to know that?'

'I'll ask the questions, if you don't mind. You waited for the *Moonstone* to return?'

'Yes.'

'Why? Was there someone onboard you wanted to see?'

Dan stared at his feet and then answered, 'Yes.'

'Olga Tratas, for instance?'

Dan looked up at Buchanan, tears in his eyes. He nodded and said, 'Yes'.

'Did you climb down onto the pontoon when the *Moonstone* docked?'

'Yes.'

'You wanted to talk to Olga?'

'Yes.'

'What about?'

Dan shook his head and looked back down at his feet.

'She was pregnant with your child and refused to have an abortion, that it?'

Dan continued to stare at the floor.

'You were angry and continued to argue with her as the *Moonstone* moved out of the lock. When you saw she was cold you gave her your coat. You continued to argue and when you reached the bridge between the harbours she fainted. Then you pushed her off the boat to drown?'

Dan looked back up. 'No, you've got it all wrong. Why would I kill her? I loved her.'

'Are you saying she killed herself?'

'No, of course not.'

'Do you know who did?'

Dan clenched his teeth and let out his breath slowly.

'How did you first meet her?'

'I was in the office, New Year's Eve. The *Moonstone* entered the lock and Sir Nathan asked if there was anyone there who would like to go out and watch the fireworks.'

'And you said yes?'

'You've seen the *Moonstone*. What would you have said?'

'Good point. Go on.'

'We stopped just off of the pier and watched the fireworks. Olga was serving drinks, we got to chatting and became friends.'

'Did you see her very often?'

'No, not as much as I would have liked, she was always busy working, then—,'

'Then what?'

'I saw her in Jukes – I think it was about February – she was with someone I didn't recognise.'

'What did they look like?' asked Street.

'He looked like he was in his forties, tall, going bald.'

'You got Abosa's photo with you, Street?' asked Buchanan.

'Yeah, here,' she said, taking the photo out of her pocket and passing it to Dan.

'Yeah, that's him. What's his name?'

'He goes by the name Abosa. We're eager to talk with him,' said Buchanan.

'So am I.'

'What happened after that? Did you confront her?'

'She said it was none of my business.'

'Did you pursue it?'

'Yes. Then she said she had asked him to find her sister.'

'Was she lost?'

Dan shrugged his shoulders. 'I don't know, she never mentioned it again.'

'You two broke up?' asked Street.

'No, we sort of drifted apart. With my shift work and her working for the catering company we didn't get much time together.'

'What was the name of the catering company?' asked Buchanan.

'Don't know, I never asked.'

'Dan, why don't you tell us exactly what happened the morning of the 30th?'

'As I said earlier I was supposed to go off shift at midnight; George came in to relieve Harry, I waited for George. I knew the *Moonstone* had gone out the previous morning, so I hung around till it returned.'

'Was that normal, for you to hang around after your shift?'

'George and I like to play poker, so yes, it was quite normal.'

'For money?'

'Not with George, it was just for the fun of it.'

'Why else did you hang around?'

'I wanted to talk to Olga, I wanted to help her, or at least make her get help. She was working in the country illegally. She told me she had been offered the job by an agency in Budapest, but when she got here her passport was taken away and she was told she could only get it back after she had paid off the cost of her travel and first three months' accommodation expenses.'

'How did she travel?'

'Don't know.'

'How did she get to the UK?'

'Don't know, she never talked about it.'

'Do you think it was on the *Moonstone*?'

'Unlikely, it's only been out a couple of times while it's been here. Check the log, you've got a copy.'

'How long has it been in the harbour?'

'It arrived just before Christmas.'

'Did Olga say where she was from?'

'No, only that she had been hired through the agency in Budapest.'

'What about her sister? Does she have a name?'

'Maria.'

'Did Olga say where Maria lived?'

'No.'

'When you were talking to Olga, did you see anyone else on deck?'

'A couple of the crew were tending the dock lines. I think one of the guests was watching. They went back in when the *Moonstone* left the lock.'

'So, you said goodbye from the pontoon?'

'Yes. And I never saw her again till I saw her photo in the *Herald*.'

'Why didn't you come forward and tell us you knew who she was?'

'I did mention it to one of your detectives, the one who had the accident in the harbour.'

'That was no accident.'

'You mean two murders in two weeks? I never realised.'

'What did you say to DS Nichols?'

'Was that his name? Just what I've told you.'

'What was his response?'

'He thanked me.'

'Did you see him again?'

'No.'

'Thanks Dan, you've been a big help.'

♦

Buchanan looked at Street's face as they walked back to his house. 'You look all in, you need a rest.'

'I wish.'

'Can't sleep?'

She shook her head. 'Next door's just had their first child, keeps me awake with its crying. I'll get used to it sooner or later.'

'No, really, why don't you take a couple of days off?'

'You can't afford not having me around.'

'Nonsense. I need you fresh and at full strength. Listen, I've got an idea. Why don't you head over to France and spend a couple of days with Karen? And while you're there you could have a wander around Dieppe and the tattoo parlours and see what you can find out about Olga's tattoo.'

'So it would be a working break?'

'Someone needs to check them out. You speak French, don't you?'

'A little.'

'Good, let's get to the house. I'll call Karen, then book your ferry ride.'

'What about the French police? They won't want me poking around on their turf.'

'You're just going over for a visit, checking out the tattoo parlours in case you want one for yourself.'

'I don't know. I'm not insured to drive in France.'

'Don't worry, I'll drive you to the ferry, and Karen will pick you up when you arrive.'

18

'Morning. Patron.'

Buchanan screwed up his face and shook his head. 'Boss will do, Hunter. Where's Dexter?'

'Just arrived, gone to get a cup of coffee and a doughnut from the Cavendish Bakery wagon, he said he missed breakfast this morning.'

When Dexter arrived, Buchanan brought them up to date on Sunday's revelations.

'I want both of you to get out to the Marina and see what you can turn up. Then head over to Greyspear's stables and see if anyone saw Greyspear there on the day Ilka died.'

'Where will you be, sir?' asked Dexter.

'Going to see Greyspear.' He was interrupted by his phone ringing and punched the speaker button. 'Buchanan.'

'Jack, it's Karen. Have you heard from Jill?'

'No, why should I?'

'She wasn't on the ferry this morning.'

'What do you mean?'

'I arrived at the terminal to collect her, the ferry was early, but when I checked the waiting room, she wasn't there.'

'Did you ask at reception?'

'Yes, but you know how lax immigration can be, all you have to do is wave a passport and they let you in.'

'Did you phone her?'

'Just goes to voicemail.'

'What about taxis?'

'They're only here when the ferry arrives.'

'I'm coming over,' he said, looking at the ferry schedule on his computer. 'Next ferry isn't till just before midnight, gets in at four am your time. I'll see you tomorrow morning at the terminal.'

'Don't miss it Jack, I'm really worried about her.'

'Don't worry, I'll be on it.'

'Was that Mrs Buchanan, sir?' asked Hunter.

'Yes.'

'And was she worried about Jill?'

'Yes, but I'm going over to see what happened to her. You and Dexter are in charge till I get back; call me if you've got any questions.'

'Yes sir, but what are we going to say if the chief calls and asks to talk to you?'

'Just tell her I'm following a lead on the tattoo.'

'With Jill?'

'With Jill. Don't worry; we'll both be back before you know it.'

♦

'Jack, I'm so glad you're here! There's not been a word from Jill since the ferry got here – are you sure she got on?'

'Yes, I checked with Border Control, she definitely got on.'

'Suppose she's still on board? Suppose she saw something or someone and stayed on to investigate?'

'It's possible, but I don't think it's likely; she would have called me if she had. Did you ask the taxi drivers if anyone gave her a ride into town?'

'I asked all that were here, but not all the taxis come out each time the ferry docks.'

'But why would she go into town in a taxi, even if the ferry was early, when she knew you were coming to collect her? It just doesn't make sense.'

'Suppose she saw someone she recognised and decided to follow them?'

'That's a possibility. Anyway, let's get a taxi and head into town and see what we turn up.'

'I've got mum's car.'

'She's still driving?'

'Not since her eye op. She said she doesn't think it wise to drive till her eyesight settles.'

'Wise lady, just like her daughter.'

'Thanks for the compliment.'

'You're welcome.'

'I've been busy; I've made a list of the tattoo parlours.'

'How many are there?'

'I only found three, but there may be more.'

Buchanan looked at his watch, 'Is it really only half past four?'

'Hungry?'

'What else at this time of day?'

'I know a café where we can get an early breakfast. Besides, the tattoo parlours won't be open for a while yet.'

♦

As Karen sipped her coffee, Buchanan said, 'I think it would be wise to have a story ready before we go making our enquiries.'

'Like what?'

'Probably best if you go in alone. It might look odd if we go in together. You could say you were looking for the place that did your daughter's tattoo as you wanted one just like it, a surprise for your boyfriend.'

'It would be, wouldn't it?'

'Don't go getting ideas, I like you just the way you are.'

'Jack, you're a prude.'

'No, I'm not. I just like you the way you were when I married you.'

'In case you haven't noticed, dear, we've both changed a bit over the years.'

'Enough of that. You speak better French than I do, so it is going to be up to you ask the questions. Be better if they think you're French.'

'And I'm a woman?'

'There's that.'

'OK, so I say my daughter has a tattoo, *and* I want one just like hers, *and* done by the same person? You have the photo with you, don't you?'

'Yes.'

'Good, let me have it and I'll show it to the tattooist.'

'OK. Where first?'

'It's just down the road from the station. We can park in the station car park and walk to all of them – walking will do you good.'

At the first parlour they drew a blank. The second was closed and looked like it wasn't likely to reopen anytime soon according to Madame Degrease in the flower shop next door. At the third, Karen went in while Buchanan stood watch at the door and waited for Karen to exit.

'What did he say, does he know where there are any other parlours?' asked Buchanan when she came out.

'He was able to tell me there is another tattoo parlour down by the docks, but he said it wasn't recommended because it has a bad reputation - untrained staff. However, he did confirm that the tattoo was the work of Raphael, and that he works there,' she said holding out the address.

Buchanan looked at it. 'Do you know where this place is?'

'Yes. It's down by the harbour, not where the private yachts are moored, it's near where the fishing boats tie up.'

He smiled, this was more like it. 'We'll drive past it, park a way down the road, and walk back.'

Karen drove slowly down the street. 'Bit seedy. If I was to be looking for a place to get a tattoo, it certainly wouldn't be here. Doesn't even look like it's open.'

'Park down there,' said Buchanan, pointing to gap in the cars and vans lined up in front of the shops. 'We'll walk back and have a coffee in the café on the corner.'

They walked casually down the pavement pretending to be tourists, stopping occasionally to look in shop windows, till they reached the tattoo parlour.

'Do you see what I see?' said Karen.

'What? Where?'

'Look at that display of sample tattoos on the board at the side of the window – there's the same one as your dead girl had.'

'Bingo, you're right! Well spotted. Let's go next door for a coffee and decide what's next.'

'Deux cafés, s'il vous plait.'

'Oui, Madame.'

When the waitress returned with their coffees, Karen asked her if the tattoo parlour next door would be open today.

Buchanan listened to them conversing in French wishing he'd paid more attention to his lessons at school.

'What did she say?'

'She said she wasn't sure, they're not open regular hours, but she did see one of the artists go in the back door about an hour ago. She said they're not very nice people.'

Buchanan smiled again. 'I sure we have found what we're looking for.'

They sat chatting and sipping their coffees and staring out of the window till Karen thought she saw someone crossing the street making for the tattoo parlour.

'Jack, I think they're open. Someone just crossed the street, and it looked like they went in the front door.'

'Are you sure you're all right going in on your own?'

'Of course, I am, I'm only going to ask about a tattoo.'

'OK, I'll have a wander down the side street and check what I can see through the back door of the parlour.'

'Why would you be interested in the back door? You're not going to do something silly, are you?'

'No, of course not, just want to satisfy a curiosity I've got.'

'Are you sure?'

'I've been running this through my mind from the moment I heard Jill was missing. I have an idea that when the ferry was early she probably thought she had time to nip into town and have a look at the tattoo parlours before you were due to pick her up.'

'Why would she be looking?'

'I asked her.'

'For goodness sake, she was supposed to be taking a couple of days' rest, not gallivanting around Dieppe on one of your mad whims.'

'I know. I've been beating myself up ever since you called.'

'Honestly, Jack, sometimes you just don't think.'

'Well, anyway, I figured she'd done what you did and made a list. She probably thought she'd make it back to the ferry terminal long before you got there.'

'And just what is this curiosity of yours?'

'When you're inside talking, I'll sneak round to the back door and, if it's open I'll pop inside and see if I can find Jill.'

'Cloak and dagger isn't your style, Jack. Sure you don't want to charge in through the front door shouting *Yippie yi yo kayah*?'

Buchanan smiled, shook his head, and said, 'thought you were going to finish the quote.'

'You know full well I don't swear.'

'Nonetheless, this is the best lead we've had so far; we can't just let it go.'

'If what you think is true, then these are desperate people. They'd probably stop at nothing to keep themselves out of the clutches of the law. For all we know they've already been responsible for three deaths; I don't want you to be the fourth.'

'Relax, it won't come to that.'

They paid for their drinks, left the café, and crossed the road. They stood, keeping a watch on the tattoo parlour front door by looking at the reflection in the shop window.

'It does look like its open, and I think I can see someone moving around. What do you want me to do?'

'You go in, best to stick to what we discussed earlier, and say your daughter had a tattoo just like the one in the window and you'd like one to surprise your boyfriend. Speak in French, don't want them getting suspicious. Keep them talking, say something about you're not sure, don't like needles, afraid it might hurt, just keep them talking.'

'Where will you be? Or should I ask?'

'As I said, I'll just be nosing around the back, see what I can see through the back door.'

'Be careful.'

Buchanan waited for Karen to go in and start talking with one of the artists before he crossed the road and wandered down the side street. He was momentarily disappointed; instead of a back alleyway he found a small car repair garage set back from the road by a small forecourt.

He had reasoned that if the café had a back door then the tattoo parlour must have one as well. His conjecture had been correct. There were two doors at the side: one for the café and the other, a couple of metres further back, for the tattoo parlour.

Buchanan realised he couldn't just stand there. Not only was the clock running for Karen, it was also running for Street. He looked around the forecourt and saw no one then glanced casually into the interior of the garage repair shop, also seeing no one. Taking the bull by the horns he walked straight back to the door to the tattoo parlour and was about to open it when a mechanic, who unnoticed by Buchanan, had been working on the far side of a Renault People Carrier, walked out of the back of the garage.

'Monsieur, qu'est-ce que vous voulez?'

'My car, it's not running right. This way to the office?' said Buchanan, opening the door.

'Non, monsieur.' The mechanic pointed to a door on the far side of the forecourt.

Grudgingly, Buchanan pulled the tattoo parlour door closed behind him; he'd only been able to make a cursory glance inside. No sign of Street.

'Over there?' he asked, pointing to the partially open door on the far side of the forecourt.

The mechanic nodded. Buchanan noted the balled fists hanging down from the greasy overalls. Now why would someone be that tense at such an honest mistake? he mused.

He crossed the forecourt, past a polished Mercedes sitting on a hydraulic jack with the driver's front wheel missing, and went into the office.

On the right, there was a well-worn counter, which extended across the office to the back wall. Tyre brochures of various manufacturers were peeping through very scratched plastic covers. There were two tattered armchairs to Buchanan's left, and a doorway on the far wall. This was definitely the other end of the spectrum from that of Greyspear's office in Greenock.

An untidy mop of blonde hair tilted back to reveal a well-travelled face with a cigarette hanging out of the woman's mouth.

'Good afternoon,' said Buchanan. 'My car is having trouble. Can someone look at it for me?'

'You English?'

Buchanan was about to give the receptionist a lesson on the differences in dialects but just grunted yes.

'We're busy. Come back tomorrow.'

'I can't, the ferry is at eight tonight.'

'What's wrong with your car?'

Buchanan shrugged. 'Difficult to start, stalls at the lights.'

'Where is your car? We don't have time to collect.'

'I'll bring it. Ten minutes, OK?'

The mop of hair nodded.

'One more thing. Do you have a toilet?'

'Through the door and down the corridor,' the mop said, indicating the door to her right.

'Thanks,' said Buchanan, as the mop went back to looking at her mobile phone

Buchanan had only a few minutes before the mop would start to wonder what the strange Englishman was up to.

The corridor ran from the street all the way to a door on the right that Buchanan surmised led into the workshop. There was a staircase on the left and Buchanan saw the toilet was underneath, *You're pushing your luck, Jack*, he whispered under his breath as he made his way up the stairs on tiptoe. At the top there was a small landing with a long corridor leading off to the right. In the dim light Buchanan saw two sets of doors on either side. He reasoned the door at the far end must lead through to the floor above the tattoo parlour. He was about to make his way down the corridor when the door at the far end opened and Abosa walked through. Buchanan ducked back out of sight and as quietly and quickly as he could made his way down the stairs 'Be back as soon as I can get my car to you,' he said, heading out the door and back to Karen.

Buchanan walked out of the office and as he walked across the forecourt he noticed the mechanic had finished with the Renault people carrier and had parked it beside the Mercedes.

'What's up? You look like the cat that's just drunk the cream.'

'In a minute. How did you do?'

'Fine. I said I'd have to think about it, made a big to-do about being afraid of needles. Now what's got you looking so pleased with yourself?

'You remember me telling you about Abosa? And how we think he's involved in this mess?'

'Yes.'

'I've just seen him.'

'Where?'

'Upstairs, above the garage. It's behind the tattoo parlour.'

Buchanan explained about the story of the sick car, him needing the toilet, going upstairs, the locked doors, and Abosa.

'What are we going to do? You can't just march in there and arrest him, can you?'

'Don't intend to, though I'd love to have a quiet word with him. No, I'm convinced the lass is somewhere in there, probably locked in one of the rooms off the corridor.'

'You have a plan,?'

'Let's get back to the car, I need to think.'

Karen glanced in the shop windows as they made their way back to the car, Buchanan ruminated.

'Karen, what time is the next ferry back?'

'Six o' clock this evening.'

'That makes things tight, I thought it was at eight,' he replied, looking at his watch, 'it's now quarter past four. Never mind, should still give us plenty of time for what I'm thinking.'

'And just what are you thinking?'

'Climb in the car and release the bonnet catch.'

Karen frowned, but did as he asked.

Buchanan lifted the bonnet and leaned into the engine compartment. 'Start the engine.'

The starter engaged, but instead of the steady purr of a well-running engine it coughed and leapt like a demented cat.

'What's wrong with the engine? What have you done?'

'Keep it running. I pulled a spark cable. We couldn't drive into the garage with nothing wrong with the engine.'

'Makes sense. What next?'

'I'm going to climb in the boot. Throw the travel blanket over me, just in case the mechanic looks inside. When you get to the garage, drive straight into the forecourt; make sure you go in on the left side, as far back as you can get.'

'You're not planning to do anything illegal, are you?'

'No, of course not, the receptionist already gave me permission to use the toilet, I just choose to wait till now. Listen, when you've parked the car, make a big fuss that it's your mother's car and you need to get it back to her this evening. Then go into the office and give them your mother's details, let them assume you live here in France. Get the receptionist to call the mechanic, say you have to explain to him what the problem is, and take your time doing it. OK?'

'But what will you do?'

'While you're chatting to the receptionist, I'll sneak out of the car and up the stairs. With luck, I'll be back down with Jill.'

'Do you know what you've just said?'

'Yes, I'll be –'

'No,' said Karen, shaking her head, 'you've just called the lass, Jill.'

He shook his head, and grinned. 'So I did. Just a slip of the tongue, that's all.'

Karen smiled. 'Be careful Jack, this isn't a game.'

Buchanan waited for the disappearing sound of the mechanic's heavy steps to tell him that he had gone into the office and the workshop was clear. But instead of quiet he heard the sound of the mechanic returning. There was a pause, then the driver's door opened and the mechanic climbed into the car and started the engine. Just as before, the car shook and rattled. The mechanic revved the engine a few times, and then closed the driver's door.

What was he up to? Buchanan wondered. Then he realised the mechanic was reversing the car into the garage closer to his workbench. Perfect, Buchanan thought. The mechanic turned off the engine, ratcheted the hand-brake and got out of the car. Once more Buchanan listened to the sound of the mechanic walking to the office. Then he pushed the rear seat forward and climbed into it. Satisfied that he was still alone in the workshop, he opened the back door of the car and crept over to the bottom of the stairs.

He made his way up them as quietly as he could. On the landing he paused and peered round the corner. All was quiet, so he walked to the first door on the right. Holding his breath, and ready for whatever might be behind the door; he turned the doorknob and gently pushed it open. There was just a desk and a couple of chairs; the walls were festooned with photos of past Pirelli calendar girls. The door on the left led into an empty room. He continued to the next door on the right. Being a little bolder, he opened it to find a room full of cardboard boxes. He pulled the door closed and was about to reach for the last door but the doorknob turned before he could put his hand to it.

Buchanan stepped back into the box room and squinted through the door jamb. He saw the last door open and could hear female voices. Then he was stunned to see Abosa backing out of the room, swearing in a language he couldn't understand. As Abosa bent over to turn the key in the lock Buchanan stepped quietly out of the room and punched him as hard as he could on the back of the neck. Being off balance, Abosa shot forward, banged his head on the doorframe, and collapsed on the floor.

No time to waste, Jack, Buchanan said to himself, while stepping over the prostrate form of Abosa. He was almost hit by a chair as he entered the room. Grabbing the unguided missile he shouted, 'Steady on, lass, that's my head you're trying to open.'

'Oh, sir, I knew you'd come!' said Street, giving him a big hug.

'No time for that, lass. Let's get out of here.'

'We can't leave them behind,' she said, pointing to the eight girls cowering on their beds.

'Who are they?' asked Buchanan.

'Next batch of young girls being trafficked.'

'OK. Let's go, before Abosa wakes up.'

'We can't just leave them to fend for themselves, can we? They don't have their passports or any money. Who knows what will happen to them if we just send them out the door. They'll probably get rounded up again by Abosa's people.'

'What do you suggest?'

'We could make a search of the building and see what we can find. Maybe their passports are here somewhere.'

'Oh, by the way, where's yours?'

Street smiled, reached down to her ankle, and pulled her well-worn passport from her sock.

Buchanan looked down at Abosa who was snoring contentedly, though he would have a sore neck when he woke. He crouched down and went through Abosa's pockets finding his wallet in the front trouser pocket. Street watched as Buchanan took everything out of it, put them on the floor, and then photographed each piece of paper before replacing them – minus the cash – and putting the wallet back in Abosa's pocket.

'You're not going to steal his cash, are you?'

'No, lass, those girls are going to need some money to get home. Abosa is just refunding them some of what they've probably paid him.'

'That's fair enough.'

'There's what passes for an office at the end of the corridor. Let's try it' said Buchanan, standing up and leading them to it. 'Street, tell the girls to wait here. If Abosa wakes, tell them to get down the stairs as fast as they can.' '

Buchanan and Street entered the office.

'Just like being on the job, sir.'

'We are. Keep looking.'

The third drawer in the desk revealed its secrets.

'Look at this, sir, there must be twenty passports here, including Olga and Ilka's, and a bundle of cash.'

'Grab the cash, our girl's passports, leave the rest for the gendarmes, and let's get going.'

As they headed for the stairs, Abosa got to his feet rubbing his neck. 'Girls first!' yelled Buchanan. Street followed directly after with Buchanan trying not to tread on her heels. They reached the bottom as Abosa took his first step on the stairs, stumbled, and fell down the rest.

'Is he dead?'

'No, lass. Just knocked himself out; he'll have one hell of a headache when he wakes up.'

Street started to laugh.

'What's so funny?'

'Jack and Jill came down the stairs, and Abosa came tumbling after.'

'Come on,' said Buchanan, shaking his head, 'let's get out of here.'

The girls and Street followed him into the reception office.

Karen reached out in a motherly embrace. 'Jill! You're safe.'

'No time for that, let's get going,' said Buchanan. 'Where's the receptionist?'

'Here, on the floor. When you started to make a ruckus upstairs, she headed for the door. I hit her with the appointment book.'

'Mrs Buchanan, is there no end to your talents? Is the mechanic still out in the workshop?'

'I think so.'

'Good, wait here.'

He went through into the corridor and along to the workshop door. The mechanic was bent over staring at the engine and didn't see Buchanan creep up behind him and slam the bonnet down on his head. Buchanan grabbed the unconscious mechanic by his arms and dragged him back over to the foot of the stairs where Abosa still slumbered. Buchanan thought for minute, returned to the garage, rummaged in the mechanic's toolbox, and returned with a handful of cable ties. Then he pulled the mechanic's arm through the baluster and cable-tied his wrist to Abosa's. Returning to the garage, he re-attached the plug lead on his car engine.

'Jill, get in the car and drive out into the road and wait for us.'

'What are you going to do' asked Karen.

'You, my dear, are going to call the police and fire department. Tell them there's a fire in the garage, and people are trapped upstairs.'

'Oh, I get what you're up to. Where's the phone?'

'Behind the desk, make sure you speak in French.'

'Good point – you're not really going to start a fire are you?'

'Just a small one, I've put a few oily rags in the dustbin. Even if the phone call doesn't make them believe you, the neighbours seeing the smoke will.'

'Why bother, if Jill and the girls are safe?'

'Because we're not officially here and I don't want Abosa to do a runner. While he's explaining why he's tied to a car mechanic, we get back across the channel and put in an enquiry as to his whereabouts regarding multiple murders.

'OK.'

While Karen dialled 112, Buchanan dashed back out to the garage and set light to the oily rags.

'Let's get out of here. Is Jill still in the car?'

'Yes, she's just backed out into the road, she'll be right in. In the meantime, what are we going to do with them?' she said, gesturing to the girls. 'We can't just let them wander off down the street – Abosa's people might grab them, and I'd hate to think what would happen.'

'That's what I was wondering as well.'

'Car ready, lass?'

'Yes, and just what are we going to do with the girls?'

'We've been discussing that. I've returned their passports to them and divided up the cash I found in the drawer and Abosa's wallet. They've all said they want to return home, except for one.'

'Who?'

'The tall one by the door with the long auburn hair, does she look familiar at all?'

215

'Vaguely.'

'She's Olga's twin; her name's Maria. She wants to come to England and help find her sister's killer.'

'And the rest want to go home?'

'So they say; there's plenty of cash to cover their train fares with some left over as a sort of compensation.'

'We should be going, Jack. Don't want to miss the ferry.'

'Good thinking, Karen. I'll head round to the café with Jill and Maria while you drive the other girls to the station.'

'With what, mum's car has only got room for four passengers and there's seven girls needing a lift to the station?'

Buchanan looked round the reception and reached for a bunch of keys hanging from a hook beside the desk. 'Here use this one, it's the key to the Renault People Carrier out on the lot, you should be able to squeeze into that, it's only a short ride.'

'Suppose Abosa comes round and sees you?'

'Unlikely, he'll be too busy with the gendarmes to go anywhere.'

'Fine. See you in twenty or so.'

Karen was back in fifteen. 'Almost couldn't get through with the police and fire engines.'

'The girls?'

'The train for Paris left five minutes ago. I stayed and watched it leave. We must hurry, the ferry leaves in twenty minutes.'

No one asked any questions when Karen purchased an extra ticket for the ferry.

♦

'What are we going to do with Maria?'

'Don't worry, I've got an idea.'

'But where is she going to stay?'

'With Street, she's got a spare room; and it'll only be till Maria gets established.'

'It better be.'

'Besides, Maria's a material witness; we've got to keep her safe till we get this mess sorted out. Where is she?'

'Jill's taken her down to the cafeteria to get something to eat.'

♦

As the ferry approached Newhaven, Street and Maria returned to the lounge.

'Jill, why weren't you at the terminal waiting for me?' asked Karen.

'As I was walking down the ramp I saw Abosa drive past. While he queued behind the traffic leaving the harbour I hired a taxi and had it follow him into town.'

'How'd you know he wouldn't head for the road out of town?'

'I didn't. I assumed he'd head into town, so told the taxi driver just to drive to the nearest market. I said I wanted to buy some flowers for my mother.'

'What happened next, lass?' asked Buchanan.

'When I saw Abosa was going in to town, I said to the driver that my cousin was driving the blue Mercedes two cars in front and could we follow him, I wanted it to be a surprise.'

'I bet it was."

'Abosa drove to the garage where you found me. I had the taxi driver drop me off at the café and I waited a few minutes then walked round to the garage. His car was in front, but I couldn't see him. I went into the office and asked the receptionist if my uncle had just come in.'

'Bit risky, lass?'

'It was all I could think of at the time. I was going to say it was a case of mistaken identity if Abosa walked in.'

'Good idea, what went wrong?'

'He came in through the corridor door and looked at me. I apologised and said I thought my uncle had just come into the garage. I don't think he believed me, because as he was talking to me the mechanic came in and grabbed me from behind. They bundled me upstairs and into the room where you found me.'

'Oh, Jill, I hate to think of what they were planning to do to you.'

'That's OK, Karen; I can take care of myself.'

'But you were locked in the room.'

'I was already working on escape when the inspector broke in.'

'You almost brained me with that chair.'

'Sorry.'

The conversation was interrupted by Buchanan's phone ringing.

'Buchanan. What is it, Hunter?'

'What did he want, sir? asked Street, as he put the phone down.

'He said the chief's been looking for me. Apparently, I've been a bad boy; I'm to be in her office at nine sharp tomorrow morning. Oh, Hunter wanted to know if you had your phone with you?'

'I left it behind; remember I was supposed to be taking a couple of days off.'

'Here, use mine; he's waiting for you to call.'

'But you have to call the chief.'

'She can wait. You call Hunter first.'

Street walked over to the far side of the lounge before dialling. She returned ten minutes later and handed Buchanan his phone.

'Better call spider woman.'

'Good luck.'

Buchanan winked at Street and put his index finger to his lips as he dialled the chief's number 'Yes, Ma'am. No, I'm in Newhaven. Yes, be in your office at nine.'

'Was she upset, sir?'

Buchanan shook his head. 'Doesn't make sense. We've only been out of France five hours and she says someone has filed a complaint against me for beating them up.'

'Do you think Abosa recognised us and has made a complaint to the French police?'

'Must be – but how? Unless he was pretending to be unconscious. Nah, that doesn't make any sense, either.'

19

'What are you going to tell her, sir?' asked Street, as they drove along the A27.

'Let's see what she asks first.'

♦

'When I agreed to take you on,' began Atkins, 'it was with the proviso that you kept your nose clean, stayed out of trouble and earned your keep. What on earth possessed you to do such a thing?'

'It was sort of self-defence, Ma'am. I had to hit him before he saw me.'

'That's not what the complaint says,' she said, picking up a report from her desk. '*I was minding my own business when the officer started asking questions. He then called me a bloody Gippo and punched me in the face.*'

'What? Let me see that.'

Atkins passed the copy of the complaint to Buchanan.

'This is bloody nonsense, a complete fabrication.'

'There are witnesses,' said Atkins.

'Liars, all of them.'

'Explain?'

'It's about Street, Ma'am.'

'What's she got to do with it?'

'She was missing, Ma'am, and I went to look for her.'

Atkins shook her head. 'I wanted you here this morning to respond to a complaint of physical violence. In the complaint you are accused of trying to make a witness confess to a crime by beating a submission out of them, and now you're blaming Street?'

Buchanan sat back in his chair, cocked his head, and shook it slowly. 'I've no idea what you're referring to, Ma'am.'

'Read the report, it's all there in black and white,' she said.

'But this is all nonsense; I wasn't even in the country when this is supposed to have taken place.'

'What are you talking about, Buchanan?'

'I was in France yesterday. The ferry didn't dock till after nine last night, two hours after this incident was supposed to have taken place. Where did it happen?' he said looking back through the complaint. 'Out back of the Black Rider Pub. Where's that?'

'Just down the road from Greyspear's stables, sir.'

'Look at this, Street. Does he look familiar?'

'He's the one I pushed over the rail at Jukes. Got that pretty face from someone in the crowd, Ma'am, it definitely wasn't the inspector who did that to him.'

'Would one of you please explain what is going on?'

'I think you may remember I went out on Saturday evening with Alice; she works at the Harbour House restaurant,' explained Street. 'While in Jukes I had my drink spiked. I don't remember much after that. PC Hunter was outside, he videoed me coming out of the club with two men. One of them was the person whose face is in this report. I pushed him over the railing and someone in the crowd beat him up for pushing in.'

'I told DS Street she should take a couple of days off to recuperate.'

'What were you doing in France?'

'Inspector Buchanan suggested I spend a couple of days with his wife.'

'But why did *you* have to go to France, Buchanan?'

'My wife called to say that when she arrived at the ferry terminal to collect DS Street, she wasn't there. That's why I took the next ferry over, to look for DS Street.'

'There's more to it than that, isn't there, Buchanan?'

Buchanan recounted the previous day's events in Dieppe.

'Well, it doesn't look like your Abosa was involved in this complaint – you had him tied to a mechanic in Dieppe at the time.'

'Hopefully he's now in a French cell. Could you check, ma'-am? See if we can have a word with him?'

'There may be a delay in that now the French police are involved. I'm afraid we are way down the pecking order.'

'But this is a murder investigation.'

'I'll see what I can do. I'll have a word with Border Control; with all the people trafficking going on, I'm sure they have direct contacts with Interpol. In the meantime, what's next?'

'I've got to catch up with Hunter and Dexter.'

'You need to wrap this up soon, Buchanan. It's getting very messy.'

'Yes, Ma'am.'

'If the French authorities still have Abosa, I'll get them to hold him. Where will you be?'

'Hammonds Drive, Ma'am. I want to hear what Hunter and Dexter found out yesterday. I sent them back to the Marina and then on to Greyspear's stables.'

'Good work, Buchanan. Keep me posted, and no more surprises, please.'

'Oh, Ma'am, if the French still have Abosa, it might be helpful if they search his phone and do a trace on where it's been. We might be able to match his whereabouts with the killings.'

'Good idea, Street.'

♦

Buchanan grabbed a coffee and headed to the incident room.

'Afternoon, sir.'

'Afternoon, Hunter. Well, what's got you so pleased with yourself?'

'As you asked, Dexter and I went to the Marina yesterday morning. We looked at where the girl –'

222

'Olga. She has a name,' interrupted Street.

'Yes, where Olga was found.'

'Find anything?'

'Sorry, sir, no. We also had a look at where DS Nichols' car had been parked, but all we found was an old pair of rubber gloves – the type mechanics use.'

'Did you bag them?'

'Yes, sir. Sent them to forensics first thing this morning.'

'Good. Anything else?'

'We were luckier in the boat repair yard.'

'Go on.'

'It was Morris's idea. We went into the repair shop and asked if anyone had been working on a boat next to where DS Nichols had been parked.'

'This where you found the gloves?'

'Yes. We thought we were going to draw a blank till one of the mechanics told us that he remembered working on a boat out on the hard – that's what they call the area beside the water where boats are stored. He'd been given the job of removing one of the propellers from a power boat. He fitted the propeller extractor and had to use a blow torch to get it off.'

'It's a club hammer we're looking for.'

'I know, sir. The mechanic said the propeller was on so tight he had to use the blowtorch to warm the propeller, then hit the extractor with a hammer to get it off the shaft. He'd been working on it for about twenty minutes when it just popped off, hitting him in the face. He dropped his tools and the propeller and dashed into the office for first aid. Apparently the cut on his face was so bad he needed to go to the A&E for stitches.'

'What about his tools and the propeller?'

'One of the other mechanics went out and picked up the propeller and the extractor, but didn't think to look for the hammer, so it lay on the ground for a couple of days. When the mechanic returned to work he noticed his hammer was missing and went out to look for it.'

'And did he find it?'

'No, sir. Someone else had, and handed it in.'

'Did they say who?'

'No.'

'Well, where is it now?'

'Tagged, bagged, and off to forensics as soon as I got back to the office. I put a rush on the request, should get the results sometime today.'

'Well done, you two. That's what I like to hear: three murders and so far three murder methods.'

'Excuse me, sir?'

'Olga drowned while on the *Moonstone*, Nichols with the hammer, and I suppose we could say Ilka and a pair of hands.'

'Doesn't really fit the pattern of a serial killer, does it?'

'No, Hunter, it doesn't.'

'Sir, then it looks like we have three separate murders and murderers?'

'You could look at it that way, Dexter.'

'Or it could be someone covering their tracks?'

'What are you saying, Hunter?'

'I once read an Agatha Christie novel where three people were killed at random.'

'The ABC murders?' said Street.

'That's the one, Jill. The killer murdered three people at random, and then when the fourth was killed everyone assumed that it was part of the same bizarre pattern, when in reality the fourth was the intended victim all along and the other three were just diversions.'

'Is that what you think, Hunter?'

'Yes, sir, it's the only thing that makes sense.'

'So we wait for a fourth murder and ignore the first three?'

'No, sir. We need to keep investigating the first three, especially if it's the same killer.'

'Good to hear that, Dexter. What did you two find out when you went to Greyspear's stables?'

'Nothing. We asked in the stable blocks, the café, and the office but both got the impression that everyone was protecting Sir Nathan.'

Buchanan nodded his head in agreement. 'Well, it looks like we have two strands to this investigation. Strand one, is the trafficking angle. Abosa seems to be the link between eastern Europe and the UK and with Interpol now involved that part is out of our hands.'

'Any suspects for this side of the channel, sir?'

'Not that we can go to court on, Dexter. I have a couple of suitable candidates, but I would rather keep that information to myself for the moment.'

'As gruesome as it sounds, sir, if we are to assume that there could be a fourth victim, can you think of who it might be? That way we could set up protection for them.'

'Interesting concept, Hunter, but I think there may be too many suitable candidates for that to be feasible.'

'What is strand two, sir?'

'Strand two, Street, is I think the trafficking angle could be more complex than it first seems. Olga's murder could be trafficking related. Nichols is connected in some way, and Ilka's murder was because we were getting too close to what Abosa was up to. If we are successful in tracing Abosa's mobile and it shows he was in the country at the time – then I think we are well on our way to solving that last death.'

'Also, there is the chance that forensics will get a DNA sample from the blood on Ilka's teeth to match Abosa's. But why kill Olga, sir? Lots of young girls get pregnant and aren't married.'

'You know so little about people trafficking, Dexter. Let me explain as best as I can. People traffickers are no better than the

225

Atlantic slave traders. Instead of rounding up men, women and children like cattle, as did the early slavers, the modern slavers entice their eastern European victims with promises of a better life in the UK. They are promised transportation, work, and accommodation when they arrive. What they are not told is they will be smuggled, like packages of contraband, into the country, their passports confiscated, wages withheld and in most cases their lives are threatened with death if they complain.'

'Surely, they could just go to the police, sir?'

'You would think so, Dexter. But these people are so traumatised into submission that they daren't. Also, some of them may still have family back home who could be harmed.'

'But that still doesn't explain why Olga was killed.'

'Possibly the traffickers saw her as a liability and were going to lose money on her,' said Hunter, and maybe Olga got pregnant by Abosa and she refused to have an abortion, so he killed her.'

'That doesn't work, Hunter. Remember Abosa wasn't on the *Moonstone*.'

'He could have got on board as it passed the bridge. Dexter and I had a look when we were down at the harbour yesterday. The gap is about ten metres wide, only two metres wider than the *Moonstone*; it would have been easy for a fit person to have jumped on board, killed Olga, then slipped away unseen when the *Moonstone* tied up.'

'But how could Abosa know that Olga would be standing outside waiting for him, sir?' asked Street.

'Hopefully by now the French police will have him in custody and we will be able to ask him.'

♦

Buchanan picked up the ringing phone. 'Buchanan. Yes, Ma'am, they did? Great — when can we talk to him? We can't? Why?' Buchanan shook his head and replaced the receiver.

'The chief, sir?'

'Yes, lass, that was the chief.'

'But what's wrong, sir? Won't the gendarmes let us question him?'

'Unfortunately, not. You saw the gendarmes arrive as we left. They found Abosa and the mechanic tied up as we had left them. Turns out that Abosa is known to the French police and they already have his DNA on record. The chief has asked them to send the details through to our lab for comparison. No word yet on the phone trace.'

'So we will be able to find out if he was the father of Olga's baby.'

'Precisely, lass. Talking of phone traces, have you had any word on Nichols' phone?'

'Nothing yet, I'll get on to it.'

Street went to pick up her phone when it rang, 'DS Street. You have? Didn't expect it so soon, by all means send it through. You've got my email address? Good.'

'Who was that, lass?'

'The lab. They've completed the DNA testing and are emailing through the results after they have compared Abosa's with the other samples. Maybe we'll have the answer to the baby's paternity within half an hour.'

'Great stuff. While we wait, anyone hungry?'

♦

The pizzas arrived as Street printed off the lab results.

'So Abosa wasn't the baby's father. Disappointed, sir?' asked Hunter.

'I'm never disappointed with positive results.'

'So now we're back to suspecting Greyspear being the father?' asked Dexter.

'Not now we've got the DNA results, Dexter; though that doesn't exclude him from the killer list.'

'What about the hammer? Whose DNA is on it?' asked Street.

'The mechanic's, Nichols', and one other, not identifiable from the samples we supplied.'

'Greyspear could have worn those gloves that Dexter and Hunter found, sir.'

'Was there anything else on the hammer, lass?'

Street re-read the report and shook her head.

'Street, get back on to forensics and ask them to check their results of the third DNA on the hammer, see if it matches the samples from the coat Olga was wearing.'

'That doesn't make sense, sir. Olga was dead before Nichols.'

'I know, lass, but the person who owned the coat wasn't.'

'Are you thinking Dan's a suspect again, sir? You think he killed Nichols?'

'It's possible, lass; he certainly had the opportunity, though I'm not sure what the motive would have been. I wonder if we check his schedule we'll find he was on duty the night Nichols died.'

'So instead of him waving goodbye to Olga,' said Hunter, 'he jumped on board the *Moonstone*, waited till they got to the bridge, then when he saw she was unconscious, he got angry, pushed her into the harbour, jumped onto the bridge and legged it back to the office. But what reason would he have to kill Nichols, sir?'

'Who knows, Hunter? It's just possible when Nichols found out that Olga was pregnant and had been trafficked into the country, he felt sorry for her. Dan got jealous, argued with Olga, and killed her. Then with Nichols breathing down his neck he arranged to meet him in the Marina.'

'Maybe Nichols was blackmailing him, sir?'

'A possibility, Hunter. Street, add to the list we need to check his bank details. Dan arranges to meet Nichols and sees him – possibly he was snoozing in the car – then sees the hammer, and we know the rest.'

'Sir, that would only work if the DNA on the hammer matched Dan's.'

'I know. Anything more from the lab, lass?'

'They're very busy, said they will have the results to us by tomorrow morning.'

'But what about the girl in the wood – Ilka?'

'Good question, Dexter. Maybe when Olga died Ilka got suspicious and asked one question too many.'

Street looked at the clock and yawned.

'I agree, lass,' said Buchanan. 'Right, I want to see all of you back here tomorrow morning at seven. Hopefully by this time tomorrow we will have made an arrest.'

20

'Morning, sir.'

'Morning, lass, where's Dexter and Hunter?'

'Stopped at Cavendish Bakery for cakes, it's Dexter's birthday.'

'Any word from forensics?'

'I'll give them a call.'

Street put down the phone, a smile on her face. 'A match, sir; the DNA on the hammer handle matches the samples taken from the coat.'

'That's what I like to hear, Street, let's go see what Dan has to say for himself. Call Dexter and Hunter, tell them to get a move on, we've an arrest to make. Tell them to meet us at the harbour office.'

'Suppose he's not at work, sir?'

'Call the harbour office and ask if he's there. If he answers, say we've something that we need him to identify.'

'OK.'

Buchanan drummed his fingers on his desk as Street called the Marina.

'Well?'

'He called in sick this morning, and he's not answering his phone. Want to know something else?'

'Try me.'

'Maria didn't come home last night.'

'Do you think they're seeing each other?'

'Possibly. She spends a lot of time on her mobile, never says who she's talking with.'

'Call her, see if she's answering her phone. Just tell her you're worried about her.'

'I am, as a matter of fact,' said Street as she picked up her phone and dialled.

Buchanan shuffled through the DNA test reports while he waited for Street to get off the phone with Maria.

'Well, what'd she say?'

'She was with him, at his place. She says he wants to help her find Olga's killer. She seems to think he thinks he knows who the killer is.'

'What was her response when you said Dan should come and talk with us?'

'She said they'd take care of it between them, it was a family matter.'

'Right, call Dexter and Hunter, and have them get Dan's home address and pick him up. We're not having any family vendettas fought out here in Eastbourne.'

♦

The uniformed PC closed the interview room door behind them. Buchanan sat in the chair facing Dan; Street took a seat beside him on the right, across from Mr Woodrow, Dan's solicitor.

'Mr Angelino, you have been informed of your rights. Are you warm enough? I can get the heating turned on if you're cold.'

'I'm fine.'

'Would you like a drink? I understand the coffee here in Hammonds Drive is quite drinkable.'

'No.'

'Do you know why you've been arrested?'

'No, of course not.'

'Your full name is Daniel Angelino; you're employed by Sovereign Marina Services as lock-keeper?'

'Yes.'

'You were on duty the night of the 29th March?'

'If you say so.'

'I'm now showing Mr Angelino a copy of the duty roster for the evening of the 29th of March. Mr Angelino, is this your name on the roster?'

'Yes.'

'What time did you go off duty?'

'Don't remember.'

'Once again I show Mr Angelino the duty roster for the 29th and 30th of March. Are these your initials indicating that you were scheduled to go off duty at midnight on the 30th of March?'

'Yes.'

'I'm now showing Mr Angelino a copy of the lock movements. Is this your handwriting indicating that the motor yacht *Moonstone* went out at nine-thirty am on the 29th of March?'

'No, that's Ted's handwriting. He was on duty till we took over at four pm.'

'We, Mr Angelino?'

'There are always at least two of us on duty through the night; Harry was with me till he had to leave early.'

'Thank you, Mr Angelino. You say you came on duty at four pm?'

'Yes.'

'And you went off at duty at midnight am on the 30th March?'

'Yes, well as I told you earlier, Harry left early and I waited for George.'

'Do you remember what time the *Moonstone* returned?'

'It will be in the log.'

'Yes, I know it will; I wanted to know if you remembered.'

'Inspector, the policeman was killed on the 8th of April. Why are you badgering my client about something that happened days earlier? Any judge would disallow this line of questioning.'

'Mr Woodrow, I will come to that, and may I remind you that in here I ask the questions. Mr Angelino, my question was, do you remember when the *Moonstone* returned?'

'About midnight.'

'Twelve thirty-five, according to your entry in the log.'

'So?'

'Tell me, when boats enter the locks at night, do you just let them through into the harbour?'

'No, not always.'

'Are you saying you sometimes you just let them through without checking to see if they belong in the harbour?'

'No, that's not how it happens.'

'Then please tell us how it happens.'

'If they are regulars, boats that are berthed in the Marina, we just let them through. We monitor VHF channel 17. Boats call us on that channel before they arrive at the lock, that way we know who's arriving before they get here. All the regulars know the drill.'

'And just what is the drill, and how do non-regulars know what to do?'

'It's standard procedure for all yachts to call the harbour on the VHF radio.'

'Even foreign ones?' asked Buchanan.

'Yes. When they arrive at the open lock gates, they motor forward slowly till they either reach the far end of the lock, or the last boat in front of them.'

'What happens next?'

'They tie up to the pontoon and wait for the gates to close and the lock to either fill or lower to the same level as the inner harbour.'

'What's the procedure for visiting yachts?'

'When they have tied up to the pontoon one of us will go down into the lock and take the details of the vessel and crew.'

'Go down? What do you mean?'

'Climb down the ladder and onto the pontoon float.'

'Inspector, once again, I must ask where your line of questioning is going?'

'Please be patient, Mr Woodrow. Mr Angelino, in the early hours of the 30th of March, you logged the *Moonstone* in to the lock. Did you go down into the lock and on to the pontoon and get the details of the crew and boat?'

'Don't need to, I know them all.'

'Let me rephrase my question. Did you go down into the lock, walk along the pontoon to the back of the *Moonstone* to talk to someone?'

'Inspector, I must insist you come to the point of your questioning.'

'Mr Woodrow, I must insist you refrain from interrupting and permit me to proceed with the interview. Mr Angelino, who did you go down into the lock to talk to?'

'You already know that.'

'Yes, but for the record, would you tell us again?'

'I went down to talk to Olga.'

'Olga Tratas?'

'Yes.'

'Did you know she was pregnant?'

'Yes.'

'Were you the father of her child?'

'You know I wasn't.'

'That was for the record, Mr Angelino. Was she standing on the back deck of the *Moonstone?* Was she waiting for you?'

'No, I mean yes. She wasn't waiting for me; I saw her leaning on the stern rail.'

'Did you talk to her?'

'Sort of.'

'What do you mean, *sort of?*'

'She was drunk, didn't make any sense. Kept on saying she was going to sort the bastard.'

'Do you think she was planning an abortion?'

'Unlikely, I think she was a Catholic.'

'And she got pregnant out of wedlock?'

234

'I'm not a church goer, I don't understand these things.'

'What do you think she meant by her outburst, then?'

'I think she meant to get even with the father by keeping the child. I got the impression that if the child was revealed as his, it would cause great embarrassment to him She said he was quite wealthy.'

'Did you climb on board the *Moonstone* and continue with your attempt to get her to talk? And when she wouldn't, as the *Moonstone* approached the drawbridge did you get angry with her and push her into the harbour? As the *Moonstone* passed the bridge abutment did you jump off and make your way back to the harbour office?'

'No. How could I kill her? I loved her?'

'Mr Angelino, did you kill Olga Tratas?'

'No.'

'Did she fall in, Mr Angelino? Perhaps you tried to grab her but missed? Maybe you saw her slip under the surface. Then you panicked and jumped onto the bridge abutment? You may have had a torch with you? You scanned the surface but there was no sign of her. You were going to get help, but realised you might be blamed for her death, so you said and did nothing?'

'No. I loved her, I wanted to take care of her, protect her from those who harmed her. Now it's too late.'

'Interview suspended at eleven thirty, due to interviewee being too emotional to continue.'

♦

Street passed Buchanan his coffee. 'Bit rough with him, sir.'

'Needs must, lass.'

'You still think he's guilty of killing Olga and Nichols?'

'That's up to the jury; all we do is collect the evidence and present it to the CPS.'

'This is a continuation of the interview dated sixth of May, with Daniel Angelino. Mr Angelino, were you interviewed by a DS Nichols?'

'Don't know the name, but yes if that was his name, I was interviewed by him.'

'Do you remember what questions he asked you?'

'Why don't you read his report? He wrote it all down.'

'Mr Angelino, I was asking you about your memory of the events.'

'He asked me if I knew Olga, and when was the last time I talked to her.'

'What was your reply?'

'I said the last time was when the *Moonstone* came through the locks. I said I'd tried to talk to her but couldn't get any sense from her. Why do you have to go over this again?'

'As I said earlier, it's for the record.'

'Don't expect me to buy a copy.'

'I will now move to the night of the 8th of April. Were you on duty that night?'

'Don't remember, I'd need to check the duty roster.'

'I'm showing Mr Angelino a copy of the lock-keeper's duty roster and indicating the night of the 7th of April. Is this your name shown as being on duty between four pm on the 7th and four am the 8th of April?'

'Yes.'

'Was it a quiet night?'

'Don't remember, have a look at the log.'

'I'm showing Mr Angelino a copy of the harbour movements log for the morning of the 8th of April. How many boats went through the lock between midnight and four am?'

'One.'

'At what time?'

'Three am.'

'And the name of this boat?'

'*Sally B*, it's a fishing boat.'

'Did you go down and talk to the crew?'

'No, they're foreigners, don't speak much English.'

'What do you mean by foreigners? Are they illegals?'

'No, they live here; they're eastern European, keep to themselves.'

'Do you ever go for a walk round the Marina at night?'

'Sometimes. Mostly if it's quiet, I carry the radio. If I'm needed I can get straight back to the office. I like to check for boats that might be in trouble: we had two sink at the dock last year.'

'Did you go out for a walk on the morning of the 8th?'

'Not that I remember.'

'You don't remember having a meeting with DS Nichols?'

'No, why would I? He knew where to find me.'

'I'm now showing Mr Angelino police exhibit, *SR2 Sovereign Ilka*. Do you recognise this hammer?'

'No. Looks just like any other hammer.'

'But it's not just any hammer. Can you explain how this one has your DNA on the handle?

Interviewee is shrugging no. So, you don't know how your DNA has come to be found on the handle?'

'I – just a minute – may I look at it? I think I do remember.'

'Don't take it out of the bag, please.'

'See these initials AS carved on the end of the handle? They're Andy Smart's. The guys in the shop are always ribbing him about that. A few days after your policeman was removed from the harbour, I was walking back from the Yacht Club to the office when I saw the hammer lying in the grass under one of the boats. I picked it up, saw the initials, and handed it in to the workshop.'

'Who did you hand it to?'

'Matt. Ask him – we had a joke about it.'

'And you had not made any arrangements to meet DS Nichols?'

'No, definitely not.'

'Interview terminated at three-fifteen.'

♦

'Did you believe him, sir?'

'It's possible he's telling the truth, but I think we'll hold onto him for twenty-four hours, let him have time to think things over.'

'Not much we can check.'

'His handing in the hammer, we can.'

'What's next, sir?'

'I had planned to go see Greyspear tomorrow, but his office says he is away till Sunday.'

'Did they say where he had gone to?'

'Fécamp, it's a coastal town on the north coast of France.'

'He'd have gone through Dieppe to get there, wouldn't he – wait a minute, you don't think he's gone to see Abosa, do you?'

21

The taxi slowed for a group of horses at the gates to Greyspear's stables, turned onto the driveway and accelerated. The driver immediately slowed at the sound of gravel being thrown up from the driveway peppering the underside. It stopped in front of the steps to the café and stable management office. Buchanan paid the fare, entered the building, and climbed the steps to the office.

'Can I help?' asked the secretary.

'Yes, I'd like a word with Sir Nathan, please; his butler said he'd be here today.'

'Do you have an appointment?'

'No.'

'I recognise you; you're that nosy policeman who was asking questions about Sir Nathan.'

'Well, now we know who's who, will you let Sir Nathan know I'm here?'

She plugged in her headset, pressed a key on her keyboard, and waited. 'Sorry to bother you sir, that policeman is back. Yes – I'll tell him.' She turned to Buchanan. 'Sir Nathan is in a meeting and can't be disturbed. He asks that you be patient and he will be with you as soon as he can.'

'No problem, I'm a patient man, and it *is* Sunday.'

'Sir Nathan also said if you go through to the club room you'll be made comfortable. I'm to let them know you're Sir Nathan's guest. He also wanted to know if you can stay for lunch?'

'As I said, it is Sunday. Tell him thank you, I'd love to have lunch with him. Oh, where's the club room?'

'Sorry, I forget you're *just* a visitor. Go through that door,' she said, indicating to a door on her right, 'along the corridor and it will take you into the club reception. Sign in as a guest at the desk and the bar is through the door on your right.'

'You know, I feel so welcomed every time I visit, I might just become a regular visitor.'

'Oh, sorry, having a bad day?'

'That's all right, we all have those, see you later.'

Lunch hadn't been on Buchanan's mind when he'd driven out that morning; he'd seen the weather forecast and decided a walk across the Downs would have been preferable.

He walked through the door and into what he expected would be a corridor. In fact, it reminded him of the one time he'd been invited to a police reception in the long room at Lords. Though not as opulent as that great room itself, this room had its walls festooned with pictures of horses going through their paces. He recognised the picture of Sir Nathan on horseback as they jumped over a fence at an event. He looked closer and saw by the label the event was at Badminton. Impressed, Buchanan walked on down the hall glancing at photographs and paintings of former champion horses. He stopped at a picture of two riders receiving awards at a dressage event. It was of Deborah Silverstein and Ayesha Bashir.

As he entered the bar he was met by the manager.

'Inspector Buchanan, how nice to meet you. Reception has called through and said to make you welcome. The members' bar is through here, if you'll come this way,' he said, guiding Buchanan by the elbow.

Buchanan chose an armchair by the window and waited for the waiter to bring him his whiskey. He picked up a copy of *Yachting Monthly* and flicked through the pages. His eyes settled on an article about the new Greyspear sailboat. The article said it had been adapted from an original design by the American designer, Herreshoff. Buchanan knew little about sailboats, but he was impressed by the 105-foot yacht's ability to carry seven guests in absolute comfort anywhere in the world; it even sported a varnished wooden bathtub.

He sat through two whiskeys and a coffee before the bar manager came over with the message that Greyspear was finished with his meeting and would the inspector return to the office.

The door to the office opened and Jacqueline Masterson came out followed by Greyspear. To Buchanan's observation they had been arguing, Masterson pocketed a tissue, shook her head, and left. When Greyspear saw Buchanan, his look of anger turned into a smile.

'Inspector! Sorry to have kept you waiting. I hope we've been looking after you?'

'I'm fine, thanks, been working on some loose ends.'

'I hear you've arrested someone for one of the deaths in the Marina?'

'We do have someone in custody.'

'Assisting you with your enquiries?'

'You could say that.'

'What about the policeman? And the girl in the woods?'

'They are ongoing investigations, sir.'

'Is that why you're here?'

'Partially; thought I'd take the morning off and see how the other half lives.'

'It's Sunday, Inspector. Most people have the whole day off – you know, the day of rest. Where's your wife? You should have brought her with you.'

'She went to church.'

'And you didn't?'

'Nah, it's not for me.'

'You surprise me. I'd have thought that a man who deals with life and death for a living would want to keep in with the man above.'

'Not everyone is investigating a triple murder, sir. Can you remember where you were on the morning of the 24th of April?'

'Not without consulting my diary.'

'And where is your diary?'

'Where it always is; back in the office in the Marina.'

'Is there anyone in the office this morning, sir?'

'No, Inspector, there isn't. But I don't need to go there; my diary is linked to my phone.'

Greyspear took his phone from his pocket and swiped the screen with his thumb a few times. 'The 24th you said? I was in my office till three in the afternoon and then I came out here to meet someone.'

'Who were you meeting, sir?'

'Not so much a meeting, Inspector. I came out here with my PA to discuss stable matters; I was making arrangements for my new horse to be stabled here.'

'New horse? How many horses do you have?'

'Personally, with Moonbeam, I have three of my own. The stables has, I believe, about ten horses available for the public to ride, and the rest are privately-owned horses that are stabled here. I would say there are about forty all told.'

'Why three horses?'

'Moonraker is getting on and struggles with the cross-country events, so I've bought a new horse to take his place, and Wallace is too old to ride, I keep him for sentimental reasons. Would you like to see Moonbeam?'

Buchanan looked at his watch.

'Inspector, it's Sunday. Relax.'

Buchanan walked round to the stable block with Greyspear, noticing the suspicious looks from the stable lads as he was introduced.

As they walked down the row of boxes occasionally a horse would neigh at the sound of Greyspear's voice. Greyspear would stop, scratch the offered forehead, and feed the horse a piece of carrot from his pocket. There was no mistaking Moonbeam, though. From a distance Buchanan saw, sticking well out from the stall, a horse craning its neck, looking eagerly at the approaching humans. His ears forward, forefoot banging at the stable door, it was as if he was trying to say 'Hurry up – where's my treat?'

'That's him, Inspector. The new member of my family – Moonbeam.'

Greyspear scratched Moonbeam's offered forehead, breathed into his nostrils, and fed him his much anticipated treat. 'I was planning to go for a ride this morning. Care to join me?'

Caught off guard, Buchanan didn't know what to say.

'Come on, Inspector, just a short ride. Then we can have lunch and you can ask all those questions that have been bothering you.'

'Haven't been on a horse in years, and I'm not really dressed for the occasion.'

'No problem, we keep freshly-laundered jodhpurs, riding jackets and boots for special visitors. I'm sure there will be a suitable set for you.'

Buchanan stood in front of the mirror, looked at his reflection, and grinned. The years may have passed, his waist filled out a little; but he still cut a fine figure in riding gear. He left the dressing room and went out into the stable yard.

Greyspear was talking with one of the lads. 'Inspector, Hans has just brought Mercury out for you; he's ready and raring to go.'

Buchanan looked at Mercury, all eighteen hands of rippling muscles. The winged messenger – would he be bringing any messages today, he wondered.

'Don't worry, Inspector, he's as tame as a puppy. Here, put this treat in your pocket and observe.'

Buchanan walked over to Mercury and stopped in front of him. He was concerned: Mercury's ears were twitching, eyes summing him up. The horse sniffed the air in front of him and then breathed out in Buchanan's face. He smiled and offered the back of his hand. 'Hello, boy.' Mercury looked down, sniffed at his hand, looked away, then bent and nudged his pocket. Buchanan reached into it, taking out the piece of carrot

Greyspear had given him. 'There, boy, there, we're going to be friends. We're just going for a short ride.'

Mercury snorted, shook his head and whinnied.

'Ready, Inspector? Your ride certainly is.'

Buchanan gathered the reins, put his foot in the stirrup and mounted Mercury. It wasn't quite like riding a bike, but he remembered to keep his hands low and close to his body, back straight, balls of his feet in the stirrups and his heels down.

They trotted out of the yard, past the café, the outdoor riding ring and on to a wide grassy boulevard. He was amazed at how much he remembered from his youthful days of riding out at Hazledean stables. Though it was thirty years since he last rode, Buchanan tried to relax and soon realised he needed days like this. He walked Mercury behind Moonbeam till they were clear of the stables then they trotted across the service road to the edge of tree-lined boulevard.

Greyspear stopped. 'How is it, Inspector? Like riding a bike?'

'Not quite, this saddle is a bit wider than the last bike I rode.'

Greyspear turned Moonbeam to the left and trotted off along the grassy boulevard. One hundred yards along, the boulevard swept in a gentle curve to the left. Greyspear stopped and waited for Buchanan.

'How are you doing, Inspector?'

'Getting there, but I think I'm confusing the horse with erroneous signals.'

Greyspear watched as Buchanan approached, 'Slacken the reins a bit, you're tugging on the horse's mouth.'

'Of course, should have realised. As I said, it's been a while since I rode.'

'We have a choice of trails to follow,' said Greyspear. 'There's one that goes into the forest, bit dark and gloomy, not much to see. The other —'

'The other is — what?'

'I was going to say, the other one heads out over the fields. Which do you fancy?'

Buchanan thought about riding through the forest: low branches, fallen trees, the inevitable ruts in the track, and possibly wild animals scaring the horses. 'What's the fields ride like?'

'Boring: it's the cross-country course. Mercury knows it well – it's just tracks alongside open fields.'

'I think I would like to be bored today.'

'OK, it's your choice. Follow me,' said Greyspear, as he set off at a canter.

Buchanan was caught off guard. As Moonbeam took off, Mercury followed, almost unseating him. In spite of Mercury's sudden departure, Buchanan managed to hang on and regain his balance. He realised that although he was in the saddle with the reins in his hand, Mercury was definitely in charge. He remembered a horse at Jock's stable that used to inflate its belly while an unsuspecting rider was saddling up and tightening the girth strap. Then, much to the animal's maligned sense of humour, at the most inopportune moment for the rider; it would take delight in deflating its belly, letting the saddle slide sidewise unshipping the rider.

Within ten lengths Mercury had caught up with Moonbeam, and, to Buchanan's horror, he realised they were reaching the end of the boulevard and Greyspear showed no sign of slowing the pace. He panicked; there was a tractor blocking the road. Greyspear turned his head and laughed. 'Follow me,' he shouted, swerving Moonbeam to the left and straight at a hedge Buchanan mentally pushed the brake pedal. *Stupid bugger, you're on a horse.* Mercury followed and side by side they flew over the hedge.

Greyspear turned and laughed again. 'Not so difficult when you let the horse do the thinking, eh Inspector?'

Buchanan ignored the jibe and concentrated on regaining his balance, hoping Hans had done up the girth strap tight enough. Then he gathered the reins and settled into the chase. He soon realised he was along for the ride. No matter how he gently tried to control Mercury, the horse ignored his signals and happily kept a length behind Moonbeam.

Greyspear looked to see how Buchanan was faring. 'Still hanging in there, Inspector?'

Buchanan looked up in time to see the next obstacle – a five-bar gate – looming in the distance.

'Relax, Inspector, just a bit of fun,' shouted Greyspear.

Fun? It's not your neck you're risking! Just what the hell are you up to, Sir Nathan? Before Buchanan had time to contemplate an answer they had arrived at the gate. He tensed then relaxed. Mercury knew the ropes – to hell with Greyspear and his joke.

Once again both horses flew over the gate, but this time Mercury landed first by half a length. The sun peeked over the horizon and Buchanan took in a deep breath. He'd become one with Mercury. He leaned forward and whispered into the horse's ear, 'Right, lad, let's show that pompous toad what real riding is all about! Let's go!' and he squeezed Mercury's flanks.

It was all Mercury needed; he was ready to show the upstart Moonbeam he still had a good gallop left in him. Within fifty feet Mercury was two lengths ahead and extending his lead with every pace.

'Inspector, hold on!' shouted Greyspear.

'Didn't think you'd like to lose,' mumbled Buchanan, as he encouraged Mercury on. He now realised Mercury had a score to settle with Moonbeam, and he wasn't about to back off.

They took the corner at the end of the field, Mercury ten lengths ahead, and raced up the hill.

'Inspector!' yelled Greyspear, 'hold up!'

Not bloody likely, I'm enjoying this, thought Buchanan.

By now Mercury was a good twenty lengths ahead of Greyspear, and no fences, hedges or five-bar gates in sight. At the top of the hill Mercury turned sharply to the left, but Buchanan sailed straight on. He landed hard, rolled twenty feet, and was arrested by the bottom strand of a rusty barbed-wire fence. Had the barbed wire not grabbed him, he would now be splattered on rocks in an abandoned chalk quarry.

Greyspear arrived moments later, dismounted and ran over. 'Inspector, are you all right?'

Buchanan lay still, contemplating. Why hadn't Greyspear warned him in time? He must have known the quarry was here.

'You knew he'd do that, didn't you?'

'I did shout a warning – not my fault if you ignore it. You can't see the quarry as you come up the hill. Thankfully Mercury turned away in time.'

You could say that, I would think differently, thought Buchanan.

They returned an hour later, horses steaming after the competitive ride across the open fields that enclosed the golf course. Buchanan dismounted and staggered for a moment, almost falling on his backside.

Greyspear chuckled. 'Inspector, you need more excitement in your life, sitting seven days in a chair makes one's legs weak.'

Buchanan laughed at Greyspear's attempt at humour; more excitement was just not what he needed. He looked at his watch and saw it was ten past one.

'Relax, Inspector, it's Sunday, the day of rest. Or don't policemen get to rest?'

'Not when there are three murders waiting to be solved.'

'Don't worry, Inspector, we've still got plenty of time for lunch. Why don't you shower and change? The lads will rub down the horses.'

♦

The waitress showed them through to a table by the window overlooking the practice putting green. When they were seated, she asked, 'Can I get you something from the bar, sir?'

'Drink, Inspector?'

'Whiskey, no ice.'

'I'll have the same, Janette, and make them doubles.' He nodded to Buchanan. 'Play golf, Inspector?'

Buchanan shook his head. 'Not my style.'

'You've obviously ridden before. Where'd you learn?'

'When I was a teenager, I had a part-time job after school and weekends helping at a local stable. I would exercise the horses when the owners couldn't. Got to ride quite an eclectic bunch of horses.'

'Where was it?'

'Busby.'

'Really? Whereabouts in Busby?'

'You turn off the East Kilbride Road and on to Field Road. When you get to the end you go over the bridge and it's on the right. I seem to remember it had stables for about thirty horses and a couple of exercise rings. Of course the beauty of the place was the availability of the country lanes and, at the right time of the year, the open fields for jumping and grazing.'

'That's bizarre. Was it run by a Jock Anderson?'

'Yes. Did you know him?'

'He's still around – must be pushing ninety now.'

'How'd you know him?'

'When I was setting up the stables here at Castlewood, I saw his advertisement selling some horses in the *Horse and Hound*. I drove up from Eastbourne, looked at the horses, and bought a couple. They were young horses he'd brought on, beautiful animals, well looked after.'

'Yes, he does have a reputation for getting the best out of young horses.'

'Why'd you give it up?'

'Joined the police force.'

'Mounted?'

'No, started as a PC and worked my way up to sergeant, then moved over to CID.'

'Your drinks, sir. Are you ready to order?'

'Give us a few minutes, Janette.'

Buchanan took a sip of his drink and picked up the menu.

'Don't worry about the bill, Inspector, this is on me. Or aren't you allowed to fraternise with me – a possible murder suspect?'

Buchanan looked up and smiled. 'Sir Nathan, in England you are still innocent till proved guilty.'

'Well then, let's order lunch. I'm famished.'

'And I will say to my soul: *Soul, you have many goods laid up for many years; take your ease; eat, drink and be merry.*'

'Didn't take you for a bible basher, Inspector.'

'Sunday school memory verse. They never leave you.'

'Can I suggest the salmon? I have it flown down every Friday afternoon, and it's not farmed.'

'Sounds fine to me, and I'll start with the soup,' Buchanan said to the waitress, who'd returned and was standing beside Greyspear.

'I'll have the same, Janette,' He turned to his guest. 'So, Inspector, what brought you out here on a lovely Sunday like this?'

'Good question. My mind's going round in circles with this case, I needed somewhere to think; was going to sit in the café and watch the horses in the ring.'

'And I've taken you away from all that.'

'I'm not complaining.'

'You know, Inspector, you're really good on a horse. Why don't you come out and ride regularly? Tell you what; I'll arrange a complimentary six-month membership for you.'

Buchanan shook his head.

'I know, I know, can't be seen to accept gratuities. All right then, forget the membership, come and ride Mercury any time you like, he's always needing exercise. I'll tell my head lad that you're to be allowed to ride Mercury whenever it suits you. How's that?'

'I'll think about it.'

Greyspear shook his head and grinned. 'You know something.'

'Sir Nathan, I know lots of things – that's what I'm paid for.'

The waitress placed their soup on the table.

Buchanan leaned over and inhaled. 'Tomato and orange. My wife makes this – one of my favourites.'

'How is your wife? I hear she had a bit of an adventure - something about your daughter running off with a Bulgarian jewel thief?'

'What on earth? Where did you hear that nonsense?'

'It's just a story going round the yacht club.'

'And the person you're calling my daughter is Detective Sergeant Street. We're working together on this case.'

'So, do you have children?'

Buchanan licked the last drops off his spoon, shook his head, and said, 'No, unfortunately, we've never been able to.' Putting his spoon down, he looked up and saw a fleeting glimmer of emptiness in Greyspear's eyes.

'That's two things we have in common, Inspector.'

'You've no children either?'

'No, unfortunately, in spite of being married twice.'

'Can't begin to understand what it must feel like to have lost two wives. Don't know what I'd feel, or how I'd cope, if I lost Karen.'

'You remember watching the tractor ploughing the field as we rode past earlier?'

Buchanan nodded as he took a mouthful of salmon.

'That just begins to show you how I felt when my first wife died. My life, in two short weeks, went from being like a pleasant meadow to a ripped-up field. I lost my will to do anything, tried to drink away the pain, but it just got worse. I lived in a perpetual dark fog.'

'What happened?'

Greyspear shook his head slowly. 'My wife was beautiful, both in looks and personality. We'd met at rugby match at Twickenham —'

'Were you playing?'

Greyspear nodded. 'It was an inter-services game between the navy and the army. I was playing for the army. Angela came along with the army team as a supporter. Her father was a Major; she was the team's unofficial mascot — we met in the bar after the game.'

'Did you win?'

Greyspear thought for a moment. 'We lost the game, but I won Angela's heart.'

'What happened?

'Shortly after we met, Angela's father had to retire from the army to run the family business.'

'Making toys?'

'You've done your homework. Yes, mostly plastic toys for children. Then one day, at a toy exhibition, he keeled over and died: heart attack.'

'How old was he?'

"Fifty-three; never got to experience retirement. His wife had died a few years prior, and since there wasn't anyone suitable to run the company, I resigned my commission and took over the family business. Turned out I had a flair for business and over the next three years the company trebled its turnover. I thought things couldn't get any better. I had a successful business, great home life and a wife who loved me.'

'Then?'

'Then came the day my world turned from summer to winter. Angela felt a lump. She went and saw the doctor. Tests were done — the results were devastating. The cancer had already spread. Two weeks later, on our fifth anniversary, I held her in my arms one last time and said goodbye.'

'*Shish.* Don't know what to say to that.'

'Nothing *to* say, Inspector. Once I'd climbed out of the fog, I got stuck into running the company. Expanded the line and yet again turnover and profits soared.'

'Were you still playing rugby?'

Greyspear shook his head and waited for the waitress to pour Buchanan another glass of wine. 'I got out of shape – all those long hours of running the business. Nope, I took up horse riding; unlike you, horses were new to me. Fell in love with them. What was it the cowboys used to say –'

'Well done, faithful steed?'

'I was thinking more along the lines of: *There may have been many faster horses, no doubt handsomer, but for bottom and endurance, I never saw the fellow* – Duke of Wellington about his horse, Copenhagen. I'm not that lyrical, Inspector. I just loved horses, regardless of size, shape, or temperament.'

'You said you'd been married twice?'

'I met Althea at the stables where I stabled my first horse. It was she who helped me to learn to ride. I would come over to the stables on Saturday at lunchtime, have a lesson, then go out for a ride. At first that's all there was to it. Occasionally, after the lesson, she'd come out for a ride with me. Then one Saturday I asked her out to dinner and she said yes. We were married three months later.'

'Karen and I were married within six months of us meeting. You should have heard the stories that went around when we announced our engagement.'

'They say she was expecting?'

'A cruel irony; if only the rumours had been true.'

'Can I get you another bottle, sir?'

'No thanks, Janette. I think we'll have the cheeseboard and coffee, and bring my brandy, please.'

'Yes, sir.'

'You sponsor Silverstein and Bashir's daughters?'

'A private indulgence, Inspector. Besides, they are exceptional horsewomen. Hope to see them at Badminton one day, and it's great advertising for the stables.'

'The Carstairs fly you where and when you wish?'

'Only on business, and as I said they are interested in buying an FBC40.'

'So they said.'

'Thanks, Janette, we'll be fine now, and I don't want to be disturbed. I'll let you know when we're finished.'

'If you don't mind me asking, what happened to Althea?'

'Inspector, my life would make perfect material for an Albee play. I am coming to the realisation that being a happily married man is not going to be my lot in life. As I said earlier, my first wife died from cancer; my second died in a car crash,'

'What happened – if you don't mind going over it?'

'That's all I did for years following the accident. As I said, we met at her stables – and they were *her* stables. She'd inherited them from a spinster aunt who'd raised Althea when her parents died in a yachting accident. We'd gone up to London to the Horse of the Year Show. Had a meal afterwards. We should have stayed overnight but one of the mares was foaling and Althea insisted we drive home that evening. We were hit head-on while southbound on the A23; drunk driver crossed the road on a corner. Althea was dead on arrival at the hospital; I got off with hardly a scrape.'

'How long ago was this?'

'Last Friday evening would have been our tenth anniversary and the fifth anniversary of her death.'

'I'm so sorry, I shouldn't have asked.'

Greyspear shook his head. 'Do you like cheese? How about a brandy?'

Buchanan glanced at his watch and was amazed to see it was almost three-thirty.

'You can't go yet, Inspector. You haven't heard the whole story. That's what you wanted, isn't it?'

'That's not why I came here today, and it wasn't my intention to pry so deeply into your personal affairs.'

'Nonsense, I haven't told you anything that I wouldn't tell anyone else.'

'I'm also a bit worried – I told the taxi to collect me at three o'clock, hope it's not still waiting.'

'I'm sure it's fine. Look, I'll check with the office, see if it showed up.'

Greyspear reached into his jacket for his phone. He scrolled through the directory and tapped its face. 'Who's this? Robin – it's Sir Nathan. Has there been a taxi looking for the Inspector? It did? Good – OK, thanks, I'll tell him.' He nodded to Buchanan 'Inspector, all is well. The taxi arrived and was told you didn't require it, but no need to worry, the driver picked up another fare so no loss to anyone. Also, your sergeant was here looking for you; she was told we were having lunch. Apparently, she has met up with Deborah and Ayesha and gone off riding with them.'

'Had no idea the lass was interested in horses; she never said.'

'Did you ever ask?'

'Now you're sounding like my wife.'

'Oh dear, forgive me; I fear I've overstepped the line.'

Buchanan shook his head. 'Doesn't matter. Are these the stables your wife inherited?'

Greyspear swallowed a piece of cheese. 'No, those stables were in London. There were too many memories for me there. It was then I found out just how valuable land in London was. I put the stables up for sale, rejected all offers for it as a going concern, and found a property developer looking for a suitable brown-field site to build expensive houses on.'

'What about this place? I understand that it'd been derelict for several years?'

'You heard right. It had last been lived in sometime in the 70's. When I bought it, the roof was still sound, but the windows had gone and most of the plaster had long since fallen off the walls.'

'Was it listed?'

'No, thankfully, and with it being in such a state of disrepair it was cheaper to gut the interior and rebuild to the latest building regulations than to try and make good.'

'Must have cost a fortune?'

'Inspector, I'm a businessman. I never sink all my own reserves into it a project – I share the risk with others.'

'And they also share the profits?'

'Of course they do. My investment in the club was the proceeds of the London stable sale. And before you ask, the names of the other investors must remain private. You do understand, don't you?'

Buchanan smiled and nodded. 'Your secrets are secure with me, Sir Nathan.' He thought that the list of names probably included Bashir and Silverstein, at least.

'I built the stables and converted the grounds into a golf course. The perimeter fields, as you saw today, I reserved for cross country riding.'

'What about the boatbuilding? How did you get into that?'

'Ah, yes, I forgot to mention that. When I sold the toy company I invested in a small boatbuilding company that was on the verge of going bankrupt. The directors had had enough and were only too eager to get out. They did have some very excellent designs, but unfortunately the factory was not fit for purpose and most of the skilled personnel had already left.'

'Bit of a risk – you not knowing anything about boats?'

'Maybe, but I did know about business and marketing. I shifted the construction to Greenock, the factory you've seen. I put an ad in the local job centre for fitters and laminators.'

'Get much of a response?'

'Mostly young men wanting me to sign their cards so they could continue to draw their dole.'

'From what I saw during our visit, you managed to turn it around.'

'It was difficult at first, but when those who stuck out the training started to spend their pay packets down the pub on Friday nights, we had more staff than we could find tools for. Today the factory wins industry awards for excellence.'

'And you've never remarried?'

'What do they say about twice shy?'

Buchanan nodded. 'I understand. Sir Nathan. I can't remember when I've spent a more pleasant afternoon, but I must really be going.'

Greyspear pushed his chair back. 'I'll walk you to the office. Maybe your sergeant will have returned from her ride – if not I'll get one of the lads to run you home.'

'One last question, Sir Nathan.'

'Ah, le coup de grâce.'

'Pardon?'

'Inspector, I've watched *Colombo*. Just as he is getting to the point, he goes to leave the room, then turns as though he's just remembered something and asks the vital question.'

'I prefer *Lewis*. Excellent scripts and the interaction between Lewis and Hathaway is as good as any detective story on television can be.'

'So, what's the question, Inspector?'

Buchanan shook his head and smiled. 'Did you have a break-in, here at the stables, last year?'

Greyspear frowned and thought for a moment. 'Yes, last November. Doesn't matter though, they were caught, and we got all the tack back. Why?'

'Do you remember the investigating officer?'

The colour drained from Greyspear's face 'Er, not sure I'd recognise him if I saw him.'

256

Buchanan took his copy of Nichols' photo from his pocket. 'Is this him, sir?'

Greyspear looked at the photo, the colour returning to his face. He sighed, 'Yes, that's him. Why'd you ask?'

'When's the last time you saw him?'

'Don't remember.'

'Did you ever meet him at his house?'

'What's that got to do with anything?'

'I'll ask the questions. Did you ever meet with DS Nichols at his house?'

'I suppose you already know the answer: yes, several times.'

'When was this?'

'Mostly last year and a couple of times this year.'

'And the last time?'

'I believe it was sometime in February, I'd have to check my diary for the date.' He looked at his phone, scrolling through the appointments. 'Ah, here it is, the 22nd. It was a Sunday.'

'Can you tell me the reason for your meeting?'

Greyspear thought for a moment, looking around to see if anyone was in earshot. 'It was an investors' meeting. You know we're going to make a movie of *The Penitent Heart* story. We needed somewhere private to do the presentation to the prospective investors. Detective Nichols was kind enough to lend us his house.'

'You mean you just asked him to lend you his house?'

Greyspear shook his head. 'When we had the break-in, Detective Nichols mentioned in passing that he also worked privately in security. We talked some more and the option of using his house was mentioned, that's all.'

'Did he charge for the use of his house?'

'Of course, he did. Really, Inspector, the government should pay you chaps better, then you wouldn't have to moonlight doing ad-hoc security jobs. Besides, he said he was thinking of giving up the day job and going into private security full-time, and this was his way of easing into it.'

'I don't, sir.'

'Don't what?'

'Have another job on the side. I can't multi-task, I'm not a woman.'

'Very funny, Inspector. Is that all?'

Buchanan cast an imaginary fly onto an equally imaginary fast-flowing river. 'When was the last time you met with Detective Nichols?'

'I told you, February.'

Buchanan began to reel in the slack line. 'That was at his house. Where else?'

Once more the colour drained from Greyspear's face. 'Don't know what you mean.'

Buchanan gave a gentle tug on the line. 'How about here at the stables?'

'I might have done.'

Buchanan could feel the fish nibbling at the fly. 'Did you meet with him here and did you have an argument with him?'

The muscles on Greyspear's face collapsed; his shoulders sagged in defeat. 'I warned him off.'

Buchanan jerked on the rod; the fish had taken the fly. 'I'd like you to tell me all about it. We'll find out anyway.'

'Look, there's too many ears here. Let's go outside into the grounds – it'll be more private there.'

Buchanan followed Greyspear out of the club reception area and over to the seats surrounding the fountain in the middle of the lawn. When he was satisfied no-one could overhear them, Greyspear said, 'Inspector, before I begin, are you recording this conversation? Do you have a recording device with you?'

Got you my beauty, thought Buchanan, plunging the landing net in the water. 'Sir Nathan, I'm an old-fashioned policeman, I catch criminals fair and square. If you're guilty of anything, rest assured, I'll get you.'

'As I previously mentioned, Detective Nichols was helping with security matters pertaining to the initial stages surrounding the financing of the film. What I'm going to say has little or nothing to do with that, or his death.'

'Go on.'

'I didn't know at the time we first met – but he was a bit of a rogue when it came to the ladies. I should have seen it coming.' He shook his head slowly. 'It was my fault entirely. He hit on Deborah.'

'Really? There must have been at least ten years between them.'

'Twelve – but these days that doesn't mean anything. They would meet here at the stables, go out riding and then have dinner. It all looked so innocent.'

'What happened to make you change your mind?'

'This would have been back at the beginning of March. They'd apparently met for lunch and had a bit too much to drink. I caught them in the feed room. They'd climbed up on the straw bales to be out of the way. I'd gone in to get some feed for one of my horses and heard her trying to fight him off.'

'What did you do?'

'I scrambled up on to the straw; the bastard was zipping up his fly. I'm sorry to say this, Inspector; but I lost it and hit him as hard as I could.'

'Then what?'

'The little shit got up and dived at me. I side-stepped, and hit him again in the face with my fist. Didn't stop him though, he was a wiry little bastard, squirmed out of my grasp and in doing so punched me in the balls. I lost my balance and fell onto the floor. He jumped down and made to punch me.'

'Did he manage?'

Greyspear smiled at the memory, 'Not a chance. I had him where I wanted him. I'm sorry now to say this, but I took out many years of my frustration on him. If it wasn't for Hans coming in to see what was going on, I might have – well, I don't want to contemplate what might have happened.'

'What did happen?'

'I told him that if he said anything, I'd make sure a charge of attempted rape would be brought against him.'

'What did he say to that?'

'He called me a few unmentionable names and left. Never saw him again.'

'Did you say anything to Deborah's parents?'

'No, she and I agreed to say nothing. She may have changed her mind and told her mother, though.'

'Thank you, Sir Nathan, this helps immeasurably. And you never saw him after that?'

Greyspear shook his head.

'Sir Nathan, just one last question.'

'Go ahead.'

'Why did you go to Fécamp?'

Greyspear chuckled and shook his head. 'No conspiracy, Inspector. I went to arrange for my company's new yacht to be entered in the Royal Escape Yacht Race. It's an annual event, the biggest event in the south east's sailing calendar.'

22

'How was the weekend, sir?'

'Where did you go, lass? I looked for you at the stables.'

'I went riding with Deborah and Ayesha.'

'Didn't know you rode.'

'Didn't know you rode, either.'

'I used to exercise horses at my local stable when I was a lad.'

'Me too, but I was never a lad.'

'Very funny. How was it?'

'Very interesting. Did you know that Deborah and Nichols had a thing going between them?'

'Heard it from Greyspear yesterday.'

'Bet you didn't know he tried it on with Ayesha as well?'

'No, I didn't. What did they have to say about it.'

'Deborah said Sir Nathan warned Nichols off. They had a fight over it.'

Buchanan nodded. 'So Greyspear said. What about Ayesha?'

'She told her mother, who then told her father. He was furious.'

'Enough to do Nichols in?'

'Don't know. Ayesha said her father never spoke about it afterwards.'

'This is very interesting. Wonder where the three of them were the night Nichols died?'

'That was Monday the sixth of April,' said Street, consulting her notes.

'I think we'll have Dexter and Hunter pay them a visit.'

'Can't, sir.'

'Why not?'

'They've been temporarily reassigned: missing child in Christchurch area. They've gone to join the search party. No telling when we'll get them back.'

Buchanan pursed his lips and let out a long sigh. 'Can't imagine what the parents must be feeling. Murder is bad enough, but not knowing where your child is –' he shook his head. 'Hope they find the child – alive.'

'Me, too.'

'Well, if we don't have the dynamic duo, I suppose we'll just have to do the rounds ourselves. Probably for the best.' He looked at his watch. 'Plenty of time today; we'll have lunch then pay them a visit.'

'Learn anything from Greyspear? Other than the bit about Nichols?'

'He likes to talk. He confirmed in detail what we already know about him, how he got started in business, his marriages, and the loss of two wives.'

'Still think he's a murderer?'

'I hope not.'

'Surely if he was guilty, he'd be careful what he talked about? He wouldn't want to give anything away.'

'Let me tell you a story.'

'Good, I like your stories.'

'This is one told me by my dad; he heard it from a sailor. You remember me telling you he used to work in the shipyards?'

'*Uh-huh.*'

'They had started on the refit of a destroyer, which had just returned from the far east. Well, this sailor had bought some jewellery and didn't want to declare it to customs and subsequently have to pay the duty.'

'What'd he do?'

'On his first night ashore he went through security and started a conversation with the guard on duty.'

'I thought this was about customs?'

262

'They don't always have customs officers on duty in naval dockyards, so the gate security takes on that responsibility. They randomly search people going out the gate for contraband. From then on this sailor went out through the same gate at the same time each night, occasionally being searched. One Tuesday night he intimated to the guard that he wanted to have a private word with him. They stepped out of the guardhouse and the sailor asked the guard for a favour. He explained he had brought a load of jewellery back from the far east and he wanted to smuggle it out through the gate. If he was successful he would reward the guard with ten percent of what he got for the jewellery.'

'Did the guard go along with it?'

'Yep, so the sailor said he would bring it out on Friday evening as he had made arrangements to sell it that night and would pay the guard on Saturday morning when he returned.'

'Bit stupid, telling the guard he was going to do a bit of smuggling.'

'Ah, but there's the trick.'

'What trick, sir?'

'The sailor assumed, correctly so, that the guard would probably agree to the deal and arrest him on the Friday evening when he tried to smuggle the jewels out.'

'So?'

'The sailor smuggled the jewels out on the Thursday evening, and when he got stopped on the Friday he was clean, and the guard couldn't do anything except look a fool.'

'Where's this story going?'

'One of you mentioned the ABC murders the other day. You remember how the story about the ABC timetable was just a red herring to cover what the murderer was really up to?'

'I get it. You think Greyspear is trying to throw you off the trail by being friendly and helpful, while all the time he is manoeuvring you away from the truth about him being the killer?'

'It's a possibility, lass.'

263

'Hadn't thought of that.'

'So, what's on this morning?'

'The Chief's here.'

'Here in the station? Why didn't you tell me?'

'Just did. She's gone to the loo, says she wants to have a word with us. I think she's getting impatient and wants the case wrapped up, especially since we have a prime suspect for at least one of the killings.'

'Is that what she said?'

Street grinned. 'Her words, not mine.'

'You want coffee while we wait?'

Just as Buchanan stood to go for their coffees, Atkins walked into the room.

'Ah, there you are, Buchanan. Has Street told you why I'm here?'

'Yes, Ma'am.'

'Good. I've got a meeting with the crime commissioner this afternoon – she'll want answers and I need something to give her. Still pursuing Sir Nathan?'

'I had lunch with him at his club yesterday.'

'Be careful, Buchanan. You need not to be seen to having your judgement clouded by getting too friendly with your main suspect. Though I'm sure the more you get to know him you'll find he's quite a decent chap.'

That will be for me to decide, thought Buchanan.

'I've heard from the authorities in France. They've traced Abosa's phone movements. He was in England on the 24th, so he may have been the killer of the girl in the wood. Here's a copy of the report.'

'Ilka, Ma'am.'

'Yes, Ilka. So now you can lay off Sir Nathan. I'm making arrangements for you to interview Abosa. It won't be right away as Interpol want to –'

'Can we have him extradited, Ma'am?'

'Unfortunately, not right away; Interpol have him at the moment. Apparently when the office at the garage was searched, a collection of passports was discovered, mostly of young women who have been reported as missing. We'll be getting a report, complete with their photographs. It will be circulated to all European forces. Maybe we'll get lucky and find some of these unfortunate girls alive.'

'He wasn't here on the 29th or the 30th, Ma'am.'

'He could have been: the phone he had in his possession was new. According to his air-time contract, it started on the 1st of April.'

Buchanan looked at the report for the 6th of April and shook his head. 'Not in the UK on the 6th either, Ma'am.'

'So, he was unlikely to have killed Olga or Nichols, Ma'am,' said Street.

'Looks that way, Street,' said Atkins.

Buchanan grinned.

'I know what you're thinking, Buchanan. Get it into your head: Sir Nathan is not the murderer.' Atkins stood and headed for the door. 'Keep me posted Buchanan, and good work rescuing Street. But next time –' she shook her head, 'let's hope there never is a next time.'

◆

Buchanan looked out the window and watched Atkins walk across the car park and get into her chauffeured car. Street excused herself and left the office. Buchanan's computer beeped at the arrival of an email.

Street returned with two cups of coffee. 'Something interesting?'

'Susan Richardson's disappeared.'

'What?'

'Her husband phoned in a missing person report,' he looked at his watch, 'about an hour ago. Front desk just emailed it through.'

'What does it say?'

> *Susan Richardson, 46, missing since Sunday morning. Husband, Rodney Richardson, said she wasn't home when he returned from the newsagents; he'd only been gone about forty minutes.*
> *She is described as being white, around 5ft 7ins tall and having shoulder-length, straw-coloured hair. Husband is unclear what she was wearing when she left home.*

'This is awkward, sir, especially since you spent the day with Sir Nathan yesterday.'

'Hmm, yes, I did. But I got to the stables at ten-thirty, and he was supposedly in conference.'

'So, what's next?'

'Rodney Richardson. Murder victims most always know their killer.'

◆

Buchanan and Street walked into Richardson's office.

'Yes sir, can I help?'

'We'd like to have a word with Mr Richardson.'

The receptionist looked at his computer screen. 'I'm sorry, he's not available today and I'm not sure if Mr Anderson has any time.'

'It's Mr Richardson we want to talk to,' Buchanan said, presenting his warrant card. 'DCI Buchanan and DS Street. We wish to talk to him about the report he made on his missing wife.'

The receptionist pressed a couple of keys on his keyboard. 'Harriet, there are two policemen in reception to talk with Mr

Richardson about his wife – I know, but they are insistent – I'll send them up.' He looked up and said, 'If you take the –'

'Thanks, we know the way.'

Richardson's secretary looked up as the lift door opened.

'Inspector, Mr Richardson has asked not to be disturbed, his wife's disappearance –'

'That's why we're here.'

She pushed a couple of buttons on her keyboard and waited. 'Mr Richardson, sorry to disturb, but there are two policemen to see you – I think they're here to ask you about your wife – I'll send them in.' She looked up at Buchanan,' Mr Richardson says to go right in.'

'Thanks.'

Richardson was leaning back in his chair staring out the window, his feet resting on an open desk drawer. There was a half-drunk whiskey bottle on the desk and a half-empty glass in his hand. He turned as Buchanan and Street entered.

'Come in, Inspector, join the wake.'

'Wake, sir?'

'Whatever. You're here to ask about my wife, the faithful Susan, the companion of my bosom?'

'Yes, sir. We're here to see if there's anything you can add to your report.'

'Ask *him*, he knows.'

'*Him*, sir?'

'Sir Nathan bloody Greyspear, that's who.'

'Could you explain that remark, sir?'

'What's to explain? It's his fault she's gone. Ask him.'

'Are you saying she's with him?'

'They seek her here, they seek her there, they seek her everywhere; that darned elusive butterfly. Have a drink, Inspector.'

'I'm on duty, Mr Richardson.'

'All I know is she's gone and it's his fault. Sure you won't join me?'

'When exactly was the last time you saw your wife, Mr Richardson?'

'Friday evening.'

'And you didn't report her missing till this morning?'

'She disappeared. I looked but didn't see her. Serves her right, the bitch.'

'I'm not sure I understand.'

'I thought she'd gone off with him.' Richardson breathed out slowly, drained his glass, and reached over for the bottle. 'Friday, who'd have thought –'

'Thought what, Mr Richardson?'

'She's actually gone, I just can't believe it.'

'What time on Friday did you last see your wife, and why was it, you reported her as being missing since Sunday?'

'Sunday meant Friday. Outside the restaurant, it was raining. I went for the car, when I got back, she was gone. 'Where was this, Mr Richardson?'

'The Marina.'

'Can you tell me where you had dinner, the name of the restaurant?'

'The Harbour House. They do good steaks, wine's not bad either.'

'You went to the Harbour House restaurant with your wife for dinner, she disappears, and you don't report it till today?'

'No.'

'No, Mr Richardson. If we're to help find your wife we need more to go on. Can you give us more details about the evening? For instance, did you and your wife argue about anything during the evening?'

'What couple don't?'

'Did you?'

'I suppose we did.'

268

'About what?'

'Don't remember, she started it anyway. I'd had enough, just wanted to go home.'

'Can you remember what time you left?'

'About ten-thirty.'

'You left your wife at the restaurant at ten-thirty while you went for the car?'

'Er – my wife, yes, I left her at the restaurant. It was raining, nowhere to park, ended up over beside Boots. Thought I'd get the car and drive over to the Marina, didn't want her to get wet.'

'And you say she was missing when you returned with the car?'

Richardson nodded and took another gulp from the glass.

'Did you look for her, go back inside the restaurant?'

'Of course, I did, she was nowhere to be seen.'

'What about the toilets?'

'I had one of the waitresses look.'

'And no one in the restaurant saw her leave?'

Richardson shrugged. 'They were busy clearing up.'

'Can you tell us why you waited so long to report her missing? Had she done this sort of thing before?'

'What?'

'I said, had she done this sort of thing before?'

'She's a bit temperamental, doesn't like to lose an argument.'

'Can you think of anywhere she might have gone? Family, or friends?'

Richardson shook his head slowly while staring at the bottom of his empty glass. 'Inspector, some people are half-full kind of people, others are half-empty kind of people; I think I'm an empty-glass-waiting-to-be-filled kind of person.' He reached for the whiskey bottle and refilled his glass.

'Thank you for your time, Mr Richardson. We'll be in touch as soon as we have further information on your wife.'

'What was that all about, sir?'

Once we walked
Hand in hand
dreams we shared
on a beach of sand.

The tide came in
and washed them away
our dreams were lost
then you went away.

'I like that.'

'Thanks, and to answer your question, I'm not sure. We'll have another go at him when he's sober. In the meantime let's check the restaurant; see if they can tell us anything.'

They parked in front of the yacht club and walked over to the restaurant.

'He couldn't have brought the car to the restaurant.'

'I see that. lass, but at least this car park is much closer than Boots. They'd only have to walk twenty yards to get to the car.'

'Do you think she wandered off after the argument?'

'Possible.'

'At least Dan's not a suspect – we had him locked up.'

'True, but all the same the pattern has changed, lass. Just like the ABC murders. Susan Richardson going missing has altered the equation.'

'You think she's dead?'

'Hope not, though I believe our killer has made a mistake. Let's go talk with the manager of the Harbour House, see what he knows.'

◆

'Well, well! Just look who's here, lass.'

'Surprised it's Maria, sir?'

270

'This your doing?'

'*Uh-huh.*'

'We're not open yet, lunch is at twelve. Oh, hello.'

'Hello, Maria, how are you? Settling in all right?' asked Buchanan.

'Yes, thanks. Have you found my sister's killer yet?'

'No. I'm sorry, we're still working our way through the evidence, should be soon now. Is the manager here? We'd like to have a word with him.'

'I'll get him for you. Please wait.'

'Nice restaurant,' said Street, 'foods good, if you like traditional English faire.'

'I'll have to give it a try one day,' said Buchanan, while looking at a menu.

'Inspector, how are you? Come to see how your girl's getting on?'

'Not this time, Mr Andreotti. We're here to ask if you remember seeing Mr Richardson here for dinner last Friday evening?'

'I wasn't here all evening. Let me check the reservation book.'

Buchanan and Street followed him over to the desk. Andreotti turned the pages back to Friday's bookings. 'Ah, here we are: Richardson, table for two at nine.'

'Would the booking be for him and his wife?' asked Street.

'I'm sorry. Sergeant, it just says table for two. I could ask whoever served the table, if that would help?'

'Yes, please, sir. Would you do that?'

Andreotti returned with Maria.

Street passed her phone over. 'Do you recognise this person?'

Maria looked at Richardson's photo. 'Yes, he was here on Friday evening.'

'Alone?'

'No, sir. He was with a woman.'

'Can you describe her for me?'

'She was tall – about your height, Sergeant – with long fair hair. She was wearing a long blue dress with medium heels.'

'Is this her?' asked Street, showing Maria a picture of Susan Richardson.

Maria looked at the photo. 'I'm not sure. She *does* look like her – but the eyes – they're different.'

'Could it be her make-up?' asked Buchanan.

Maria shook her head. 'No, sir. the eyes are a different shape, and her hair – the lady I saw, her hairline was much further back.'

'And you didn't see them, Mr Andreotti?'

'Sorry, Inspector, we had a run on our other restaurant last Friday evening and I spent most of the evening there.'

◆

As they walked back to the car Buchanan said, 'Street, we need a picture of Richardson's secretary, then go see if Maria recognises her.'

'Doesn't make sense. Why would Richardson take his wife and secretary out to dinner at the same restaurant, on the same evening?'

'I don't think he did.'

'Ah, he took his secretary out to dinner and his wife caught them in the act?'

'A working hypothesis for now, lass.'

'But what happened to the wife? Where is she?'

'Let's go back and have word with Richardson's secretary. While I'm talking to her, see if you can get her picture on that phone of yours.'

◆

'Back so soon?'

'Is Mr Richardson's secretary in?'

'You just missed her; she's gone down the pub for lunch.'

'Where?'

'Cross the street, turn left and it's about a hundred yards, can't miss it. It's called the Wheatsheaf.'

'Are you the regular receptionist?'

He shook his head. 'I'm sitting in for Liz.'

'Was she here last week?'

'Yes, she's always here, never misses a day.'

'Till now.'

'I've been working here for almost four years and she's always been here, except for –'

'Except for what?'

He lowered his voice. 'I shouldn't say this, but when old man Richardson is away on business, she skives off.'

'On holiday?'

'Don't know about that.'

'Do you think she goes with him?'

'Unlikely – you should see his wife, she's a looker. No, it's just odd, her being gone when he is, that's all.'

'Thanks.' Buchanan turned to Street. 'Come on, lass; let's go for an early lunch.'

♦

The clock above the fireplace struck twelve o'clock as they entered the pub.

'Do you see her?'

'No – wait a minute, is that her over in the corner, beside the fruit machine?'

'That's her, lass, and look who's with her. Wonder if he's drinking lemonade? There's an empty table close by. You go sit and I'll get us something to drink. Sit with your back to them, and when I sit down pretend to take my picture, but do that thing with the lens and get hers instead.'

'OK. Since you're driving, I'll have a glass of white wine, make it Pinot Grigio, and if they have a menu?'

Buchanan grinned. 'You win, lunch it will be.'

He returned with a glass of his favourite whiskey and Street's wine. 'We are having lunch. I'll be fine to drive after.'

The sound of his voice had the required result. Richardson's secretary's eyes opened like an owl that's just spied dinner.

Street took the cue and had Buchanan pose for his photo.

'Did you get it?'

Street nodded and grinned.

Buchanan feigned surprise and stood. 'Mr Richardson! Feeling better?'

Richardson squinted and tried to focus. 'Inspector, fancy meeting you here. Having lunch?'

'Yes, we were just passing and thought we'd drop in. Any word from your wife, sir?'

'That's your job. Why don't you go out and do it?'

Richardson's secretary turned to Buchanan. 'I'm sorry, Inspector; Mr Richardson is under a lot of strain with his wife going missing.'

Buchanan went over to their table and sat down.

'Where's your sister, Miss – ?' Her face turned white and tears formed in her eyes. She shook her head. 'Davies, it's Patricia Davies. I don't know, she didn't come to work this morning. I called her flat, but there was no reply. She does this sometimes when something bothers her and she won't talk to anyone for days. Then she acts like nothing has happened and is as right as rain. I expect we'll hear from her when she's ready.'

'Are you close, you, and your sister?'

'Suppose so, we're identical twins, we're sometimes mistaken for each other, but that's where the resemblance ends.'

'Thank you, Miss Davies, I've interrupted enough for one day. Please excuse me.'

'Not at all, Inspector. I hope you find Mrs Richardson soon.'

'I'm sure we will, and hope your sister comes home soon, as well.'

♦

'What was that all about?'

'Here's something very interesting, lass. Would you say that Susan Richardson and Richardson's secretary's sister look alike?'

'There is a basic resemblance, why?'

'Let's have our lunch, don't want to discuss it here.'

♦

As they drove back to the office, Street asked, 'Why didn't you want to talk in the pub? And why the reference to the likeness between them?'

'As you observed, there is a basic resemblance between Susan Richardson and Richardson's secretary's sister. I've found that when a married man strays from the matrimonial bed he unconsciously chooses a woman that resembles the wife, not necessarily an exact copy, but close enough. And from that I'm guessing that Richardson is having an affair with his secretary's sister. Likely as not they've had some sort of disagreement and she's gone off in a sulk.'

'This doesn't make sense. Susan Richardson and Richardson's mistress both disappear at the same time. You said Greyspear was angry when you arrived at the stables yesterday?'

'Yes.'

'No, that's a crazy idea.'

'What is, lass?'

'Suppose Susan Richardson found her husband and mistress at it and got angry.'

'As you would.'

'She kills the girlfriend, then scarpers.'

'Where's the body?'

'Where they always are these days.'

'In the Marina?'

'Why not, sir? Richardson and girlfriend go to the Harbour House in the Marina for dinner. Wife sees them together in the restaurant, sees red, and waits for them to come out. She watches as Richardson goes for the car and then she makes her move. She attacks and kills the girlfriend then shoves the body into the Marina, suffers remorse and does a runner.'

'That works, but where is Mrs Richardson? Who's hiding her?'

'Greyspear. He's the obvious one.'

Buchanan shook his head. 'Somehow I don't think so. If he was, why were he and Jacqueline Masterson at loggerheads yesterday morning?'

'Why don't we go ask her?'

'Why not.'

As they drove, Street asked, 'what did Dan say when you let him go?'

'Of course, you don't know.'

'Know what?'

'Before you arrived this morning, I went down to make arrangements for his release and you'll never guess who was waiting for him.'

'Go on, surprise me.'

'Maria.'

'Really? Was she angry?'

'No, not in the least.'

'What about Dan? What'd he say?'

'Not much, shrugged and said I was just doing my job. He knew he was innocent and had nothing to fear.'

'So what about Maria?'

'She was sitting in the reception area; I asked her why she was there. She said she'd heard that Dan had been arrested,'

'How'd she and Dan get together?'

'Olga had written to Maria and told her about Dan and how he looked after her and had tried to make her see sense. Maria

276

said she just wanted to tell him how grateful she was to him for looking after Olga.'

'That makes sense.'

'I went through to the cells and brought Dan out. You'd think it was a family reunion the way they hugged and cried together. I wouldn't be surprised to find out that something good comes out of this miserable affair.'

'You mean romance?'

'Why not? Olga and Maria were identical twins; who knows what bonds will grow out of their common grief.'

'That would be nice, just realised how many sets of sisters we've got mixed up in this sorry tale.'

'Go on.'

'There's Olga and her sister, Susan Richardson and her sister, and now Richardson's mistress and her sister.'

'Wonder if Ilka had a sister?'

♦

Buchanan drove into the stables and parked in front of the office.

'This way,' he said, climbing the stairs two at a time and ushering Street into the office.

'Yes sir, can I help? Oh, it's *you* again.'

'Yes. It's me again. We'd like a word with Mrs Masterson.'

'You can't – I mean she's not in.'

'And where might she be if she's not in?'

'She said she had to go and see one of our suppliers, won't be back till tomorrow.'

'Is Sir Nathan here?'

'No sir, he was here yesterday, but I don't suppose knowing that would be any good to you?'

'You'd be surprised if you knew what was good for me. Come on lass, back to the station and see what the tide's brought in.'

♦

As they went past the front desk, the duty sergeant called out to Buchanan, 'Got something for you, sir.'

'What is it?'

'That missing woman, sir, we think it's her handbag. Bin men found it this morning, it was in one of the harbour rubbish bins. Looks like someone picked it up, got scared and just tossed it. It's been logged as evidence.'

Buchanan took it up to his office.

'Not much in it for a woman's handbag, Street. Karen's is like a Tardis on a strap,' he said, opening the evidence bag and emptying the contents onto his desk.

'What do you think, lass? You're a woman. What's missing?'

Street stared at the assembled detritus on the desk for a moment then said, 'If that was my handbag there would be at least a mobile phone, purse, and make-up.'

'Exactly. What conclusion do you draw from that?'

'A female purse snatcher?'

Buchanan smiled, shook his head and said, 'Interesting deduction, you may be closer to the truth than you realise.'

He picked up the small bunch of keys and looked at the initials on the key fob. 'SMR, no guesses whose they are.' He passed them to Street.

'One Mercedes car key, rest house keys?'

'I'll tell you about the keys, lass. The large one is no doubt a Mercedes car key, this one is an office door, this one will be to the front door of the matrimonial home, and the last one I wouldn't be surprised to find fits an expensive flat or house somewhere in town. It's a secure key, not easy to get copied.'

'Richardson must be quite a senior partner to afford a flat in town.'

'I didn't say it was *his* flat. Secure key, should be possible to trace.'

'Do you want me to do the rounds and see if we can find this flat?'

'Just what I was going to ask. You never know who we will find living there. Give me a call on the mobile when you find it – I'm going out.'

'Where to, sir?'

'Greyspear Yachts' sales office in town, then Litlington and Mrs Richardson's mother – the Chief says that's where we will find Mrs Richardson.'

'What do you think?'

'More likely to find cheese on the moon.'

♦

Buchanan parked in the visitors' parking slot between a green Aston Martin DB7 and beige Mercedes SLS AMG.

'Good morning, can I help?' asked the receptionist.

'Yes, I would like to see Sir Nathan Greyspear.'

'Do you have an appointment?'

'This is my appointment,' he said, producing his warrant card.

'Been a robbery?'

'Not quite. Now could I have a word with Sir Nathan, please?'

She pressed a key on her telephone. 'Sir Nathan, there's a policeman to see you. No, he doesn't have an appointment – no, not sure what he wants – yes, ok.'

She hung up. 'His office is the on the left at the top of the stairs.'

Buchanan knocked and walked in to Greyspear's office.

Greyspear stood as he entered.

'Inspector, we meet again. Change your mind about buying a boat?'

'Not on my salary, sir. I'm here to ask you if you've heard from Mrs Richardson; and can you tell me when you last saw her?'

'She was at work last Thursday. We had a phone call this morning to say her mother was unwell and she would be taking a few days off to be with her.'

'Who placed the call?'

'It might have been her husband. Julie at reception took the call, you can ask her.'

'And you have not heard from her since?'

'No – what's wrong, Inspector?'

Buchanan saw a look of concern grow on Greyspear's face.

'Is there something you would like to say, sir?' he asked.

'No, sorry, Inspector. I just hope she's all right.'

'I'm sure she is, sir,' said Buchanan. He walked over to the window and looked down at the sales yard. 'The yard looks busy?'

'Yes, we've just had our local spring boat show, finished last Thursday.'

'Take many orders?' asked Buchanan.

'We don't usually have customers order new boats at these local shows. Most customers are trading up from previous models and are looking for deals on more current models. Customers for larger yacht come along at our invitation to discuss the final details of the yacht that they have already ordered.'

'Was Mrs Richardson at the show?'

'Yes, it's all hands-on deck when it comes to the boat show.'

'Where do you hold the show?'

'Top end of the north harbour; we set up temporary docks and sales office.'

'Did you notice if she spent time with anyone in particular?'

'She's a very attentive person, Inspector; I'd be disappointed if she didn't spend time with our guests.'

'Quite expensive, the boats you build?'

'Not all. Some of the previously owned yachts cost as little as a second-hand car.'

'But not a FBC40?'

'No. Yet for some of our clients, buying larger yachts is no more expensive that buying a summer house on the Riviera.'

'Thank you, Sir Nathan. I'll be in touch.'

Just before he closed the door Buchanan asked, 'Can you tell me Mrs Richardson's maiden name and where her mother lives?'

'Yes, it's Latimer and they live in Litlington, just past the pub.'

'Thank you, sir,' said Buchanan, smiling to himself as he shut Greyspear's door behind him.

♦

He turned left out of the office and headed towards the A259, Seven Sisters, the road to Litlington and the Latimers.'

Susan Richardson's parents' house was a large four-bedroom cottage. Parked on the spacious driveway was a luxury motorhome, a powder-blue Mercedes 280sl and a black Porsche Targa convertible.

Buchanan rang the doorbell and was greeted by, he assumed, Mr Latimer. He presented his warrant card. 'Mr Latimer? Detective Chief Inspector Buchanan. I wonder if I could come in? It's about your daughter, Susan.'

He followed Mr Latimer into the conservatory. 'Constance, this is Inspector Buchanan. He wants to speak to us about Susan.'

'What is it?" asked a worried-looking Mrs Latimer. 'Has there been an accident?'

'Not that we're aware of, Mrs Latimer. Can you tell me when you last saw your daughter?'

'Last Wednesday evening. We had dinner together, here at the house.'

'And you haven't heard from her since?'

Mrs Latimer looked at her husband, turned back to Buchanan, and shook her head.

'Have you called her house, Mrs Latimer?'

Mrs Latimer again looked at her husband, who answered, 'I called, *he* answered and said he thought Susan had gone off on a business trip, said he didn't know when she would be back.'

'Did you call her office?'

Mr Latimer answered. 'Yes, they said she was at home, apparently she had called in sick.'

'Had you and your daughter argued about anything last Wednesday evening?'

Buchanan noticed the nervous look between them. Mrs Latimer nodded to her husband.

'Inspector, things weren't well between Susan and her husband, there were many arguments; he drank a lot and when he was drunk he used to hit her. We said she should leave him, at least for a time till she could think things over.'

'And did she?'

Mrs Latimer shook her head. 'She just went deeper into her work, worked all hours, and went on as many business trips as she could. I told her she needed to rest, that she would make herself ill, running around like she was. And now?' She burst into tears; her husband put his hand on her shoulder and gave it a gentle squeeze.

'And last Wednesday, you argued over this?'

Mrs Latimer nodded, wiping her nose with her ever-present handkerchief. 'And now she's avoiding us –won't speak to us.'

◆

Buchanan was driving along Beachy Head Road, admiring the view of Eastbourne, when Street called.

'I've found it, sir, in Meads. Big house with a monkey puzzle tree in the front garden, on the left as you drive down King Edward's Parade.'

'Good work, lass. Be with you in a couple of minutes.'

Buchanan followed Street's direction and parked in the driveway.

'Had to arm twist the locksmith to get the address,' said Street, as Buchanan entered through the front door.

'Looks like someone was going on holiday,' she said, pointing to the suitcases sitting in the hallway.

Buchanan stopped and picked up the post.

'Look at this, lass.'

Street nodded. 'Do you think she was having an affair, sir?'

'Most likely. PA to all that money and a husband using her as a punch bag – no contest.'

They were interrupted by Greyspear walking in through the front door.

'What the hell's going on? How did you get in?'

'Mrs Richardson's key,' said Buchanan.

'Where is she?'

'We are still looking for her, sir.'

'How did you get her key?'

'Her handbag was turned in to the police station, her key was inside.'

'Why didn't you tell me earlier?'

'Why didn't you tell me about your relationship with Mrs Richardson?'

'It wasn't any of your business.'

'Missing persons *is* police business, sir.'

'I thought she was staying with her mother.'

'Her mother hasn't heard from her since the middle of last week. When did you last see her, sir?'

'I told you earlier last Thursday, but it was really Friday.'

'Was that at work, sir, or afterwards?'

Greyspear's shoulders slumped; he leaned against the wall and swept his hair back with his hand and thought for a moment. 'Her marriage had broken down long before I met her. She came to us looking for work, initially to get out of the house and put some money aside for the day she did finally leave him.'

Greyspear took a deep breath and continued, 'Within weeks she knew more about our yachts than anyone else on the sales team – our clients would ask for her by name – she was becoming such an asset I couldn't afford to lose her, so I decided to promote her to my PA and that, as they say, was that.'

'And Friday?' asked Buchanan.

'We went out to dinner Friday evening, she told me her husband had left a message on the answering machine to say he would be home Saturday instead of Monday. We had planned to spend the weekend together. I was angry with her, told her to sort things out with her husband.'

'What did she say?'

'What didn't she say? Mostly that I didn't understand how difficult it was for her. Did you know that when he was drunk he would beat her? You should have seen the bruises; I kept pleading with her to leave him.'

'Why didn't she?'

'She said a woman her age needed security.'

'And did you offer her any?'

Greyspear breathed out and smiled.' I was going to propose during dinner, even bought an engagement ring – here ,' he said, taking a ring box from his jacket pocket and showing Buchanan and Street a huge diamond engagement ring.

'Any girl would be dead proud of that,' said Street.

'What went wrong, sir?' asked Buchanan.

'My impatience, that's what went wrong. I kept pushing her to make up her mind and leave him. I was a fool, I didn't see it coming. She just stood up, said she was going to the toilet, and that's the last I saw of her.'

'What did you do?' asked Buchanan.

'I had one of the waitresses go into the ladies and see if Susan was in trouble.'

'And was she?'

'She'd gone; nowhere to be seen.'

'Bit awkward isn't it, sir?'

'What do you mean, Inspector?'

'Dating another man's wife – bit awkward.'

'Yes, but that's life. You play with the cards you're dealt.'

'Thank you, sir,' said Buchanan, 'as soon as we have any news, we'll get in touch. Oh, by the way, where did you go for dinner on Friday evening?'

'Luigi's. It's a new restaurant in the Marina.'

♦

'Was he was telling the truth?'

'*Oh what a tangled web we weave when first we practise to deceive.*'

'Walter Scott, sir?'

'Well done, lass well done. There's hope for you yet.'

Street smiled. 'Isn't Luigi's the sister restaurant to the Harbour House, sir?'

'I do believe it is.'

23

Tuesday morning, Buchanan had been in the incident room since six. His second cup of coffee of the day dispatched; two Sudoku puzzles completed and by six-thirty his preliminary report on Susan Richardson's disappearance had been emailed to the Chief. Not bad, he thought.

He re-read the initial statement by Rodney Richardson, of how they had gone out to dinner on Friday and she'd gone off with Greyspear. Bunch of tosh, Buchanan mumbled.

He put down his copy of the report and was about to head for the canteen when he was interrupted by Atkins.

'Ah, there you are Buchanan, I want a word with you.' She walked into the office and sat in Buchanan's swivel chair, turning to stare out of the window.

Collecting her thoughts, rummaging for just the right balance of insult mixed with encouragement, thought Buchanan.

Her ruminations over, Atkins turned back and stared at Buchanan while brandishing his report like a fly swatter.

'I've read your report on Richardson's wife's disappearance and I don't like your conclusion one bit. He's a highly respected member of the Rotary. Killed his wife? I don't think so. His family have lived in this area for generations; he's raised thousands for the children's hospital trust and I've been led to understand that there's royal blood in the family.

Probably from the wrong side of the blanket, thought Buchanan.

'You need to get the big picture, man; you can't go running off with your fancy notions like that.'

'I am working on it.'

'Working on it? How many gallons of ale has the Smugglers pulled while you work on it? Have you checked with her mother?

No, I bet you haven't, they probably don't have the same variety of ale in Litlington.'

Atkins turned back to look out of the window. 'It'll probably turn out they had a bit of a barney and she walked out; went home to mother, that's more likely.' She swivelled back and gave Buchanan a patronising look. 'I know you've got your own way of working these things out, but please, for once, would you just follow procedures? Now get on with the job and sort this mess out, and remember, I don't want to see your face in the *Herald*. We get enough adverse publicity as it is; don't need you adding to it.'

Buchanan smiled back and said, 'Golden Tipple, Ma'am.'

'What?'

'Golden Tipple, Ma'am. An excellent ale from a local brewery and it's available at the Plough and Harrow in Litlington.'

Atkins shook her head, got up from Buchanan's chair and left.

♦

On Friday morning Buchanan telephoned Street.

'Street, I need you, we're going back to see Richardson.'

'But, sir, I've a special dinner date tomorrow; it's my day off and I've got to finish cleaning the flat.'

'Needs must, lass We have a body. I'll be with you in fifteen minutes.'

♦

'Car in the garage, sir?'

'Sort of, someone thought it funny to slash all the tyres and finished it off by jamming a fence post through the radiator. The mechanic said the car isn't worth repairing to service standard, so will be withdrawn and sold. This, shiny, almost new BMW is my new car; for now, anyway.'

'Well, at least it's got more room inside. Where we off to?'

'Morgue.'

'Where did they find the body?'

'In the bay; looks like it was washed out of the Marina when the lock gates were opened. I'm afraid that people drowning in the Marina is becoming a regular occurrence.'

♦

'What can you tell me, Doctor?' Buchanan asked Mansell.

'Female, mid to late forties, five feet nine, slim build, been dead about seven days.'

'Cause of death?' interrupted Buchanan.

'Drowned in the Marina, although appearances could be misleading, as you can see,' said Mansell, unzipping the body bag. 'Most of the face gone. Propeller, I'd say, and a big one at that. By the looks of the injuries she'd been caught on something under the waterline and dragged backwards out into the bay.'

'How'd you determine that?'

'The water in her lungs matched samples taken from your earlier dead girl, who also drowned in the Marina.'

Buchanan momentarily turned away and stared at an anatomy chart on the wall. 'Had she been assaulted?'

'I can give you the full details when I have completed my autopsy.'

'Yes – do that – please. Any ID on the body?'

'There was a laundry tag on the skirt with the initials EH.'

'I'd hate to have his job,' said Street, as they walked over to Buchanan's car. 'Bad enough job cleaning out a chicken.'

He shook his head and said, 'Get in, lass; I want to talk to Richardson again.'

As they drove, Buchanan asked,' Conclusions from the visit, lass?'

'Pretty gruesome sight.'

'Not that. What was she wearing? You looked in the bag?'

'Not sure. Only saw the face – or what was left of it – my mind was in overload, didn't really look at the clothes.'

Buchanan shook his head. 'She was wearing a long blue dress, black court shoes, white blouse and cardigan. Does that sound like a PA to an MD of a major international company to you?'

'Not all PA's wear high heels and short skirts, sir.' Street was quiet for a moment, then said, 'Then if that wasn't Susan Richardson, who was she?'

'Good question, lass, good question.'

'I don't follow you, sir.'

'Street, there are two women in this tragedy, both missing. Given the fact that the body in there isn't Susan Richardson, it has to be Elizabeth Henderson.'

'But how can you be sure about that, sir?'

'Wait and see, lass, wait and see.'

'Where to now? Or should I not ask?'

'We're going back to talk to Richardson. His story has more holes in it than a pound of Swiss cheese.'

As they drove, Street closed her eyes and thought of Saturday evening, and the special dinner she was preparing for Stephen. Buchanan thought of his conversation with Atkins. She was right; he should spend more time with Karen. If she'd only spend more time at home instead of dashing off to see her mother every time there was a family emergency.

♦

Buchanan drove into Richardson's driveway and parked behind a well-used Saab convertible.

Richardson opened the door.

'I've been expecting you. I heard on the radio that you've found a body in the harbour.'

'Can we come in, sir? Don't want the neighbours talking, do we?'

Richardson led them through to the lounge, sat down in an armchair by the fire, and poured himself a large whiskey.

289

'Drink, Inspector?'

'No, thanks. Friday evening when you went out for dinner, you didn't go with your wife, did you?'

'No. You married, Inspector?'

'Yes, sir, and very happily.'

'You don't know how lucky you are.'

'The night in question. sir, can we get back to it, please?'

'I had been away during the week. I called Susan to say I'd be back sometime late on Saturday, instead of Monday. I actually got back on Friday at lunchtime. We finished about eight and I suggested to Elizabeth we go out and get something to eat.'

'Elizabeth is your secretary?'

'No, she's my secretary's sister.'

'Did you call your wife, sir?' asked Buchanan.

'I don't remember.'

'What happened after dinner?'

'We got up to leave, I saw it was raining and since Elizabeth hadn't brought a coat, I told her to wait inside and I would get the car. When I came out of the restaurant I ran into Susan. She was in a foul mood. I tried to walk away, avoid a scene in front of the restaurant, but she kept on at me, just like she always did.'

'What did you say, sir?'

'You know,' he said, smiling, 'I almost divorced her once; glad I spared myself the expense. I confronted her about Greyspear, she said she didn't care, said she was leaving me. I called her a whore; she swung at me with her handbag, the strap broke and it flew off into the road. I slapped her; she stepped back, lost her balance, and fell in the harbour.'

'So you left her to drown?'

'I panicked – I can't swim. By the time I found a lifebelt it was too late, she was gone.'

'What did you do next?'

'I went for the car, but when I returned Elizabeth had gone as well. I figured she'd witnessed the fight, got scared and left. She hasn't been in to work. I've tried to phone her, but she won't return my phone calls – she's like that.'

'And then?' said Buchanan.

'I went home and had a couple of drinks. The next thing I knew it was eleven-thirty the next morning. Strange thing, Inspector, I had the best night's sleep in years. I often wondered what it would be like to be single again. Now I know, I can't say I'm sorry she's gone.'

'Who's gone, sir?' asked Buchanan.

'Why, Susan of course. She drowned in the Marina – I saw her go in.'

'I wouldn't be so sure about that. I have reasons to believe your wife may still be alive, sir.'

'Then who? Oh no, it can't be! Tell me it isn't Elizabeth?'

'We haven't had the results of the post mortem yet. As soon as we do, we'll get in touch,' said Street.

'Is it possible that there was a fight, and Susan killed Elizabeth? No, no, it's too horrible to contemplate.'

♦

'What do we do now, sir?' asked Street, as they drove off. 'Could Richardson's wife have killed his mistress?'

'Interesting lass. Let's keep an eye on Greyspear for a couple of days; see what he gets up to.'

'But if not her, who then? I'll bet Greyspear's hiding her somewhere, getting ready for a getaway, that's why the suitcases were in the hall.'

'All things are possible, lass. In the meantime, shall we go see Bashir and Silverstein?'

'Just what I was going to suggest.'

'Who should we bother first?'

'How about we shake Silverstein's tree? I'll call his office and make sure he's in.'

'Just a minute, lass, if they're in it together, I don't want them having the chance of concocting a story, though if they are then they'll have already worked out some sort of alibi. No, we'll just show up and shake the tree.'

'Pity we can't get them both down the station at the same time, make them sweat a bit.'

'You've been reading too many Chandler stories.'

'Actually, I'm working my way through the Hammett short stories at the moment. Must be interesting to work as a PI in California, they get to shoot the villains there.'

'Well, at least most of our villains don't carry guns – on second thoughts, give Bashir a call, ask to talk to the daughter and see if the father is in. I'll call Silverstein, chat with the wife, and ask if hubby is at work today.'

◆

'Bashir's in, sir, how about Silverstein?'

'He's at the dentist, having his teeth deep-cleaned, won't be back for an hour and a half. Apparently, they have to knock him out for treatment.'

'In that case, Bashir it is.'

◆

'Good afternoon, Mr Bashir.'

'Inspector, Sergeant, what brings you here?'

'Can we come in, sir? We'd like to ask you a few questions, it won't take long.'

'Sure, come in. I'm sorry I can't offer you tea or coffee, my wife isn't here, gone shopping with Ayesha.'

'That's OK, sir.'

They followed Bashir through into his office. He offered two chairs and went behind his desk and sat down. 'Now, Inspector, how can I help?'

'Can you tell us where you were on the evening of the sixth of April?'

Bashir smiled. 'Can you tell me where you were?' he said, looking at his diary.

'I was in hospital, sir.'

'Sorry to hear that, but all seems to have worked out. Ah, here we are: we were in London on the sixth of April. We went to listen to Deborah and Aaron playing at St Martin in the Fields.'

'And you were there to listen to them play what?'

'They weren't the only performers, but I believe everyone had mainly come to listen to them.'

'What did they play?'

'Schubert's *Arpeggione*, all three movements.'

'Lovely piece, I have a recording done by Britten and Rostropovich.'

'Inspector, I'm a busy man and I'm sure you didn't come here to talk music.'

'What was the concert in aid of?'

'It was a fundraising event for the victims of terror in Palestine.'

'Was it just the two of you who went to listen?'

'No. Ayesha went along with us, as did Mrs Silverstein.' 'What time did you get home?'

'Not sure, I do remember it was well after midnight. We got held up on the A23, lorry had rolled over and spilled diesel all over the carriageway. Took ages for them to reopen the road.'

'Why not take the train?'

'Sir Nathan offered a ride in his car, it was chauffeur driven, a very pleasant ride.'

'Can you try and remember what time you got home, sir? It is important.'

Bashir leaned back in his chair and stared at the wall behind Street. Buchanan turned to see what Bashir was looking at: another Osborne – this one was of a striking sunrise over a beach.

'Inspector, I do remember, it was just after one. I recall thinking that one in the morning for us was six in the evening in California. I called a business acquaintance.'

'Bit odd.'

'Not at all. When we got in the door I turned on the TV to catch the news. There was an item on Al Jazeera about an ISIS attack on an oil pipeline in Iraq. I reasoned the price of oil would rise so I called my friend and together we bought some oil futures.'

'Did it pay off?'

'Yes, the price only shifted marginally, but enough for us to make a tidy profit.'

'Who was dropped off first?'

'That was the Silversteins, in deference to Deborah and Aaron having played for us.'

'And that would be just before one?'

'Yes, I suppose it would have been.'

'Was anyone else with you?'

'Yes, my wife and daughter.'

'What about Sir Nathan?'

'Yes, of course he was there, it was his car we were being driven in. Besides, he's the patron of the charity. It makes a big difference to the size of the donations when you have a titled patron.'

'Was he alone?'

'Depends by what you mean by alone.'

'Was he accompanied by anyone?'

'Mrs Richardson. She's his PA.'

'Did she go home with Sir Nathan?'

'Not sure. She was still in the car when we were dropped off.'

'Did Sir Nathan receive any phone calls during the evening?'

'Don't remember – oh, just a minute. He did get one, just before he was to go up on stage and give a speech.'

'How did he react?'

'Bit annoyed at first, but then seemed to relax and said something to the effect that it was OK and he would see them later.'

'Mr Bashir, I would like you to come down to the police station and give a statement to these facts.'

'Am I being arrested?'

'No, not at all; it just helps the investigation to have official statements. We have professional stenographers who will transcribe what you have to say. Would tomorrow be convenient? We'll send a car for you.'

'After ten, I'm too busy before that and don't bother sending a car.'

'We will also be asking Mr Silverstein for his account of the evening.'

'And Mrs Richardson and Sir Nathan's?'

'Thank you, Mr Bashir. We'll see you at the station tomorrow.'

24

'Just read Silverstein's version of the evening of the sixth, sir,' said Street.

'Anything stand out for you, lass?'

'No. Practically word for word the same as Bashir's account of the evening.'

'Did you check about the accident on the A23?'

'Yes, it was reported at ten-fifteen, traffic didn't start to flow till near midnight.'

'So that would have got them home about – one in the morning.'

'Just like they said in their statements.'

'Wish Mrs Richardson was here to interview.'

'You still don't think she's dead?'

Buchanan shook his head. 'Unlikely, but where is she? Who's hiding her?'

'Sir Nathan?'

'Don't think that's likely, you saw how panicked he was when we were going through his love nest.'

'Anything from Interpol about Abosa yet?'

'I talked with the Chief earlier this morning; she says Abosa will be charged with trafficking and held pending investigations into a couple of unsolved killings in France. If they can't get anything to stick, they'll hand him over to us. Either way, we're way down the pecking order when it comes to Abosa.'

'At least he's out of the picture for now, and that makes one less murder suspect for us to pursue.'

'Maybe, but let's not be too hasty in eliminating him. Either way we still need to process the paperwork. Well now, that just leaves us three murders, one suspicious death and a missing PA to sort out.'

'Talking of which, any conclusions about the statements by our friends?'

'Points to Greyspear again. He did get a phone call during the evening. If it was from Nichols then we've got a case for bringing Greyspear in for questioning under caution. I think we'll get a warrant for his phone call record, see if he did get a call from Nichols during the evening.'

'And if he didn't?"

Buchanan shrugged. 'Do we have his mobile number?'

Street consulted HOLMES. 'Yes, got it, and the airtime provider.'

'Good, get moving on it, then we're going for a conference.'

'Smugglers?'

Buchanan smiled and shook his head. 'Starbucks. This type of conference requires caffeine.'

♦

'Grab the settee in the corner, I'll get the coffee, I suppose you want a –' Buchanan looked up at the selection of drinks available, 'an Iced Caramel Macchiato?'

'No. How about a Mango and Passion Fruit Frappuccino, instead?'

Buchanan grinned and ordered a large Americano for himself.

'Thanks, sir,' said Street, taking a sip. 'Where shall we start?'

'In a minute. Ever wonder what people do for a living?'

'Sometimes curiosity gets the better of me.'

'Go on.'

'A friend and I used to go out for tea in the village tea room and afterwards we'd discuss what we heard other people talk about. Quite revealing and possibly embarrassing for them had they realised we could overhear what they were saying!'

'What about doing a Sherlock Holmes'

'What do you mean?'

'Have a look at that chap at the counter. What can you tell about him?'

'Neatly dressed. Office worker, I'd say.'

'That all?'

Street shrugged her shoulders.

'Right, let's start with the obvious. Yes, he's smartly dressed, shaved head, with a neatly trimmed beard, and the grey suede shoes make a statement. His jacket doesn't match his trousers, shows signs of hanging on a peg, so he's used to working without it, ergo he probably works in an office environment, probably without air conditioning. But the jacket says he has to go out and meet people and still look smartly casual. He does a lot of driving, look at the creases in the back of his jacket.'

'So, Sherlock, what does he do for a living?'

'Not a nine to fiver. Used car salesman? Nah, don't think so. Social worker more likely, some sort of job where he's able to keep his shoes clean.'

'How about banking?'

'Nah – trousers too wrinkled.'

'He could be one of us – see the way he scans the room.'

'Maybe. Or of course he could be an IT engineer.'

'Not with those shoes and those trousers, I would say he spends most of his time sitting at a desk or driving.'

'Taxi driver?'

'Not at Starbucks, they don't make enough money to buy coffee here.'

'That's an unfair assumption.'

'OK, I'll give you that. I think he's a teacher, probably secondary, I'd say he teaches something technical.'

'That makes sense. Shall we get back now to why we're here?'

'Let's go back to the beginning then. This whole story rotates round Greyspear, so that's where we'll begin.'

'We know his wealth came from his two marriages.'

'The money may have come from his two wives, but it was his genius at business that turned his paltry inherited wealth into the empire that it is today.'

'Granted, lass. During his rise to prominence he has demonstrated a flair for making money and making that money work for him. So it is quite reasonable that he would attract others of like ilk to his circle.'

'Like Silverstein and Bashir. Between them they know more about Greyspear's wealth than the great man does himself.'

'Good point, but let's get back to why we're here. Last November there was a break-in at Greyspear's stables; a large quantity of tack was stolen. Greyspear said the loss could have been in the multiple thousands, though thankfully it was soon recovered.'

'I read about that. Customs got a tip-off and a week later a lorry was searched at Newhaven. Those on the lorry had no paperwork to prove they had ownership of the contents, and it was impounded. They were arrested on suspicion of being in possession. Could Nichols have set it up to get close to Greyspear?'

'He shows up as the investigating officer, all smiles that the tack has been found, then makes a pitch to Greyspear about supplying a private security service, possibly hoping Greyspear will fund his plans. He also offers the services of his house as a discrete meeting place for the investors Greyspear has put together for the movie idea. As a result of these meetings, Nichols makes friends with –'

'You mean he hits on Silverstein's daughter, Deborah.'

'She's smitten. Maybe he comes over as a big executive in his own security firm and before she realises what's happening Nichols is trying his best to get into –'

'Don't forget he was trying it on with Ayesha as well.'

'That's true lass; he gets caught with his pants down by Greyspear, who gives him a lesson on what you don't do with the family of his friends.'

'I had thought it possible the fathers and Greyspear had done Nichols in, but now it doesn't look like it.'

'Either way, as soon as Greyspear gives Nichols his lesson in etiquette, he disappears from the scene, till he turns up dead in the Marina.'

'What a way to go.'

'As part of Greyspear's way of doing business he takes the investors out for the day while demonstrating to the Carstairs how well the *Moonstone* handles.'

'Wonder if they actually bought one?'

'They'd probably lease it; no business likes to unnecessarily tie up cash like that.'

'That makes sense.'

'That's beside the point. Anyway, on returning from the pleasant day out, one of the guests pushes Olga off the transom and leaves her to drown.'

'We haven't talked to the crew yet.'

'Add that to your list of things to do, but I think we'll draw a blank.'

'You know, we are assuming that Maxton was really sleeping off his sea sickness. No one saw him all day. He could have pushed Olga off the boat.'

Buchanan shook his head, 'Metzger told me he gave Maxton a couple of pills to help him sleep, also told him not to drink alcohol with them.'

'And did he take the advice?'

'Apparently not, Maxton slept for twelve hours straight. His wife had to wake him up when they tied up at the dock.'

'We also found that Nichols was renting a bedroom to Olga. Why was that?'

'She was very attractive; just have a look at her twin.'

'But she was pregnant.'

'Do you think that would have put Nichols off – especially now we know what a womaniser he was?'

'Just doesn't seem right.'

'Of course it's not. Women all over the world have to put up with characters like Nichols treating them like playthings.'

'Didn't take you for being a women's libber.'

'I'm not; I just think women deserve more respect, regardless of how they look.'

'Is that how you see me?'

'No, of course not, you're different.'

'Hmm, I think we should get back to why we're here. It's possible that Nichols was actually working on the trafficking angle and providing Olga with a safe haven. Pity we'll probably never know the truth.'

'What about Nichol's notebook, and all those funny entries?'

Buchanan smiled. 'I was coming to that. Last night I was looking through the photos I took of the documents inside Abosa's wallet and quite by chance I had a moment of inspiration.'

'With you there's no such thing as chance.'

'Thanks for the compliment. As I was saying, the amazing deductive power of my little grey cells made me compare Abosa's scribbles with that of the copy of the lock movements and Nichol's diary. That's when the light came on.'

'Please explain.'

'Nichols had been keeping track of the comings and goings of certain fishing boats, see the entry on the 14th February: *MB out@1855* relates to the entry on the lock gate movement log, see here it is: *MB passed through lock outbound at 1907.*'

'And Abosa's notes? How do they tie in?'

'Different fishing boat names; but if you work out how long it takes to get just past the middle of the channel, it all ties up.'

'So, late in the evening, one of the fishing boats in Dieppe gets loaded with Abosa's trafficked girls. They sail out to the middle of the channel and transfer the girls to the waiting UK fishing boat. Then the fishing boat motors back like they've been out fishing all night, and no one's any the wiser.'

'That's the theory for now.'

'But we've got channel patrols out twenty-four seven. How can the traffickers know they'll not get boarded and inspected?'

'The patrols are looking for illegal fishing, not girlfriends of the fishermen on board. The girls would probably be drugged before boarding, so if the boat is inspected the girls would be found asleep in a cabin on board and no one would be the wiser.'

'You've got it covered. The girls would arrive in the Marina, probably with one hell of a hangover and when it's dark and no one's around they would be taken ashore and placed in their accommodation. It would be explained to them just what was expected of them and what would happen if they broke the rules.'

'Do you suppose that when Olga got pregnant she was seen as a rule breaker and was punished, or was used as an example to the other girls?'

'I hate to say this, but it's just possible that she was told to get rid of the baby, refused, and was disposed of like yesterday's rubbish.'

'Pity. I'd like to get the bastard who thought Olga was rubbish and –'

'Let's keep to the discussion on hand, lass. I suppose we are assuming that either Abosa or the father of Olga's child killed her. And Nichols was attempting, for whatever reason known only to himself, to track the traffickers and killer down. He'd probably arranged to meet up with the killer the night he died.'

'So, we're right back on Greyspear's doorstep again.'

'I wish I could be sure. He does seem such a decent chap who, despite his wealth, deserves a better hand in the game of life.'

'What about Richardson? I'd rather believe he's capable of murder. You've seen how he respects women,' said Street.

'Yes, the beautiful but feisty Susan. Wouldn't want to be on the end of one of her tongue lashings.'

'I'm sure it wouldn't happen if she was treated with respect. You surmised that she and Greyspear were having a relationship.'

'You saw the flat.'

'As I was going to add, which became clear when we saw the flat. But you saw how worried he was when he realised that she really was missing and we were also looking for her.'

'Interesting point, lass. Both Richardson's wife and girlfriend go missing in one evening. I wonder—'

'I've been thinking about that. You're sure Susan Richardson's still alive?'

'Could be she has been fed up with the husband treating her like a punchbag and waiting for Greyspear to take her under his wing by proposing marriage, so she's done a runner.'

'But where to, sir?

'Unlikely she's gone to Greyspear, nor her parents, and certainly not home.'

'What about Metzger? You said he specialised in women's issues.'

Buchanan shook his head. 'Very unlikely, I don't think he deals with psychological issues, though it is just possible that they have someone in the practice who does.'

'I'll check on that, just on the off chance.'

'No, don't do that. It's time I went and stood on his toes.'

'What're we going to do about Greyspear?'

'Would you go out to the stables and talk to the sister, see if she's heard from Susan? The sister's name is Jacquelyn Masterson. Try the sympathetic sister act. I've a feeling she knows more than she's letting on.'

'OK, I'll go first thing in the morning.'

'You never explained why you came out to the stables on Sunday. Was something bothering you?'

'Er – no, I just wondered –'

'Wondered what, lass?'

She shook her head. 'I was bored and went into the office. I spent the morning going over the case notes. I wanted to discuss what I was thinking with you, that's all, nothing sinister. And now we've talked I'm satisfied, I know where the case is going.'

'Are you sure?'

'Perfectly.'

'OK, I'll run you back to the office and see you tomorrow after you've been to the stables.'

Buchanan stared out his office window and watched Street drive out of the compound. He was unsettled. Why had she come out to the stables to see him? Was it something in one of the reports she'd read?

♦

'Damn, blast, where is it?' Buchanan muttered to himself as he rummaged through the pile of papers on Street's desk. He was worried about her evasiveness when he asked her what was bothering her. He continued to search till he found what he was looking for: Hunter's report on Metzger. It was stuck behind the cushion on Street's chair.

He grabbed the phone and dialled. It rang and went to the answering service. He wasted ten minutes trying to get the answering service operator to believe the call was urgent and he had to talk to Doctor Metzger.

'Inspector, how can I help?' asked Dr Payne.

'Is my sergeant in with Doctor Metzger?'

'I'm sorry, Inspector; I'm not allowed to discuss patient information over the phone.'

'Listen, you thick-headed plonker, it's a matter of life and death that I talk to my sergeant.'

'Inspector, we have rules here.'

'You're rules are an ass. I'm on my way, and if anything untoward has happened I'll make it my life's work to see you pay for it.'

♦

It took Buchanan five and a half precious minutes to get to the clinic with his blues to navigate through the Eastbourne commuter traffic. He parked beside Street's car at the front door and charged into the outer reception.

'I need to get through,' he said, showing his warrant card to the startled receptionist. 'Quick, it's a matter of life and death!'

Startled by Buchanan's outburst the receptionist buzzed him through. He almost bowled Payne over as he barged into the main waiting room.

'Where are they? Quick man, hurry, we've no time to waste worrying about the niceties of doctor-patient confidentiality?'

It must have been the look on Buchanan's face that made Payne act. Without speaking he ran to the secure door to the consulting rooms and buzzed Buchanan through.

'Which door? Quick man, which bloody door?'

'First on the right. Wait – it's maglocked from the inside, you need the key to unlock it.'

Buchanan prayed he'd not be too late, while Payne took the lanyard from his neck and tapped the magnetic key against the pad on the wall.

Buchanan placed his hand on the door handle and with the peace he didn't feel, gently opened the door, entered, and closed it behind him. He was committed now, the maglock clicked: they were locked in.

Street was standing with her back to Buchanan, her arms outstretched, both hands holding what Buchanan realised was her mother's Walther PPK. The barrel was pointed directly at the forehead of Dr Metzger as he knelt on the floor, backed up against the wall.

'Steady lass, steady.'

'For God's sake, Inspector! Stop her, she's crazy!'

'Dr Metzger, please relax. No one's going to get hurt.'

'Don't be too sure of that, sir. The scum deserves to pay for what he did.'

'Killing Dr Metzger is not going to solve anything, lass.'

'Maybe not, but at least it'll stop him from killing any more children.'

'Performing terminations is not killing children,' whined Metzger.

'That's your lie. Have you ever taken the trouble to talk afterwards with the women whose children you've murdered? No, I'll bet you haven't. Just too busy, I'll bet.'

'What – what have I ever done to you? I've never seen you before in my life.'

'You don't remember, do you? A scared little girl who'd been raped and fallen pregnant, another little inconvenience for you to take care of.'

'I'm really sorry for your grief, but you've must have me confused with someone else.'

'He'd be fifteen on his last birthday. He'd be getting ready to sit his GCSE's, thinking about A levels, university and his future. There's not even a grave marker for me to put flowers on, I've nothing but emptiness and nightmares. How many children did you kill to pay for your nice, shiny, silver Rolls Royce, Doctor?'

'Please, I don't kill children– I perform terminations, it's all legal and above board.'

'Huh, you're just a bloody prostitute, selling your skills to the highest bidder. You'll never wash the blood from your hands.'

'Inspector, please – stop her before she does something she'll regret for the rest of her life.'

'Who'd blame me if I did? I assure you, *Doctor*, I'll have no regrets.'

'Jill, are you sure this is what you want? If you go through with this, it will mean jail, probably for life.'

'What's the difference? My whole life is a prison sentence. Do you know how often I've sat on the edge at Beachy Head, and been too scared to jump and too scared to face another day with the loss of what might have been? At least this way I'll have done something about it, got vengeance for my son.'

'Jill, you don't even know it was a boy.'

'There, you're at it as well.'

'At what?'

'You said *it*. The, *it* you referred to, was my son, a boy.'

'Sorry, Jill. Your son.'

'Would one of you please explain what the hell is going on? I'm the one facing down the barrel of a gun.'

'Dr Metzger, fifteen years ago you were the house doctor at Radleigh School for the children of diplomats. One evening you attended an accident in one of the private bedrooms. The PE teacher, Mr Salter, had been shot and lay there dying from a single gunshot wound. You weren't able to save him and when you checked you found out there was no next of kin. Along with the Mother Superior it was decided, for the good of the school's reputation, to say nothing about the shooting. You filled out the death certificate showing cause of death to be chronic heart failure and had the deceased cremated. Am I correct?'

'How on earth do you know that, Inspector? There were no witnesses.'

'I'm coming to that, Dr Metzger. The reason Mr Salter had been shot was that a young teenager, afraid for her very life, shot him in self-defence. With the very gun whose barrel you are staring down.'

'So this is what it's about. You're taking revenge, see it as some kind of poetic justice. Hah, you're no better than how you paint me! Even so, you won't get away with it. Even if you shoot me, you'll never get my body out of here without someone seeing you. The whole clinic is covered with CCTV cameras, and the camera feeds go off-site.'

'CCTV won't do you any good if you're dead.'

'Too late. As soon as I saw the look on your face I pushed the panic button. Even if they're not here yet, the police are on their way.'

'Dr Metzger, in case you haven't realised, we *are* the police. There's no one else coming to your aid. You're all alone.'

Buchanan looked over at Street, trying to judge how unstable her emotions were. He saw, with trepidation, her right thumb quivering over the safety catch. Up till this moment she couldn't have pulled the trigger, but now Buchanan was concerned. He needed to end this standoff.

'Signing the death certificate wasn't the only crime you committed that day,' said Buchanan.

'And what was that, Inspector? Surprise me.'

'You administered an abortion pill to a minor and in doing so almost caused her death by causing her to spontaneously abort the child she was carrying.'

'For heaven's sake man! she'd been raped and was pregnant. I was just looking after her best interests. She'd get over it, plenty of time to think about having a family later.'

'You're the lowest of the low. You were only thinking about the school's reputation and your job. You knew if the story got out you'd all be finished.'

'Tell him, sir, make the bastard sweat.'

'Surely you're not going to believe this fairy tale, Inspector?' said Metzger, getting to his feet. 'She's obviously mentally unbalanced; I've seen it all before. Made an orphan at an early age, creates a fantasy world, mind full of self-pity, looking for someone to feel sorry for her. I'd send her to the company psychiatrist if I were you; she's a danger to herself and the public.'

There was an audible click as the safety catch was released. 'Back on your knees. You called me a stupid girl, you and that bitch, the Mother Superior. How was I supposed to know what was happening to me? I was only fourteen; I'd never had a boyfriend or been on a date. I was still a child.'

'And you're still a child. Brought your dad along to watch you get your vengeance?'

'*My dad*? I don't need anyone to fight my battles for me. I've killed before; one more is not going to make any difference.'

'Please, I need to go to the toilet.'

'Go piss yourself. How many children have you killed in the past fifteen years, Dr Metzger? How many inconvenient accidents have you taken care of? How you manage to sleep at night with all those dead children crying out for justice is beyond me. I've dreamt about this day for the last fifteen years. The only pity is that bitch isn't here to suffer along with you.'

'She's dead: heart attack.'

'Hope it was a painful death. Dr Metzger, today you have been tried and found guilty of the murder of one little boy, my son. Your future will, oh dear, unfortunately you don't have one. I, on the other hand, have nothing to look forward to except the nightmares and feelings of emptiness. Lying awake through the long nights thinking of what could have been. It will be very easy for me to pull this trigger and send you into hell where you belong – but I'm not going to. I've found out that it's better to forgive – to put down the burden of the hurts, the anger, and the desire for revenge – than it is to seek to hurt those who hurt you. Dr Metzger, I choose to forgive you. Today is the first day of the rest of your life; don't waste it.'

'Jill, I think it's time to call it a day,' interrupted Buchanan, reaching over and putting his hand on the pistol. 'Come on, lass, let me have the gun. Dr Metzger has got your point. He'll never forget today, I'm sure of that.'

'I'll sue you both, and the police,' said Metzger, trying to get up off the floor and from the ever-expanding pool of urine. 'You'll both go to jail for this. It's nothing but police brutality – threatening to shoot someone is still a crime in this country.'

Buchanan chuckled and held up the gun. 'With this? It's a toy, Dr Metzger, Twenty quid on eBay,'

Metzger fainted. The maglock released and a very worried Payne entered. As soon as he saw Metzger on the floor he rushed over, bent down and cradled him in his arms.

Buchanan put Street's gun in his pocket, turned to her and saw tears forming in her eyes. 'Come here, lass,' he said, arms open wide. She stepped into his embrace, tears streaming down her face and hugged him.

'He called you my dad,' she said, between sobs.

'Is that a problem?'

She shook her head and snuggled into his embrace.

◆

'So, Jill, Jack says you stood on the edge today – for the last time?'

Street nodded. 'I think so – oh. how I hope it's so.'

'Jack, we need some milk. Pop out and get some, would you?'

'OK. I hear it's one penny off at Morrison's in Brighton.'

'I heard it's two pence off in Christchurch.'

Buchanan smiled, and nodded in understanding. 'Back in a while.'

◆

When Buchanan entered the house, the only light came from the living room lamp on the side table. An empty wine bottle stood lonely on the coffee table, two empty glasses beside it. Karen

310

snored quietly on one end of the settee; Street lay with her head in Karen's lap.

Karen stirred at Buchanan's presence.

'Thought I'd try the price of milk in Southampton. How is the lass?'

'Cried herself to sleep an hour ago. I think she'll be fine, just needs some tender loving care.'

'Can't send her home now, wouldn't be right.'

'Jack, carry her through to the guest room, I'll put her to bed.'

Buchanan returned a few minutes later and stood at the bedroom door as Karen tucked the sleeping Street into the bed. 'We've waited a lot of years to be able to do this.'

'It's been worth it. You know what she said when you were out?'

Buchanan shook his head.

'She said the doctor called you her dad, and you said you didn't mind. Is that true?'

Buchanan put his arm round Karen and pulled her close.

'You know Stephen has proposed to her?' she said.

'No, he never breathed a word.'

'I've invited them to dinner this Saturday.'

Buchanan chuckled. 'In one day I've become a father and now I'm gaining a son-in-law. What a day.'

25

The sun rose in a clear blue sky. Buchanan dressed and went down for breakfast. He recognised something about today as being one of those rare days that occurs in every investigation: they were near the end.

'Bacon and eggs, Jack?'

'Sounds great. How's Jill?'

'Sleeping like a baby. Toast's in the toaster; do you want your coffee now?'

'Please. Been quite a couple of days, can't remember when we've had so much excitement.'

'How about the time you cornered Johnnie Stark down the tunnel he'd dug out the back of Maggie Wylie's to the bank across the street?'

'How could I forget? He'd completed his digging and was about to blow a hole in the vault floor when I stopped him.'

'He threatened to blow you to kingdom come, if I remember?'

'Oh, aye, that was a close one.'

'What was a close one?'

'Morning, Jill. Just one of Jack's old cases when he was a PC in Port Glasgow.'

'I'd love to hear about that – but first, is there any coffee left? I could do with one.'

'Just made a fresh pot – milk, sugar?'

'Black, two sugars, please.'

'Coming right up. We didn't want to wake you, thought you needed your sleep.'

'No, I was just dozing, my mind's too full.'

'How'd you sleep?'

'Like a baby. Sorry to have caused you so much trouble yesterday.'

'No trouble at all, lass.'

'I'm a bit worried about Dr Metzger. What I did was wrong, I know that, but it did feel good.'

'Don't worry, lass. He deserved it, and more. Besides, his troubles are just starting.'

'What do you mean, just starting? It's mine that are just starting, if he makes a complaint.'

'What you did yesterday was wrong, but good will come out of it, eventually. I'm sure of that.'

'Sorry, you've lost me on that.'

'No matter how Dr Metzger justifies what he has done for a living, he now has a decision to make. You actually helped him with what you did.'

Street shook her head. 'I still don't understand.'

'As I see it, when someone like Dr Metzger goes through life, their actions impacting on other's lives, and does it without contemplating the fullness of their actions, they will inevitably one day have to look at their reflection in the mirror.'

'But not everyone does what Dr Metzger does for a living.'

'Good point. It could be anything though – even being angry with someone. For instance, did you watch the news last week, about the shooting at the church in California?'

'Yes, but I don't get your point.'

'Some of the congregation were allowed to speak to the gunman via a video link. The camera didn't show them, just the killer.'

'I missed that. Bet they were angry.'

'No, they actually forgave him. One woman told him how sad she was at her loss, how nothing could ever replace her daughter and husband, but through her tears she still forgave him. Here he was, guilty, and stripped of the cloak of anger that he'd worn for many years, the very same anger he'd used to justify his hatred, and actions. He was now, to all intents and purposes, standing naked in front of his victims' families, with no justification for what he had done.'

'And you think that's what Dr Metzger did yesterday, even though he was staring down the barrel of the gun?'

Buchanan nodded and took another sip of coffee. 'It's always easier for someone in that position to continue in their denial, always harder to face up to their actions. As I see it, had you been angry and maybe even taken a shot at him –'

'Couldn't – the gun wasn't loaded. Just wanted to scare him, couldn't trust myself.'

'So I subsequently found out. Anyway, had you taken a shot, and not killed him, he would then have been angry and would have justified his life and actions. The fact you didn't shoot and forgave him means he now has a lot of soul-searching to do.'

'What about the gun? I suppose I'll have to surrender it and put up with the consequences of owning it.'

Buchanan shook his head. 'It's all sorted.'

'How?'

He looked at his wife. 'The next time Karen goes to see her mother by ferry, she'll just drop the gun over the side in mid-channel.'

'Is that legal?'

'No, but it's an extremely expedient method of getting rid of something unwanted.'

'I'm still worried about Dr Metzger. He's had time to sleep on it – maybe he'll file a complaint.'

'Don't worry, he's a smart man. He won't risk that kind of publicity, consider the matter closed. And you, my young lady, are taking the day off. Too much stress in your life these last few days.'

'But what about you? There are still two murders to solve.'

'Tell you what, since Dexter's still away, I'll call Hunter. You can work with him today.'

'What's he doing?'

'Tidying up loose ends. I'm going to send him out to Castlewood and go through the reports, see if we've missed anything. And besides, I hear you'd be quite happy to spend the day with him?'

'You know?'

'Karen told me last night when you were sleeping. Congratulations.'

♦

'They make a lovely couple, don't they, Jack?' said Karen, as Hunter and Street headed off to Castlewood.

'Yes. And I've got work to do – see you at tea time.'

♦

Buchanan sipped on his coffee and was about to make a phone call when his phone rang.

'Buchanan. I'm in the office – no, not that one – Starbucks. What is it, lass? You've found her? Good girl. Hold on till I get there and don't let her know you've seen her.'

♦

Buchanan drove out to Castlewood, windows down, car heater on full and singing along with Tony Bennett that he'd left his heart in San Francisco. He parked beside Hunter's police car.

'How did you find her, lass?'

'Bit of luck, really. The café was busy, and Stephen and I wanted to discuss some private matters, so we decided to go for a wander through the grounds. As we passed the cottage I saw Susan Richardson through the open window.'

'Where's Hunter?'

'I told him to wait outside the cottage and keep an eye on it – don't want her to scarper.'

'Makes sense. Where's the cottage?'

'You go around the stable block and turn right towards the woods. There's a gravel driveway that leads into the forest. The cottage is just around the corner, used to be a gamekeeper's lodge.'

'And you're sure it's her?'

'Yes, I had Stephen go to the door and ask for directions. I hid behind a bush and watched. It's definitely her.'

'Come on then, lass, last chapter. Let's hear from the fair Susan herself.'

♦

'Good afternoon, Mrs Richardson.'

'Oh, it's you again! How did –'

'Old-fashioned police work, Mrs Richardson. Can we come in, please? We have some questions we'd like to ask you.'

'Er, yes, come in.'

She led them through to the open-plan living room and kitchen.

'Very cosy, Mrs Richardson. Does Sir Nathan know you're staying here?'

'No, and please don't tell him.'

'Can we go back to the evening of Friday the first of this month? Will you tell us what happened to cause you to go missing?'

'I suppose it will come out eventually. That Friday, Nathan and I went out to dinner.'

'Where was this?'

'Luigi's – it's in the Marina.'

'See anyone you knew?'

'I wasn't looking for anyone.'

'What time did you leave?'

'*We* didn't; *I* did.'

'Can you explain?'

'Nathan and I had an argument and I went to the Ladies. When I'd composed myself I came out and noticed a fire exit door at the end of the corridor. Instead of turning right, back to the restaurant, I turned left and went through the fire door. It was subsequently a decision I regret. I wandered round towards the car park and ran into Rodney; he was just as surprised as I was.'

'What happened next?'

'I thought you'd have talked to him and know what happened next?'

'He's made a statement. I'd like to hear your account of the events of the evening.'

'I admit I was angry, especially when I realised Rodney was with *her*. He'd told me he would be in London till late Sunday, the lying bastard.'

'What did you argue with Sir Nathan about?'

'The usual.'

'And what was the usual?'

'He wanted me to leave Rodney.'

'And why wouldn't you?'

'Inspector, when a woman reaches my age, she wants security. In spite of Rodney's philandering, he at least provided for us.'

'Surely Sir Nathan would have done that for you? He's a very wealthy man?'

'Possibly, but he never offered, and besides, money's not everything. I needed him to make a commitment.'

'Like marriage?'

She nodded. 'I'm an old-fashioned girl, Inspector. I need the security of marriage, good or bad.'

'So, you confronted your husband. What happened next?'

'He kept walking off. I think he was headed for his car, he just kept ignoring me. I – I'm sorry to say I snapped. I ran at him and tried to hit him with my handbag. The stupid strap broke and the contents flew out. He moved back away from me and when I ran at him again he stepped to the side and stuck out his foot. I tripped over it and fell headlong into the harbour.'

'You managed to find the steps and make your way up on to the quayside?'

'Sort of. I grabbed the dock line of one of the fishing boats and waited while I caught my breath. I then swam to the steps and when I got to the top I was confronted by my husband's mistress. She lunged at me with a broken bottle – I dodged, and she went in where I had just got out. I looked, but there was no sign of her. Being attacked twice in one evening was enough for me.'

'You found your handbag, took out your purse, makeup, and mobile, then threw the handbag in the bin?'

'Yes, it was an old one; I was going to replace it anyway.'

'What about your husband?'

'I guess I'll be replacing him as well, oops – that's not quite what you meant, is it? Anyway, I hid in the doorway of the gift shop till he gave up looking for her. He kept calling her name, not mine. He'd given up on me, and I suppose he wondered where she'd got to, because he kept going into the restaurant. He kept on calling for her; he didn't give a shit about me.'

'What did you do next?'

'I started walking.'

'Where to?'

'Nowhere in particular, I – I just started walking. I didn't want to be found. I turned right at the main road and ended up in Pevensey Bay, sore, tired, and soaking wet.

'Is that when you called your sister?'

She nodded. 'She picked me up, and we drove for ages.'

'Where to?'

'No idea, we just drove. It was Jacq –'

'Jacq?'

'Jacq, Jacqueline, my sister. It was she who suggested I stay at the holiday cottage in the grounds; that way she could keep in touch without letting on where I was.'

'Smart lady, just like her sister.'

'Thanks. I needed time to think, things had to change. I was afraid he'd do it again if he found out what I was contemplating.'

'Who'd find out what, Mrs Richardson?'

'Inspector, you're after the wrong man.'

'And just who am I after, Mrs Richardson?'

'Sir Nathan's not the killer; I now realise he's the most gentle, loving, caring man I know. He'd never intentionally hurt anyone.'

'And who should I be looking for?'

'The day we went out on the *Moonstone,* I told you my husband was with me all the time. Well, he wasn't.'

'Go on.'

'Oh, he spent most of the time in the pantry all right. He wasn't working though, he was flirting with the waitresses; he thought I didn't notice, but I did.'

'Any one of them in particular?'

'There was one; I remember her trying to avoid him, made him angry.'

'Is this the girl, Mrs Richardson?' asked Street, showing the photo of Olga.

'That's her. Very pretty.'

'Not now she isn't.'

'Why – what happened to her? Oh no, she's the one who fell overboard and drowned, isn't she? Pregnant, I read in the newspaper. Surely you don't think Rodney had anything to do with her death, do you, Inspector?'

'Can you recall any time that your husband was definitely out of the pantry?'

'Just before we tied up, one of the catering team wanted to ask him a question, something about a future engagement, I think.'

'When did you see your husband next?'

'It was just before we tied up, I remember the boat lurched. Nathan said Harry Carstair was manoeuvring us alongside the dock and put on too much reverse thrust.'

'So your husband was gone for, say, about twenty minutes?'

'No – couldn't be more than fifteen.'

'Does the name Abosa mean anything to you?'

'Yes, he's a business acquaintance of Rodney's.'

'Was he out on the *Moonstone* on the 29th?'

'No, definitely not.'

'Do you remember seeing Dr Metzger on the 29th – the day you went out on the *Moonstone?*'

'I suppose you'll find out anyway, you seem to know a lot already.'

'Find out what?'

'One of the crew tripped and fell in the engine room. He cut his arm quite badly, made a bit of a mess, dripped blood all over the crew passageway on deck two. Someone went to look for Dr Metzger. He was found in one of the staterooms, powdering his nose.'

'Powdering his nose?'

'He had his nose to the dresser, sniffing up lines of cocaine. Nathan was furious when he found out, wanted to turn him over to the police.'

'Why didn't he?'

'Metzger threatened to blow the story of the syndicate raising money for the film.'

'Why would that be an issue?'

'Money for movies is hard to raise, and besides, we didn't have the rights to the film at that point. If it got out that Nathan was putting together a syndicate, and the fact that Dr Metzger was found snorting cocaine on Nathan's boat, well, who knows where the price for the rights would end up, or if we would even be able to get a deal. As soon as we got back, Nathan had Dr Metzger escorted off the *Moonstone.*'

'What was to stop Dr Metzger making good his threat?'

'He'd already made a sizable investment in the film and he was told he'd have to wait till hell froze over before he'd get it back if he went to the press.'

'And did he get it back?'

'We got the rights agreed last week and Dr Metzger's cheque went in the post the next day, second class post.'

'Abosa: what's the arrangement he has with your husband?'

'Abosa runs an employment agency in Hungary, sends girls over to work in restaurants and bars. Rodney hires some of them when he needs a catering team.'

'Is that all?'

She sighed, tears coming to her eyes. 'If I tell you, can you assure me I'll get police protection?'

'I'd need to hear what you have to say before –'

'Will I get police protection? If not, I've nothing more to say.'

'If what you have to say warrants police protection, I guarantee protection will be provided.'

'All right. I think those girls that Abosa hires are actually trafficked.'

'Do you have any proof of that?'

'The girl in Abbotts Wood, the one who was strangled – Rodney said she was one of Abosa's girls, said she needed to be taught a lesson not to talk.'

'When did he say this?'

'Monday the 27th. I remember it because we'd been to the Pashley Manor Gardens Tulip Festival. Rodney didn't want to go, but I made him. On the way back, he had a phone call; it was from Abosa. They argued. I'm sorry, Inspector, I hate driving. The A21 was full of commuter traffic and I was concentrating on my driving. I don't remember much of the conversation. All I do remember was that Rodney was furious with Abosa and went back out as soon as we got home.'

'Did he say where he was going?'

'No, just said not to wait up, he'd be late.'

'Can you tell me what time he went out?'

'Yes, I was listening to the radio and *I'm Sorry I Haven't A Clue* just came on.

'That would be about six-thirty?'

'Suppose so.'

'What time did he return?'

'The news had just come on, so I guess that would be about ten.'

'How'd he look? Was he still angry?'

'No, he looked weird, like a child being caught after doing something wrong and now looking for sympathy. His hand was injured – he'd wrapped his handkerchief round it; the handkerchief was soaked in blood.'

'Did you ask him about the injury?'

'He said he'd hurt it changing a tyre. He was lying.'

'How do you know?'

'He wouldn't know how to change a tyre if his life depended on it. Years ago – we hadn't been married long – we were on holiday in the Lake District. A tyre blew out and he had me stand beside the car while he went and hid behind a tree, hoping that someone would take pity on me and change the tyre for us.'

'What happened to the handkerchief?'

'Who knows? Probably in the bin – it wasn't in the laundry when I did the wash.'

'Did he get medical help for his injury?'

'He tried to bandage it himself, but gave up.'

'Did he go to A&E?'

'Don't think so. He made a phone call, and then went back out. When he returned, his hand was properly bandaged.'

Buchanan took out his phone. 'Who's this? Bill, I need a forensics team to go to the Richardson's' house asap.' He turned and looked at Susan Richardson.

'Go ahead, there's a key in the flowerpot beside the door.'

'Thanks, Mrs Richardson.'

'You're absolutely welcome. Just hope it's still there.'

'Bill, you don't require a search warrant, owner's given permission to enter. The address is. The Oaks, Beach Copse, it's in Meads. You'll be met by DS Street and PC Hunter. DS Street's SIO for this, she'll tell you what to look for.' He put the phone back in his pocket 'Jill, Stephen, as soon as we are done here, head over there, and make sure you find that handkerchief.'

He turned back to Susan Richardson. 'Mrs Richardson, the night you returned from London and the concert. Did your husband go out again?'

'Yes, but I didn't wait up for him. I'm not sure when he got in.'

'Does he have his own car?'

'Yes, it's a dark blue Saab convertible; you can't miss it, one wing's only got primer paint on it.'

'Why's that?'

'Someone backed into his car, and dented the wing, didn't stop to leave details. Rodney didn't want to call his insurance and got a quote from a garage. They started the repair, but when he heard how much they wanted for the paint, he fell out with the garage. He said he'd get it done cheaper somewhere else, but he never did.'

'CCTV again, sir?'

'Yes, lass, you know what night.'

'Mrs Richardson, do you know if he supplied a team to DS Nichols' house when the syndicate met there?'

'Don't know a DS Nichols.'

'This is DS Nichols, Mrs Richardson,' said Street, showing her the photograph of Nichols.

'Yes, that's him, but didn't know he's a policeman.'

'He *was*, Mrs Richardson. I'm afraid that several people your husband knows are currently reclining in the Eastbourne morgue.'

'I'm sorry, Inspector. I know very little about Rodney's business deals.'

'What will you do now?'

'I suppose I'll stay here for a few more days. before moving back to the house. I'm having dinner with Jacq this evening. I need to get life back to normal, whatever that is these days.'

'What will you do about your husband?'

'Need to find him first, unfortunately.'

'Do you know where he is? We'd like to talk to him.'

She shook her head. 'I had Jacq call the house, no answer. She also tried his office, but they said he hadn't been in for several days and didn't know when to expect him back.'

'What about Sir Nathan? Will you contact him, let him know you're ok?'

'I'll call him in the morning; do him good to miss me one more day,' she said, as a smile grew across her face.

'Thank you, Mrs Richardson. That will be all for now, unless there's anything else that comes to mind?'

'Inspector, all I can say is it's a pity they don't hang murderers anymore.'

♦

It was the end. An excited peace prevailed; Buchanan was staring out the window singing quietly to himself.

'We got it, sir,' exclaimed Hunter, bursting in to Buchanan's office.

'It was in the cupboard under the washbasin in his bathroom,' added Street.

'Well done, you two. Get it off to forensics; tell them we want the results yesterday. Also, have them compare Olga's baby's DNA to Richardson's – pound to a penny he's the father. Next Jill, you two head over to the harbour office and hopefully get a copy of the CCTV recording of Richardson driving into the

Marina car park; should be easy to spot it with that bodged paint job.'

'And then, sir?'

'And then,' Buchanan said looking at his watch, 'I think, then will be tomorrow. Especially by the time you check for his car and we get the DNA test results back.'

♦

Buchanan walked into his office. Street and Hunter were waiting for him, huge grins on their faces.

'OK, what's got you two so excited, as if I didn't know?'

'Bull's eye on all three counts, sir,' said Hunter. 'DNA test on the blood on the hanky is Richardson's; mixed with the blood was saliva from Ilka, positive DNA on that – and he was the father of Olga's baby.'

'And the CCTV shows him driving into the Marina car park, near to where Nichols was parked the night he died.'

'Right, Jill, let's go grab a killer. Hunter, you have your car, follow us to Richardson's office, you can have the honour of bringing him in.'

'He's still not at his office, sir, I just called to check,' said Street.

'Hunter, get on to control, give them Richardson's description and the details of his car, you can't miss it with that bodged paint job, and I would like you to go and bring Mrs Richardson down to the station. Take someone with you. Have Mrs Richardson dictate a full statement, can't have her suffering from amnesia at some future date.'

'Then what, sir?'

'Have a look around the harbour, you might just get lucky.'

Street followed Buchanan down to the lobby.

'Oh, Inspector, Dr Mansell just called, wants you to call him back, it's urgent he said, apparently there's a message for you, from – a Dr Metzger?'

325

'Where is Dr Mansell, did he say?'

'At the morgue.'

♦

Buchanan and Street made their way through the busy hospital and down to the morgue. It took them a few minutes to track down Dr Mansell.

'Ah, Inspector, you got my message.'

'Something about Dr Metzger? Is he here?'

'You don't know?'

'Know what?'

'Last night, according to his office, just before sunset he set off in his Rolls and drove down to Pevensey Bay. He must have waited till no one was around, because no one saw him drive his car over the shingle bank and down on to the sand, all the way out to the edge of the incoming tide.'

'Stupid bugger, a car that heavy would get stuck in the sand.'

'It did, right up to the door sills.'

'How'd he get it out?'

'He didn't, had to wait till low tide this morning. First they tried with a tow truck but it didn't have a long enough cable, so they used one of the fishing boat winches on the beach.'

'So, where is the doctor?'

'The last time I checked he was in ICU on life support. I've been told that it's not likely he'll survive. Dr Payne is with him.'

'What on earth happened to him?'

'In the early hours of this morning some fishermen on the beach waiting for the tide to come in saw the car and called the coastguard. They in turn called the lifeboat. Dr Metzger was lucky, another thirty minutes and he'd have drowned.'

'You said he was the lucky one?'

'According to the paramedics, when Metzger was brought ashore he kept on saying, "*Where is he?*'

'Did they ask who *he* was?'

326

'They put his ranting down to hypothermia and shock.'

'Did they look for anyone else in the car?'

Mansell shook his head. 'Apparently the weather turned nasty last night. The lifeboat crew couldn't see any sign of anyone else in the car and since it was too dangerous to send anyone in, they had to wait till this morning to recover it.'

'When was this?'

'About an hour ago.'

'What did they find?'

'When they got the car out of the water, it was empty except for some short pieces of rope and a blanket on the floor in the back.'

'You said there's a letter?'

'In my office. It's addressed to you; I didn't open it.'

'Had he been drinking?' Buchanan asked, as they followed Mansell down the corridor.

'Yes, but he had probably only had a couple of drinks, not enough to be incapacitated. His blood test was interesting: he'd ingested enough cocaine to kill a horse.'

'So, to all intents he was away with the fairies as the tide came in?'

'Looks that way.'

'Does it look like attempted suicide to you?'

'Sorry, Inspector, I determine time and type of death, not the motives behind it. If it was attempted suicide, it's the most bizarre one I've ever come across. Anyway, we'll probably never know; the incoming tide took care of any evidence there might have been. Of course, in the unlikely case that Metzger should regain consciousness, you could ask him.'

'And you're sure there are no injury marks? Bruising to the head, or signs he put up a fight?'

'I've had a good look at him; any marks he has are at least several days old.'

'No bite marks on the palms of the hands for instance?'

327

'Sorry, Inspector, no. His hands are slender and supple; perfect surgeon's hands, not a bite mark on them, but his right hand is badly injured.'

'What do you mean?'

'Looks like it's been run over by a tank: his right hand is crushed beyond use.'

'Self-inflicted?'

'Who knows? People on drugs do strange things. I once heard of a student, high on LSD, jumped out of a fourth-floor window believing he could fly.'

'I've heard worse.'

'Oh, here's the letter.'

'Thanks, very kind of someone to put it in a sealed plastic envelope.'

'That's the way it was found, inside Dr Metzger's jacket pocket. Whoever did it, intended you to read it. Aren't you going to open it?'

'Yes, but not here.'

'Where to, sir?' asked Street.

'Let's go see Dr Metzger. If he's lucid, be better if we get the story straight from the horse's mouth.'

'Inspector, I'll just check and see if he's still with us,' said Mansell.

'Good point. Thanks, Doctor. We'll wait out in the hall.'

'This way, Inspector,' said Mansell, after his phone call to the ward. 'Remarkable man, our Dr Metzger; he's regained consciousness and says he wants to talk to you.'

'Lead on then, Doctor.'

They followed Mansell up to the wards. Metzger was propped up in bed in a private room, the door ajar. Payne was sitting beside Metzger, reading to him from a book.

'Looks like Metzger really has come to, sir.'

'Inspector, it might be better if you both wait out here. I'll go in and see if he really is well enough to answer your questions.'

'Fine with me.'

Dr Mansell knocked on the door; Payne looked up and nodded. Mansell went in.

They watched as Dr Mansell examined Metzger, said something to Payne then turned and left the room.

'How is he, Doctor?'

'Not good. Under normal circumstances I would have put his chances of recovery at better than seventy-five percent, but – well, it's his heart. The stress of a busy life and burning the candle at both ends, and the near-drowning has taken its toll. I'm sorry to say, in spite of the fact he's woken, he probably won't last twenty-four hours.'

'Will he stand being questioned?'

'Oh, yes, he insists on it, probably the only thing that's keeping him going.'

Buchanan and Street entered Metzger's room and stopped at his bedside opposite Payne.

'Good morning, Dr Metzger. How are you?'

'They say I'm doing as well as expected – liars, all of them. I'm in transit, Inspector, waiting for the ferryman to carry me across the Styx.'

'Don't say that, Alois. A few days bed rest and you'll be fine,' said Payne.

Metzger shook his head. 'It's too late for that, Anthony.'

'You know why we're here, Dr Metzger?'

Metzger nodded.

'You sure you're up to answering my questions?'

'Yes, I'm sure. I hadn't intended to end life this way; I had plans for a long retirement with Anthony,' he said, turning to look at Dr Payne.' I'm sorry about that, Anthony, but you'll get over it. You're still young and have the rest of your life to look forward to.'

'No, don't say that, Alois. You'll recover, you can't die!'

'Youth, Inspector; ever optimistic.'

329

'You wished to tell us about what happened, sir?'

'Yes, of course, let the poison flow out. That's what old Professor Perkins would say, better out than in. It had to end, Inspector, your young lady made me realise that, but she wasn't the main reason. It was Rodney, he just kept on; he never gave up demanding.'

'Could we go back to the beginning, sir?'

'Why can't you leave him alone? Can't you see he's ill?'

'It's all right, Anthony, it's better if it all comes out in the open.'

'If you're sure?'

'It all started when I got my first appointment as a doctor. I was fresh out of medical school and after applying for several positions in London clinics, I landed what I thought was a dead-end position, as doctor in residence at Radleigh School for Girls. It's near Exeter, not many people know of it.'

'I do,' said Street.

'Yes, I'm aware of that now. I'm sorry you have those memories. Inspector, moving out of London to the country was a bit of a shock for me, especially after my time training in London. That's where Anthony and I first met. Happy times, eh, Anthony?'

'We can have them again, Alois. We could sell up and move away, give you time to recover.'

Metzger shook his head. 'I enjoyed my time at Radleigh. The Mother Superior and I got along fine. Being an all-girls school wasn't a problem for me, and it was probably my ambivalence to the female form that helped me to fit in so well. Your young lady wasn't the only one who required my expertise as a doctor, Inspector. Young girls out of the reach of parental control can, and do, get in to all sorts of trouble, – pregnancy being one of them. During my time at Radleigh I helped many young girls with the inconvenience of an unwanted pregnancy. Your young lady was, I thought at the time, just another one of those accidents. Honestly, I thought I was doing what was best.'

330

'You never asked me. To you I was just another little problem that needed taking care of.'

'I've already said I was sorry for that. The first mistake I made was assuming you were just like all the other girls I helped out. The second was the assumption that the sports master was a nonentity, with no one to miss him. Little did I know he was the top run-maker in the village cricket team; but fortunately for me, by the time people started asking questions, his body had already been cremated. Due to the local gossiping, Mother Superior and I reluctantly decided that in the interest of the school I should resign and move out of the district.'

'How convenient for you, Doctor. I had to change school and start all over again, all the time with the memories of what had happened to me tying my mind in knots, and no-one I could talk to.'

'Well, at least you have a future and by the look of things I'd say you now have someone to talk things over with.'

'Dr Metzger, can we get back to your statement, please?' asked Buchanan.

'Yes, sorry, Inspector. I moved back to London and that's where I ran into Anthony again. He told me he'd just inherited a house in Eastbourne and it was too large for him on his own. He invited me down to stay for a weekend and that's where we got the idea of turning it into a Well Woman Clinic.'

'Where does Rodney Richardson come into the story?'

'When we set up the clinic we realised we needed an accountant to look after our affairs. There are many excellent firms to choose from in Eastbourne, but Rodney's firm seemed to be just what we required. It wasn't long before we became friends, though with hindsight I wish we had chosen someone else. At first the relationship was very business-like. We'd meet at his office once a month; he'd show us how to keep our accounts in order. He was very good at keeping us away from the clutches of the taxman.'

'Maybe that should have been a warning.'

'Maybe. One evening in the pub he asked me if I could write him a pain relief prescription. He said he had a reoccurring sinus headache and he'd been told there was a medication that he could take to relieve the pain; I suppose it was his way of sounding me out. I said the only one that came to mind was cocaine hydrochloride, but it was only used as a local anaesthetic and could become additive if used too frequently. I said it would be better if he approached his own GP. We bantered back and forth till he admitted it was cocaine he wanted. I told him I didn't deal in drugs and I could only write prescriptions for legitimate medications.'

'Good advice. Did he take it?'

'No, I'm afraid he didn't. He was nothing but persistent. He said if I couldn't help him, he couldn't help me. I asked him what he meant by his remark and he said that the taxman might be interested in our trading records.'

'Was he cooking the books?'

'Yes, though it took us years to figure out how he was doing it. Inspector, did you know that the company accountant usually knows more about the company's finances than the owners do, and has access to all the company cash with the means to hide their tracks?'

'Didn't you ever have the company's books audited? Surely that's a requirement of HMRC?'

Metzger shook his head. 'Rodney took care of all that; he used to boast that it was part of the service his company provided.'

'How did you figure out what he was doing?'

'We didn't: it was my sister, she's a trained auditor. One-way Richardson cheated us was to send a bill to the clinic from a non-existent company, which of course he'd created, for non-existent supplies, and then simply write out a cheque and deposit it in his own bank account'.

'You're not the first company that's been hoodwinked by its accountant.'

'I'm sorry to say I gave in to his demands. We were so busy in the clinic we never had time for bookkeeping. Like a lot of people in high-demand jobs, I did use cocaine on occasion – just to help me relax you understand, but I was never addicted to it. I told him I might be able to find someone who could provide him with what he needed.'

'Would you care to tell us who your supplier is, Doctor?'

'Too late – they were arrested last week.'

'That's good to know.'

'Rodney said he'd rather get it from me as he trusted me and it would be better to keep that sort of thing in-house. It was a simple job for me to contact my supplier and up my regular amount. Over time I found that some of my clients benefited from the occasional use; they said it helped them to relax and live with the after-effects of their procedures.'

'So you became a drug dealer. What about the Hippocratic Oath, *Doctor*?' asked Street.

'I didn't see any conflict, Sergeant. The basis of the oath says I am to put my patient first, serve their interests, be polite and caring, and to empower them to make decisions about their own care.'

'That's bullshit, Doctor; many lives and families are destroyed by that sort of lie.'

'Maybe, maybe not, Sergeant; anyway, it didn't take long for the worm to turn. I thought I was doing Rodney a favour, but in actuality he was setting me up. One day he came to my office, said he'd found someone who could supply me cocaine cheaper than I was buying it; and not to try buying from my regular supplier anymore. He was adamant about this. Once again I gave in and was now purchasing my supply from Rodney.

'Do you know where he was getting his from?'

Metzger shook his head. 'This was just the start of the story. When I tried to move our accounts to another firm, Richardson said that would be a foolish act. I confronted him about this, but he just laughed and replied that if I did anything about it he'd be in the clear and we would go to jail for defrauding the taxman. He said it was a case of swings and roundabouts; the money he withdrew was his fee for supplying us with our cocaine supply. He had the nerve to say we were foolish if we didn't make it up, and more, when we supplied our clients. Inspector, I'm a doctor, not a businessman. I had looked at our accounts and they looked fine to me. I'd no idea what he meant; we were at his mercy.'

'Ignorance of the facts is no excuse, Doctor.'

'Inspector, do you file your own tax returns?'

'No, my accountant does that; I'm too busy catching criminals.'

'My point exactly.'

'I'll give you that.'

'One particular day I got a call from Rodney – actually it was in the evening. He called me in great distress, saying he'd had an argument and the other person had died. He said he needed my help to make it look like an accident.'

'Where was this?'

'At the Marina.'

'When?'

'Weeks ago, I don't remember the date.'

'Go on.'

'We met in the car park and walked over to where the incident had taken place. There was a man sitting in a car; he looked dead.'

'Why did you come to that conclusion?'

'He was a young man, sitting behind the steering wheel, the side window was broken. Richardson said they'd had a fight in the car and the man had hit his head on the window, breaking it.'

'Did you check to see if he was dead?'

Metzger nodded and Payne handed him a glass of water. 'He was quite dead.'

'Do you remember seeing the dead man again?'

Metzger once again nodded. 'I did the autopsy.'

'What was your diagnosis?'

'I said he hit his head on the window causing unconsciousness and was drowned when the car rolled backwards into the Marina.'

'Is that what you really thought?'

Metzger shook his head. 'There was evidence to show he'd been struck on the temple with a hammer. It was Rodney who told me what to say in my report.'

'Did you do any other favours for Richardson?'

'I sutured some cuts in his right hand.'

'When was this?'

'A few weeks ago.'

'Did he say what caused the injury?'

'He told me he did it changing a tyre.'

'Did you believe him?'

'No, they were definitely bite marks. I didn't think much about it till Dr Mansell told me about the autopsy he'd just done on a young girl. She'd been choked to death and bitten the hand of her killer.'

'How did you end up in your car in Pevensey Bay?'

'Inspector, as I said, it had to end. I was desperately looking for ways to end it.'

'Committing suicide is never a way out, Doctor,' said Street.

'It's easy for you to say that, Sergeant. You never had Rodney breathing down your neck. A few days ago, he came to me and said he needed my help. He made up some cock and bull story about having a fight with his wife: she'd chucked him out of the house, and he needed somewhere to stay till he figured things out.'

'Disgusting man Inspector, he didn't even let the water out of the sink after he shaved.'

'That's all right, Anthony, he's gone now. Oh, also he said he needed money.'

'Why would he say that? He must have had plenty of his own?'

'He said he was being investigated by HMRC, they'd blocked his bank accounts, and the police – probably meaning you – were getting to close to him. I told him he could stay with us, at the clinic. I was adamant it would be just for a few days.'

'And did he just stay for a few days?'

'Looked more like he was moving in; he said it was the perfect place for him to stay till things quietened down. It was awkward the first couple of days and by the third day I decided it just wasn't working and he'd have to leave.'

'What did he say?'

'When I told him he had to leave, he was livid and demanded the keys to Anthony's car. He'd gone to London on business, said his car was at his house and he wouldn't be seen dead in the Rolls. He actually threatened me with a knife, and then forced me out to the garage. Inspector, I couldn't remember where Anthony kept his car keys, and the more he threatened me the more confused I got.'

'Inspector, unfortunately I had taken my keys with me. If only I'd know what was going to happen,' said Payne.

'You weren't to know, Anthony,' said Metzger. 'Anyway, by now Rodney had become manic, nothing I said assuaged him. That's when he put my hand in the vice and crushed it – the spiteful bastard. I'm finished, Inspector. I'll never operate again.'

'What happened next?'

'I fainted, and when I came to I was in the lounge sitting in an armchair. Rodney was pacing the floor, swearing. When he saw I was awake he became all apologetic, said he didn't know what had come over him. That's when I made my decision. Anthony was away in London so it was just the two of us. I excused myself and went into one of the treatment rooms where we keep bandages and drugs for our procedures. I did my best to bind up my hand then returned to the living room. Rodney was pacing the floor again, and swearing and kicking the furniture. I suggested he might like a drink; I spiked it with Rohypnol. Funny thing, he'd asked me for some a few weeks ago, said he wanted it for a young girl he was pursuing.'

'The bastard – that was for me,' said Street.

'Sorry, I didn't know.'

Buchanan reached over and gave Street's shoulder a gentle squeeze. She looked at him and sniffed. 'Thanks.'

'What happened next, Doctor?'

'I managed to get him in the back of the car. I found some bits of rope in the garage and tied his hands and feet. I didn't want anyone to see him, so I covered him with a blanket, and you know the rest.'

'No, sir, I'm sorry – I don't. How did Mr Richardson escape?'

'Escape? What do you mean?'

'You were rescued by the lifeboat crew and when your car was recovered this morning, there was no-one in the back of your car. All that was found were some bits of rope.'

'So, he's still alive?'

'It looks like that, Doctor.'

'Oh, shit. What will I do now, Anthony?'

'Inspector, Alois needs to rest; he's had quite a shock,' said Payne, as he pulled up Metzger's blankets.

'Indeed, he does, Dr Payne.

◆

'What are we going to do now, sir?' asked Street, as they drove back to the office.

'Call Hunter, ask him if he's seen Richardson at the Marina. There's no telling what he'll get up to now he knows we're on to him.'

'And if he hasn't?'

'Tell him to meet us at the office.'

◆

'So, no one's seen him, Hunter?'

'No, sir, I went to his office, hasn't been in for days. They're in a panic, though.'

'Why's that?'

'HMRC have been in and walked off with all the company books and computers. Everyone's staring at the phones, hoping they don't ring.'

'What about his house, did you check there?'

'Mrs Richardson says she hasn't seen him.'

'Did you go in?'

'No.'

'How did she look?'

'I'd say she was frightened.'

'What makes you think that?'

'She only partially opened the door, it was on the chain, and she'd been crying.'

'Is Dexter back yet?'

'Yes, he's in the canteen.'

'Jill, page him and tell him he'd wanted here, now.'

'Will do.'

'While we wait for Dexter, Hunter, what did you uncover at the Marina? Did you see Dan Angelino?'

'Not much has changed at the Marina, and Dan's not in till eight this evening. Why? Do we need to talk with him again?'

'No, not immediately, but it wouldn't surprise me if he features once more in this investigation before it's done.'

'You think he's going to do something stupid, sir?'

'Hope not, Jill.'

'Sorry for the delay, Chief,' said Dexter, as he rushed in. 'Wife's got morning sickness and I forgot to make a lunch.'

'Another one, Dexter? How many is that now?'

'With this one on its way, makes six.'

'Jammy so and so. Right team, here's what we're going to do. We'll take two cars and head for Richardson's. Pound to a penny he's holed up there now that Metzger's place is not an option.'

'Should I give her a call, sir?' asked Street. 'See if he's there? I could ask her if she's settled back in all right.'

'OK, but make it casual. Say you've got a couple of questions to ask her about her statement before you close her missing person's report.'

Street dialled the number. It rang and then the ringing stopped. 'Mrs Richardson? It's DS Street, could I –'

'What happened, lass?'

'She answered, but as soon as I introduced myself, the phone went dead.'

'He's there. Right, let's go.'

'Just the four of us, sir?'

Buchanan nodded. 'But just in case, Jill, get on to control and tell them we need support for a possible forced entry. Have them meet us at Richardson's, no, wait a minute, what's the name of the pub down the road?'

'The Lamb, sir.'

'Thanks, Dexter. Jill, tell them to meet us in the car park, I'll brief them there, and tell them to be there in,' he looked at his watch, 'fifteen minutes. We need to wrap this up before it gets dark, can't have him give us the slip again.'

◆

'Sergeant Molloy, take two of your men –'

'Sam's got the dog, sir. Want him to go as well?'

'Good idea –'

'Two men and a dog, sounds like the start of a joke.'

'Another time, Sergeant, this is business – we're here to apprehend a possible armed, serial murderer, wife beater, people trafficker and fraudster.'

'Sorry, sir.'

'That's all right, just shows you're human. Right, Sergeant, as I said, take two men and the dog. Go round the back, there's an alleyway that runs down behind the houses and station yourselves so as to cover all escape routes; you know the drill. Give us a call on the radio when you're in position.'

'Yes, sir.'

'Hunter, Dexter, you two come with us. We'll walk down to the house and hide behind that white van, should give us a clear line of sight to the front door. I'll call the house on my mobile and see what happens.'

'No answer, sir?'

Buchanan shook his head.

'Doesn't look like anyone's home, sir,' said Street, as they crept up the path to the front door.

Buchanan bent down and peered through the letter box. 'There's a light on in the back of the house. Hunter, Dexter, go round the side and wait close to the kitchen door.'

Buchanan rang the bell, the hall light came on, and then the front door opened. Susan Richardson, as before, peered round the partially opened front door.

'Good evening, Mrs Richardson. Is your husband here?'

'Oh – thank God, it's you. I thought he'd come back.'

'I presume you mean your husband, Mrs Richardson?'

'Who else?'

'Can we come in, please?'

'Yes, of course, just a minute.'

She closed the door, undid the security chain, and then re-opened the door wide for them to enter. They followed her through to the kitchen.

'I was making myself a cup of tea, would you and your men like one, Inspector?'

'No thanks, Mrs Richardson. Do you know where your husband is?'

'He was –'

Her answer was interrupted by the shrill ring of the front door bell.

'That'll be my men, Mrs Richardson. Go let them in Stephen, and tell Sam to keep the dog outside. Mrs Richardson, do you know where your husband is?'

She shook her head.

'When was the last time you saw him?'

'About an hour ago.'

'Did he say where he was going?'

She shook her head again.

'We've checked the area, Inspector, nothing. Do you want us to stay on?'

'No, Sergeant, you can stand down for just now; if we need you we'll get you through control.'

'Thanks, maybe see you later.'

'Would you go over what has happened since we last saw you, Mrs Richardson?'

'After you left I decided to stay on for a few more days. I needed the rest and wanted to be ready for when I next met up with Rodney, Before I left this morning I called the house to see if he was home.'

'And was he?'

'If he was, he didn't answer the phone. On the way home I stopped by the market and bought some groceries and a newspaper. That's when I read about the body being found in the bay. I felt guilty; I suppose I should have called the police – but at the time, I'd had enough, and she'd attacked me. I parked in the driveway and noticed something unusual: the garage door was partially open. I peeked inside and saw his car was in there.'

'Why was that unusual?'

'He never does that; he's too lazy to go to the trouble of getting out of his car and unlocking the door. I think he was hiding from you – you've got him scared.'

'Don't like that, scared people do stupid things.'

'He's certainly that, Inspector.'

'When you got home, was he inside?'

'Yes, he was hiding in the upstairs bedroom like a naughty child. His clothes looked like he'd been wearing them when they went through the wash. As soon as I walked into the room he grabbed me by the throat and threatened to kill me if I called the police. His eyes – they reminded me of – of a photo I once saw of a fox cowering in a ditch, waiting for the hounds to rip it to shreds.'

'Did he actually hurt you?' asked Street.

'No, though I truly believe he meant what he said. Did he strangle that poor girl in the woods?'

Street nodded. 'The evidence points that way.'

'He hadn't shaved in days and smelt of booze, of course that's quite normal for him when he comes off of one of his binges. It was terrible, Inspector, I think he actually would have killed me had I given him an excuse.'

'That was this morning, and he kept you captive here all day?' She nodded.

'Did he make or receive any phone calls during his stay?'

'Several.'

'Can you remember who from?'

'Other than the normal junk PPI calls, all the rest, but for one of them, were someone with a French accent; they always asked for Rodney.'

'Did they give a name?'

'Not that I was able to find out. Each time the phone rang, Rodney would stand beside me and listen in, if the caller had a French accent, he would pull the phone away from me and take it into the next room to talk.'

'What about the one that didn't have a French accent?'

'Just asked for Rodney, mumbled something about an outstanding account. Rodney talked to them – I think it was in some sort of code, because it didn't make any sense to me.'

'Who do you get your phone service from, Mrs Richardson?'

'BT.'

'Jill, get on to BT and see if we can trace any of those calls. Shouldn't be too difficult for them, they've only got today to look at.'

'Do you have any idea what your husband's likely to do?'

'Run away, that's his style.'

'Jill, anything from BT?'

She shook her head, 'I'm on hold, they've gone home for the day, need to get onto the duty supervisor.'

'Keep on them; make sure they understand how important it is.'

'Mrs Richardson, when your husband left, did he take anything with him – like a passport for instance?'

'I'll check his room.'

'BT, sir. They say it'll take time to check the French calls, but it looks like they all came from the Dieppe region.'

'And the non-French call?'

'The Marina.'

'The arm is waving at me, lass. Tell BT thanks, we've got the information we need.'

Street hung up the phone. 'What next, sir?'

'Call the Marina, see if Dan's there.'

Four faces watched as Street dialled the harbour office. She turned to Buchanan and gave a thumbs up.

'Get him to the phone. I need to talk to him before he does something stupid.'

She shook her head. 'He's was in the office earlier. Apparently he's gone to meet someone.'

'Ask them where he's gone.'

Street asked the question. 'They don't know, but they say they watched him head over towards the restaurants.'

'Hang up, lass. We're off to the Marina, and if I'm correct, we should have one Rodney Richardson in custody within the hour. Better call control and get the backup unit to meet us there, just in case.'

Buchanan waited while Street called control. 'Be with us in about twenty minutes, sir. It's the best they can do.'

'No sign of his passport, Inspector.'

'Thank you, Mrs Richardson. Please let us know if your husband gets in touch with you. In the meantime, I'll make arrangements for someone to keep an eye on your house.'

'Thanks, Inspector, but I don't think that will be necessary.'

'It's for just in case, Mrs Richardson. You are now a key witness.'

♦

'Which way, sir?' asked Street, as they climbed into the car.

'Ah, good point, lass. Let's come in by Atlantic Drive; at least we won't get stuck behind the bollards again.

They parked on the gravel in front of the locks, walked across the lock gates and up to the harbour office.

'Yes, can I help?'

'DCI Buchanan. Is Dan Angelino here?'

'Was a minute ago, not sure where he's gone.'

'Did he go to meet someone?'

He shrugged, 'All I know is he got a phone call and left.'

'Was he alone?'

'Yes.'

'Which direction did he go in?'

'As I told your sergeant on the phone, I think he went towards the restaurants.'

'Do you think he was going for dinner?'

'Unlikely, he's just come on shift.'

'Sorry, I didn't catch your name?' Buchanan asked the lock keeper.

'It's George, George Butterworth.'

'Tell us, George, what you *do* know.'

'Dan had just come to work when he got a phone call. I think it was from his girlfriend because he said to meet him by the Harbour House and they would sort it out together.'

'What did you think he meant by sort it out?'

'I didn't want to ask, he can get quite angry if you pry into his affairs, and he was plenty angry when he arrived for work.'

'Would you call the restaurant and ask them if Dan's there, please?'

'I'm sorry, I need to watch the locks for traffic.'

'It's a matter of life and death. Please call the restaurant and ask if he's there, and if he's not at the Harbour House would you try the other restaurants, please?'

They waited and watched the wind blow a small rowboat, complete with skipper, across the harbour.

'No, sorry, Inspector, he's not at any of them.'

'Can you think of anywhere he might have gone, then?'

'If he's not at the restaurants – ah, wait a minute – he might have gone to the yacht club; I'll give them a call.'

Another shake of the head told Buchanan all.

'Is the boat repair yard open?'

'No, not at this time of night.'

'What does that leave? What else would get him to go over there?'

'The fishing boat fleet?'

'Of course, stupid me, why didn't I think of that?' said Buchanan. 'Do you have a CCTV camera in that area?'

'Yes, the monitor's over here. Let me bring it up for you. There are three cameras that cover that area. Now let's see. Voilà, there he is, talking to one of the crew of the *Sally B.*'

345

'Is that Maria with Dan, sir?' asked Street.

'Looks like her, lass. George, isn't that the boat where Dan says the crew keeps to itself?

'Yeah, Dan's always having run-ins with them.'

'Does he have a radio with him?'

George turned and looked at the radio base station. 'No, it's over there,' he said, 'it's still in the charging stand – he left it behind.'

'What about a mobile phone? He must have one of those?'

'Be a waste of time, he leaves it off, usually goes to voicemail.'

'Would you try for me, if you don't mind?'

'OK'. He pressed a key on the console. The disembodied sound of ringing could be heard emanating from the speaker on the wall.

'No one say anything, let me talk to him,' said Buchanan, as he watched the monitor, willing Dan to answer his phone. After five rings, Dan reached into his jacket and removed his phone. 'Dan, it's Inspector Buchanan. Don't hang up, please, just listen.'

Five pairs of eyes watched as Dan turned away from the fisherman. 'What d 'you want?'

'Listen, Dan, I know why you're there. They didn't kill Olga.'

'Then who did?'

'Come back to the office and I'll tell you.'

♦

Dan, followed by Maria, climbed the steps, and barged into the harbour office.

'All right, Mister Know-it-all,' he said, breathing hard, 'who did kill Olga?'.

'Calm down, Dan, and I'll explain,' said Buchanan.

'I am calm.'

'Do you remember the night the *Moonstone* came into the lock?'

'How can I forget?'

346

'You remember you said you went down on to the pontoon to talk to Olga?'

'Of course, I do, you all but accused me of killing her.'

'Do you remember who was on deck on the *Moonstone*?'

'Olga, I already told you that.'

'Anyone else?'

'Yes, three of the crew.'

'Any guests?'

'I told you before.'

'Then tell me again, were there any guests on deck?'

'One.'

'Can you tell me where this guest was standing?'

'Yes, he was standing at the back of one of the open decks.'

'How close would you say he was to you?'

'I suppose, maybe about ten to fifteen feet.'

'Would you recognise him, if you saw him again?'

'I think so – yes, of course I would. Now I remember, I caught him staring at Olga.'

'Did you say anything?'

'No, he just looked away when I stared at him.'

'Why do you think you'd recognise him again? It was night time.'

'The deck was lit with bright deck lights.'

'How easy would it be for him – you did say it was a he?'

Dan nodded.

'To get down to the stern of the *Moonstone*?'

'Simple, there's a flight of steps on the port side.'

'Could you provide us with a description of this person?' asked Buchanan, as Street turned on her phone.

'I would put him at about five foot nine and thin. He had an angular face, short hair going thin at the front. Oh yes, he was wearing glasses – sort you'd see on a lawyer.'

'Is this him?' asked Street, showing Dan her phone and the photo of Richardson.

'Could be, yes, I'd say that was him. Why?'

'We're just verifying statements made by all those on board the night Olga died.'

'That's not really why you're here, is it? That person, the one you just showed me the photo of, you think he killed Olga. You think he's here in the Marina?'

Buchanan nodded. 'We believe he may be trying to make an escape on one of the boats from the Marina.'

'He'd have a hard job stealing one of those. All the dock gates are locked and so are most of the boats. No, I don't think he'd get away with that, Inspector.'

'Why were you talking to the crew of the *Sally B,* Dan?'

'It's no use, Dan,' said Maria, 'they know more than we do, and if we want to find my sister's killer, we should tell them all we know.'

'Excellent advice, Maria,' said Buchanan. 'Dan, let's start with why were you talking to the crew of the *Sally B?*'

'It was Maria's idea. She called one of her friends back home and asked her to see if they knew anyone who had been trapped into working in England; especially anyone who had managed to get away and return home.'

'And did she?'

'It wasn't easy. Most of the girls that go over, never return. But she did find one: Anna. She said she'd been lied to about her job and the benefits.'

'Did she say how she was smuggled into the UK?'

'Yes, she was put on a French fishing boat and then some time later they were transferred to another one that brought them to the Marina.'

'And you assume the fishermen on the *Sally B* were the ones who brought them into the UK?'

'Yes,' said Dan,' I'm sure of it. I've been watching them for months now. They go out twice a week and always return empty.'

'How do you know they just aren't bad fishermen?'

'No one would spend money the way they do, go out twice a week and not catch any fish. Besides you should see the cars they drive.'

'Like what?'

'One of them –'

'Wait a minute,' interrupted Buchanan. 'Let's start from the beginning. How many of them are there?'

'Mostly just two, and the captain; though sometimes they are joined by a third one.'

'Could you describe them?'

'The captain's a big fellow, about your size – maybe two, three, inches taller than you – with thick curly hair and a bushy beard. The other two are about five nine, slim, shaved heads, one's got a moustache, the other's covered in tattoos.'

'Sounds like our two miscreants from Jukes, Jill,' said Hunter.

'What about the third man? What's he look like?' asked Buchanan.

'Don't know, he always wears a hoodie, with the hood up, never seen his face.'

'What about the cars?'

'Captain drives an AMG Mercedes. You can hear the engine a mile away, especially the way he drives it. Mustachio drives a series seven BMW and the other drives an Audi, not sure what model.'

'What about the mystery man?'

'For someone who tries to be incognito he does a poor job of it. His car is an ancient Saab with a damaged wing. Looks like he was going to have it painted then changed his mind. Also, I followed a couple of them to the pub one night – they spent money like there was no tomorrow.'

'Thanks Dan, Maria.'

'Where are you going now, Inspector?' asked Dan.

'Dan, is there a spare radio I can borrow?'

'Sure, here, it's already on channel one,' he said handing one of the harbour radios to Buchanan. 'Why do you need it? Thought all you guys had your own radios?'

'We do, but not connected to your control room. I don't want to get all the way over to the *Sally B* and find she's gone.'

'Makes sense. You do know how to use one, don't you?'

'Press and speak.'

'What shall we do if the *Sally B* wants out?'

'Hold it till we get back here.'

'OK, will do.'

'Oh, also, keep an eye out for any fast-looking boats bearing a French flag.'

'OK, I'll give you a shout on the radio if any turn up.'

'Jill, Hunter, Dexter,' said Buchanan, 'let's go have a word with the crew of the *Sally B*. Hopefully they'll still be onboard.'

They followed Buchanan down the stairs and over to the *Sally B*.

'Quite nondescript, sir. Perfect if you want to blend into the background.'

'Good point, Hunter. Dexter, you go to the bow and Hunter, you take the stern. Don't want any of them jumping ship when we announce our presence.'

Buchanan gave Hunter and Dexter a moment to get into position then knocked loudly on the hull of the *Sally B*. 'On board, this is the police.'

Nothing stirred. Buchanan picked up a metal bucket and threw it at the cabin roof. 'Police! I want to talk to your skipper.'

Finally, a hatch in the wheelhouse slid back and a bald head came into view.

'You the captain?' asked Buchanan.

'I'll get him.'

This time a curly-haired, short-necked brute appeared. 'Whatcha want?'

'You're the captain of the *Sally B*?'

'Might be. Who's asking?'

'Detective Chief Inspector Buchanan, Sussex CID.'

'So?'

'We're looking for a man. This one,' said Street, holding up her phone with the photo of Richardson.

'Never seen him.'

'Try coming closer, the image on the phone is quite small,' said Street.

They waited for the captain to open the door, exit the wheel-house, and step down on to the side deck.

Street held up the phone again. 'Here, take a good look.'

He made a fuss of taking out his glasses and balancing them on his nose. 'No,' he said, shaking his head, 'never seen him before. What's he done?'

'He's wanted for the deaths of three people, tax avoidance, and embezzlement,' said Buchanan. 'Are you sure you've never seen him? There's a substantial reward for his capture.'

'And you say he's killed three people?'

'A policeman and two young girls,' said Street. 'You might have read about it in the papers?'

'Let me see that photo again. Hmm, now I look again he does look familiar. Seen him down on the docks a couple of times. Try the *Walpurgis*, few boats down the dock; I think I've seen him there.'

'But never on your boat?'

'No,' he said, shaking his head like a naughty child, 'never my boat.'

'Mind if we come onboard and have a look around?'

The colour drained from his face. 'Not good just now, we're painting; get paint on your clothes. Some other time.'

'Hunter, Jill, down the dock, the *Walpurgis*, have a look at her.'

The standoff continued till Hunter and Jill returned.

'Well?'

'Clean. Nobody's been on her for months, all the padlocks are rusted shut.'

'Thanks, Hunter,' said Buchanan. 'Captain, you can let us onboard now, or we all stay here till the search warrant and search party shows up. Your choice.'

'I make phone call, not my boat. You wait here.' He clambered back into the wheelhouse, shut the door and slid the hatch shut. The momentary silence was broken by the sound of security bolts being slid into place.

'Take your time, we've got all night,' shouted Buchanan, worrying that all night they certainly didn't have. Time was passing and still no sight of Richardson.

'Hunter,' said Buchanan, 'get on to control, ask them where our back-up has got to.'

While they waited for control, Buchanan paced up and down the dock.

'Sir,' said Hunter, 'they're on their way, be about fifteen minutes.'

'We can't wait that long. Follow me, we're going below, invited or not.'

They clambered on board and into the wheelhouse. Buchanan picked up a large rusty spanner and started hammering on the hatch.

'Captain,' he bellowed, 'are you going to let us in or do I have to batter my way through this hatch?'

'No need to wreck my boat, Inspector,' came the captain's voice as he unfastened the security bolts. The hatch slid back and a large gnarled hand pushed open the door. 'Why don't you go away? We don't want you here!'

'Can't, Captain. I believe you are harbouring a wanted fugitive. We are coming in to make a search.'

The captain grunted and backed down the companionway steps, followed by Buchanan and team.

The cabin was cosy. On the right there was a small galley with a table and chair in front of a wall of navigation electronics. Facing them was a door through to a forward cabin, which Buchanan assumed would be the sleeping quarters. On the left was a full-length settee with a table fastened to the floor in front. Two, bald-headed crew sat on the settee, half-empty glasses in their hands. On the table were two empty glasses and an almost empty whiskey bottle.

'Been celebrating, Captain?' asked Buchanan.

'Nothing to celebrate, why you ask?'

'Just wondering, and it's just the three of you?'

'Yes.'

'Your crew don't appear to be pleased at our presence. I wonder why?'

'The one on the left, sir,' said Street. 'He's the one who tried to abduct me.'

'And, if I'm not mistaken,' said Buchanan, 'I'm supposed to have assaulted the one on the right. Book them, Street'.

As Street read the two fishermen their rights, Buchanan asked, 'You sure there's no one else on board, Captain?'

'No, Inspector, no one else on board.'

Buchanan walked forward and put his hand on the doorknob to the forward cabin. As he turned the knob the sound of a hatch being opened and scrambling footsteps told him someone was trying to make a hurried getaway. By the time they had climbed the steps and got on to the deck Richardson was nowhere to be seen.

'Hunter, Dexter, head to the control room, go by the bridge; Jill and I'll go round by the restaurants and meet you at the lock gates. Hopefully one of us should catch sight of him.'

Buchanan and Street climbed the shingle bank in front of the southern lock. The pedestrian barriers were down and the harbour lock gates were open to let a sailboat through.

'Busy harbour today,' said Street, as they watched a sleek, long, powerboat slowly approach the lock gates, 'and is that a French flag I see flying from the stern?'

'Well spotted, lass.'

'See anything, Hunter?' Buchanan yelled.

'Nothing, he's just vanished – must be hiding somewhere.'

Buchanan pulled the radio from his pocket, 'Dan, It's Buchanan, can you see Richardson from up there?'

'No, Inspector.'

'Is there anywhere he could be hiding?'

'Wait one, I'll check.'

The sleek power boat turned away and idled its motors. Dan clambered down the steps from the control room and walked behind it. Doors opened, doors closed, bins clattered. Then Richardson made a dash for freedom. He clambered over the closed pedestrian barriers and waved at the power boat.

The boat revved its engines and started to back up, drifting sideways. Richardson leapt over the closing gate of the north lock, across the central island and on to the southern lock gate. Dexter and Hunter patiently waited for the north gates to close.

Buchanan climbed over the south lock barriers to get closer to Richardson and subsequently cut off his escape route.

They were six feet apart, separated by the open lock gates; the roar of the outer harbour water filling the inner harbour was deafening. 'Give it up, Richardson,' shouted Buchanan, 'you've got nowhere to go.'

Richardson looked at Buchanan, then over to the power boat waiting to speed him away to safety. 'You're too late, Inspector. In case you haven't noticed, that's my ride. I'll be in France in a couple of hours, bit of plastic surgery and it's the start of a new life for me.'

Buchanan shook his head. 'The game's up, Richardson. The coastguard's on its way, you'll never get out of the bay.'

Richardson turned back to look at the powerboat. It was having trouble balancing its position against the current of water flowing in to the lock. It revved its engines to maintain position.

'Dan,' radioed Buchanan, 'close the gates. Richardson's going to jump – can't let him get away.'

Seconds later the pumps started, and the gates creaked as the rams started to pull them closed. The sirens of the approaching backup team could be heard wailing through the Marina. The torrent slowed and the powerboat, no longer holding its position against the flow, shot forward. In desperation, Richardson jumped and started to swim towards the boat.

26

'Drowned, you say?'

'Yes, a case of poetic justice,' answered Buchanan. 'Richardson drowned in the same harbour where he started his crime spree.'

'What happened?' asked Greyspear.

'When the gates started to close Richardson must have realised there was nowhere to go, so he jumped into the harbour and started to swim to his getaway ride. Unfortunately for him he didn't realise the power of the water as it rushed through the lock. The powerboat skipper saw the difficulty Richardson was having and reversed to get closer. Unfortunately, he reversed to fast and ran him over, severing his left arm at the elbow.'

'Oh, how awful, even for someone as bad as Richardson.'

'With only one good arm and haemorrhaging from the stump, Richardson couldn't swim against the current and was dragged backwards by the water flow. He ended up being trapped underwater between the closing gates. Wasn't a pleasant sight when the body was recovered later that night.'

'How did you deduce he was at the Marina? He could have gone to earth anywhere.'

'During the day, while he held his wife hostage, he'd frantically been making phone calls to his friends in France. He finally made contact with someone who was prepared to motor across the channel and pick him up at the Marina.'

'Surely he'd be seen?'

'I suppose that's the risk he was prepared to take; besides it was night time, not much traffic about.'

'But how was he to get onboard his ride to France?'

'According to the testament of the powerboat skipper, Richardson was supposed to be waiting at the foot of the lifeboat pontoon.'

'And the *Sally B*?'

'As we suspected, it was used for people trafficking and drug running. We've kept that part out of the newspapers as there is a very nice evidential trail to follow back.'

'Ever thought you'd see this day?'

Buchanan smiled, 'Sir Nathan –'

'For goodness sake, call me Nathan, all my friends do. Surely what we've been through warrants that, at least?'

'Nathan, every time I start an investigation I never know where it will go, or what I'll discover.'

'Ever think about retirement, or a change of direction in your life?'

'What do you mean?'

'Ah, ever the policeman – always looking for suspects under the bed.'

'Not quite. But I have from time to time contemplated retirement, and now living down south, I've got a different outlook. Trouble is though, I love my job.'

'Which part? Being a policeman, or the chase?'

Buchanan, sipped on his drink while contemplating an answer. 'I suppose it's the chase, I'd gladly give up the bureaucracy in a minute.'

'Well, come work for me.'

'Doing what? I know very little about boatbuilding and my knowledge of horses is extremely limited.'

'Not quite what I meant.'

'What exactly do you mean?'

'As you know, my business interests are not just in boatbuilding. I have Castlewood, the film studios, my factory in Scotland, sales offices here and there in the UK, Carstair –'

'Wait a minute; I thought Harry and Jasmine owned Carstair?'

'They do; I helped finance it. Also, there are the overseas boat shows to look after.'

'I don't know. Can't imagine what Karen would say.'

357

'Additionally, there's now the matter of the movie I'm about to make.'

'What? You're going ahead with making the movie of *The Penitent Heart*?'

'The very same.'

'But where would you make it? And who'd do all the filming? Surely your present film company is too small to handle making a full-length movie?'

'You've seen the factory in Greenock. I have one whole factory section empty at the moment; I'm having my lads convert it into a film set. The actual making of the film will be contracted out to professionals.'

'So where would I fit into all of that?'

'You'd be looking after all the security requirements while the film's in production.'

'What, on my own?'

Greyspear shook his head. 'No, of course not, you'll need a team for that.'

'Never hired anyone before.'

'You won't actually need to do that yourself. You would work with my HR people in London. All you'd need to do is let them know what type of people you'd need, and they'd take care of the hiring.'

'I'm a bit old to start a new career.'

'Nonsense, what's age got to do with it? All those years in the police force, all those skills, connections, and knowledge – you'd be perfect for the job.'

'So just what are you proposing?'

'What I'm proposing is, to set up a separate security company, wholly owned by my corporation, and have you as the managing director.'

Buchanan shook his head. 'I don't do the sitting behind a desk well. My old sergeant once told me to, "Never polish your arse in a chair," and I've tried to follow his advice all my working life.

'You will of course have shares in the company, and when you travel it will be first class.'

'But I've no experience in running a company.'

'Maybe in your eyes you haven't, but I've seen you at work and I'm a good judge of a man's capabilities. Think about it, will you?'

'Your table is ready, Sir Nathan. I've put you in the alcove, as you like.'

'Thank you, Angie.'

'Champagne, Inspector? Or, I suppose if you're going to call me Nathan, I should call you by your first name. What is it? Can't call you Buchanan.'

'It's Jack.'

'Well now, Jack, let's drink to what has become a successful outcome and an exciting new venture.'

'Hang on! I haven't said yes, yet.'

'You will, you will. And now a toast: to Rodney Richardson, brought to justice, Susan and I to get married and you, at your age, becoming a dad and soon to be a father-in-law.'

'Nathan, I'll drink to that.'

The End

Extract from, **The Falcon**. The new novel from the pen of Alex Willis. Available to order early 2016

◆◆◆◆◆

I heard the thud and cursed Dizzy's cheap heart. I'd worked till gone one in the morning doing the setup on his bass guitar, and now I was going to have to shell out for a new string at the least. *Don't change the strings,* he'd said; *they were new three gigs ago,* he'd said. Three months of hard gigging more likely.

He'd dropped the guitar off late Saturday – no, it was just gone Sunday morning, and said he would pick it up on the way through to the Newhaven ferry on the Monday morning. If he hadn't been a friend, I'd have told him where could have shoved his guitar.

I looked at the digits on the bedside clock: two-thirty. At least there would be plenty of time to replace the offending strings and get back to bed before the inevitable whirlwind that was Dizzy showed up.

I turned on the bunk light, threw back the blankets, and swivelled out of bed, watching not to bump my head on the side deck. Living and working on a restored WW2 tugboat had its good points and of course inevitable drawbacks. Having a bunk that was partially under the side deck was one of those drawbacks.

Without turning on the passageway lights I groped my way through to the workshop and almost tripped over the body. I turned on the light and saw it had a neat hole in the forehead where the bullet had entered; the mess of blood, bone, and brains told me where it had exited.

◆◆◆◆◆

I hope you have enjoyed reading, *Buchanan, The Case of the Bodies in the Marina.* This book is the first in the series about the Glasgow policeman, Jack Buchanan, seconded to Eastbourne. If you would like to read more about Jack Buchanan and his cohorts, plus the other books I have written, please click on this link. More about Alex Willis.

I would be eternally grateful if you would write a short review of your reading experience.

Write a review

You can follow Alex via his website and occasional blog, http://www.alexwillis.me.
http://www.alexnwillis.blogspot.co.uk/

Some reviews from Amazon readers of
The Penitent Heart by Alex Willis

By <u>S Leads</u>
Format: Paperback

A fast-moving story written in a style reminiscent of the late Desmond Bagley. The author interweaves a series of themes within the novel but never loses sight of the main issue, a man running from problems of his own creation. A really good read which I can thoroughly recommend.

By <u>Simon</u>
Format: Paperback

A proper old-fashioned adventure story; with a couple of neat twists along the way. Alex creates a couple of, very believable; villains and this reader took great delight in their eventual downfall. A perfect bit of escapism and ideally suited for a pool side read.

By <u>J. A. Eyers</u>
Format: Paperback

Bill Drysdale is middle aged and has a comfortable middle-class existence. But he's basically just the househusband of a successful QC. Restless and dissatisfied, he drinks more than he should. Then a fatal accident on the road changes Bill's life forever. He wasn't directly responsible for the death and isn't imprisoned, but the guilt slowly creeps up on him, exacerbated by a driving ban that leaves him feeling trapped. Taking a sober view of his life, he spirals down towards a breakdown.

Alex Willis's novel is like Joseph Conrad's Lord Jim rewritten as a modern thriller. Both are about someone fleeing from his past mistakes rather than truly facing up to them, and walking a rocky road towards any kind of redemption. There's more than a slight nod towards Conrad's Heart of Darkness too with the section of the book set on the expedition downriver. Bill's emotional plight is very much at the centre of the fast-moving plot, which makes this a character-led thriller, written in a dialogue-led style.

Alex Willis

Alex spent his early years listening to the sound of riveting hammers on the Clyde ringing in his ears. At the tender age of 17, Alex left school and joined the Royal Navy. This was not a mutually happy arrangement and after three years being trained as an engineer, Alex left to explore other avenues for a career.

His family emigrated to the USA in early 1967, and he joined them later that year. He was hired by the local phone company to maintain the switching equipment and short haul carrier systems.

Not being challenged enough with his full-time job he took to building and racing motorcycles on the clubman circuits of Northern California. One engine blow-up to many saw him changed direction and declare he was going to build a boat and sail the oceans of the world.

Plans for a 45-foot ferro-cement (later stretched to 51 feet by adding a bowsprit) ocean going ketch were purchased. As the building of the boat progressed he met and married Nancy. Three years after starting construction, the boat was launched and suitably named, *Nancy L.* It wasn't long before the sound of tiny feet could be heard running up and down the deck.

After sailing the San Francisco bay and short trips up and down the Pacific coast it was decided to sell the boat and relocate to England and a re-establish a career in telecommunications.

As a hobby Alex took to making acoustic guitars. From his love of making guitars came his love of writing, and talking about guitars. The highly successful book *Step by Step Guitar Making* was the result of this endeavour and the inspiration for his present career in creative writing.

Alex now spends his days writing, giving talks, being a househusband and gregarious grandfather, going for walks with his wife, cycling, and tending his allotment.

22359060R00210

Printed in Great Britain
by Amazon